"Why are you questioning Julia?" Frank asked.

Detective Hammond gave a noncommittal shrug. "Routine procedure." He snapped his notebook shut and gave them all a bland smile. "I'm finished here—for now," he added, looking at Julia.

"The detective thinks I did it," Julia said after he'd left. "He didn't come right out and say it, but I could tell by the way he questioned me and looked at me that he thought I killed Paul."

"But that's ridiculous!" Penny exclaimed. "Why would he think that?"

"He had good reason to be suspicious," Julia said quietly.

As expected, her comment brought a quick look of surprise from both Frank and Penny. "I was parked outside Paul's house shortly before he was killed," she explained.

"What *were* you doing there?" Frank asked. "What is it, Jules? What aren't you telling us?"

"As betrayals and dirty secrets surface, the pace moves along smartly.... Heggan throws in enough twists to keep readers guessing...."

—*Publishers Weekly* on *Deception*

Also available from MIRA Books and
CHRISTIANE HEGGAN

SUSPICION
DECEPTION

Watch for Christiane Heggan's newest blockbuster

ENEMY WITHIN

available March 2000
only from MIRA Books

TRUST NO ONE

CHRISTIANE

HEGGAN

ISBN 1-55166-536-0

TRUST NO ONE

Visit us at www.mirabooks.com

Printed in U.S.A.

For my pal, Christina Skye
With love and admiration

Prologue

The meeting took place in a luxurious hilltop villa eight miles north of Monterey and five and a half miles from the nearest house. From the sun-drenched terrace one could see the Pacific Ocean curling majestically around the coastline. In the distance, oblivious to the beauty that surrounded them, sea lions barked happily as they frolicked in the water.

All but one of the five men present had arrived the night before, from different parts of the country and at irregular intervals so as not to arouse suspicion, though such precaution was hardly necessary. The fifth man, who was also the group's host and its leader, had bought this house because it was remote and accessible only by way of a long private road. Both features made it virtually impossible for anyone to spy on his activities.

Dressed in casual clothes, the men sat on comfortable, high-backed wicker chairs, sipping freshly squeezed orange juice from Baccarat glasses and chatting. As usual, the conversation was light and friendly. One of the men, who had recently become a grandfather, proudly passed around snapshots of the newborn, while others teased him about getting old.

Anyone eavesdropping on the conversation would have sworn they were old friends—former classmates, perhaps, or army buddies who had come here for a reunion.

Although they were wealthy, they came from all walks of life. Some had inherited their fortune; others were self-made millionaires, tough guys no one dared to push around. Highly respected in their communities, each gave generously to various charities, supported youth programs and contributed to the prosperity of their respective hometowns.

Wearing blue Bermuda shorts and a colorful Hawaiian shirt, their host listened to the chatter but did not take part in it. He didn't like to talk about himself, or divulge any more of his private life than he had to, even to those he trusted.

Short and wiry, he had a broad chest and thick, powerful arms. His light brown hair, in a military crew cut, accentuated the angular features of his face and made him look younger than his fifty-six years.

His eyes were by far his most arresting feature. They were a pale, almost transparent blue and totally devoid of expression. Staring into them was like looking at a very clear lake, yet being unable to see what lay beneath.

After allowing his guests to chat for another minute or two, he clinked his fingernails against his glass. "All right, gentlemen. Enough small talk. We'll have plenty of time for that at lunch. Right now, we have an important decision to make."

The group instantly fell silent.

"I take it you've all had time to give our little problem some thought." His eyes rested briefly on each of the four men and, though there was no change in his expression, the tension on the terrace was almost palpable.

The new grandfather cleared his throat. "I'm not sure we should proceed as previously agreed," he said, glancing uneasily at the others. "For one thing, this is American soil. The risks, if we are caught, will be high."

"The risks will be greater if we don't act," the leader

said sharply. "And the time to act is now. We'll never have a better opportunity."

"I agree," the man on his right stated. He glanced at the newspaper clipping in front of him. It showed the picture of a tall, handsome man standing on a podium, addressing a large crowd. "That news conference our *friend* has scheduled is a godsend, one we can't afford to ignore." The emphasis on the word *friend* earned the speaker a couple of chuckles.

Looking pleased, the leader leaned back in his chair. "In that case, shall we put the matter to a vote?"

One of the men who hadn't yet spoken glanced at the newspaper clipping. With his jaw clenched, he gave a short nod. "I make the motion that we kill him."

"I second the motion," the leader of the group said. "All those in favor raise your hand."

Three hands went up simultaneously. Only the new grandfather hesitated. Then, as the other four men stared at him and waited, he, too, raised his hand.

One

"What you need," Penny Walsh said, panting as she helped Julia carry a heavy clay pot from the trunk of her red Miata to The Hacienda's cobblestone patio, "is a man. Preferably one with a strong back, broad shoulders and a talent for handiwork."

A slow smile pulled at the corners of Julia's mouth. Although Penny had once sworn she'd never get married, she had fallen head over heels in love with Frank Walsh of the Monterey PD the moment Julia had introduced her to the handsome policeman. Now blissfully happy, Penny never missed an opportunity to extol the virtues of marriage or drop hints for Julia to give love another chance.

"Right here is good," Julia said, lowering the flowerpot next to a stone bench. The planter, with its swirling grapevine design, was one of Penny's latest creations and looked perfect in this corner of the small, shaded courtyard.

"Did you hear what I said?" Penny asked.

"Every word." Crouching, Julia began to fill the planter with potting soil she scooped out of an open bag. "Unfortunately, man-hunting was never one of my strong points."

"But that's just it. You wouldn't have to do anything except come to the policemen's ball with Frank and me next month. The place will be filled with eligible bachelors, every one of them drooling at the thought of escorting one of Monterey's most beautiful women."

Julia laughed, a little self-consciously. Then, tucking a blond curl behind her ear, she gazed fondly at her friend. Now there was a beautiful woman. With that long brown mane held at the sides with two barrettes, those wide hazel eyes and those sober trailing skirts she always wore, Penny looked like a modern version of Jo, the older sister in *Little Women.*

And, like dependable Jo, her mission in life was to look after the people she loved.

"What do you say, girlfriend?" Penny nudged her gently with her sandaled foot. "Can we count on you? I'll help you pick an outfit."

Julia shook her head. "I'd make a lousy date, Penny. And the poor soul I'd choose would hate you forever for introducing us."

Sitting on the bench, Penny rested her elbows on her knees and cupped her chin between her hands. "Still not ready, huh?"

Julia shook her head, remembering her disastrous six-year marriage to Paul Bradshaw. "Afraid not. And to tell you the truth, I'm not sure I'll ever be. One bad relationship is enough. Besides," she continued, "I have too much on my mind right now to worry about romance. Every ounce of energy I have is focused on two things—my son and making The Hacienda a success."

The Hacienda was a small inn Julia had purchased soon after her divorce a year ago. Because few businesses made money the first year, or the second, she had held off hiring help and handled all the chores herself—the cleaning, gardening and cooking, which at the moment consisted only of breakfast and four o'clock tea. In a couple of years she'd look into expanding into a full-service inn, with gourmet dinners and even a monthly cooking class.

For the time being, the upkeep of the place and taking care of Andrew, her six-year-old son, kept her busy enough.

"How's business these days?" Penny asked.

Julia made a face. "My only two guests will be leaving next week, and unless I fill the vacancy quickly, I'll have to dip into my savings again."

Savings that, unfortunately, were getting smaller every day. The two hundred and fifty thousand dollars she had received as her divorce settlement had seemed like an enormous amount of money at first. The Hacienda, however, had taken nearly every cent.

"It's that damned resort." Although Cliffside wasn't visible from the inn's courtyard, Penny threw a malevolent look up the hill, in the general direction of the new ritzy establishment. "No matter where you advertise, you can be sure Cliffside will be there, with an even bigger spread and raves about their four-star restaurant, their sauna, their impeccable service." She blew a breath that sent her bangs fluttering. "They make me so mad."

"Oh, I don't mind a little friendly competition," Julia said as she kept filling the planter. "It's those ridiculously low introductory rates that are killing me."

"Surely those can't last."

Julia took a clump of pink impatiens and stuck it into the fresh soil. "More important, will I?"

"It's that bad?" When Julia nodded, Penny came to squat next to her and handed her the next clump of flowers. "Look," she said after a short hesitation. "I've been holding back saying this because I know you'll give me a hard time, but Frank and I had a little talk the other night and if you need a loan, enough to tide you over until things stabilize, well...we have some money saved and we would be more than happy to loan it to you."

Touched by the generous offer, Julia hugged her friend.

Penny had hinted about a loan before, but Julia had remained stubbornly unresponsive. Buying The Hacienda had been her idea, her dream, and whatever problems she was having, they were hers alone.

"Thanks," she said, hoping her refusal wouldn't hurt Penny's feelings too much. "It's very sweet of you to offer, and I truly appreciate your generosity, but another loan right now would only get me into a deeper hole."

"There'd be no rush in repaying us."

"I know." Julia gave her an apologetic smile. "I still can't accept it."

Penny let out a disappointed sigh. "All right, I won't mention it again. Just know the money is there if you need it, okay?"

"Okay."

Penny gave Julia's shoulder a little squeeze. "You're going to make it, you know. Frank says you're too damned stubborn not to." She glanced at her watch. "Speaking of dream boy, I've got to run. He's working the eight-to-four shift this week and I want to slip into something sinful before he gets home."

Julia rolled her eyes. "You're incorrigible."

"I know," Penny said wickedly.

Arms around each other, the two women walked toward the Miata. "Thanks for the birthday present." Julia glanced over her shoulder to admire the now overflowing flower planter. "It was just what I needed for that corner. It even made turning thirty-four less painful."

"Good." Penny slammed the trunk shut. "Don't forget, dinner *chez moi* on Sunday."

"Andrew won't let me forget. Can I bring anything?"

Penny threw her a sly look. "Your linzer torte? It's Frank's favorite."

Julia laughed. "The linzer torte it is."

Leaning against the gurgling fountain in the middle of the courtyard, Julia waved as Penny's car headed down the gravel driveway. When it had disappeared from sight, she walked to the curb to pick up her mail, then walked back, admiring, as she always did, the inn's sheer beauty.

Although in Monterey one could never be far from the sea, it was the proximity to the ocean and the spectacular view of the bay that had first attracted her to the three-story Spanish Colonial on Via del Rey.

The structure itself, while sound, had been in a terrible state of disrepair. But Julia, who had graduated from college with a degree in business and had always dreamed of running an inn, had immediately seen its potential.

When she had found out that the owner was willing to let the property go for a mere two hundred and twenty-five thousand dollars, she used part of her settlement money for the purchase and took out a loan to cover the restoration costs.

Three months later, the nineteenth-century ruin had been transformed into a stunning five-bedroom inn complete with red-tiled roofs, archways and balconies that reflected the beauty and unique history of Monterey.

She had kept the downstairs—kitchen, two bedrooms and one bath—for herself and Andrew, paying particular attention to the large kitchen where she and her son spent most of their time. Sparing no expense, she'd bought state-of-the-art appliances, a round oak table, six matching chairs and a hutch to display her collection of antique Spanish plates. A cooking island with an impressive assortment of copper pots hanging over it was the focal point of the room. In a corner near the tall, arched windows, two easy chairs in a soft butter shade, a coffee table and a television set formed a small living area.

Once inside, Julia walked to the kitchen window and

opened it to let in the late May breeze. Halfway down the hill, a stake marked the spot where she planned to install a hot tub. But that, too, would have to wait until her financial situation improved. Hopefully, that would be soon.

"You're beautiful when you daydream."

At the sound of the familiar voice, Julia jumped. In spite of all the months that had passed since she had left Paul, she never felt quite safe when he was around. Telling herself she no longer had anything to fear, she turned to face him.

With his brown hair perfectly combed, his handsome smile in place and his suit jacket held casually over one shoulder, he looked exactly like the image he had been projecting for the past twelve years—that of a charismatic, friendly, caring politician.

Julia knew another side of him.

"You could have rung the bell," she said with more bravado than she felt.

He tossed his jacket on a chair. "I thought The Hacienda had an open-door policy."

"That's for guests only." To give herself something to do, she started to put away a set of glasses she had left drying in a wooden rack by the sink. "What do you want, Paul?"

"To talk to you."

Dropping by for an occasional visit was a habit her ex-husband had developed soon after she had left her mother's house and moved into The Hacienda. Although he always pretended to be checking on Andrew's academic progress, Julia knew better. Those impromptu drop-ins were his way of checking up on *her,* making sure there was no one new in her life.

"What do you have to say that couldn't wait until Saturday when you pick up Andrew?" Her tone turned sarcastic. "Or are you here to break another date with your son?"

"I didn't come here to fight, Julia, so could you please take off the gloves?"

She gave him a long, speculative look. He appeared so sincere, so earnest, that if she didn't know him so well, she might have believed him. But she had seen that same expression too many times to be fooled. "All right." She leaned against the sink. "You have five minutes. Talk."

He looked at her, that familiar half smile playing on his lips while his gaze traveled from her face to her gardening overalls. "I've been such a fool, Julia," he said, suddenly serious. "I should never have let you go."

"Let me?" She gave a short laugh. "As I recall, you didn't have much of a choice."

"I could have tried to change sooner."

She didn't miss the subtle insinuation that he *had* changed, but made no comment.

"The truth is," he continued, "I'm miserable without you."

She opened a cabinet and set the glasses on a shelf. "I find that hard to believe. From what I read in the papers, you don't seem to be lacking female companionship."

He made a dismissive gesture. "None of the women I date mean anything to me. They're just a distraction. They could never replace you."

Julia sighed as she hung the towel on a hook. "Why are you doing this, Paul?"

"Because I love you. I will always love you. And because I'm sorry for what I did to you, for the way I hurt you."

"It's a little late for apologies."

"It's never too late." Unexpectedly, he closed the distance between them and gripped her shoulders. "Marry me again, Julia," he said, his voice low and husky. "Let's forget the past and start fresh. I promise I'll do it right this time."

For a moment, Julia was so stunned that she could do nothing but gape at him.

"Don't look at me like that." There was a pained expression on Paul's face. "It's not such an unreasonable request, is it? Not when you know how I feel about you."

Julia shook her head in disbelief. "I can't believe you would ask me to marry you after all you've put me through, the physical abuse—"

"I told you I'm a different person now."

"So am I." With a shrug, she freed herself from his hold. "And this Julia doesn't love you anymore."

"Is there someone else?" he asked sharply.

Julia let out another tired sigh. Even now, after nearly a year, he was still jealous. "No, there's no one else. But even if there was, my private life is no longer any of your business."

"I know. I'm sorry." His voice softened. "I shouldn't have asked you such a stupid question. You're a beautiful woman, Julia. I wouldn't blame any man for wanting you. It's just that..." he ran the back of his index finger down her cheek "...I can't bear the thought of another man touching you, kissing you."

She jerked her head away. "Stop it."

He didn't seem to have heard her. "I miss you so much, baby. There are nights when your face, your body, are all I can think of."

Before she could stop him, he yanked her to him and crushed his mouth to hers in a kiss that was as familiar as it was revolting.

Splaying her hands over his chest, she shoved as hard as

she could, coming just short of slapping him. "What's the matter with you? Have you lost your mind?"

"Tell me you didn't feel anything." His breath was coming faster; his eyes had grown darker, more intense. He pulled her toward him again. "Tell me that kiss didn't awaken old memories, old needs."

This time she did slap him, hard. "No, it didn't," she snapped. "And don't ever do that again."

His expression changed and, for a fleeting moment, the old rage was back, ready to explode. Then, as quickly as it had surfaced, it was gone. His hand went to his cheek. "I guess I deserved that."

"Yes, you did." She withdrew a couple of steps. "Now please leave. Andrew will be home soon and I want to spare him an ugly scene."

"You're right." Paul picked up his jacket and threw it over his shoulder. "But this conversation isn't finished."

"For me it is."

He gave her his dazzling smile again, as if they had been discussing nothing more than a PTA meeting. "I'll be here on Saturday morning. Make sure Andrew wears a tie, will you? We'll be having lunch at the club with my father."

"You did what?" His predinner martini forgotten, former California governor Charles Bradshaw set his glass on the ebony coffee table with a bang and stared hard at his son.

"I asked Julia to marry me."

"I heard what you said. What I want to know is why in God's name you would do a dumb thing like that?"

"Because I love her."

"Well, get over it. The woman is no damn good for you. She never was." Charles tugged at an impeccable white cuff. "She comes from different stock, son. I tried to tell you that years ago, but you wouldn't listen." His gaze hardened. "For God's sake, if you want a woman that bad, look around and take your pick. This town is full of beautiful, sophisticated women who would kill to be the next Mrs. Bradshaw."

"I don't want another woman, Dad. I want Julia."

Paul's tone made Charles wince. He'd had two children, one an idealistic rebel, the other a whiner. And as much as he'd hated Sheila's free spirit, he now wished Paul had inherited some of her backbone. Sometimes he wondered how the boy had managed to get himself elected to town council. The Bradshaw name, that's how, he thought bitterly. Without it, God only knew what Paul would be doing right now.

Following him to the window, Charles laid a hand on his shoulder. "Let her go, son. She's not worth the effort."

Paul spun around, his eyes suddenly bright. "Why are you fighting me so hard on this, Dad? Can't you see that if I get Julia back, I get Andrew, too? Isn't that what you want? To have him back in the family?"

Charles's gaze sharpened. By God, he hadn't thought of that. Andrew. Of course he wanted him back. He should never have lost him in the first place. But for reasons that still escaped him, Paul had refused to contest Julia's request for custody.

"I don't want to put Andrew through a bitter courtroom battle," Paul had offered by way of an explanation. "And he's better off with his mother, anyway."

It was one of the few times, maybe the only time, Paul had ever stood up to his father, and nothing Charles could do or say had changed his mind.

The thought that he might get Andrew back after all erased Charles's bad mood. He loved that boy. Andrew was everything Paul wasn't—spirited, smart and too damned stubborn for his own good. Like Charles, and in more ways than he cared to admit, like his daughter, Sheila.

Curious to hear Julia's reaction, he asked, "What did Julia say when you asked her to marry you?"

"She turned me down." Not appearing to be particularly upset, Paul walked over to the well-stocked liquor cart and poured himself a generous Scotch. "Which is exactly how I expected her to react."

"And you still asked her?" Charles chuckled. "Are you that much of a masochist?"

Paul turned around, drink in hand, a smug expression on his face. "She'll change her mind."

Charles frowned. "What makes you think that?"

"I bought her something." He twirled the ice around in his glass before taking a sip.

"If you think an expensive trinket is going to change her mind, you've wasted your money. Julia hates jewelry."

"It's not jewelry."

"So why didn't you give it to her today, when you proposed?" Charles asked impatiently. "You might have saved yourself a rejection."

"Because today wasn't the right time." Paul gave him another smug smile. "But I will give her my present after the news conference on Saturday. She'll be in a much more receptive mood by then. I can guarantee that."

Charles's gaze narrowed. "Ah, yes, that mysterious press conference." He pursed his lips, waiting for Paul to elaborate further. When he didn't, Charles came straight to the point. "I thought that had to do with your work with the Crime Commission."

"It does. In part.

"So where does Julia fit in?"

Paul's expression turned teasing. "You'll just have to wait and see, won't you?"

Charles's own expression remained troubled. He didn't like when Paul kept secrets from him. It reminded him too much of the many blunders, *costly* blunders, the kid had made over the years. Whatever announcement Paul planned to make on Saturday, Charles wished he would run it by him first.

Paul took another sip of his Scotch, smacking his tongue in appreciation. "By the way, I just got word that the news conference will be televised, so be sure to tune in." The smug smile turned into a cocky grin. "I think you're going to be proud of the kid, Dad."

Two

Julia parked her black Volvo in front of the Monterey Bank on Alvarado Street and turned off the engine.

She'd traded her gardening overalls for a narrow pink skirt that emphasized her slender waist and a plain white cotton blouse with the sleeves rolled up to the elbows.

Remembering she hadn't had time for a touch-up, she pulled out a small kit from her purse, dabbed a little powder on her freckled nose, slicked a thin coat of mocha lipstick on her lips and ran a brush through her hair in an attempt to tame the cap of blond curls. Then, declaring herself businesslike enough, she got out of her car and strode briskly toward the one-story stucco building that housed one of Monterey's oldest banks.

Though she tried not to worry, she was a bundle of nerves. Phil Gilmore had called earlier requesting that she stop by his office, but had not told her why. As owner and president of the bank, Phil was the only banker in Monterey County who had been willing to loan her the money to restore The Hacienda. And when Cliffside had opened its doors four months ago, taking a huge bite out of her business, Phil had once again come to her rescue by agreeing to let her split her mortgage payments—half on the first of each month and the other half on the fifteenth—until business picked up again.

Phil's secretary was at her desk, going through the afternoon mail. Usually friendly and talkative, LuAnn Snider looked up briefly but did not meet Julia's gaze.

"You can go right in, Julia," she said, nodding toward the door to her left. "Phil's expecting you."

The banker, a short, rotund man in his early fifties, was already rising when Julia entered his office. One look at his face, and she knew something was very wrong.

"Thanks for coming on such short notice, Julia." He waited until she was seated before doing the same.

"Is something wrong?" Julia didn't bother to disguise her anxiety. Phil's behavior was making her nervous, and whatever he had to say, she wanted it over with.

Clearly uncomfortable, Phil pushed a few papers around his desk. "I don't know if you're aware of this, but I've been trying to sell the bank for some time now."

"Sell the bank?" Julia gave him a puzzled look, not sure why he was telling her this. "It's been in your family for over a hundred years."

"I know, but things haven't been the same since my father died. And times have changed. All those mergers, big banks getting bigger, smaller banks being driven out of business..." He shook his head. "It would take too much time and money for me to try to compete with all of them."

"I'm sorry to hear that." Julia chewed nervously on her lip, aware that Phil's decision to sell the bank would undoubtedly affect their arrangement regarding her payment plan. Was that what he wanted to tell her?

"Unfortunately," Phil continued, "I'm having difficulties finding a buyer. The owner of Commerce Bank in Carmel is ready to make an offer, but on one condition—that I get rid of some of my...riskier loans."

Julia's heart skipped a beat. She gave Phil a long, level look. "Do you consider my loan risky, Phil?"

"No," he said quickly, looking embarrassed. "Not at

all. I know you, Julia. You're a hard worker, and you're reliable. Getting The Hacienda off the ground might take you a little longer than we had both anticipated because of the new hotel next door, but it will happen." He picked up a pencil from his desk and twirled it between two fingers. "Unfortunately, Arthur Finney at Commerce doesn't see it that way."

"How does he expect you to get rid of certain loans?"

"By selling them to whomever is willing to buy them."

"Can you do that?"

Phil tossed his pen on the desk. "Small banks aren't bound by the same rigid rules as larger institutions. And it's a perfectly legitimate transaction. It's done all the time."

"So you're going to sell my loan to a third party? Is that it?"

Eyes downcast, Phil remained silent for a moment, then said quietly, "I already have."

Julia sat upright in her chair. "What?"

"I had no choice, Julia. It was either that or lose the sale. Yours was the last loan I sold, and believe me, it wasn't easy. No one I talked to wanted anything to do with The Hacienda."

She didn't even try to keep the anger from her voice. "Don't you think you should have discussed it with me first?"

Phil sighed as if he had been expecting the question and hated to give the answer. "Normally I would have, but the buyer asked me not to. He wanted the transaction to go through before you found out."

"Why is that?"

"Before I answer that question, let me assure you that nothing will change. The buyer gave me his word that the arrangement you and I have regarding your payments will be honored.''

Julia heaved a sigh of relief. For the first time since entering the bank, she was able to relax. ''Why didn't you say so sooner? Who is this wonderful person?''

Phil held her gaze. ''Your ex-husband. I sold your mortgage to Paul.''

Stunned, Julia just stared at him.

''I didn't seek him out, Julia,'' he said, as if this in some way made everything all right. ''He heard about my problems and came to me.''

''How could you do this?'' Julia asked, sitting on the edge of her chair.

''I had no choice—''

''You and I have known each other for twenty-seven years,'' she cut in. ''I opened my first savings account right here, when I was seven years old. You typed up my five-dollar deposit in my bank book yourself.''

Phil licked his lips. ''I know.''

''I thought we were friends, Phil,'' she said reproachfully.

''We are.''

''Friends don't stab each other in the back!''

''Julia, you make it sound as if The Hacienda is in jeopardy. I assure you it's not.''

She couldn't argue with him. She couldn't tell him that Paul had bought her mortgage because he was once again trying to control her, no more than she could tell him what a monster he really was. ''What can he do?'' she asked.

''I beg your pardon?''

She waved a hand impatiently. ''If Paul suddenly decided he didn't want to honor the verbal agreement you and I have, could he request—demand—full payment on the first of every month?''

"I suppose he could, but—"

"And if I can't do that? Can he foreclose?"

Phil's prominent Adam's apple jerked up and down. "Julia, that's just not going to happen."

Julia fell back against the chair. He had answered her question.

Suddenly that marriage proposal that had seemed so ridiculous a few hours ago now made perfect sense. Paul had wanted to reconcile with her for a long time but he hadn't had any leverage to use against her. Now he did. Or *thought* he did. She wasn't totally helpless, she reminded herself. She still had those pictures of herself she had taken on that last horrible night in her husband's house. And she had the doctor's report.

"Maybe you ought to talk to Paul," Phil suggested, sounding relieved that no major argument had erupted. "It'll set your mind at ease."

Julia rose. "I'll do that."

Too distraught to say another word, she gave Phil a curt nod and walked out.

The Monterey open-air market on Cannery Row was a weekly event, attended by people from all over the county. Exotic fruits, vegetables and flowers bursting with color were lavishly displayed, their smells mingling with the intoxicating aroma of roasted coffee beans from the nearby coffee factory.

With her mother at her side, Julia strolled down each aisle, stopping at a favorite stand every now and then, selecting ripe strawberries she would serve with her morning scones, and apricots she would make into delicious jam.

"Look at this beauty," Grace Reid said as she picked up a large purple plum and held it at eye level. "Where else but in Monterey can you find such perfection?"

Julia smiled. "The Chamber of Commerce should have never allowed you to retire, Mom. You've always been its best spokesperson."

Only two weeks past her fifty-seventh birthday, Grace Reid still retained much of her youthful beauty and vitality. The years had added a roundness to her figure, but she concealed the few pounds well with perfectly tailored slacks and blowsy shirts in brilliant jewel shades.

Abandoned by her husband twenty-three years ago and left to care for two small children, she had met the difficult challenge with a courage and dignity Julia deeply admired. She was now retired from the Chamber of Commerce, where she had worked for nearly four decades, but kept busy with her volunteer work at the hospital and a weekly game of canasta with her friends.

"I'm glad I finally got a reaction from you," Grace said in answer to Julia's comment.

"What do you mean?"

"You've been miles away since we got here." Grace returned the plum to its pyramid and looked at her daughter. "Is something wrong?"

Julia held back a smile. She had never been able to hide anything from her mother. "Not really," she said, not wanting to worry her. "I was trying to decide what to serve my two guests for afternoon tea, that's all."

"Really?" Grace gave her a skeptical look. "I find that hard to believe. You usually have your menus prepared days in advance. You're the most organized person I know."

"That's no small compliment coming from you."

"Don't change the subject." Grace picked up a cantaloupe, smelled it, then handed it to the woman behind the stand. "Something is bothering you and I want to know what it is."

There was no point in hiding the truth any longer. Grace was every bit as stubborn as Julia and wouldn't give up until she knew all the details.

Julia waited until her mother had paid for the melon and they were walking again before asking, "Did you know that Phil was trying to sell the bank?"

Grace waved at someone she knew, but didn't stop. "I've heard rumors. How did *you* find out?"

"Phil told me." Then, because she had been dying to get the whole thing off her chest, she told her mother the bad news.

Grace's reaction mirrored her own as shock spread over her attractive face. "Phil sold your mortgage to Paul? Without telling you?"

"Apparently Paul asked him not to until the deal was signed and sealed." They had reached the lot where the Volvo was parked. Julia popped open the trunk and laid her and Grace's purchases on the black mat.

"Why would Paul want to buy your mortgage?"

"To force me to do something I don't want to do."

The two women walked around the car and got into their seats. "Like what?" Grace pressed.

Feeling her mother's concerned gaze on her, Julia stared out the windshield for a moment. Grace was the only person who knew about Paul's abuse, but because Julia had been anxious to put the past behind her, they rarely, if ever, discussed it.

"Paul came to see me yesterday." She turned in her seat. "He asked me to marry him."

"Dear God!" This time Grace's hands flew to her mouth. "Why would he ask you something like that? Does he think you have a death wish?"

"He said he's changed, that he's miserable without me and wants to start over."

Grace's eyes filled with horror. "Oh, Julia, you didn't say yes!"

"Of course not. I told him a reconciliation was out of the question." She thought it wise not to mention Paul's heated kiss or that she had slapped him. It would only worry her mother more.

"How did he take it?"

"Actually, he was sort of...amused by my reaction, as if he knew something I didn't." Her smile turned bitter. "Now I know what it was."

"Oh, Julia, I can't believe he would try to use that loan to get you to marry him. It's insane. And besides, you have something on him, too, remember? He can't ignore that."

"You wouldn't think so, would you?"

Grace shook her head. "He's always been so possessive of you. I should have known he could never give you up." A flicker of worry flared in Grace's green eyes. "What happens now?"

Julia inserted the key into the ignition. She had lain awake all night, wondering how to handle the situation. Her decision to confront Paul didn't thrill her, but she saw no other alternative. "I'm going to wait until Paul gets home from tonight's council meeting," she said. "Then I'll go to the house and talk to him. See what he's up to."

"Maybe he's not up to anything."

Julia put the car in reverse and backed out of the parking space. "Paul never does anything without a reason, Mom. You know that."

"Maybe so, but I don't like the idea of you going to his house."

"I'll be fine."

"Then at least let me go with you."

Julia shook her head. "No, Mom. This is between Paul and me." Reaching over, she squeezed her mother's hand.

"I'll be all right. Paul isn't stupid. He's not going to hit me now that he's running for county commissioner." She smiled. "Besides, he wants to marry me, remember? As long as he believes there's a chance I'll change my mind, he'll be on his best behavior."

"If you say so."

But Julia could tell by the way Grace sat with her hands tightly clasped on her lap that she wasn't convinced.

Even now, after twelve months, Julia still found it difficult to look at the house where she and Paul had lived for six years without a shudder of fear running through her.

The two-story Tudor had been a wedding present from Charles, a grand gesture meant to impress his new, very impressionable daughter-in-law. She had been such an innocent in those days—and totally dazzled that Paul Bradshaw, a Monterey city councilman many said would someday be governor of California, had chosen *her* to be his wife.

At first, he was the perfect husband—loving, attentive and devoted. Eager to please him, Julia had agreed to put her career in hotel management aside in order to help her husband further his own, the way Paul's mother and grandmother had done before her.

But on the day of Andrew's first birthday, everything changed. As Julia cut the cake, Charles proudly announced that his grandson would be following in the Bradshaws' tradition by attending one of the oldest and most exclusive boarding schools in the country—the James Clark Academy in Alexandria, Virginia.

"I had to call in a few favors," he said with a chuckle. "But I got my boy on the list."

Shocked to have been left out of such an important decision and upset with Paul for agreeing with his father, Julia stunned the two men by telling them her son would not be going to a boarding school and that, from now on, any plans regarding Andrew would have to be discussed with her.

When she and Paul returned home that evening, the argument escalated even further. His face livid, Paul had accused her of being ungrateful and of wanting to turn Andrew into a sissy, a mama's boy. Angry, Julia fought back and paid dearly for it. With no warning, Paul had backhanded her. The force of the blow snapped her head around and slammed her against the bookcase.

As she slid to the floor and stared at him in horror, Paul rushed to her. Taking her in his arms, he murmured words of love and apology and swore that nothing like that would ever happen again.

It had. Many times.

At first, Julia was convinced his outbursts were her fault. She was too immature, too unsophisticated. She didn't fully understand the responsibilities her husband faced, not only as a Bradshaw but as the son of California's most popular former governor. She often felt that his frustrations stemmed from a deeply rooted fear that, no matter how hard he tried, how much he accomplished, he could never be as good as Charles.

Because she loved her husband, she tried desperately to be the kind of wife Paul wanted. She joined several charitable organizations, began addressing various women's groups, and, when Paul began campaigning for his reelection, she stood right by his side until that victorious night.

But as his popularity grew and they began to socialize more, a new beast emerged—Paul's insane, unfounded jealousy. Soon he was accusing her of flirting with other men and even of cheating behind his back.

Her fierce denials, which he took as another form of betrayal, enraged him even more.

When it became obvious the abuse wouldn't stop, Julia gave Paul an ultimatum. Either he seek help through counseling or she would leave him.

The look on his face that night was something she would never forget. He'd stared at her for a long moment, his expression unreadable. Then, laying his hands on her shoulders, he'd gently pushed her down on the sofa. In a voice that was frighteningly calm, he'd told her that if she left him, she would never see Andrew again. Charles would see to that.

When she threatened to press charges of abuse against him, he only laughed. Who would believe her? he asked. How would she substantiate such ridiculous claims? Did she have any witnesses? Had he ever left a mark on her? Or raised his voice in public? Had she ever confided in anyone about those so-called beatings?

As he talked softly, slowly, almost as if he were addressing a child, she realized the hopelessness of her situation. She knew, without a doubt, that Paul's promise to never let her see Andrew again was no idle threat. Charles Bradshaw was a wealthy, powerful, influential man who could do anything, even buy the custody of a child.

She had no choice but to back down from her ultimatum. She would stay, pretend to give in, and the next time Paul hit her, she would retaliate, not by fighting back, which was useless, but by putting together the proof she needed to get out of the marriage—with Andrew.

That day arrived sooner than she expected. It was a mild spring evening, and as they drove back from a fund-raiser, Paul had immediately picked a fight. It started over nothing, an innocuous comment Julia had made about one of their male friends. The rage hadn't stopped until Julia was on the floor with a bloody lip.

The following morning, sore, frightened, but determined, Julia took pictures of her bruised face and drove to Santa Cruz to see a doctor.

That same evening, after dropping Andrew off at her mother's, she had gone back to the house. Feeling almost giddy with her newfound power, she had laid out her demands—her silence in exchange for her freedom. And full custody of Andrew.

Aware of what she could do, Paul had agreed to the deal. He was an ambitious man, with large-scale plans for his future—a future that, with one word from her, could end up in shambles.

Moments later, she had walked out of that house for the last time.

Now, sitting in the Volvo, Julia stared at the big, brightly lit house, remembering every argument, every accusation, every blow. She gripped the steering wheel even tighter. How could Paul believe she would want back into such hell? Even with The Hacienda at stake?

Opening the driver's-side door, she hesitated, suddenly filled with doubts. Was she doing the right thing by confronting Paul about the loan? Showing him she was worried? Yes, she wanted to know what he was planning to do, but what if her mother was right and he had no ulterior motives? She certainly didn't want to give him any ideas.

She closed the door again. She hated to feel this way, frightened and undecided, but that was how Paul affected her, even now.

It took her another five minutes to finally make up her mind. Once she did, she put the car in Drive, pulled away from the curb and headed home.

* * *

"Aw, Mom, do I have to wear this stupid tie?"

Holding back a smile, Julia crouched in front of her six-year-old son. With his blond hair, blue eyes and compact little body, he was a constant reminder of her late brother, Jordan. And like Jordan, he was a tornado of energy who couldn't sit still for a minute.

"Yes, you do," she said, straightening the Windsor knot Andrew had just pulled askew. "You're having lunch at the club with your grandfather later on and you know what a stickler he is when it comes to appearances."

"But I'm just a little kid. I shouldn't look like a grown-up. Plus it's Saturday."

Andrew's common sense, keener than that of most adult men she knew, brought a chuckle from Julia. "I know, sport." She patted the necktie and winked at the boy. "Just humor me, okay?"

Andrew blew out a sigh. "I hate going to the club. It's full of old men with yellow teeth and smelly cigars who keep telling me 'When I was your age...'"

At Andrew's perfect mimicking of an old man's trembling voice, Julia burst out laughing. "You're quite a comedian, you know that?"

As he inserted a finger between the tie and his shirt collar, trying to loosen the knot, she pulled his hand away. "I'll make a deal with you. Leave your tie alone, behave at lunch, and when you get back we'll go to the video store and rent a movie. Your choice."

Andrew's expression went from irritation to sheer delight. "Can we get *Revenge of the Ninja?*"

"Again? You saw that movie twice already."

"So what? Jimmy saw it four times."

She laughed. "Oh, well, in that case..."

His smile grew mischievous. "And afterward, can we stop at Ben and Jerry for some rocky road?"

"You drive a hard bargain, sport." She pushed the cowlick back. "All right, I guess we can splurge on a couple of cones."

"Cool." Suddenly anxious to go, Andrew glanced at the kitchen clock. "Dad's late."

Julia sighed, hoping Paul wasn't going to be a no-show again. Now that he was running for county commissioner, his son was low on his list of priorities.

"He'll be here soon," she said halfheartedly.

She waited another ten minutes, then decided to call the house. To her surprisc the phone was answered on the first ring, not by Paul but by a man whose voice she didn't recognize.

"Hello?"

"Ah..." She hesitated. "May I speak to Paul Bradshaw, please?"

"Who is this?"

"Julia Bradshaw. Paul's ex-wife. Who are you?"

There was a brief silence, then the man said, "My name is Detective Hank Hammond of Monterey PD I'm afraid I have bad news, Mrs. Bradshaw. Your ex-husband's been shot. He's dead."

Three

Julia went numb with shock. Paul couldn't be dead. She had talked to him only two days ago. He had stood right here, in this kitchen.

"What did you say?" Her voice sounded far away, as unreal as the words she had just heard.

"Councilman Bradshaw is dead, ma'am," Detective Hammond repeated. "I'm sorry."

"But that's impossible. He..." She stopped, not sure she should mention Paul's recent visit.

But the homicide detective was quick to pick up on her hesitation. "He what, Mrs. Bradshaw?"

"Nothing." She glanced at Andrew, who was still fussing with his tie. God, how was she going to break the news to him? "Do you know what happened?" she asked. "Or who did it?"

"Not yet." The homicide detective sounded matter-of-fact, as though he answered such questions routinely. "I'll need to talk to you, Mrs. Bradshaw. Where can I find you?"

Didn't he know? Didn't everyone in Monterey know? "I run an inn on Via del Rey—The Hacienda."

"I'll be there shortly."

Andrew was watching her, his expression suddenly grave. Crouching in front of him again, Julia took his hands in hers and looked at them for a moment. Because of Paul's busy schedule, he and Andrew had never been close, but the boy loved his father with the total, unconditional love of the young, and the loss would hurt.

"What's wrong, Mom?" he asked. "Who were you talking to?"

"A policeman." She looked up. "I'm afraid there's been an accident."

The blue eyes grew fearful. "Is it Dad?" He searched her face. "It is, isn't it? What happened to him? Where is he?"

A knot formed in Julia's throat. "You're going to need to be very brave, Andrew. And very strong."

"What happened to Dad?" His voice shook as though he had already guessed.

Julia drew a breath, hating herself for the pain she was about to inflict on him. "He's dead, sweetheart."

As if a tremendous weight had suddenly come down on him, Andrew's slim shoulders sagged. He pressed his lips together in a desperate effort not to cry. Then, unable to hold back the tears, he let out a wrenching sob and fell into Julia's arms, burying his face against her shoulder.

Shattered by his grief, Julia held him tight, her mouth pressed against his hair. "I'm so sorry, Andrew. So sorry."

After a while, his face blotchy and his eyes red, Andrew pulled away. "Was it a car accident?" In a gesture that reminded Julia of his toddler days, he wiped his tears with the back of his sleeve.

"No." There was no point in lying to him. Paul was a famous man. A few hours from now, the circumstances of his death would be all over town, as well as in the schoolyard. "He was shot."

Andrew's eyes widened as if the thought was too shocking for him to comprehend. Then, through the veil of tears, anger sparked, quick and hot. ''Who did it?'' he demanded. ''Who killed my dad?''

''We don't know yet, darling.'' She brushed the endearing cowlick back, only to see it fall forward again. ''The police are there now. They'll find out who did it.''

Another tear rolled down his cheek, but this time he ignored it. ''I was mad at him last week,'' he said in a small voice.

''Why, sweetie?''

''Because he didn't take me to the baseball game like he promised.''

She understood the guilt. She had felt it, too, last year when her brother, Jordan, a detective with the Monterey PD, was killed. ''Your father knew you loved him,'' she said gently, hoping to ease the pain. ''And he knew the reason you were mad was because you wanted to spend time with him.''

''But he didn't like to spend time with me.''

The words went right through her heart. ''Oh, Andrew, that's not true,'' she lied. ''He didn't have a lot of free time, that's all.''

His head bowed, he asked, ''Does Grandpa know?''

Charles. Julia closed her eyes briefly, remembering his grief at the death of his daughter eight years ago. And now Paul.

Suddenly all animosity toward the man was gone, replaced by a feeling of deep sorrow. ''I'm sure the police called him right away. You can talk to him a little later if you'd like.''

She glanced at the clock. Detective Hammond would be here any moment, and she didn't want Andrew to be present when he questioned her. ''Right now, I'm going to call Grandma and ask her to come over. Is that okay with you?''

He nodded. One hand around his shoulders, Julia picked

up the cordless phone from the desk and punched the speed dial with her thumb. With a minimum of words, she told her mother the news.

Before Julia could even ask, Grace said, "I'll be right there, honey."

After she hung up, Julia led Andrew toward one of the easy chairs in the corner of the room. From the open window came the cry of a seagull as it swooped toward the ocean. Sitting down, Julia drew Andrew into her arms and held him.

They remained linked that way until Grace arrived.

Detective Hank Hammond was a medium-sized, slightly overweight man with thinning black hair and hooded, sleepy eyes that made him look as if he had just finished working a double shift.

"Mrs. Bradshaw?" When she nodded, he flashed a badge. "I'm Detective Hank Hammond."

Julia let him in. Fortunately, The Hacienda's two guests were early risers and had already left for their respective sightseeing expeditions.

"Have you learned anything more since we talked?" Julia asked, as the detective followed her into the kitchen.

"Just that the motive wasn't robbery and that there was no sign of forced entry. Whoever killed your ex-husband either had a key or was let in."

He glanced around the kitchen before returning his gaze to her. The sleepy eyes looked at her steadily. "Do you still have a key, Mrs. Bradshaw?"

Inexplicably nervous, Julia shook her head. "No. Not anymore."

"That's good." He pulled a small notebook from his breast pocket, flipped through the pages before finding a blank one. "Did your husband have any enemies that you know of?" His voice was as bland and flat as the rest of him. "Anyone who would want him dead?"

"Vinnie Cardinale is the only name that comes to mind." It was no secret that, since being named to the crime commission, Paul had waged a fierce war against the San Francisco mobster. Not only had he blocked Cardinale's attempts to open a nightclub on Cannery Row, but he had vowed to dig into Cardinale's activities in Monterey until he had enough to put the man behind bars once and for all.

"And besides Cardinale?"

"Paul and I didn't discuss our private lives, Detective, so I couldn't say—"

"But you saw each other."

She took a steadying breath. "Occasionally, when it was his weekend to have Andrew."

"And...was this one of those weekends?"

"Actually, today was a makeup day. Paul missed the last two parental visits."

She regretted the words the moment they left her mouth. The remark made her sound reproachful, even accusing, and the last thing she wanted was to give the police the impression she held a grudge against her ex-husband.

"So the last time you saw him was...when?"

Julia hesitated. "Thursday afternoon," she said reluctantly. "He stopped by for a few minutes."

"To see his son?"

Though there was hardly a change in his expression, she felt herself grow uncomfortable. She shifted her weight from one foot to the other. "No. He came to see me."

The policeman's gaze left her face for a moment as he made an entry in his book. "Any particular reason?"

She shrugged, trying to appear casual. "He just wanted to talk, nothing important."

"Tell me anyway."

The thought of lying to him came and went. She was a terrible liar. And why should she lie, anyway? She had nothing to hide, nothing to feel guilty about. "He asked me to marry him." The words sounded even more ridiculous now than when she had first heard them.

The calm brown eyes settled on her. "Really. What did you say?"

Julia tried to hold his gaze without flinching. "I turned him down."

"How did he take it?"

"Well enough," she said truthfully. "I think he already knew what my answer would be, but he still asked."

Hammond kept writing. "What happened after that?"

Julia's heart did a little somersault. It was a direct question, one she couldn't easily avoid. "What do you mean?" she asked, stalling for time.

"I mean, did he try to change your mind? Ask you on a date? Or did he just leave?"

"He left shortly after." Bracing her hands against the sink behind her, she forced herself to look at him, praying he wouldn't guess that she was lying by omission. "He said he'd be back on Saturday morning to pick up Andrew."

"And you never saw him again?"

"No."

Pursing his lips, Detective Hammond looked around him again, as if trying to commit each item, each corner of the room to memory. "This is a great house. It used to belong to old Sandi Garcia, didn't it?"

A little surprised by his sudden interest in the inn, Julia nodded. "Yes, it did."

He nodded. "You did a great job of restoring it."

"Thank you."

His gaze returned to her. "Where were you between eleven o'clock and midnight last night, Mrs. Bradshaw?"

The question, though expected, sent her heart racing. Her face must have shown her anxiety because he added, "It's just a routine question. It helps eliminate the suspects."

"I understand." She tried to swallow, but the dryness in her throat made the simple task nearly impossible. "I was right here." It was true, though barely. She had arrived back at The Hacienda moments before the eleven o'clock news. "Is that when Paul was killed?"

"It's just a rough estimate. We'll have a more exact time of death after the coroner is finished with the autopsy."

A more exact time of death. It still didn't seem possible that he was talking about Paul.

Hammond tapped his pen against his chin. "Was anyone here with you? Someone who could verify that you were home?"

Another routine question? she wondered. Or hadn't he eliminated her as a suspect yet? "My mother was here."

He looked surprised. "Does she live with you?"

"No. She..." Julia resisted the temptation to press a hand against her stomach, where a cold feeling was slowly spreading. "She sometimes spends the night, when...when I need her to stay with my son."

The hooded eyes no longer looked sleepy. "Did you need her last night, Mrs. Bradshaw?"

Oh, God, had she really believed she could keep something like that from him? "Yes." Her heart was beating so hard, she wondered if he could hear its mad thumping. "I had to go out for a while."

"Where?"

A few seconds passed. "To Paul's house," she said in a whisper.

Under the rumpled brown jacket, the detective's shoulders stiffened slightly. "I thought you said you never saw Paul Bradshaw again after he left The Hacienda on Thursday afternoon."

"I didn't." Relieved that the truth was finally out, her voice grew stronger. "I drove to his house but I never went in. I just sat in the car, trying to make up my mind. After about ten minutes, I decided not to go in and went back home."

"You went to his house and just parked there? Why?"

Julia glanced out the window. The morning fog had lifted, leaving behind a cerulean sky and bright sunshine. A mild ocean breeze blew in through the open window, bringing with it the crisp, salty scent of the sea. Everything looked so peaceful, she thought. Just another ordinary day. Yet she knew, from this moment on, nothing in her life would ever be peaceful and ordinary again.

"I had found out something that day," she said reluctantly. "Something I needed to discuss with Paul."

The look the detective shot her was sharp and probing. "What was that?"

She might as well tell him, she thought, fighting the panic. He'd find out sooner or later. She pulled away from the sink where she had been anchored for the past ten minutes and crossed over to the island. With a hand she tried to keep steady, she took the butter dish from the counter and put it back in the refrigerator. "The day after Paul's visit, I found out that he had bought my mortgage on The Hacienda from the bank." Pretending to be busy, she didn't look at the detective as she spoke. "That's why I needed to talk to him."

"So you drove all the way to Mr. Bradshaw's house, late at night, and when you got there, you changed your mind and came back."

Those were more or less her exact words, yet out of his

mouth, the premise sounded totally unbelievable. "Yes." She squared her shoulders as she turned back to face him. "That's exactly what I did."

"Why did you change your mind?"

The anxiety in her gut wound tighter. Like a noose, she thought. "I didn't think I should be the one to bring up the matter. I figured he would tell me himself, eventually."

Lips pursed again, as if trying to make up his mind about something, Hammond continued to look at her. "Do you own a gun, Mrs. Bradshaw?" he asked suddenly.

His habit of lapsing into silences and then firing incriminating questions was beginning to get to her. "No."

"But your ex-husband did. We found a permit in a desk drawer."

"He bought a Beretta a couple of years ago when one of our neighbors was robbed at gunpoint." She watched him scribble the information in his book. "When we separated, however, the gun stayed with him."

"I'm surprised. A woman living alone, with a small boy—I would have thought you'd want protection."

"This is a peaceful neighborhood, Detective. And I don't like guns," she added. "Especially with a child in the house."

"Do you know where the Beretta is now?"

"Paul used to keep it in a closet in the master bedroom. Why are you asking me that?"

"Because the gun is missing, Mrs. Bradshaw."

"Paul was shot with his own gun?"

From the courtyard came the sudden screech of tires. A car door slammed, then another. Moments later, the front door was flung open and Penny, followed by Frank, burst into the kitchen.

"Oh, Julia, I came as soon as I heard." Barely glancing at Hammond, Penny ran to Julia and embraced her.

Frank did the same, then released her and held her hand. He was a handsome man, with thick black hair, hazel eyes and a raspy voice all the girls at school had been wild about. "Where's Andrew?" he asked.

"In his room. My mother is with him."

"You're okay?"

Julia nodded. "I'm fine. "Detective Hammond was just asking me a few questions."

Frank let go of her and approached the detective. "What's going on, Hank?" he asked, his tone sharpening slightly. "Why are you questioning Julia?"

Hammond gave a noncommittal shrug. "Routine procedure, Frank. You know that." He snapped his notebook shut and gave them all a bland smile. "I'm finished here—for now," he added, looking at Julia.

He handed her a business card. "If you remember anything that might be helpful, give me a call."

After he was gone, Julia sank into a chair. Elbows on the kitchen table, she pressed her temples, where a fierce headache had begun to throb. "He thinks I did it," she murmured. "He didn't come right out and say it, but I could tell by the way he questioned me and looked at me that he thought I killed Paul."

"But that's ridiculous!" Penny exclaimed. "Why would he think that?"

"That's just Hank's style," Frank said reassuringly. "It doesn't mean a thing."

"He has good reasons to be suspicious," Julia said quietly.

As expected, her remark brought a quick look of surprise from both Frank and Penny. "I was parked outside Paul's house shortly before he was killed," she explained.

Frank was silent for a moment, then sat down across

from her, his fingers interlaced on the tabletop. "What were you doing there?"

She repeated what she had learned from Phil at the bank and her decision to confront Paul. When she mentioned her ex-husband's marriage proposal, Penny stared at her, bewildered. "Marriage? What made him think you'd even consider such a thing?"

"Maybe he thought he could use the loan as leverage, I don't know. I could never figure him out." She looked down at her hands, afraid to say anything more.

Frank was watching her closely. "What is it, Jules?" he asked, using the nickname he had given her years ago. "What aren't you telling us?"

"Nothing."

"You're lying."

Penny threw him a scolding look. "Frank! What are you doing? Can't you see she's upset?"

"Of course I can see she's upset. I can also see she's not telling me everything." Turning back to Julia, he said, "I want to help you, Julia, but unless you level with me, I won't be able to do that."

"I don't want to bring you into this."

"Forget about that. Is there something you didn't tell Hammond?"

Julia nodded.

"What?"

She looked up. "Paul grabbed me and kissed me."

"That snake," Penny muttered under her breath.

"I overreacted," Julia continued. "I...I slapped him. That's why I couldn't bring myself to tell Hammond. Now if he finds out..."

"He won't," Frank said with a firm shake of his head. "Knowing how Paul hated to lose face, I doubt he told anyone you slapped him. And even if Hammond does find out, so what? A slap isn't proof you killed your ex-husband." He patted her hand. "Don't worry about it, okay? It's no big deal."

He glanced at his watch. "I tell you what. I'll go back to the station and see how the investigation is progressing. I imagine Charles Bradshaw has already put pressure on the chief to give this case top priority, so things should start popping soon."

Feeling better, Julia nodded. "Thanks, Frank."

He looked toward the back of the house. "Okay if I check on my pal? He might need a little man-to-man talk."

Julia gave him a weak smile. "He would love that."

Four

In a smoky tavern in downtown Sacramento, former army master sergeant Cooper ''Coop'' Reid sat at the bar, nursing a Coke. From time to time he looked up at the TV set above the counter, where a baseball game between the San Diego Padres and the San Francisco Giants lumbered at an excruciating pace.

Coop took another sip of his Coke and grimaced. God almighty, how could people drink this foul stuff and like it? The metallic taste reminded him of the cough syrup his mother used to pour down his throat when he was a kid. He hadn't liked it then and he sure didn't like it now.

A sigh caught in his throat as he set the glass back on the water-stained counter. What he really longed for was a shot of Johnny Walker. Or a cold draft. Anything that would take the edge off. And chase away the medicinal taste of this damned soda.

The longing remained just that—a longing. He had made a promise. Not to his wife or daughter, both of whom he hadn't seen in over twenty years; not to his landlady, who had kicked him out for disturbing the peace; and not even to his parole officer, who had sworn he'd haul his sorry ass back to jail if Coop so much as sniffed another drink.

No, sir. This time he had quit because he wanted to. After reaching rock bottom and going to hell and back, Coop Reid had decided he'd had enough.

Glancing up, he caught his reflection in the mirror behind the bar and shook his head in disgust. Time and booze had taken their toll, adding pouches under his eyes and lines around his mouth as deep as crevices. Most of his fiery red hair had turned a dull shade of gray, and even now, after twenty-five days of sobriety, his eyes still looked the way they used to after a three-day binge.

A hand that had once been steady enough to shoot a running rabbit at fifty feet went up to his face and rubbed the day-old stubble. He was glad to see he no longer had the shakes, though he doubted he'd ever be able to shoot a gun with any accuracy again.

As they often did when he was sober, his thoughts turned to Grace, the beautiful, courageous wife he had left behind. Would she recognize him if she passed him in the street? Probably not. He, on the other hand, would recognize her in a heartbeat. How could he forget those beautiful green eyes? Or that gentle smile?

At the thought of all he had loved and lost, his heart filled with sorrow. Twenty-three years since he'd seen his family. Twenty-three years since that fateful night when he had told Grace he had lost another job because of his drinking. That's when she had finally turned on him, angry and fed up.

"I can't take it anymore, Coop," she had said, with tears of despair streaming down her cheeks. "I've had it with the binges and the bar brawls, with having to bail you out of jail. Julia is eleven years old now, and Jordan is nine. I can't hide things from them the way I used to when they were younger. And I don't want them growing up with a drunken father for a role model. Either you sober up, for good this time, or you leave."

But Coop knew he could no more stop drinking than he

could stop breathing. Not even with Grace's ultimatum hanging over his head.

So the following morning, while his wife and two beautiful kids slept, he had kissed them goodbye, and, like the coward he was, he had walked out on them, convinced they'd be better off without him.

As the years passed, he had drifted from city to city, job to job, dingy motel room to dingy motel room. Because he had left their meager savings with Grace, he had no money except what he managed to earn doing odd jobs.

He had kept in touch with only one person—his old army buddy, Spike Sorensen. The two men had served in Vietnam together, in the elite Fifth Special Forces. Upon his discharge, Spike had found a job with an oil company and now spent most of his time traveling the high seas on an oil rig. Every couple of years, he returned to his hunting cabin in the Santa Lucia Mountains, twenty-five miles east of Monterey, for well-deserved R and R. If there was a message from Coop on the answering machine, Spike always called back, and if he could, he would give him news of his family.

That's how Coop had learned of Jordan's death.

He closed his eyes, remembering that day as if it were yesterday. And he remembered the pain, as if someone had plunged a knife in his gut.

Eventually, he had pulled himself together and made plans to go home for the funeral. And if Grace let him, help her through the ordeal. But halfway home, he had met with another bottle and never made it past Modesto.

Three weeks ago, following a bar brawl, Coop had found himself in jail with no recollection of how he'd gotten there.

It had scared the hell out of him. That evening, he had

gone to an AA meeting, another of many he had attended in the past, vowing to stay with the program.

And now here he was, twenty-five days later, and to his amazement, still sober. He had even found a new job, some light carpentry work the owner of a hardware shop had offered him. It didn't pay much, but it put food in his stomach and a roof over his head.

In time he would find something better. For now, this was enough. As for his sobriety, he would take that challenge one day at a time—AA's credo—and keep his fingers crossed.

Coming into Clyde's Tavern every day and drinking something he didn't like was a test of his own strength. Though not one recommended by AA, it worked for him. The bartender knew what he wanted—the special of the day and a Coke—put it in front of him and left him alone.

Taking a last gulp of the cola, Coop raised his gaze to the TV again. The ball game was finally over and the six o'clock news had already begun.

Suddenly, as photographs of a young woman and a little boy filled the upper right corner of the screen, Coop almost dropped his glass. His heart in his throat, he took in the blond curls, the wide-set green eyes so much like Gracie's, the generous mouth, the proud chin.

Julia. His Julia.

"Hey, Joe." Coop didn't take his eyes off the screen. "Turn up the sound, will you?"

Joe took the remote from under the counter, pointed it at the TV and pressed a button.

"...Councilman Paul Bradshaw is survived by his father, former California governor Charles Bradshaw, and his six-year-old son, Andrew. Police are still searching for Bradshaw's killer, and while no arrest has been made, a report confirmed that the councilman's former spouse, Julia Bradshaw, was being questioned as to her whereabouts on the night of the murder. Mrs. Bradshaw was not available for comments regarding the allegations that she may be a suspect. In other news..."

"Julia," Coop whispered, still looking at the screen even though the snapshot was no longer there. "My little Julia." He wouldn't have recognized her if it hadn't been for the newspaper clipping Spike had sent him after Jordan's funeral. And the boy. Dear God, that boy was his grandson.

He started to bring the Coke to his lips, but his hand shook so badly he had to put the glass down. His little girl suspected of murder. How could that be? She was the sweetest, kindest girl he knew. She had cried the day their neighbor's cat had died, not only out of grief for the feline but because the cat's owner, a nice old lady who always baked the kids cookies, was inconsolable. Julia had gone to the shelter, paid the required fee using her own money, and had brought back a little black kitten for her neighbor.

So what the hell were they doing talking of allegations and calling his Julia a murder suspect?

He had to talk to Spike, find out exactly what kind of evidence the police had. He wasn't sure his friend was back, though. Coop hadn't talked to him since Jordan's death a year ago. But it was worth a try.

His legs more steady than they'd been in years, he walked to the public phone against the far wall, put a handful of quarters in the slot and dialed his friend's number from memory. At the fourth ring, Spike's machine clicked on. Coop waited for the short message to end before leaving his number at the hardware store.

Back at the bar, he put his elbows on the counter and took his head between his hands.

"Another Coke, chief?"

Dragging his hands down his face, Coop nodded. He needed something to chase away the dryness in his throat.

And he needed to see his little girl.

The thought of going home had crossed his mind more than once in the last twenty-five days. Each time he had rejected it, certain his family didn't want to see him.

But it was different now. Julia was in trouble. And there was the boy. Now that Coop had seen his face, he couldn't get him out of his mind. A small, sad smile played on his lips. How would it feel, he wondered, to be a grandfather? To take the kid fishing, play catch with him? Do all the things he hadn't done with his own son?

Maybe he should go and find out. Julia had always been a forgiving soul. And she needed him.

The stupidity of that thought made him laugh. Who was he kidding? She had done without him for twenty-three years. What made him think she'd even want to look at him? That she wouldn't slam the door in his face?

He wasn't even sure his parole officer would let him leave the county. Maybe it could be arranged, though, as long as he reported to another P.O. in Monterey. And stayed out of trouble.

Coop sat at the bar for another half hour, turning his glass around and around, making water rings on the already ringed surface. At the back of the bar, someone had dropped a quarter in the jukebox and the mournful sounds of Reba McEntire lamenting over her lost love filled the room.

After a while, Coop stood up, took a few bills from his pocket, enough to cover the bill, then added another five-buck tip. What the hell, it was only money. And Joe had treated him right.

Then, with a two-finger salute to the bartender, he walked out of the tavern and into the damp night.

Five

More than three hundred people had come to El Camino Cemetery, high in the Monterey hills, to pay their last respects to Councilman Paul Bradshaw.

Julia wasn't surprised at the large number of mourners. Since the day Paul's grandfather had been elected first mayor of Monterey in the late 1800s, the Bradshaws had enjoyed a tremendous popularity in the area. But it wasn't until Charles had inherited the family fortune and donated huge sums of money to help the needy and to embellish the town that the people of Monterey began to treat the Bradshaws like gods.

Next to Charles, a handful of distant relatives Julia hadn't seen since her wedding seven years ago stood by the freshly dug grave, their expressions as coldly detached as those of strangers. Not one of them made eye contact with her. But then, they hadn't been overly friendly at the wedding, either.

A few feet away, camera crews from all over California filmed the arrival of several city dignitaries—the chief of police, who was also Charles's best friend; the district attorney; the mayor and his three remaining councilmen.

Although Charles's lawyer had informed Julia of the funeral arrangements, only Andrew had been asked to ride in the limousine with Charles. He stood next to his grandfather now, a solemn, sad-looking little boy in his Sunday suit.

No sooner had the townspeople begun to arrive than tongues started wagging.

"The nerve of her showing up here," a woman whispered, loudly enough for Julia to hear.

"As if she hadn't done enough harm."

"The one I really feel sorry for is the boy."

"If you ask me," another female voice chimed in, "Charles should take him, give him a proper upbringing."

It took all of Julia's self-control to hold on to her temper. Stoic and dry-eyed, she tuned out the malicious gossip and stared at Reverend Barlow, the same minister who had married her and Paul.

She was well aware that the people of Monterey had never liked her. At the news that Paul Bradshaw was marrying the daughter of a drunk, a man who had abandoned his family, no less, a wave of horror had rippled through the small town. Why her? they had asked. What contribution could a girl like Julia Reid possibly make to Paul's future?

Six years later, they had blamed her again, this time for divorcing their golden boy. Even though she and Paul had claimed irreconcilable differences, people had been quick to point a finger at her. Why hadn't she tried to make the marriage work? How could she be so heartless and leave him, when his career was just taking off?

And now he was dead. And they blamed her again.

Watching the mourners as they filed past to offer their condolences to Charles a few minutes later, Julia wondered how they would feel if they knew the man they had come to mourn, the man in whom they had placed so much faith and hope, was a wife beater.

Would they even believe her?

"Julia?"

Julia turned to see Barry Specter, the mayor of Monterey. Specter and Paul had been friends once, but Paul's recent decision to run for county commissioner and campaign against his boss had put a serious damper on the relationship.

Behind him, her gaze heavy with resentment as she stared at Julia, was Paul's devoted secretary, Edith Donnovan. Rather than offer words of sympathy, Edith leaned toward the mayor, said something only he could hear, and left.

"What a terrible thing." Specter, looking grave, pressed Julia's hands, then glanced down at Andrew, who had returned to Julia's side. "I want you both to know that I'll do everything in my power, spare no expense, to find out who did this."

"Thank you, Barry." Julia had never liked Specter. Nor did she trust him. It didn't take a crystal ball to know that he not only didn't give a damn about Paul's death, he was probably celebrating it. With such a formidable opponent out of the way, his election as the new county commissioner was more or less a certainty.

Andrew tugged at her sleeve. "Are we going to Grandpa's house now, Mom?"

Julia wished she could say no. The thought of mingling with people who resented her so much, feeling their stares and listening to their spiteful comments, was more than she could endure.

But Andrew obviously expected to spend more time with his grandfather and she didn't want to disappoint him. Or give Charles another reason to criticize her. And who knew? Maybe in his moment of grief, her former father-in-law would finally let bygones be bygones and be civil to her.

"Yes, Andrew. You'll excuse us, won't you?" she asked Specter.

"Of course."

As the mayor and his small entourage left, Julia turned to her mother. "Will you come, too, Mom?" Leaning toward Grace, she whispered, "I may need a little moral support."

Grace gave a discreet nod of her head.

As the mourners drifted toward the long stream of waiting cars that lined the road, Julia wrapped her arm around Andrew's shoulders, and together they made their way toward the Volvo.

The Bradshaw mansion, overlooking Monterey Bay, had been built by Charles's father, a man with tastes as lavish as they were ostentatious. Victorian and grandiose, the famous landmark harbored twenty-two rooms and tons of antiques whose past was as illustrious as the family itself. In back of the property was a magnificent rose garden Paul's late mother had begun when she and Charles had moved into the house forty years earlier. After Sarah Bradshaw's death in 1982, her practice of opening the garden once a year to the public had continued. The event still attracted the curious by the thousands.

Pilar, Charles's longtime housekeeper, was surveying the buffet table when Julia arrived. She was a small, round woman with thick gray hair, a bronzed complexion and kind eyes. Opinionated and outspoken, she was Charles's greatest supporter and his harshest critic. Their heated arguments were legendary, and many wondered why Charles tolerated such behavior from a servant.

The truth was that Pilar, fiery temper and all, had become an indispensable part of the Bradshaw household, and Charles simply could not manage without her.

Looking up, the housekeeper saw Julia and rushed to greet her and Andrew, offering her condolences to both.

"How are you doing?" Julia asked, knowing how much Pilar had loved Charles's children.

"It's a sad day, *señora.*" Pilar gazed down at Andrew, one hand on his shoulder. *"¿Y tu, pequeño?"* she asked, using the Spanish she had taught him over the years. *"¿Como estas?"*

"I'm almost seven," he replied. "You don't have to call me *pequeño* anymore."

Pilar chuckled. "Sorry, big guy," she said in her accented English. "I'll try to remember that. In the meantime, can I get you some food? A soda?"

Andrew shook his head. "No, thank you, Pilar."

"¿Como?" Pilar cupped her ear. "I didn't quite understand that."

Andrew smiled. *"No, gracias, Pilar."*

"Much better." She ruffled his hair. "What about you, Mrs. Bradshaw? Mrs. Reid? I'd be glad to fix you a small plate."

Julia shook her head. Her stomach was in such knots, she couldn't have swallowed a thing. "We won't be staying long." Julia's gaze swept over the room in search of Charles. She hadn't yet had a chance to offer her condolences, and wanted to get that ordeal over with as quickly as possible. "It's been a trying day for Andrew. He needs to be home."

"He needs to be here," a cold voice said behind them. "Where he belongs."

Grateful to Pilar and Grace, who quickly took Andrew away, Julia turned to face her former father-in-law. At sixty-six, Charles Bradshaw had remained an imposing man. Well over six foot, he had an athletic build he maintained with daily rounds of tennis. Snow-white hair, blue eyes and dark eyebrows that met in a thick, straight line gave him a predatory look. Standing before her, his lips pressed together, he pinned her with one of his implacable stares, as if daring her to defy him.

Julia refused to be intimidated. The days when she shrank at the mere sight of him were long gone. "Andrew needs to grieve, Charles, not to be put on public display."

"What do you know about grieving? You killed my son."

"I did not." Because she hated scenes, she kept her voice just a notch above a whisper. "And you know it."

Charles made a sarcastic sound. "All that phony sincerity may have fooled the police, but it's not fooling me. I know about the mortgage loan Paul bought from Phil, and I know about your visit to Paul's house last Friday night."

She wasn't surprised to find him so well-informed. Charles had spies everywhere. "Then you must also know that I never went inside the house," she said, enduring his hard stare.

"I know that you hated him."

For good reason, Charles. She kept that thought to herself. Even now, with Paul dead, she had no intention of breaking her promise to him. Or shatter Andrew's life by letting him find out that his father had abused her. "I didn't hate Paul," she said in reply to his remark. "But even if I did, that wouldn't make me a killer."

Hands behind his back, Charles surveyed the room, nodding at an acquaintance every now and then. Without looking at her, he said, "You'll soon find out so I might as well tell you. I intend to file for custody of Andrew."

Julia felt as though she had been sucker-punched. She gripped the edge of a small table next to her. "File for custody?" she repeated dully. "You want to take my child? Have you lost your mind?"

"Everyone agrees he'd be better off with me."

"I don't give a damn what everyone agrees to." Aware that a small group had turned around and was looking at them, she took a deep, head-clearing breath. When the shaking inside her subsided, she spoke again, much more calmly this time.

"Andrew is my son, Charles, and nothing you have—not your money, not your power, not your connections—is going to change that."

The cold blue eyes glistened with animosity as they assessed her. "And who will look after him if you go to prison? Or if your business collapses and you have to go to work?"

"I will not go to prison," she said, her anger increasingly difficult to control. "And, as much as you would like it to, my business will not collapse."

"Are you sure about that?" Charles's mouth curved in a thin, nasty smile. "You may not be aware of the terms of Paul's will just yet, but that mortgage he bought from the Monterey Bank is now mine. And I'm afraid I won't be as accommodating as Phil, who ran that bank into the ground, or Paul, who had marshmallows for brains. *I* will insist on being paid according to the terms of your loan agreement in full, on the first of every month."

She didn't flinch. "You'll get your money."

His penetrating eyes still held hers. "How? I checked you out. That new resort up the hill is killing you. My guess is you'll be filing for bankruptcy before the end of the summer."

"Don't count on it." She moved to stand in front of him. "And don't underestimate me, Charles. Or what I can do when I'm pushed."

His eyes burned with a cruel light. "I already know what

you can do when you're pushed, Julia. Now all I have to do is prove it."

Exercising all the willpower she could muster, Julia bit off a sharp reply. Then, knowing she couldn't bear spending another second in this house, she turned away and went to look for Andrew.

"Are you sure you're all right?" Grace asked when the three of them were back at The Hacienda. "You've hardly said a word since we left Charles's house."

Though Julia was still shaken from her confrontation with Charles, she didn't let it show. The last thing she wanted right now was to worry her mother. "I'm fine, Mom. It's been a trying day, that's all."

Turning to Andrew, Julia helped him take off his jacket. "What about you, sweetie? Are you tired? Hungry? I could make you a sandwich."

With a hand that seemed to weigh a ton, Andrew pulled off his tie and shook his head.

Concerned, Julia crouched in front of him and held him by the waist. "Then why don't we ask your friend Jimmy to come over?" she suggested. "He could even stay for dinner if you'd like. I was thinking of making your favorite—sloppy joes and fries."

But instead of a smile of approval, Andrew gave another shake of his head. "I'd like to go to my room, please." His big blue eyes, usually so sparkling, looked dull and sad. "May I?"

"Yes, of course, darling." She pushed back his cowlick and kept her hand there. "Would you like me to come with you?" she asked hopefully.

"No."

Dismayed, she watched him disappear down the hall.

"Oh, Mom," she said, throwing her mother a helpless look. "He's hurting."

"I know, baby." Grace wrapped a comforting arm around Julia's shoulders. "And I know that you want to help him, but children have their own way of grieving, and if he wants to be alone right now, you have to respect that. He'll let you know when he needs you."

Julia nodded. Her mother was right. Children needed their space just as adults did, but seeing him looking so dispirited tore her heart. In an hour or so, she would go and check on him. Maybe by then he'd be ready to talk.

"I'm going to make you some tea," her mother said, already busying herself at the stove. "You look like you need it. You've been on edge all day."

Julia almost laughed. *You'd be on edge, too, Mom, if someone had just threatened to take your business* and *your child.*

She had barely finished that thought when the phone rang. She picked it up. "Hello?"

"Mrs. Bradshaw?" The voice was young, female and hesitant.

"Yes. Who is this?"

"You don't know me, Mrs. Bradshaw. My name is Jennifer Seavers. I'm Eli Seavers's niece."

"I'm afraid I don't know an Eli Seavers, either."

"I wasn't sure if you did or not." There was a pause. "My uncle is ill, Mrs. Bradshaw. He has Alzheimer's and has been confined to a nursing home for the past six months."

Julia glanced at Grace, who was watching her, and gave a puzzled shrug. "I'm sorry to hear that."

"The reason I called is because my uncle was watching your ex-husband's funeral on TV earlier today, and when he heard the name Bradshaw, there was a flicker of recognition in his eyes, which is strange, considering he hasn't recognized anyone in months."

"Did your uncle know Paul?" Julia asked.

"I don't know. But he became very agitated, even more so when the camera spanned across the crowd and he saw your little boy. That's when he started saying his son's name—Joey—over and over."

"Then maybe you ought to have this conversation with his son," Julia suggested gently.

"My cousin died when he was just a little boy, Mrs. Bradshaw. That was thirty-two years ago. My uncle hasn't mentioned Joey's name once since he was admitted to Pine Hill Nursing Home. And like I said, he hasn't recognized anyone, including me, for several months. But today, the Bradshaw name triggered his memory."

Julia stiffened, though she wasn't sure why. "Triggered how? What did he say?"

"He didn't say anything. He just...reacted."

"I'm not sure why you're calling me, Miss Seavers." Julia nodded her thanks as her mother put a mug of tea in front of her. "I can't help you. Or your uncle."

"I think you can," Jennifer said earnestly. "This is the most encouraging sign we've had since my uncle was admitted to the nursing home, and I thought if you could...I mean, I was hoping..." She made a small choking sound and let the sentence go unfinished.

Julia felt sorry for the girl. She seemed to genuinely care for her uncle, though Julia wasn't sure what all this had to do with her. "You were hoping what?" she asked gently.

Jennifer cleared her throat. "That you could come to Pine Hill." She said it quickly, as if afraid she might lose her nerve. "I know it's a lot to ask on a day like this, and believe me, Mrs. Bradshaw, I wouldn't if I didn't feel your visit might help my uncle somehow. Or at the very least, calm him down.'' In a rush, she added, ''Pine Hill is in Carmel Valley, only thirty minutes or so from Monterey.''

''I suppose I could stop by for a few minutes,'' Julia said. ''But not today. Today I need to be here, with my son. Would tomorrow be all right?''

''That would be fine. Thank you so much, Mrs. Bradshaw.''

Julia picked up a pad and pen on her desk. ''All right then. Give me the address.''

Six

Pine Hill Nursing Home was located in the highlands above Carmel Valley just north of San Jose Creek. From the gnarled, rocky promontory where the sprawling medical building sat, the sweeping view of Monastery Beach was spectacular. And judging from the number of patients sitting on the lawn by themselves, or with a visiting relative, the site was one of the most popular in the entire facility.

Jennifer Seavers was waiting at the nurses' station when Julia arrived. She was a pretty young woman with light brown hair cut in a short pixie style, brown eyes and a quick step as she hurried to meet Julia.

"How's your uncle?" Julia asked as they shook hands.

"Still agitated, though not as badly as he was yesterday."

They walked down the green-floored hallway, Julia's heels clicking with each step.

Jennifer led Julia into a sparsely furnished room with green walls, a small dresser and a bed. A few personal items and photographs yellowed by time stood on the dresser, the only reminder that the patient in room 106 had once been a normal, functioning human being.

A man with his back to Julia sat in a rocking chair, staring out the window. Moving closer, she was shocked to see how fragile he looked when she saw his face. Deep lines bracketed his mouth and only a few wisps of gray hair remained on his head. He wore tan pants, a neat white shirt opened at the neck and a beige cardigan two sizes too big.

He didn't look at Julia or Jennifer, but seemed totally absorbed by the pastoral scene outside his window.

"Uncle Eli?" Jennifer crouched beside the still figure and took his limp hand in hers. "Julia Bradshaw is here."

The man's head turned and his dull gaze met Julia's.

Julia smiled. "How are you, Eli?"

The man's dry, white lips began to move and the look in his eyes, so blank a moment ago, grew fearful.

"Uncle Eli, please don't be afraid." Jennifer gave his trembling hand a few reassuring pats. "No one is going to hurt you."

Julia took a step back. "Is that what he thinks? That I'm going to hurt him?"

"It's not you. He's afraid of everyone. Paranoia is one of the illness's many symptoms, as well as a loss of memory."

From a nearby tray, Jennifer took a paper cup half-filled with water, and brought it to Eli's mouth. He took a small sip, then another, but didn't thank her.

"I can't believe how quickly he's deteriorated," Jennifer continued. "Ever since he was admitted here, all he does is stare at the television or out the window, in complete silence."

"How old is he?"

"He turned sixty-four yesterday. I know," she added as she caught Julia's look of surprise. "He looks a lot older."

"Did he live here in Carmel?"

"In Salinas. And I live in Ventura, which makes it difficult for me to come up as often as I'd like. I'm working my way through college by waiting tables," she explained.

Julia was thoughtful for a moment. "I'm trying to recall

if my ex-husband ever mentioned knowing someone in Salinas, but I can't. What did your uncle do?"

"He used to teach economics at UCLA a long time ago. Then when Joey died of leukemia, everything changed. Uncle Eli left his job, stopped seeing his friends, shut everyone out. On the first anniversary of his son's death, he told my aunt he was filing for divorce. He left her everything he owned and moved to the Middle East, where he took a teaching job at the American University in Beirut. He stayed there for twenty years, but came back every summer to visit. Eventually he moved back to California, but I didn't find that out until six months ago."

Julia watched as Jennifer took a tissue from a box and dabbed the dribble at the corner of Eli's mouth. "You seem very fond of your uncle."

The young woman's eyes filled with tears. "I wasn't born when he left L.A., but I have wonderful memories of his yearly visits and the presents he always brought me—beautiful dolls in Middle Eastern costumes, colorful bags, jewelry."

"And he never contacted you when he came back permanently?"

Jennifer straightened up and discarded the tissue. "I don't understand it, either. Now that my father is dead, Uncle Eli is all the family I have left. And I know he cared for me." The small sound she made seemed perilously close to a sob. "But for some reason, he didn't want to see me."

Julia felt a lump in her throat. Such a young girl to have no one left but this man who no longer knew her. "How did you finally find him?"

"When my uncle was diagnosed with early Alzheimer's a couple of years ago, his neighbor began looking in on him from time to time. Then this past December, she found him wandering outside his house, disoriented and frightened. After calling a doctor, she went through Eli's papers in search of relatives and found my name and address."

"So he knew where you lived?"

She nodded, looking sad. "Apparently. When Mrs. Hathaway—that's his neighbor—called me, I came right away. He was pretty sick by then and I knew I had to put him in a facility where he would get proper care. I would have liked to have him close to me, but the only opening was here at Pine Hill."

Jennifer moved aside to make room for Julia. "Maybe if you started talking to him and told him your name again, he might respond to you."

"Of course." Julia pulled out a chair and sat down. "Hi," she said softly as Eli turned to look at her. "I'm Julia Bradshaw. Have we met before, Mr. Seavers? Or perhaps you knew my ex-husband? Paul Bradshaw?"

At the name, Eli shrank back in his chair. For a few seconds, as his mouth opened, he looked as if he was about to cry out. Then his expression grew vacant again and he returned his attention to the rolling hills outside the window.

"Jennifer tells me you saw Paul's funeral on TV," Julia continued. Remembering that Eli had confused his son with Andrew, she added, "And I understand that you saw my son."

Eli began to rock, slowly at first, then with more vigor.

"His name is Andrew," Julia continued. "He's six years old—almost seven, actually. And quite a handful." She smiled. "You know how little boys are."

Eli continued to rock.

Feeling as if she had let the young woman down, Julia looked at Jennifer and shook her head. "I'm sorry. I'm afraid I'm not reaching him."

"I'm the one who should apologize," Jennifer said with a sigh. "I made you come all the way here for nothing."

Julia squeezed the young woman's hand. "You couldn't have known. And you were trying to help him."

As Julia stood up, a cold hand clamped over her wrist, startling her.

She glanced down. Eli was staring at her, his eyes suddenly very bright, almost feverish looking. With a strength remarkable for such a frail man, he pulled her down toward him. "*Gleic Éire* did it," he whispered.

Julia felt a sudden chill. *Gleic Éire?* The Irish extremist group that had killed Paul's sister eight years ago?

Eli darted a quick, frightened look around him. "Be careful," he said in a raspy whisper. "Don't let them take Joey." He tugged on Julia's wrist until her face was only a few inches from his. Up close his eyes seemed to burn with a light so intense, Julia tried to pull back.

His gnarled fingers tightened around her wrist. "Trust no one," he whispered.

Julia sat down again and looked deeply into the man's eyes. "Are you saying that *Gleic Éire* killed Paul Bradshaw?" she asked in a low voice.

The flame in Eli's eyes faded. His hand let go of Julia's wrist and fell back on his lap, limp.

"Eli, please, talk to me." Desperate to bring him back, she took his arm and shook it gently. "Do you know who killed Paul Bradshaw?"

But Eli didn't seem to hear her. His eyes blank, his mouth slack, he began to rock again.

Julia stared at him for a long moment. Had the man experienced a moment of lucidity? she wondered. Or were his imaginary fears worse than she had realized?

She looked up at Jennifer, whose face had gone pale. "Has he ever mentioned *Gleic Éire* before?"

Jennifer shook her head. "No. When he was first admitted to Pine Hill, his fears were focused on marching soldiers, men he believed were coming to get him."

Julia's hands clasped on her lap. *Gleic Éire,* which meant the "Irish Struggle" in Gaelic Irish, was a small but well-organized, well-armed Irish militant group that had spread terror throughout Ireland and England for the past four decades.

Eight years ago, while Julia was interning at the Fairmont Hotel in San Francisco, Sheila Bradshaw had been killed by a terrorist bomb as she was walking past the British Consulate in Manhattan. The attack, meant to kill the visiting British prime minister, took the lives of three people, including Sheila, and injured a dozen others.

Immediately following the blast, the *New York Times* had received a taped message in which *Gleic Éire* had claimed responsibility for the bombing.

The FBI, assisted by Scotland Yard, had conducted a massive search for the killers, both in the U.S. and in the British Isles, but the group, rumored to be headed by wealthy Irish Americans, had remained as elusive as air.

Julia glanced at the pitiful figure slumped in the rocker. For a brief moment, he had sounded so sure of himself, so…passionate. Could he have been telling the truth? Or had he been hallucinating?

Those were questions that needed answers—answers Eli couldn't give her. Not now that he had retreated into his own solitary world.

Maybe Frank would know how to handle him. Or Detective Hammond, though how much credibility he'd put on the ramblings of a sick, old man was anyone's guess.

Only mildly hopeful, Julia said goodbye to Jennifer and left the nursing home.

* * *

After calling her mother and asking her to watch Andrew a little while longer, Julia drove directly to Penny and Frank's house.

The couple had purchased the charming Cape Cod two years ago. Penny, who loved the outdoors, had transformed the simple yard into a lush English garden that was a perfect showcase for her sculpting talents. Whimsical clay animals, mostly rabbits, squirrels and chipmunks, were everywhere, peeking from behind thick rhododendrons, lining the brick pathway, even guarding the front door.

Frank, who was on the midnight-to-four-o'clock shift, let Julia in just as Penny walked in from her studio in the back of the house. She wore a long, wraparound navy apron and had piled her long brown hair on top of her head in a haphazard bun.

"I called the inn to find out how you made out with Charles at the funeral," she said, looking concerned. "But your mother said you had gone to see someone in a Carmel nursing home?"

Julia told them about her puzzling visit with Jennifer's uncle and his startling accusation.

"Are you sure that's what he said?" Frank asked when she was finished. "*Gleic Éire?* You couldn't have misunderstood?"

Julia shook her head. "His niece heard it, too. She said it was the most lucid thing he had said in weeks."

Penny looked from Julia to her husband. "Wait a minute. Are we talking about the terrorist group? The same people who bombed the British Consulate in New York City eight years ago and killed Sheila Bradshaw?"

Frank nodded, his expression grim. "They're the ones." He turned to look at Julia. "But why would they want to kill Paul? They have only one cause and that's to separate Northern Ireland from Great Britain. Why would they come after a small-town American politician? It makes no sense.''

''It does to me,'' Penny interjected. ''Don't you remember how angry Paul was when Sheila died? How he vowed to find the leaders of *Gleic Éire* and bring them to justice?''

Frank chuckled. ''That resolve lasted all but two months, if I recall. Long enough for him to take advantage of the publicity and get himself elected to council.''

That was true, Julia thought. Not a particularly brilliant politician, Paul had a knack for manipulating the press that was second to none. The publicity surrounding his sister's death had been brilliantly, even cunningly orchestrated, and in the end, it had won him a landslide victory.

''Maybe he had decided to reopen Sheila's case,'' Penny suggested. ''And in the process found new evidence.'' She gripped her husband's arm. ''What if that's what he was planning to announce at the news conference?''

A frown creased Frank's handsome face as he looked at Julia. ''Did Paul say anything to you about the news conference, Jules? Give you any hint at all of what it was about?''

''Not a word,'' Julia said, remembering her conversation with Paul. ''All he seemed to have on his mind that day was that stupid marriage proposal.''

''Hmm.'' Frank was silent for a moment. Then, having apparently made up his mind about something, he slapped the chair's armrests. ''Let's call Hank. He may not be able to get much more out of Eli Seavers than you did, but he can run a background check on the guy, see how he occupied his time after he returned to California.''

Julia gave a short, bitter laugh. ''Why should Hammond even bother to investigate other suspects when he already has one, fully endorsed by Charles Bradshaw?''

''Because he's a good cop,'' Frank replied.

He stood up and walked over to the phone. He only had to wait a few seconds for his call to be transferred to the homicide detective.

"Hank, it's Frank Walsh," he said, turning so he faced the two women. "Julia Bradshaw is here, at my house, yes. She has information I think you should hear."

He glanced at Julia. "Do you want to talk to him here or at The Hacienda?"

"Here," Julia said quickly. "I don't want Andrew to hear any of this."

Frank relayed the message and hung up. "He's on his way."

Seven

Sitting alone at the kitchen table, Julia sipped her chamomile tea and tried to relax. It was no use. The events of the last forty-eight hours—the funeral, her quarrel with Charles and her visit to Pine Hill Nursing Home—had her nerves wound tighter than piano wire.

Her earlier conversation with Detective Hammond had gone pretty much as expected. Though intrigued by Eli Seavers's accusation, the detective had been skeptical about the validity of the man's words.

"I'll check it out," he had told her as he took notes in the same little black book he had used when he had questioned her. "But I wouldn't get my hopes too high if I were you. Police departments all over the country, as well as the FBI, receive hundreds of calls a year from people who claim to know where *Gleic Éire*'s leaders are holed up. We check them all out. We have to, but we haven't turned up anything yet."

And the way her luck was running these days, Julia thought in a rare moment of self-pity, they wouldn't turn up anything this time.

The sudden sound of shattering glass followed by a loud thump made her jump out of her chair like a shot.

Too startled to be frightened, she ran into the foyer. The broken remains of the small stained-glass window above the front door lay at her feet. Among the colored shards was a package—a brick, she realized, loosely wrapped in newspaper and secured with a rubber band.

From the road came the sound of screeching tires as a car sped away. Anger bubbling up, Julia yanked the door open and ran outside. She was too late. The car had already disappeared into the thick fog.

Her heart thudding in her chest, she walked back toward The Hacienda, worried that the noise might have awakened Andrew. But instead of her son, she found her two guests, a retired schoolteacher from Joliet, Illinois, and a Seattle accountant, standing in the foyer. Their robes untied over their pajamas, their mouths open, they stared at the gaping hole where the window had been.

"Mrs. Bradshaw!" Emilie Harris exclaimed. "What happened?"

"That's plain as day to me." The accountant, Jack Woods, cranky by nature, looked at Julia as if she were somehow to blame for the incident. "Some joker threw a goddamned brick through the window."

Ignoring his belligerent tone, Julia picked up the package and unwrapped it. And immediately saw the message scrawled across the page in big red letters. A cold, clammy feeling swept over her as she read the single accusing word.

Murderer.

Emilie Harris's hands were clutched to her breasts. "What does it say, Mrs. Bradshaw?"

Her hands trembling, Julia quickly folded the newspaper. "Nothing. It's prom week, so I'm sure it's just—"

"Like hell, it's nothing." Jack Woods walked toward her, jabbing his index finger at the newspaper. "We're guests in your house, Mrs. Bradshaw. If that's a threatening note, something that might endanger our lives, we have a right to know."

"It's not a threatening note."

But before she could stop him, the accountant snatched the paper from her hands, glared at the scrawled word, then back at Julia.

"Will someone please tell me what it says?" Mrs. Harris's voice was filled with panic. When Woods held the newspaper out to her, she let out a gasp. "Oh, my God!"

"Who are they calling a murderer?" the accountant demanded. "You?"

"Yes, but there's no truth to it," Julia protested. "I didn't kill anyone." She hoped her candor would somehow appease him. It didn't.

"They're talking about the murder of your ex-husband, aren't they?" Emilie Harris's small eyes glistened with sudden curiosity. She turned to Woods. "The man across the street told me the police were here last week, questioning her."

Woods's gaze hardened as he looked at Julia. "They think you killed your ex-husband?"

"No, of course not." Faced with such hostility, Julia tried desperately not to lose control of the situation. "If they did they would have already arrested me."

Woods brandished the newspaper like a sword and shook it. "But someone obviously thinks you did kill him or they wouldn't be calling you a murderer."

"Mr. Woods, please," Julia implored. "There's no need to shout. You'll wake up Andrew—"

Her plea had no effect on him. "Tell me, Mrs. Bradshaw," he said sarcastically. "What can we expect to come flying through the window tomorrow night? Bullets?"

"I told you it's just a stupid prank."

"Well, prank or not, I have no intention of being a target for some lunatic with a vendetta against you." He peered out the side window. "Obviously, I can't go anywhere in this fog, but I'll be leaving first thing in the morning." He gave a curt nod. "Have my bill ready."

"Mine, too," Emilie Harris said pointedly, and followed him up the stairs.

Dismayed, Julia stood watching them, wondering what else could possibly go wrong with her life. In the space of just four days, she had become a murder suspect, been threatened to have her child and her business taken from her, and now this. As her eyes welled up with hot tears, she stared at the glass debris on the floor. She wasn't sure what upset her more, losing her only two guests or realizing someone hated her enough to hurl a brick through her window and call her a murderer.

The need to give in to her despair was strong, but somehow she managed to fight it. She had to pull herself together, for Andrew's sake.

As Julia heard both upstairs doors slam shut, she brushed away her tears, turned around and stopped dead in her tracks.

Andrew stood in the doorway that separated the kitchen from the foyer. His eyes were huge with fear and disbelief.

"Andrew." Quickly, she set the brick and the newspaper on a small table and rushed to him. "What are you doing up?"

"I heard Mr. Woods's voice." Big trusting eyes searched hers. "He said you killed my dad."

Julia felt a wave of panic. She had tried so hard to shield Andrew from the malicious gossip, and now, because of one careless, angry man, the child was more confused than ever.

"He's wrong, Andrew," she said in a tone she hoped was both soft and reassuring. "I didn't kill your dad. I would never do anything like that."

"Then why did he say you did?"

Julia held his hands in hers and stroked them gently. "I don't know, Andrew. Sometimes people need to blame someone, and often that someone is a husband or a wife, or another member of the family. But I swear to you I didn't do it." Suddenly, nothing else mattered but having her little boy's trust restored. "You believe me, don't you?" she asked anxiously.

To her relief, he nodded vigorously, but still seemed worried as he looked past her, toward the foyer. "Did somebody really throw a brick through our window?"

"Oh, that's nothing, darling." She worked up a smile. "Just some stupid kids with nothing better to do."

"Mr. Woods said they were going to shoot us."

Julia took his dear face between her hands and kissed the tip of his nose. "Mr. Woods doesn't know what he's talking about. No one is going to shoot us."

"But what if those people come back?"

"They won't." When her reply failed to reassure him, Julia turned him away from the mess on the floor. "I tell you what. Why don't you help me fix that ugly hole? It so happens that I have a piece of plywood in the carport that will fit perfectly. The problem is, I need a pair of strong arms to help me carry it in." She grinned. "Do I have a volunteer?"

The worried expression disappeared. "I'll help you."

Ten minutes later, Julia had nailed the plywood over the hole. While Andrew looked on, she climbed down from the ladder and stepped back to admire her handiwork.

"Hmm. Not bad if I say so myself. What do you think, sport? Do I have a future as a window repairwoman?"

Andrew made a face. "I don't know, Mom. That plywood is pretty crooked."

Julia tilted her head to the left and tried to sound cheerful. "Not if you look at it *that* way."

Andrew laughed, the first heartfelt laugh she'd heard since Paul's death four days ago.

She ruffled the blond hair. "Now that we have that settled, what do you say I tuck you in again? It's getting pretty late."

He looked up, a flush of embarrassment rising to his cheeks. "Could I sleep in your bed, Mom? Just for tonight?" He hesitated. "I'm a little scared."

Julia felt a quick pang of pain. Poor sweetheart. After all that had happened, violence had now invaded the only place where he felt truly safe—his home. No wonder he was frightened.

Knowing it had taken a lot for him to admit he was scared, Julia kept her tone light. "Okay, but only if you promise not to hog the covers."

The ploy worked. "*You're* the one who hogs the covers."

After Julia had put him to bed, leaving the door open so the kitchen light would filter through, she walked over to the phone and picked it up. But as she started dialing the police station to report the broken window, she stopped.

If she filed a police report, the news that The Hacienda had been vandalized would be all ovcr town by morning. Was that what she wanted? To have Charles think the inn wasn't safe, giving him additional ammunition he could use to take Andrew from her?

Slowly, Julia put the phone down.

For the time being, it was best to keep the incident quiet.

This time, the meeting at the luxurious hilltop villa was somber. There was no chatter on the sunny terrace, no pleasantries, no talk of newborn grandchildren.

Having taken the same precautions they always did, the

four men had arrived moments before, aware that an unexpected crisis demanded their immediate attention.

Their host, Ian McDermott, waited until his butler had served the ritual crystal goblets of orange juice and disappeared, before addressing his four partners.

"As you already know," McDermott said as he picked up his glass, "Councilman Bradshaw is dead, and some crazy old fool in a nursing home is pointing the finger at us."

Spencer Flynn, the head of one of the country's most successful security companies, was the first to react. "What I want to know is who the hell is Eli Seavers?"

"Good question." McDermott turned to Aaron Briggs, the owner of the one-hundred-year-old *San Francisco Star* and his second-in-command. "Aaron, you've had reporters covering the story. What do you know about the man?"

Lowering his gaze, Briggs read from an open folder. "So far, not much. He's lived in Salinas for the past seventeen years. Two years ago, he was diagnosed with Alzheimer's, but wasn't admitted to Pine Hill Nursing Home until last December. His only relative is a niece the police and the FBI questioned extensively. According to Jennifer Seavers, her uncle became agitated as he viewed Paul Bradshaw's funeral on TV. That's why she asked Julia Bradshaw to come over, hoping she'd somehow trigger the old man's memory."

"And just like that," McDermott said sarcastically, "he told her we killed her ex-husband?"

Briggs nodded. "His exact words were '*Gleic Éire* did it.' However, when Detective Hammond attempted to question him, Seavers remained silent as a tomb, which is good news."

"Damn." Sitting across from Briggs, John Adams drummed impatient fingers on his chair's armrests. A former naval officer and now the head of his family's frozen-food empire, Adams was a mild-mannered man and the group's new grandfather. "This could jeopardize our mission next month."

McDermott's jaw tightened. "The mission will *not* be jeopardized. We have worked too hard perfecting every phase of it to see it fail now."

"I agree." Flynn turned to look at the publisher. "Aaron, maybe you should investigate Seavers yourself rather than have one of your reporters cover the story. Safer that way."

Briggs nodded. "That's fine with me." He looked around him. "If everyone agrees."

Four heads nodded in unison.

"I'll get right on it, then." The publisher glanced at his host. "What do we do if Seavers turns out to be a threat?"

Holding his Baccarat glass up to the light, McDermott turned it a fraction, allowing the expensive crystal to catch the morning light. "We kill him."

Eight

Briggs's much awaited phone call arrived at noon the following day. McDermott, who, in spite of his earlier optimism, had slept no more than a couple of hours, picked up the phone on the first ring, before his too-efficient butler had a chance to answer.

"Yes?"

"I traced Seavers."

McDermott could tell by the sound of his associate's voice that the news wasn't good. "Who is he?"

"We knew him as J. C. Spivak."

McDermott drew a breath and let it out slowly. A self-proclaimed mercenary with no particular allegiance to any country, J. C. Spivak had been their chief arms negotiator, the man who had, single-handedly, arranged an enormous arms deal between *Gleic Éire* and Libya in 1986 and 1987.

They had known virtually nothing about the man, except that he was reliable, highly competent as an arms negotiator and a bomb expert, and didn't come cheap. At the time that had been enough.

Then one day, when they had needed him again, Spivak hadn't answered his phone. Not even Spencer Flynn's sophisticated network of security operatives had been successful in tracking the man down. He had simply vanished.

"Are you sure it's him?" McDermott asked.

"Positive. I checked the nursing home's personnel files.

Spivak's folder had a photograph taken in 1986. There's no doubt. It's the same man. Different name, but the same man."

"Damn." McDermott ran the palm of his hand over his brush cut. "He knows who I am, where I live."

"Come on, Ian. Spivak or Seavers, or whatever you want to call him, is a sick man. These days he doesn't even remember his own name."

But he had remembered theirs.

McDermott stared into the distance for a moment, trying to think calmly, rationally. The good news was that the police hadn't been able to get anything out of him. The bad news was that they'd probably try again.

Which meant, McDermott reflected, he had to act quickly.

"Do me a favor," he told Briggs. "Check the nightly routine at the Pine Hill Nursing Home and get back to me."

The voices had returned. They always came at night, when the room was dark. And when he was alone.

He couldn't tell how many there were. Or what they were saying. But he knew they were coming for him. He knew because he could hear the marching getting closer and louder.

Lying in his bed, Eli pulled the covers up to his chin and tried to remember. But remember what? His head felt like a big balloon that never stopped bouncing. He didn't know what frightened him more—the bouncing ball or those marching boots.

Suddenly, the door to his room opened slowly, allowing a sliver of light from the hallway to shine through. Framed in that light, a shadow loomed, more frightening than anything Eli had ever seen.

His eyes wide, his heart beating like a drum, Eli held his

breath and sank deeper into the covers. The shadow closed the door and walked slowly toward his bed.

The marching stopped. And for that Eli was thankful.

Up close, the shadow transformed itself into a man, a smiling man, dressed in the familiar nursing whites.

"Hello, J.C," the man whispered in Eli's ear. "That is your name, isn't it?" He tugged the covers from Eli's grip and pushed them aside. "Let's go, J.C. We're going for a little walk."

Confused, frightened, but always obedient, Eli let his visitor pull him out of bed. Together they walked over to the window.

Wearing gloves, the stranger manipulated the intricate latch, then held Eli's arm, coaxing him gently. "Come on, J.C. Over the sill." The voice was soft, almost musical. Eli felt he should know it, but couldn't remember why. "Left leg first, then the other. That's it. Good job, J.C."

The cold wind nipped at his face and the grass felt damp under his bare feet. As they hurried across the vast expanse of lawn, Eli, with nothing on his back but his nightshirt, shivered. Where was he going? Who was this man?

The sound and smell of the surf were getting closer. Soon he and his companion stood on the edge of a cliff, an area he vaguely remembered as being off-limits. Down below, the sea churned angrily and crashed hard against the boulders. He closed his eyes when a fine mist hit his face.

The man let go of Eli's elbow. Without the support, Eli rocked back and forth, and for a moment, he thought he was going to fall.

The man caught him. And smiled. "Have you ever wanted to fly, J.C.?" he asked. "Like a bird?"

Panic rose in Eli's throat. He shook his head. And again wondered what he was supposed to do.

"Oh, come on, J.C. You won't know how much fun it

is unless you try it." The man's hand was on Eli's back. "You're not afraid, are you, J.C.? You never used to be afraid of anything or anyone. But I guess you don't remember that."

The marching had begun again, slowly, a small rumble that grew increasingly louder.

"Fly, J.C.," the man whispered. "Fly."

Eli never felt the push. All of a sudden, he was over the cliff. As a gust of wind caught him and lifted him, he soared like a bird, arms extended. For a moment he felt exhilarated.

Eli heard laughter and wasn't sure if it came from him or from the man on the cliff.

This wonderful moment of euphoria was short-lived. Without warning, gravity took over and Eli plunged into the darkness below.

In spite of Julia's efforts to keep her two guests from leaving, both had politely declined breakfast, settled their bills and checked out at precisely nine-fifteen the following morning. For the first time since the inn's grand opening nine months ago, The Hacienda was empty.

At that thought, Julia was filled with overwhelming despair. At first the inn had been nothing more than a means of supporting herself and Andrew while doing something she loved. Now, with Charles's threats still so fresh in her mind, she was only too aware that The Hacienda's success or failure could greatly influence a judge's decision in a custody battle.

Clenching her hands into fists, she pressed them against her mouth. I won't let it happen, she vowed silently. Whatever I have to do to keep The Hacienda going, I'll do it. And the first item of business was to get that window replaced. She'd deal with the rest later.

But what she had assumed would be a simple task turned out to be another source of frustration. After listening to her request, Larry Sims at the hardware store told her he was terribly backlogged and wouldn't be able to do the job.

Angry, she hung up on him. Something about the way he had edged around her questions made her doubt he was that busy. More likely he was one of the many people who believed she had killed Paul and wanted to express their resentment.

Even the widely distributed *Monterey Journal*, where she had a standing weekly ad, had run today's issue without it.

"I'm sure it was an oversight," the sales manager had told her when she'd called to complain earlier. "We'll make sure to have your ad in next week's issue. No charge."

Oversight, my foot. They were all determined to drive her out of business. One way or another.

Before her thoughts could turn to self-pity, the phone rang. Unable to shake off her sour mood, she picked up the receiver and mumbled a quick hello.

"Julia, it's Jennifer Seavers." The young woman's voice shook as though she was on the verge of tears. "I thought you'd want to know…my uncle is dead."

Shock was Julia's first reaction. "Oh, Jennifer, no. What happened?"

"It was an accident. He got up during the night and wandered off outside. He…" A sob broke through. "He fell from the cliff. They found his body early this morning, sprawled on a rock fifty feet below."

Julia sat down, filled with sorrow for Jennifer, who had loved her uncle so much, and for herself. Whatever Eli had known, whatever secrets his confused mind had harbored, had died with him.

"The staff can't explain it," Jennifer continued, her

voice growing steadier. "Nothing like this has ever happened before. Except for a few rare cases, the patients at Pine Hill are very passive. And all the windows have an elaborate locking device none of them could open on their own."

"Is that how your uncle got out? Through the window?"

"They found it open, so it's fair to assume he figured out how to unlock it, which doesn't surprise me. He always did have a mechanical mind. When I was little, I used to watch him take things apart and put them back together. Maybe that's something the disease didn't totally destroy."

Her voice faltered again. "This is all my fault. If I hadn't pushed him to remember, he wouldn't have been so restless."

At those words, Julia as well felt a twinge of guilt. She had been just as insistent, just as eager to hear what Eli knew, for no other reason than to clear her name.

"Don't blame yourself, Jennifer," she said, wishing she could take her own advice. "You were only trying to help him."

"I guess you're right. I'll make myself crazy if I keep thinking I somehow contributed to his death."

Julia had another thought. "Are you sure he was the one who opened the window?" she asked. She hated to instill fear into Jennifer's mind at a time like this, but if there was a possibility that foul play was involved, Detective Hammond had to know.

"I'm not sure of anything." Jennifer sighed. "And neither is the doctor, which is why he called the Carmel police. A local forensic team came to dust for fingerprints and will send a copy of the results to Detective Hammond in Monterey."

Julia doubted they'd find any suspicious fingerprints. *If* foul play was indeed involved, whoever had killed Eli was not stupid enough to have left such damaging evidence behind, just as Paul's killer hadn't.

"Have you made funeral arrangements yet?" she asked.

"Yes." Jennifer's composure had finally returned. "I'm going to bury him in L.A. next to his wife and son. He left no burial instructions in his will, but I think that's what he would have wanted."

"I think so, too, Jennifer." The thought of attending the funeral vanished quickly. L.A. was six hours away and would require an overnight stay. Julia couldn't possibly leave Andrew for that period of time, not when he had just lost his father. She'd send flowers instead, or make a donation to the Alzheimer's research foundation.

"Let me know if there's anything I can do," she said quietly. "You still have my number."

"Yes. Thank you, Julia."

As Julia hung up, sadness and guilt gave way to more haunting questions. Was Eli's death truly accidental, as everyone seemed to think? Or had he been silenced? She had no choice but to wait until Detective Hammond received the fingerprint report from the Carmel police.

Realizing there was nothing she could do, Julia picked up the phone book and began searching for another window repairman.

"Dammit, Garrett," Charles Bradshaw thundered. "Don't tell me you're buying that fairy tale about *Gleic Éire* being involved in Paul's murder. As much as I would love to catch the bastards who killed my daughter, I don't believe for one minute that an Irish terrorist group would come all the way to Monterey to kill Paul. It's just a ploy on Julia's part to shift the suspicion away from her."

Standing in front of his old friend's desk, Charles waited for Garrett's reply, which, as usual, took a while to come.

A lanky man with a laid-back attitude his men knew better than to take at face value, Chief of Police Garrett Browning was a good cop, but his unhurried ways could be infuriating at times. This, Charles decided, was one of those times.

"That fairy tale," Garrett said without so much as batting an eyelid, "still has to be investigated. Especially if Paul had discovered something vital about the group that could help the FBI track it down."

"If that was the case, he would have told me."

"Not necessarily. Paul was a showman. He liked to surprise and he liked to dazzle. And that's exactly what he had planned on doing at that news conference. That's why he gave it so much hype."

"The news conference has nothing to do with Paul's death," Charles said stubbornly as he resumed his pacing in front of Garrett's desk. "Julia killed my son. You know it and I know it, so why the hell aren't you arresting her?"

"Because I need proof, Charles."

"You have proof. One," he said, touching his thumb, "she hates Paul with a passion. Two, you have her at the scene of the crime at the time of the murder. Three, you know Paul had just bought her loan on The Hacienda, something that couldn't have made her very happy." He spread his arms wide. "What the hell more do you want?"

Garrett leaned forward, long hands clasped on his desk. "An eyewitness would be nice. So would a set of fingerprints, or the murder weapon." His calm gaze remained on Charles. "But no one saw her going inside Paul's house, and of all the fingerprints the lab team lifted, none belong to Julia. As for the gun..." He shrugged. "It's nowhere to be found."

Garrett's logic was beginning to get on Charles's nerves. "That's because she probably tossed it in the ocean."

"Or maybe someone else killed Paul, someone with a

better motive. Like Vinnie Cardinale, for instance. In my opinion, he's an extremely likely suspect, even if he was in Sacramento that week, appearing in front of a grand jury. The problem is, we'll never be able to prove he or one of his henchmen did the job."

Charles shook his head. "Cardinale didn't do it. The man may be a snake but he's not stupid. He wouldn't have Paul killed right after his request to open a nightclub on Cannery Row was denied. He might as well have signed a confession."

"And you think Julia *would* be stupid enough to kill Paul so soon after learning that he had purchased her loan?"

Charles let out a sigh of irritation at the chief's total lack of imagination. Did he always have to spell things out for people? "Maybe she didn't mean to kill him, Garrett," he said patiently. "Maybe she went there to get the loan papers back, and when he wouldn't give them to her, she lost her temper. It doesn't take much, believe me. The girl always did have a short fuse."

"So what you're saying is that, sometime during that heated argument, Julia walked into Paul's bedroom, took the gun out of its hiding place, provided, of course, he still kept it on that upper shelf, and then came back and shot him? And Paul just stood there and let her do it?" Garrett's smile was mildly condescending. "Come on, Charles. Even *you* have to know that's stretching it."

Garrett's deliberately patronizing tone ignited another spark. "Does that mean you're letting her off the hook?" Charles demanded.

"It means that, until I have something more concrete to go on than those wild assumptions of yours, I'm not going to do anything rash. And unless you want to risk being slapped with a lawsuit, I wouldn't advise you go around town accusing Julia of murder either."

That remark drove the point home, perhaps because Charles's attorney had been worried about the same thing. "Who the hell's side are you on, anyway?" he muttered, determined to have the last word.

"I'm on the side of the law, Charles."

Out of answers, Charles threw his hands up in the air and stormed out of the chief's office. Incompetents, he thought as he strode down the long hallway. That's what he was surrounded with. Total incompetents.

Sitting on his terrace, McDermott puffed gently on a slender cigar and stared up at the cloudless morning sky. He felt proud of himself. Except for a tense moment last night when a nurse had come into the supply room where he had been hiding, his little expedition to Pine Hill Nursing Home had gone off without a hitch.

And how fitting that this accomplishment should have come on the eve of his thirteenth anniversary as leader of *Gleic Éire.*

Thirteen years already. He took another puff and sent the smoke curling upward. He had come a long way since his days as a young boy growing up in the slums of west Belfast.

The son of republican activists, Ian McDermott and his younger sister, Lizzy, had had centuries of hatred between England and Ireland drummed into their young ears since the day they were born. But it wasn't until their parents were killed by British troops during a violent demonstration that Ian, only eight years old at the time, understood just how deep that hatred ran.

His young heart simmering with a resentment he couldn't contain, he had flown the Irish flag, an illegal act, in front of his house on the day of his parents' funeral. When the police took the flag down with a pickax, Ian retaliated by throwing stones at them. Soon another riot erupted. Wounded, Ian fell to the pavement as tears of pain and frustration streamed down his cheeks. That night, in the hospital, he had made a solemn vow—to someday avenge his parents' deaths.

Unfortunately, Granny McDermott had other plans. Afraid her two grandchildren would suffer the same fate as her son and daughter-in-law, she decided to take them away from their beautiful but war-torn country.

In October of 1950, with the help of a distant relative, what was left of the McDermott family immigrated to the United States and settled in San Francisco.

At first, Ian hated everything about the United States. He wanted to go back to Ireland, be with his friends and make good on his promise. But in time, the rebellious youth adjusted to his new life and became an American citizen, a day Granny celebrated with great fanfare.

Because everything about the sea fascinated him, he eventually went to work for a boatbuilder in Marin County. Syd Rupert, who was childless, took an instant liking to the hardworking teenager and taught him everything he knew about the boatbuilding business.

Shortly after his grandmother died in 1965, Ian went back to Belfast for a vacation. While there, he joined *Gleic Éire,* the small but powerful party his parents and their parents before that had belonged to. Standing tall, he had pledged allegiance to the same forbidden flag the British had torn down from his house seventeen years earlier.

From that moment on, every dollar he could spare from his salary was sent to the party.

By the time Ian turned thirty, his boss had come to rely on him so much that he made him a full partner. And when old Syd Rupert died in 1981, he left the boatyard and his entire estate, valued at several million dollars, to Ian.

The inheritance was like a sign from heaven. Eager to take a more active role in the party he had supported all these years, Ian immediately flew to Belfast, where he met with the leaders of *Gleic Éire.* Impressed by Ian's vision for the future, and his money, they listened to his plans, agreeing that, in order to reach their goal faster, a more aggressive approach was needed.

In 1985, convinced that McDermott's strength and leadership qualities were exactly what the party needed, the twelve-man committee had named him president.

One of McDermott's first priorities as *Gleic Éire*'s new leader was to schedule a series of medium-scale bombings in central London meant to bring Downing Street to its knees. The Brits, though upset and angry, didn't budge from their position.

And so the time came to move to the next level—the destruction of the British Empire. But to achieve such a tour de force, Ian needed help. He needed men of power, men with wealth, men with the same fierce desire to free Ireland from oppression and see it become a sovereign state.

His search had taken him three years. Three years to find four extraordinary, passionate, deeply committed men.

Because the five partners' activities had to be conducted in absolute secrecy, Ian sold the boatyard and bought the secluded hilltop house on Point Cobra. Soon the surrounding communities came to know him as a private but generous man, who raised orchids and bought boxes of Girl Scout cookies every year.

By 1990, after five years of terror in the streets of London, the British were forced to admit that *Gleic Éire* was indeed a force to be reckoned with and would have to be included in future peace talks.

But unlike other republican parties who favored the

peace agreement, *Gleic Éire* persistently refused to sit down with the British and bargain for something they felt was already theirs. What they wanted, Ian wrote in a letter to the editors of the *London Times,* was the swift and unconditional withdrawal of British troops from Ireland.

Rival republican parties, worried that *Gleic Éire*'s radical views would disrupt the peace process, had denounced the organization as a group of irresponsible, ruthless extremists who didn't give a damn about Ireland. The statement, made when Ian and his four partners were meeting with J. C. Spivak regarding a possible Libyan arms deal, had amused McDermott.

"We'll see who gets results first," he had told his little group.

The first major bombing, which J.C. had orchestrated, took place in a London restaurant where three members of the British Parliament were having lunch. Though they were only wounded, the blast killed eleven people, two of them American, and made headlines all over the world.

Outraged, the international media had called the bombing "an act of barbarism and cowardice."

McDermott called it justice.

A few weeks ago, McDermott and his four partners had begun planning their most daring coup yet—the assassination of the leader of the Ulster Unionist Party. In addition to being a strong sympathizer of England, Patrick O'Donnell had been particularly vocal about *Gleic Éire* and their so-called "atrocities."

O'Donnell's visit to the U.S., meant to garner support for UUP's proposed peace agreement, would take place in a downtown Chicago hotel. It was there that O'Donnell planned to hold his much publicized news conference.

When the subject of providing security for O'Donnell and the six members of his entourage had been raised, there had been little debate. The job should go to the largest, most reputable firm in the U.S.—Flynn International.

Seconds after being notified of the selection, an exuberant Spencer Flynn had called McDermott to give him the good news.

McDermott grinned as he clamped the cigar between his teeth. Those poor bastards wouldn't know what hit them.

Nine

Steve Reyes was stretched out on a deck chair, his head tilted to the hot Floridian sun and his Red Sox baseball hat pulled over his brows.

It was one of those hot, easy, lazy afternoons that required nothing more than a minimum of clothing—in this case frayed denim shorts and beat-up sneakers—and an ice-cold Corona, which Steve had just pulled out of the cooler next to his chair.

Feeling perfectly content, he brought the bottle to his lips and took a long, satisfying pull.

As an occasional motorboat sped across the Intracoastal Waterway, ripples of water lapped against the hull of *Time Out,* the houseboat he now called home.

Behind the dark aviator sunglasses, his eyes remained closed. Yet he was aware of every sound and every movement around him. It was a habit he had developed early in his journalistic career and had never lost.

Though he had shaved earlier today, a heavy dark stubble, a legacy of his Cuban heritage, already shadowed the bottom half of his face. His thick black hair, most of it hidden under the hat, hadn't met with a barber's scissors in weeks and was beginning to curl at the neck, but he didn't care. Here at the Fort Lauderdale Marina, where he had lived for the past seven years, the beach bum look reigned supreme.

In the slip next to his, T-Bone's forty-foot sloop pulsed to the beat of salsa music and female laughter. The champion wrestler was an old friend, and though Steve had been invited to the weekly bash, he had once again declined. Unlike his flashy neighbor, who liked to be surrounded by noise, music and slinky bodies, Steve Reyes preferred his own company.

"Hey, good looking. Want to have some fun?"

At the sound of the teasing female voice, Steve opened one eye, then the other.

Standing at the bow of the luxurious sloop, a leggy blonde in a hot pink bikini smiled at him seductively and leaned over the railing, offering a view of her cleavage even a blind man would have noticed.

"Some other time," he said. Pulling his hat lower, Steve closed his eyes again.

He would have dozed off, but a shadow suddenly blocked his sun, causing him to open his eyes again.

Jesus Delgado stood before him. He was a small, slender man with an easygoing personality and a passion for the sea. An actor by profession and a handyman by necessity, the Cuban native divided his time between casting calls and the Fort Lauderdale Marina, where he did a variety of odd jobs.

Steve had met him the day he had come to the boatyard in search of a houseboat. Jesus had taken him to look at a 55-foot Kingscraft, a handyman special the owner was willing to let go for a song.

"I'll be glad to help you put her back in shape," Jesus had offered with that infectious smile of his. "And when she's ready, I can crew for you. There's a lot of money to be made with a boat like this. You could take tourists to the Keys, on fishing trips, or just cruise up and down the coast."

Within weeks, Steve and Jesus had transformed *Time Out* into a seaworthy vessel, and in the process, the two men had become good friends.

Steve brought the bottle of Corona to his mouth. "You're blocking my rays, amigo."

Jesus didn't move. "There's a gringo at the gatehouse who says he wants to see you."

"Tell him tomorrow's charter is full."

"He doesn't want to go fishing. He said his name is Tim Malloy."

Steve let out a groan. He hadn't seen his former editor in seven years, not since the day Steve had resigned from the *New York Sun* and moved to Florida. Tim still called occasionally, mostly to ask Steve to do a story, one he claimed only he could handle. Steve always turned him down.

"So," Jesus said. "Who's the dude?"

"A pain in the ass."

Jesus chuckled. "That I believe. He said he's not leaving here until he talks to you."

"Stubborn son of a bitch." Turning his head, Steve caught a glimpse of Tim at the gatehouse. Sitting on a folding chair with his legs spread wide, the editor kept wiping his face and neck with a handkerchief that by now had to be soaked clear through.

"Oh, what the hell," he muttered, feeling sorry for the guy. "Send him over before he melts."

A few minutes later, Steve heard the sound of footsteps coming down the narrow gangplank. Looking up, he chuckled. Holding on to the thick rope on each side, Malloy cautiously made his way toward *Time Out* while trying to keep his balance.

He was a big man, six-three, with a broad chest and a

belly that had grown a little pudgy, thanks to his fondness for his wife's wonderful Italian cooking.

"Hey, kid! How're you doing?"

Steve rested the Corona on the chair's armrest. "What the hell are you doing here?"

"Is that any way to greet an old friend?"

"Friends usually call before showing up on someone's doorstep."

With a sigh of relief, Tim stepped onto the deck and took a minute to catch his breath. Pushing his hat back, Steve focused his gaze on his visitor. Despite the fact that the heat was getting the best of him, there was an undercurrent to the man, a contained excitement Steve's keen sixth sense picked up instantly. After working with Malloy for ten years, he had learned to read him like a book.

"What's the matter?" Steve asked. "World War III broke while I wasn't looking and you've been elected town crier?"

Malloy lowered his bulk into a chair and dipped his chin toward the bottle in Steve's hand. "Why don't you give me one of those before I die of thirst, then we'll talk."

Steve reached into the cooler and pulled out another beer. "You retired yet?" he asked, handing Tim the bottle.

"Hell, no." Malloy twisted the cap off. "The job is the only thing that keeps me sane, though some would disagree." He took a long pull of the Corona and let out a deep, satisfied sigh. "Damn, that's good. I can't remember the last time I had a beer."

"Marie always did keep you on a tight leash."

"Marie has nothing to do with it. The doc's the one who cut me off. No booze, no fat, no cigars." He tapped his index finger against his massive torso. "Ticker problems."

"Sorry to hear that."

"It could be worse. He could have said no sex."

Steve laughed. "I see you're still the same dirty old man."

"A man's got to have his fun." He gave Steve's chest an envious look. "You haven't changed, either. And you should have, dammit. Look at you. You lay there all year long, burning yourself to a crisp, guzzling all the beer you can drink, and you still look like a college kid. How the hell do you do it?"

"Just lucky I guess."

Malloy loosened the knot on his tie. Sweat was once again beading on his forehead and above his lip. "One thing I don't envy you, though, is this damn heat. I've only been in south Florida an hour and already I feel as if I've been swallowed by a furnace."

"You get used to it."

Tim looked around the houseboat, the teak deck Steve and Jesus kept polished to a high shine, the topside controls with the overhead, green-striped canopy. "Nice boat. You still take people fishing on this thing?"

"Yup."

"And you make a good living at it?"

"I make a living." Steve gave his sunglasses a little shove up his nose. "Did you travel fifteen hundred miles to chitchat about nothing? Because we could have done that over the phone."

Malloy's fat stomach shook with laughter. "Still blunt as ever, I see." He bobbed his head in agreement. "Okay, you're right. Enough bullshit." His expression sobered. "I have an assignment for you. One you won't be able to turn down."

Steve just shook his head.

"You don't even know what it is."

"Doesn't matter." Steve took another lazy sip of his beer. "The answer is still no."

Tim finally yanked off his tie and stuck it in his jacket pocket. "A California politician was murdered earlier this week. Came from a powerful, influential family."

"I don't care if he came from royalty, I'm not interested."

"I'll double your old salary and give you unlimited expenses."

Steve heaved a long, tortured sigh. The man could be a real mule when he put his mind to it. "I don't give a rat's ass about the money, Tim. You know that. These days I set my own schedule. I work when I feel like it and slum the rest of the time. Now, tell me, why would I want to trade that for another shot at the rat race?"

The blonde in the pink bikini sashayed by again and gave both men a tantalizing smile.

"Don't you listen to the news?" Tim asked, his eyes on the girl's shapely rear end.

"Not if I can help it."

The blonde disappeared behind the cabin and Tim turned his attention back to Steve. "Then you haven't heard."

"Heard what?"

Malloy leaned back in his chair, looking smug. "The murder victim was Paul Bradshaw, Charles's son."

Steve, who had been about to take another slug of his beer, slowly lowered his arm. He took a few seconds to absorb the news. "Paul?"

Malloy nodded. "He was shot at his home last Friday night."

"You're sure it's Paul who was killed? Not Charles?"

"I'm sure."

"Too bad. I might have considered your offer if it had been the other way around, if for nothing more than to find the killer and buy him a beer."

Malloy held Steve's dispassionate gaze. "That's not all.

There's a strong possibility that the killer, or in this case, *killers,* are old acquaintances of yours."

"Oh, yeah? And who might that be?"

"*Gleic Éire.*"

This time Steve's whole body tensed. The indifference he had displayed a moment ago vanished and was replaced by something cold that wrapped around his gut and squeezed. Bile rose to his throat, nearly choking him. The sights and sounds from the party boat next door dimmed until there was nothing left but the erratic beat of his heart.

He wasn't sure how long he sat there, fighting the demons, letting the familiar name roll around in his head while the hatred in his heart spread like a quick-acting poison.

When he felt as if his lungs could function again, he took a deep breath, then another. "You have any proof *Gleic Éire* was involved in the murder?"

"Paul Bradshaw's ex-wife, Julia Bradshaw, talked to a man who claimed the group killed the councilman."

"Who's the man?"

"His name is Eli Seavers."

Steve searched his memory, trying to remember the many informants he had talked to in the past. "Never heard of him."

"I didn't think you had. No one seems to know much about him. A police investigation revealed nothing out of the ordinary. He was a retired professor of economics, first at the University of California at Los Angeles, then at the American University in Beirut. He came back to the States in 1981 and settled in Salinas, California. Two years ago, he was diagnosed with early Alzheimer's, and this past December his only relative, a niece, moved him into a nursing home in Carmel."

Someone on the party boat had given the signal for a

limbo contest, and the intoxicating music began to throb. Steve barely heard it. "Why would Seavers make an accusation like that? Does he have ties with the group? Any kind of proof to substantiate his claim?"

"If he did, he didn't tell anyone. And he never will." Tim paused, then added, "Eli is dead."

Steve raised a questioning eyebrow.

Tim chuckled. "I knew that would get your attention."

"How did he die?"

"Seems the old man wandered off in the middle of the night and conveniently fell off a cliff."

Tim had always been every bit as suspicious as Steve. That's why they got along so well. "Foul play?"

"Not according to the cops." With a shrug that said he didn't put much stock in what cops said, Malloy added, "After the forensic team was finished, they found Seavers's fingerprints on the window he left from and those of the cleaning crew. They ruled his death accidental."

"Which means they're not buying the *Gleic Éire* theory."

"More importantly Charles Bradshaw isn't buying it."

The name brought a bad taste to Steve's mouth. "Why not? They killed his daughter."

"He thinks Paul's ex-wife killed his son. And he intends to prove it."

"Do they have anything on her?"

Tim shrugged. "Circumstantial evidence. She admits being parked outside Bradshaw's house at the time he was killed. Then she changed her mind about going in and returned home. Or so she says."

That last remark brought another spark of interest. "You think she could have done it?"

"Maybe." Tim shed his jacket. "But my money is on *Gleic Éire.*"

Steve thought of all the bombings for which *Gleic Éire* had been responsible, one bombing in particular, one that had destroyed his life. "Shooting someone at close range isn't their standard MO," he pointed out.

"Neither is shoving a sick old man off a cliff, but I'll bet a year's salary they did it. Besides being a councilman, Bradshaw was also a member of the crime commission and was scheduled to hold an important, televised news conference the following morning.

"Some of the townspeople my reporter talked to say the councilman was about to bring enough evidence against a local crime boss to warrant an indictment. Others believe the news conference was about *Gleic Éire.* A few even claim Paul had found out the group's base of operation, but that's pure speculation on their parts." He paused to take another sip of his beer. "Look, I know you've been trying to put what happened to Sheila behind you." His voice held a compassion he rarely showed. "And believe me, if I didn't feel that you were the best man for the job, I wouldn't be here."

The best man for the job. Steve held back a self-deprecating chuckle. That's what he had thought, too, when he had taken off after those bastards eight years ago. A lead from a former IRA soldier had taken him all the way to California. But after a few days, the trail had grown cold and he'd had to admit that he wasn't as good as he'd thought.

The possibility that they may have been there all along made him want to slam his fist into a wall.

"If they're in California," Tim said, as if he had read his thoughts, "you're the only one who can flush them out."

Steve gazed down as his fingers curled around the neck of the bottle. What he wouldn't give to catch the head honcho, wrap his hands around his throat and watch him expel his last breath.

He'd had dreams about it, dead-of-the-night nightmares that always ended with him bolting up, his heart thudding, his body drenched.

And now there was actually a chance he might catch up with his faceless enemy, after all, a man some said was so diabolically clever that not even the FBI had been able to get a single clue as to his whereabouts or his identity.

"Has the FBI been called?" Steve asked.

"The local police notified them a couple of days ago, but don't expect any help from them. You know how snotty those feds can be when it comes to giving out information to the press."

A long silence fell between them, which neither man tried to break for several seconds.

"What do you say, kid?" Tim looked at him. "Want to give it one more try?"

Slowly Steve refocused his gaze on his former boss. "Why are you suddenly so keen on me doing this story? At the time of the bombing, you did everything in your power to stop me from going after *Gleic Éire*. What changed your mind?"

"Eight years have gone by. You're calmer now, more logical. After Sheila died you were like a madman. You had no plan, no strategy, just a fierce desire to kill. You let your rage rule you and that's why you failed. It'll be different this time."

Beer in hand, Steve stood up and walked over to the bow rail. He could think of a dozen reasons why he should turn down Malloy's offer. The most important was he had carved himself a nice, comfortable life here. There were days when he could almost convince himself he was happy. Or at least content.

"I'm not sure I could do the job, Tim." He kept his eyes on the horizon. "It's been a while since my days as an investigative reporter. I'm rusty."

"Reporters like you don't get rusty, Steve. Whatever you think you forgot will come back to you quickly."

Steve chuckled. "Pretty sure of yourself, aren't you?"

"No," Tim said quietly. "I'm sure of you."

In spite of his reservations, Steve could already feel the adrenaline pumping through his system, like in the old days. Jesus would be glad to cover for him as far as the charters were concerned—no questions asked. Steve's mother would be a tougher sell. Prone to excessive worry about her grown children, she wouldn't be happy to hear Steve was back on *Gleic Éire*'s trail.

Another lengthy silence stretched out as he let his thoughts toss around in his head, knowing all along he'd never have a moment's peace until those men were captured.

Meeting the editor's gaze at last, Steve's mouth pulled into a smile. "Did you say double my old salary?"

Tim's big belly laugh nearly drowned out the music next door. "I did. Me and my big mouth."

"Then you've got yourself a deal."

"Terrific." As though doubt had never entered his mind, Tim reached inside his jacket pocket, pulled out a thick envelope and handed it to Steve. "In here you'll find a plane ticket, a thousand dollars in cash, an ATM card and a reservation at The Hacienda, the inn Julia Bradshaw owns and operates. Your weekly check will be Federal Expressed to the inn every Friday. Holler if you need anything else."

Steve glanced inside the envelope. Always thorough, Tim had included a written report and a snapshot of Julia Bradshaw. Steve took a moment to study the attractive face.

"What can you tell me about Bradshaw's ex-wife?" he asked, intrigued by those incredible eyes.

Tim pointed to the envelope. "It's all in there. You can read it on the plane." His mission accomplished, he stood up. "You leave at eight tomorrow morning."

Ten

Knowing he wouldn't be able to find a parking space within five blocks, Steve waited until a delivery van had pulled away from the curb on Calle Ocho before sliding his ten-year-old Jaguar into the vacated space.

Miami's Little Havana was a unique blend of sights, sounds and smells unequaled anywhere in the world except Havana itself. But it was during the hustle and bustle of the late afternoon hours that this Cuban neighborhood really came alive.

Hands in his pockets, Steve walked down the crowded thoroughfare and headed toward his mother's house on Thirty-first Street.

He had been only two years old when he and his parents had fled Castro's Cuba and immigrated to Miami. All he had ever known about Havana was right here, in the air rich with the aroma of *café Cubano;* in the shops where you could buy anything from religious artifacts to *cocofrio,* an iced coconut milk popular with tourists; and in Domino Park, where old men in white cotton guayaberas played dominos while reminiscing about the old country.

Steve's grandfather had talked of returning to Cuba someday, a *Cuba libre,* where fear and oppression would no longer exist. But Steve's father, Luis Reyes, had known better. After thirty years and no change in Castro's politics, Luis had given up on ever seeing his homeland again.

That's when he had begun making plans to rescue his younger brother. Ricardo, more idealistic than Luis, hadn't wanted to flee Cuba at the time of Castro's takeover. Years later, when he had realized the dictator's promises would never materialize, it was too late.

In the spring of 1989, Luis, who owned a small charter airline, had taken off at midnight in one of his planes. Flying low in order to avoid Castro's radar, he had headed for a deserted beach on the northern coast of Cuba.

The mission had ended tragically. Luis's plane had been shot down by one of Castro's Migs, and Ricardo and his family had remained in Havana, waiting for the Cuban dictator to change his mind about immigration policies.

Pushing the unpleasant memories aside, Steve turned south on Thirty-first. Fruit stands and cigar shops had made way for simple, well-kept little houses with tiny yards and clothes hanging on the lines. As he passed an open window, the sounds of a languid bolero he remembered from his teenage years stirred a few lusty memories, making him smile.

His mother's house was at the end of the block, a small bungalow made of ancient coral rock and painted a light shade of peach. The single yellow swing he and his sister had fought over was still there, coming alive only when Lena's kids came up from Coral Gables for a visit.

As always, Steve's mother was waiting for him on the sidewalk. When she saw him, her face broke into a smile. She was a tall, regal woman with dark hair pulled back into a slick bun, high cheekbones and a long, aristocratic neck.

"You just missed Evita," she said, kissing him on both cheeks. Then slyly, she added, "She looked very pretty today."

"Good for Evita." Sensing his mother was in a matchmaking mood, he distracted her by sniffing the air. "Mmm. Is that *puerco asado* I'm smelling?"

Anna Maria Reyes beamed. "Would I make anything else when you come to visit?"

"You spoil me, Mom."

She pushed the small white gate open and walked ahead of him. "Somebody has to."

The remark was her not-so-subtle way of reminding him that, at thirty-eight, he still wasn't married, a status she often tried to change by introducing him to some of Little Havana's most eligible young women. Evita, of course, was one of them.

Steve was in no hurry to get married, or to even form a serious relationship. While there had been other women after Sheila, none had awakened the kind of passion he felt was necessary for a lifelong commitment.

Arms wrapped around each other, he and his mother walked up to the screened porch, where a pretty table, complete with daisies from the garden, was set. Two tall glasses of iced coffee, the Reyeses' favorite drink, were already waiting.

"So." Anna Maria handed her son one of the glasses. "Are you going to tell me why you didn't want your sister to join us this time?"

"Because I have something to tell you—"

She gave him a mocking glance. "Something you don't want her to hear?"

He smiled. His mother had always been quick to read his mind. "Something I don't want her to hear from *me*. Because if she does, she'll go into one of her lectures and frankly, I'm not in the mood for that."

"Coward."

Steve chuckled. "When it comes to Lena, yes. The girl is brutal."

"If Lena speaks her mind it's because she loves you and has your best interests at heart."

That was true. As kids, he and his younger sister had been inseparable, but at some point, he couldn't remember exactly when, Lena had turned into a big sister, dispensing advice freely and scolding him on his beach-bum life-style. A happy homemaker and the mother of two rambunctious boys, she, too, believed it was time for Steve to put the past behind and get on with his life, which, if he knew Lena, meant getting married and starting a family.

"What is it, Stefán?" Anna Maria asked, using Steve's given name. "What's troubling you?"

For a brief moment as he drove down from Fort Lauderdale, Steve had considered not telling his mother about his decision to go after *Gleic Éire*. Not only because she wouldn't approve—he already knew she wouldn't—but because she would worry.

But deception had never been an option in the Reyes family. And it wasn't an option now.

"Tim Malloy came to see me today," he said casually. Then, as Anna Maria's brows furrowed slightly, he told her why.

Worry blinked in Anna Maria's dark eyes. "I thought those men were out of your system."

"So did I."

"Are you sure they're in California? Or is this another false alarm?"

"Tim doesn't think it is."

Anna Maria gave a disapproving shake of her head. "It's been so long, Stefán. Can't you let it go? Can't you move on with your life and let the authorities do their job?"

Steve gazed into his iced coffee. That was a question he'd asked himself hundreds of times while he had hunted those animals before. "No," he said simply. "I can't."

His mother's probing eyes stayed on him. "Do you still love Sheila? Is that why you want to do this?"

He shook his head. "No. Sheila is gone, and I have accepted that. What I haven't accepted is that her killers went free. I want to make them accountable for what they did, Mom."

Not too surprisingly, Anna Maria nodded. She was a remarkable woman, Steve thought. Proud, compassionate and as deeply committed to justice as he was.

"I guess I've always known you'd go after them again someday," she said, her voice tight with emotion. "Everytime I hear the name *Gleic Éire* linked to another bombing, I brace myself for your call, thinking this is it. This is the day Stefán will decide to go after them again."

She studied him for a long second before adding, "I don't approve—you know that. What mother would? But I understand why you have to go." Long, slender fingers touched his cheek. "You're so much like your father—loyal, passionate. And you always had this crazy need to right the wrong, just like he did."

Steve put his empty glass on the table. "Now you sound like Lena."

"She is not going to like this, you know."

He laughed, relieved that they had passed the difficult hurdle and could still laugh. "That's why I'm leaving you with the exciting task of telling her. *After* I'm gone."

"You will be careful," Anna Maria said seriously.

"That's one thing I can promise you."

She gave a short nod. "Good. Now let's eat before the food gets cold."

Moments later Steve was devouring his mother's delicious Cuban-style roast pork and chatting about the latest neighborhood news, the way they did every time he came to Miami.

He made the most of his visit, repairing a section of the fence a thunderstorm had taken down and helping his mother program her new VCR. With Lena's children being such video fanatics, Anna Maria had finally entered the twentieth century and purchased a video recorder.

By seven o'clock, well fed and satisfied he hadn't left a single task undone, Steve once again promised he'd be careful, kissed his mother goodbye and left. Before turning the corner, he glanced in the rearview mirror. Anna Maria stood on the sidewalk, waving.

Steve gave a single toot of the horn and waved back.

It might be a long time before he came home again.

He stood at the stern of *Time Out,* his elbows resting on the railing, and watched dusk turn the Intracoastal a deep shade of blue.

A slick Donzi, with a man at the controls, was slowly making its way toward the marina. Next to him, a little girl laughed happily as the wind blew her blond hair in a dozen directions. She was about seven years old.

The same age Steve's child would have been. Had she or he lived.

The memories he had fought so hard to forget rushed forth—pictures of Sheila's happy grin when she had told him she was pregnant, the way he had lifted her off the ground and spun her around, then quickly put her down, worried he had hurt her or their baby.

Sheila had laughed, that clear, bubbling laugh that always filled him with joy.

"You didn't hurt it," she had said, cupping his face between her hands. "A baby needs to feel loved, wanted. That's what you just showed him. Or her," she had added, with a new sparkle in her eyes.

They had first met in Central Park, on a bright April

afternoon. Sheila, who worked part-time as a window dresser while studying interior design at New York University, was flipping through a book of fabric swatches when he strolled by, a bag of sunflower seeds in his hand. Intrigued, he had struck up a conversation while feeding the pigeons and had told her he was a reporter for the *New York Sun.* After ten minutes, he was totally charmed by the vivacious Californian.

Though he had heard of the famous ex-governor, Charles Bradshaw, he didn't know much about his children.

"I guess you could call me the black sheep of the family," Sheila confessed as she tried to explain the Bradshaws to him. "I hate money. I also despise politics, which is my family's lifeblood. Of all the high-powered careers my father had envisioned for me, I chose to become an interior designer, an occupation he deems far beneath the Bradshaws' social status."

At the news, three months later, that Sheila had met someone and intended to marry him, Charles's reaction was exactly as she had predicted. He had told his twenty-one-year-old daughter that she was too young and shouldn't make such a decision without coming home and discussing it with him. When she wouldn't listen, he hung up.

Weeks later, when Sheila had called him back to say she was pregnant, Steve was exposed to a side of Charles Bradshaw Sheila hadn't mentioned—his bigotry.

"No daughter of mine," the ex-governor bellowed loudly enough for Steve to hear from across the room, "is going to marry some low-life exile and bear his child, do you hear me? I want you to end this relationship immediately and come home. We'll take care of the pregnancy when you get here."

Charles's reaction had angered Steve and shattered Sheila, who, despite her differences with her father, loved him very much. Too stubborn to give up, she waited a week—enough time, she hoped, for him to cool off—and called again.

This time it was she who slammed the phone down.

A few days later, Steve's perfect life was changed forever. As Sheila was walking past the British Consulate on her way to work, a bomb had exploded outside the building, killing three people, including Sheila.

And her unborn baby.

Within a half hour, an Irish militant group calling itself *Gleic Éire* had claimed responsibility for the bombing.

Steve turned into a madman. Swearing to avenge Sheila's death, he spent the day going through the *Sun*'s archives in search of anything he could find about the feared organization and its leaders.

Like many terrorist groups, *Gleic Éire* craved media attention. Angry with a government they claimed had robbed them of their country, their president, who never signed his name, wrote long, eloquent letters to the editors of the *London Times* and the *Irish Voice* demanding Britain pull out of Ireland.

From time to time those demands were followed by threats, and when those threats weren't met, *Gleic Éire* struck. Their targets were always centralized, populated areas where detection was almost impossible. The attack on the British Consulate in New York City had followed a request that Great Britain cancel the visit of the British prime minister to that city.

When the request was ignored, the threat was carried out.

During his year-long search for Sheila's killers, Steve had talked to everyone willing to give him a morsel of information about the group—local police, FBI agents, Scotland Yard, as well as a number of Irish informants he had met along the way.

The hunt had proved futile.

At the end of that year, weary and disappointed, Steve had given up the search, sold his Manhattan apartment and moved to Florida.

And now here he was, ready to try again. Would he succeed this time? Or would this turn out to be another goose chase?

Down below he could hear Jesus putting away the few remaining supplies needed for the trip tomorrow. As expected, his friend had been thrilled to take over the charters, and though he had been curious, he had respected Steve's need for privacy and asked no questions. Not even regarding Steve's return date.

Steve couldn't have answered him anyway.

Julia hit the last key with a flourish and turned to look at Penny, who had been reading over her shoulder. "Well? You're the artist. What do you think?"

Penny nodded approvingly. "I love it," she said, her gaze sweeping up and down the flyer. "It's short, eye-catching and straight to the point. I couldn't have done better myself."

"But will it bring me customers?"

"Tons, if you distribute it in all the right places."

"I'm planning to concentrate on surrounding communities like Pacific Grove, Pebble Beach and even Carmel. Those towns aren't as deeply entrenched in the Bradshaw mystique as Monterey is. And by adding some extra features, like the dining and discussion afterwards, I've made the classes unique enough to make people want to join."

Penny waved a hand. "Go ahead. Print it."

Julia hit the print function. Within seconds, a cream-colored sheet of paper slid out of the laser printer. Penny took it from the tray and read out loud. "Weekly gourmet cooking classes now forming. Learn to cook delightful meals, from appetizers to desserts, in four easy, hands-on sessions. Your instructor, a graduate of the French Culinary Institute, will conduct each class in pleasant, countrylike surroundings. The $300 fee will include four classes, dining on the premises and discussion afterward. Call The Hacienda at 555-3943."

Penny dropped the flyer on the desk. "People will be lining up at the door."

"I hope so." Filled with new hope, Julia took a stack of paper from a ream on the desk, fitted it inside the tray and hit the print function again, this time programming a hundred copies. "Except for that one reservation starting today, The Hacienda is empty. And empty means no income, so I had to come up with something."

"Didn't you say you were planning to revamp your ads in *Travel & Leisure?*"

Julia nodded. "Already did. The new version should begin with the next issue. In the meantime," she added, watching the flyers stack up as they came out of the printer, "this should help. Even if I limit the classes to twelve people, which I intend to do, I'll gross thirty-six hundred dollars a month."

"How much will that net you?"

"About twenty-eight hundred—enough to pay Charles and get him off my back, at least as far as The Hacienda is concerned."

Penny's face clouded. "Have you discussed the custody thing with an attorney?"

The word *custody* always filled her with dread, and Julia pressed her hand against her stomach and rubbed it gingerly. "I called my former college roommate. She practices family law. Legally, Charles has no rights to Andrew and would have a difficult time convincing a judge to grant him custody."

"But you're still worried."

"When a man with this much power sends a threat like that, you bet I'm worried." She returned her attention to the printer. "That's why I'm doing this, Penny. As long as I show a profit, Charles doesn't have a leg to stand on. I hope," she added with a skeptical shrug.

As the last flyer came off the printer, Julia took out a small stack and handed it to Penny. "And you can help by passing those around to your customers. From what you told me," she added with a smile, "some of them could learn a thing or two around the kitchen."

By the time Julia came back from the post office, where she had dropped off her five thousand flyers for bulk mail delivery, a trim, handsome man was sitting on her front step, apparently waiting for her.

"Mrs. Bradshaw?" He gave her an engaging smile. "My name is Ron Kendricks. I'm with the *Los Angeles News*—"

Before he could say another word, Julia shook her head. "I have nothing to say to the press, Mr. Kendricks."

Her sharp tone didn't seem to faze him. "I'm not here to harass you, Mrs. Bradshaw. In my opinion, you've had too much of that already." Matching her quick stride, he walked beside her as she hurried toward her front door. "But I do have a proposition for you, one you may want to consider."

"Goodbye, Mr. Kendricks."

"You don't understand," he said earnestly. "I'm on your side. I think the way this town and Charles Bradshaw, in particular, are treating you is despicable."

Julia stopped in her tracks. "How do you know how Charles Bradshaw treats me?"

His chin went up a fraction, as if she had just paid him the ultimate compliment. "I was at the cemetery on Tuesday. I saw how he looked at you, how the rest of the mourners looked at you. I even heard some of the comments they made."

"Very good, Mr. Kendricks. You get a star for being observant. It still doesn't change my mind about the interview."

He was blocking her way to the door, and she gave him a frosty look and waited for him to move. He didn't.

"I want to tell your story, Mrs. Bradshaw," he said with the annoying persistence so typical of certain reporters. "You talk to me and I'll make sure your message gets out. I'll portray you as the victim rather than the suspect—an innocent, hardworking woman, shunned by an entire town and trying to stand up to her rich and powerful ex-father-in-law."

Julia finally understood what he was after—a juicy story that would outsell every newspaper in the country. "What kind of garbage are you—"

"We'll play all the angles," Kendricks interrupted. "Maybe there's something in Charles's past we could use to discredit him, or in your ex-husband's. And we'll use your son, too—show his struggle as he is torn between his love for you and his loyalty toward his grandfather. The public will eat it up. There could even be a book in it for us. Or a movie deal. I have connections in Hollywood."

Julia gave him a scathing look. "You're as despicable as the rest of the reporters who tried to worm their way into this house." She almost spat the words. "How dare you drag my son into this sordid plan of yours, trying to capitalize on the grief of an innocent six-year-old?"

"You don't understand—"

"I understand perfectly. Now get out of here."

"You're turning your back on an opportunity to make a couple of million dollars?" He gave a short, incredulous laugh. "You can't be serious."

Annoyed that he still wasn't letting her through, Julia jabbed him in the chest with her finger. "I'll give you five seconds to get out of my way and another five to vacate my property. If you don't, I'll show you how serious I am."

Kendricks's smile turned nasty. "Then I guess I'll have to write my story without you."

"If you do, you'd better make sure you have your facts straight. Because if you print one word that isn't true, I'll sue you and your publisher for everything you're worth. You have three seconds left."

She could tell from his smug smile that he had been threatened before and was still around to talk about it. Making one last pitch, he reached inside his shirt pocket, pulled out a business card and laid it on the stone bench.

"I'm staying at the Monterey Arms—"

"One second."

The look in her eyes must have finally convinced him he had worn out her patience because he took a step back, then another. "Give me a call if you change your mind."

After he was gone, Julia shut the door, leaned against it and closed her eyes. It wasn't enough that an entire town despised her. Now the press wanted to turn her bad luck into some kind of soap opera.

For an irrational moment, she thought of going to Charles. He hated to have the Bradshaw name dragged through the mud. One word from him and Ron Kendricks would be back in L.A., writing the obituary page.

On the other hand, Charles was still her worst enemy. The reporter's threat and the possibility that he might pursue Andrew could give Charles one more reason to think his grandson would be safer with him.

Once again, a feeling of total helplessness swept over her. What was she doing wrong? Why was it, that as soon as she had solved a problem, another popped up, more ominous than the one before?

Taking several deep, calming breaths, Julia reopened her eyes. She would not let a vermin like Ron Kendricks get her down. And whatever battle was looming on the horizon, she would handle it the way she always did, all on her own.

Eleven

"What's the matter, sweetie?" Julia asked as Andrew toyed with his macaroni and cheese. "Not hungry tonight?"

His eyes downcast, Andrew shook his head.

Sensing what was troubling him, Julia pushed her chair back and patted her knees. "Come here."

He climbed onto her lap, and as she closed her arms around him, he laid his head on her shoulder.

"Are you feeling sad again?" she whispered in his ear.

She felt him nod, and wished she could take care of this kind of wound as easily as she patched up a scraped knee. "It's okay to be sad, Andrew."

He looked up, his eyes bright with tears. "You were sad, too, weren't you, Mommy? When Uncle Jordan died?"

"That's right. And after a while, thanks to you, Grandma, Aunt Penny and Uncle Frank, I started to feel better. And you will, too, Andrew, I promise."

He blinked as if trying very hard not to cry. "But...what if..." He bit his lip.

"What if what, darling?"

"What if you die, too?" he asked in a trembling voice.

"Oh, Andrew." She hadn't expected that. And the thought that he had lived with such a fear for days and not said a word shattered her. "I'm not going to die," she said, hugging him fiercely. "I'm going to be right here, with you."

"Connie Monroe's mom died last year." With his mouth against her shoulder, the sound of his voice was muffled.

"That's because Connie's mom was very sick," she reminded him. "I'm not sick, baby. I'm very healthy and I'm not going to die."

His arms wrapped around her neck. "You swear?"

She kissed the top of his head. "I swear. I'll always be here for you, Andrew. Until I'm old and wrinkled and I talk like those old men at Grandpa's club."

As he pulled away from her, his cheeks were moist from the tears he had tried so hard to hold back. But at the same time, he was smiling, and for that, Julia was grateful. "Feel better?" she asked.

He nodded.

"Good." The macaroni and cheese was cold by now, and she asked, "What do you say we forget about dinner and drive down to the Little League ball field? If we hurry, we can catch the last couple of innings."

Behind the tears, his eyes gleamed. "Okay."

Sheila Fay Bradshaw
Beloved daughter and sister
1969-1990
Paul Maximilian Bradshaw
Beloved son
1958-1998

White blooms from a nearby almond tree were scattered over the marble headstone, partially covering Sheila's name.

Crouched in front of the grave, Steve gathered them into

a small bunch and laid them next to the bouquet of wildflowers he had bought at the cemetery flower shop.

It was his second visit to Sheila's grave in eight years. The first, on the day of the funeral, was still vivid in his mind. Though Charles hadn't allowed him to attend the services, Steve had come, anyway, only to be stopped at the gate by two uniformed officers. While Charles looked on, they had politely informed him that this was a private burial and he should leave.

Out of respect for Sheila, and because he knew a fuss would be pointless, he had resisted the urge to punch his way in. Instead, he had waited until the last mourner had left, then had walked over to his fiancée's grave to say one last goodbye before going after her killers.

"I'm back on the trail, Shel," he said, looking around him now. "Think I'm crazy?"

It was a warm June afternoon, pleasantly refreshing after the sweltering heat of southern Florida. Listening to the sound of the surf and inhaling the crisp, clean air, he understood why Sheila had loved this part of California and why she had looked forward to showing it to him.

His gaze swept across the well-tended grounds, where dozens of other headstones were scattered. "Pretty fancy digs your father picked for you," he said. "Nothing around but hyphenated names for the ladies and thirds and fourths for the gents."

He felt amazingly calm. The raw grief and blind rage he had experienced shortly after Sheila's death were gone and he was once again in control. Maybe Tim was right. Going after a madman half-cocked had been a lousy idea.

It would be different this time.

"I'm going to get him, Shel," he murmured, squinting against the bright sun as he looked into the distance. "And when I do, I'm going to make him pay for what he did to you. And to our baby."

He stayed there until a funeral procession started to make its way up the steep asphalt road.

His thoughts already on the task ahead, he started walking toward the green Land Rover he had rented at San Francisco International airport.

The hunt had begun.

Maneuvering the sport utility vehicle through the Monterey traffic, Steve swung onto Via del Rey and headed uphill in search of The Hacienda, admiring the town's incredible beauty as he drove.

Once the capital of the Spanish and Mexican regimes, Monterey had become a mecca of culture and tradition and was one of the most sought out vacation spots in the country. As he climbed higher into the hills, he understood why. From up here, the view of the peninsula, which extended from the glittering bay to surrounding upland pine forests, was breathtaking. Not even the dark, threatening clouds that were moving in from the sea could mar its beauty.

The Hacienda was less than a mile from the hub of Cannery Row's activity, yet remote enough to make him feel as if he had just entered a green, serene oasis.

At the end of the gravel driveway, Steve parked the Land Rover under the shade of a huge oak and glanced out the window.

With its purple bougainvillea cascading from the second-floor balconies, its flower-filled courtyard and gurgling fountain, The Hacienda looked like one of the sumptuous mansions popular with the Spanish noblemen who had once reigned over the area.

The data Tim had compiled on Julia Bradshaw had revealed that, besides graduating from college with a degree in business, she had interned in a large San Francisco hotel, where she had worked on feasibility studies and marketing programs.

The experience had apparently paid off. The Hacienda, located on a five-acre bluff overlooking the Pacific, was one of the most attractive pieces of property in the entire area. It was pure bad luck that a luxurious resort, complete with tennis courts, a sauna and a four-star restaurant, had opened shortly after The Hacienda's grand opening, making it difficult for the smaller inn to compete.

After another minute, he stepped out of the Land Rover and walked up to the front door. Ignoring the decorative doorknob in the shape of bull horns, he rang the bell.

Steve's first thought when he saw Julia Bradshaw was that the photograph Tim had given him didn't do her justice.

In the snapshot she had looked pretty, in an understated way. In person, her beauty was almost staggering. He judged her to be about five-six and no heavier than a hundred and twenty pounds. Her hair was a muted shade of blond and framed her face in a mass of curls and tendrils. She had a wide, sensual mouth that could probably reduce the strongest of men to blubbering idiots, and wide-set green eyes that, at the moment, assessed him coolly.

The bright yellow halter dress was a far cry from the severe dark suit she had worn in the photograph. It hugged her small waist, swelled over round, firm breasts and bared two of the most beautiful shoulders he had ever seen. Except for a practical, inexpensive watch, she wore no jewelry.

For a moment, his head went a little hazy.

"May I help you?" she asked politely.

Realizing he had been gawking, Steve gave himself a mental kick and cleared his throat. "Mrs. Bradshaw?"

Her expression grew even cooler. "Are you a reporter?"

"As a matter of fact, I am. My name—"

The door slammed in his face.

Stunned, Steve stood for a moment, his nose inches from the lethal door knocker. Obviously the lady had a strong dislike for the press.

Which meant he needed another approach, something that didn't require a lot of conversation but would make its point. Quickly.

He knocked again.

This time, when Julia answered the door, Steve held his room confirmation in front of her nose.

She glanced at it. "Oh." She took a step back. "You're my new guest."

Smiling, Steve spread his arms wide. "Unarmed, and I assure you, not dangerous."

She didn't look amused. "The person who reserved the room failed to mention you were a reporter."

"Should he have?"

She gave him another noncommittal appraisal. "Not normally, but given the way some of your colleagues have been behaving, I wish he had."

"Would you have rented me a room if you had known?"

"No."

No smile, he thought. No sugarcoated answer, just a plain, flat response that left no doubt as to her true feelings. He liked that, even if his chances of getting a room at The Hacienda were becoming slimmer by the second. "I'm sorry my colleagues have been harassing you, Mrs. Bradshaw. And I'm sorry if my reservation created some sort of misunderstanding. The truth is I had nothing to do with it."

"Look, Mr...."

"Reyes." He steeped forward, offering his hand. "Steve Reyes of the *New York Sun.*"

After staring at his hand for a second or two, she took it, somewhat cautiously, then quickly withdrew her own.

"I'd be very grateful if you'd let me stay," he added before she had a chance to finish what she had been about to say. "In exchange, I promise to be quiet, to respect the rules of the house and to make myself useful in any way I can."

He flashed her what he hoped was his most engaging smile. "What do you say, Mrs. Bradshaw. Do we have a deal?"

After taking a few seconds to consider his question, she seemed to mellow a little. "If I do agree to let you stay," she said cautiously, "you understand there will be no interviews. Whatever you need to know about my ex-husband's murder, you'll have to find out on your own."

"That's fine."

"And my son is off-limits, as well."

"Fair enough."

Her voice remained brisk and businesslike. "I need your word on that."

Hands in his pockets, Steve bowed slightly. "You have it. Anything else?"

"Not at the moment." At last, she opened the door wider and moved aside. "Why don't you come in and sign our guest book?"

He bent over the small table and wrote down his name and address.

"Florida?" she asked, sounding suddenly suspicious. "I thought you said you were with the *New York Sun.*"

"I'm not on the *Sun*'s regular payroll," he said as he kept writing. "I only do special assignments for them—from Florida."

"I wasn't aware that the death of a local politician would interest a newspaper like the *New York Sun.*"

"Ah, but we're no longer dealing with *just* the death of a local politician, Mrs. Bradshaw." He laid down the special feathered pen. "Now that *Gleic Éire* is in the picture, your ex-husband's murder has reached a new level. Not to mention Eli Seavers's suspicious death—"

"Suspicious?" Though she tried to sound casual, he sensed a sudden excitement. "I thought his death was accidental."

"Accidents of this nature, at least to an old hand like me, are always questionable, especially since Eli died only a couple of days after mentioning *Gleic Éire* to you."

She gave him a long look, as if she couldn't quite figure him out. "For the new kid on the block, you're very well-informed."

"An investigative reporter is only as good as his sources, Mrs. Bradshaw. Mine happen to be excellent." He looked around him, rubbing his hands together. "So," he said playfully. "Where do I bunk?"

"That's up to you. Since you're my only guest, you can have any of the five rooms on the second floor. I'll get your keys."

As she walked into a large, sunny kitchen, Steve followed her and gave one quick sniff. "Brownies?" he asked. "Double fudge?"

She raised a brow. "Are you an authority on brownies, Mr. Reyes?"

"Since I was yea tall." He held his hand at knee level. "I could smell them clear across town." He sniffed again. "I haven't smelled anything that good in many years."

The remark earned him a smile, her first. "Flattery doesn't work in this house," she said, brushing past him. "But I'll remember to put some out for you later."

Her scent, which he guessed to be a subtle blend of jasmine and honeysuckle, enveloped him like a seductive cloud. "Thank you."

Steve followed her into a large room with twenty-four-foot-high wood-beamed ceilings, a brick fireplace and heavy Spanish furniture polished to a soft patina. Plush sofas and chairs in rich burgundy velvet were arranged in small groupings. An oak bookcase occupied an entire wall and was crammed with books, old and new. On another wall, landscapes of Monterey recalled a former, gentler era.

The gleaming baby grand was a surprise. Draped with an antique shawl and topped with a brilliant arrangement of red peonies, it was tucked into a corner, just under the broad, curving staircase.

Steve stopped to admire it. "You play?"

She paused, one hand on the banister. "Unfortunately, no. The instrument came with the house, and for a while I actually thought of selling it. At the last minute I decided to keep it and had it tuned and refinished instead.

"By the way," she added, "the parlor is for my guests' enjoyment, so feel free to come down anytime. Tea and coffee are always available. Over there." She pointed to a table by the bay window where a coffeemaker and an assortment of gourmet coffees and teas were neatly arranged. "Feel free to go in the kitchen for water and cream or whatever else you may need. Oh, and the books are there to be read. We have everything from Faulkner to Clancy."

Steve watched her as she talked. Though she seemed to make an effort to remain distant, his practiced eye caught something else beneath the armor—pride. And passion. He tried to picture her killing someone in cold blood and couldn't quite manage it. "Thank you," he said in answer to her invitation. "I'll be sure to take a look."

"Breakfast is served either in the parlor or in the courtyard,'' she continued. ''You can have anything you want—pancakes, eggs, cereals, fruit. All you have to do is let me know the night before.''

Together they walked up the staircase. ''No need for you to fuss,'' he said. ''Black coffee is all I ever have.''

''Very well.''

After being shown the five bedrooms, each of which had a personality of its own, Steve selected the one simply called the Green Room. Devoid of frills, it was furnished with the same heavy Spanish furniture he had admired downstairs. The color scheme was dark green and reminded him of his stateroom onboard the *Time Out.*

On the way back downstairs, Steve found his gaze drawn to the patched-up window. He turned to Julia, his tone teasing. ''An aggressive bird?''

''Vandals.'' She stopped at the bottom of the staircase. ''I'm having problems getting someone to do the repairs, so you may have to put up with the homemade job for another couple of days. I hope you don't mind.''

''Not at all. Did the police catch who did it?''

''I didn't report it.'' Obviously reluctant to discuss the incident any further, she held up a large, old-fashioned key. ''This is for the downstairs door,'' she explained. ''The smaller one is for your room, should you feel the need to protect yourself from female murderers.''

As if sensing the unexpected remark had taken him off guard, she smiled sweetly. ''Any questions?''

''No. I…''

''In that case,'' she said, looking as though she was enjoying the startled expression on his face, ''I'll let you get settled.'' She took his hand and dropped the keys into his palm. ''Let me know if you need anything.''

Standing at the sink, Julia had a clear view of her new guest as he pulled a couple of large duffel bags from the trunk of a Land Rover.

She hoped she hadn't made a mistake in allowing him to stay. The experience with Kendricks the day before should have been enough to convince her that all reporters were potentially dangerous, no matter what they claimed. Or how charming they appeared to be.

This one, however, seemed different, she mused as she watched him walk toward the house. There was something unthreatening and wholesome about him, a boy-next-door quality that inspired instant trust.

He was also handsome, in a rugged, outdoorsy sort of way. His thick black hair was a little too long for her taste, but the rest of him—the glittering dark eyes that looked as though they missed nothing, the quick smile and the broad shoulders—would satisfy the taste of even the most discriminating woman.

From somewhere inside her mind, a small warning bell rang. She had felt that same way about Paul. He, too, had been charming and easy on the eye. He, too, had inspired that same kind of blind trust.

Unlike Paul, however, there was nothing cocky about Steve Reyes's attitude, no arrogance, no smugness. Just an easy self-confidence that was too effortless not to be genuine.

As he walked into the foyer, bumping into the door with his luggage, she quickly turned away. And caught herself smiling.

Twelve

When Julia walked into her kitchen the following morning, the first thing she saw was Steve Reyes, perched on a ladder in the foyer and working on her broken window.

Eyes wide, she looked from the plywood on the floor to the clear glass panel that had replaced it. "What are you doing?"

The reporter turned around, putty knife in hand, and gave her the same disarming grin she had found so unsettling the day before. "I hope you don't mind. I'm an early riser and I needed something to do after my morning jog."

"And installing a window is the first thing that popped into your mind?"

He shrugged. "I told you I liked to make myself useful."

"Where did you get the glass?"

"Larry's Hardware. Fortunately, they cater to contractors and open early."

Julia blinked at him in surprise. Larry's Hardware was the store she had called. "Larry told me he was too busy to even cut the glass. How did you get him to change his mind?"

"I just asked him."

"Did you tell him it was for me?"

Using his fingers, Steve pushed some putty into the groove that ran along the window frame. "Yup. He was a little reluctant at first, so I told him I'd be glad to do the cutting myself." He scraped his finger against the rim of the can. "He gave me no trouble after that."

Arms folded, Julia studied her new guest with renewed interest. "Why do I have the feeling you did a lot more than suggest to cut the glass yourself?"

"I don't know. Why?"

"Call it instinct."

"Larry and I are cool." He gave the smudged glass a spritz of Windex he must have found in the shed along with the ladder, and wiped it off with a paper towel. "By the way, he's going to call you about the stained glass. It's a special order so it could take up to a month, maybe more. In the meantime, this should do fine."

"I'm sure it will. I mean...thanks." Still baffled that a complete stranger would go to such lengths to help her, Julia walked over to the desk where she kept her purse and came back holding her wallet. "How much do I owe you for the glass?"

"No charge." Wiping his hands, he came down the ladder. "Larry's way of apologizing for his rudeness the other day. He said he didn't mean to give you a hard time. He's been under a lot of stress lately."

Julia let out a bewildered laugh. Stress wasn't a condition she would have associated with Larry, but who was she to argue? "Well...all right. But since you won't take any money, at least let me make you breakfast. Somehow, black coffee doesn't seem adequate enough for what you've done."

As she talked, she walked over to the freezer and pulled out a plastic bag. "How about some waffles?" she asked, waving the bag at him. "They're Andrew's favorite and it won't be any trouble popping a couple more in the microwave."

Steve eyed the bag in her hand. "Are we talking *home-made* waffles here?"

"Nothing but in this house. I'll even throw in a few strawberries, fresh from my garden."

"Why do I suddenly feel ravenous?"

She laughed and took a colander from the counter. "I'll take that as a yes."

His elbow resting on the ladder, Steve watched her walk away as she headed for the back door. Faded jeans hugged her round behind like a second skin, and there was enough swing in her hips to send a surge of pure lust through his system. The unexpected reaction surprised the hell out of him. Back home, gorgeous bodies were a way of life, and he never gave any of them a second glance. Well, almost never.

So why Julia Bradshaw? A woman he hardly knew? A woman who, from what he had already heard and read, could be a cold-blooded killer?

"Hi."

At the sound of the young voice, Steve shook himself out of his lusty trance and turned around. A handsome boy with blond hair and intelligent blue eyes was watching him with interest, his head tilted to the side.

"Hi yourself."

"I'm Andrew," the boy said, coming forward with his hand extended.

As always when he found himself face-to-face with children, Steve felt something familiar—a mixture of longing and pleasure—tug at his heart. "Steve Reyes." He took the boy's hand, which was firm and cool.

"Are you the window repairman?" the boy asked.

"Actually, I'm your new guest."

The back door banged shut again as Julia returned.

"Ah," she said. "I see you've met Andrew." She put the colander, now full of small, red strawberries, in the sink and began to wash and hull them. "Mr. Reyes was kind enough to fix the window, Andrew, so I invited him to have breakfast with us."

"Cool."

"By the way," Steve said, as he swung the ladder over his shoulder, "I'd much prefer if you both called me Steve." He nodded toward the back door. "Okay if I go this way?"

"Of course." Julia Bradshaw gave no indication that she had heard his request to call him by his first name.

By the time Steve had put everything back into the shed, Julia had the table set for three and was pouring a tall glass of milk for Andrew.

The boy attacked his waffles with the hunger and enthusiasm of the young. "What do you do for a job?" he asked as he wolfed down his food.

"Andrew!" Julia chided.

"That's all right." Steve cut a waffle in four, speared a morsel with his fork and swirled it in the thick maple syrup. "After all, if I'm going to live under his roof for a while, he has a right to know what I do for a living.

"I'm what you call an investigative reporter," he continued. "Which means I get to poke around town, ask a lot of questions and snoop into people's business."

Andrew's eyes were serious. "Like the police do."

"Exactly."

"My uncle Frank is a policeman." Andrew sloshed more syrup over his waffles. "He's not *really* my uncle, but I call him that, anyway. We do a lot of stuff together."

"I see." Steve caught Julia's amused glance. "What kind of stuff do you like to do?"

Andrew shrugged. "Baseball mostly. I'm on the T-ball

team at school. I play shortstop, but next year I want to pitch." He looked up. "You like baseball?"

"Very much. Unfortunately, I only get to play when my friend is in town."

Andrew chewed earnestly. "Who's your friend?"

"Andrew, that's enough." Despite Julia's effort to sound stern, the little smile at the corner of her mouth was a dead giveaway that she was having a good time.

"I don't mind," Steve said. "I have two nephews about his age, and grilling people is second nature to them, too." He looked back at Andrew. "My friend's name is Gary Sheffield. You may have—"

The boy's eyes filled with awe as his fork stopped midway between his plate and his mouth. "*Gary Sheffield* is your friend?"

"I see you've heard of him."

"Are you kidding? The whole world knows who he is. He plays outfield for the Florida Marlins. He's *awesome*."

Steve laughed. "I'll tell him you said that. Maybe I can talk him into sending you an autographed ball."

"Wow." Andrew's face was red with excitement. "That would be great."

From the street came the double beep of a horn.

"All right, sport," Julia said, leaning over to straighten the boy's shirt collar. "Awesome outfielders will have to wait. Your bus is here."

Andrew gulped down his milk and gave his mother a quick kiss. "Will you be here when I get home?" he asked Steve.

"What time do you get home?"

"Two forty-five."

Steve found himself mentally reshuffling his schedule. "I'll be here."

The boy grinned, showing a gap where his two front baby teeth had been. "Cool."

Grabbing his school bag from the kitchen island, Andrew slung it over his shoulder and ran out the door.

"Cute kid," Steve commented as he picked up his coffee cup.

"He's also relentless," Julia warned. "So unless you're as passionate about baseball as he is, watch out, or he'll have you tossing balls to him until your arm falls off."

Steve sipped his coffee and watched her above the rim of the cup, glad that she no longer seemed to regard him as the enemy. "Does that mean you're beginning to trust me? A little?"

Julia smiled. "It's difficult to distrust someone who gets up at the crack of dawn to fix your broken window. Besides," she added, "Andrew seems to have taken an instant liking to you. He doesn't do that very often."

"The feeling is mutual." Picking up a ripe strawberry with his fingers, he bit into the juicy fruit. "How is he handling his father's death?"

Julia topped off his coffee, her eyes on her task. "He has his ups and downs, but he's adjusting. I try to keep his life as normal as possible. Unfortunately, when people throw bricks through your window and send you nasty notes, normalcy has a way of getting overshadowed."

"By nasty notes, you mean…threatening?"

Her gaze lifted to his again. "More accusing than threatening." Julia chewed on her lip for a second or two, as if debating how much to tell him. Or if she should tell him anything at all.

When she spoke again, her tone was cool, almost detached. "As I'm sure you already know, a lot of people in this town believe I killed my ex-husband. I suppose one of them decided to express his or her opinion a little more forcefully."

"Why didn't you report the incident to the police?"

"Because my only two guests bailed out the very next morning, afraid they'd be shot, either by a stray bullet or by me." She took a sip of her coffee. "The fact is, I didn't want to risk scaring off potential customers, so I kept quiet. Between El Niño fouling up the weather, and the luxury hotel up the hill, business isn't exactly booming these days."

He hadn't realized how much her situation was affecting her business. Nor had he guessed how truly worried she was—until now. "So you have no idea who did this to you?" he asked.

This time she didn't bother to conceal the bitterness in her voice. "It could be anyone in town. Take your pick."

"I'm sorry," he said. "This must be difficult for you."

The pride he had glimpsed earlier surfaced again. "No need to feel sorry for me, Mr. Reyes. I've learned to take care of myself."

When she rose, making it clear she was ending the conversation, Steve did the same. "Let me help you," he said, gathering the dishes.

"No," she said, taking the plates from him. "You've done more than enough already." She smiled. "And about Andrew, please don't feel that you have to be here for him this afternoon. As I said, he can be pushy."

"I'll be here," Steve said. "Not because I feel obligated but because I want to." He winked. "Thanks for breakfast. It was terrific. You may convert me yet."

Then, before he wore out his welcome, he left the room.

Steve's first priority after he left The Hacienda had been to stop at the police station and introduce himself to the detective in charge of the case, a man by the name of Hank Hammond. Though surly at first, the veteran detective had warmed up considerably when he found out he and Steve shared a mutual passion—hockey.

Thirty minutes later, Steve had been given a brief but thorough account of the information Hammond had made available to the press so far, including the names of witnesses he had questioned. Those ranged from people who knew the councilman well to a San Francisco crime boss by the name of Vinnie Cardinale.

Of all the names, only two had interested Steve—Jennifer Seavers, whom he hoped would let him search her uncle's house, and Edith Donnovan, Paul's longtime secretary. He decided to start with the latter.

Rather than go to her office, he waited in the small park outside the municipal building, where, according to the receptionist Steve had talked to earlier, Edith Donnovan ate her lunch every day.

Thanks to a brief description the same receptionist had given him, he recognized Edith the moment she walked out of the building. As the forty-something secretary headed for a shaded bench near the south end of the park, Steve stood back and took in the plain features, the mousy brown hair held back with a scarf, the low-heeled black loafers and the sensible gray suit.

Hands in his pockets, he walked over to her and stopped in front of the bench just as she was opening a small brown bag. "Miss Donnovan?"

Calm hazel eyes looked up. "Yes?"

Without being invited, Steve sat down and tried to sound as unthreatening as possible. "My name is Steve Reyes. I'm an investigative reporter for the *New York Sun.* I was hoping you could answer a few questions for me. It's in regard to Paul Bradshaw's murder."

Edith took a plastic-wrapped sandwich from her bag. "I already talked to the press," she said rather curtly.

"I know, but I've just arrived in town, which means I have some catching up to do."

"Then why don't you talk to your colleagues? I'm sure one of them will—"

"They wouldn't." At her look of surprise, he added, "Reporters are a very competitive breed, Miss Donnovan. And they never share information." It was an unfair statement, but unless he found a way to appeal to her softer side, provided she had one, he was up the proverbial creek.

The hazel eyes assessed him a moment longer, and he thought he saw a flicker of compassion in them. "I suppose I can talk to you while I eat." She unwrapped her sandwich, which was split into two neat triangle halves—no crust.

"Thank you." Spotting a soft drink vendor a few feet away, Steve fished into his pockets for a five-dollar bill. "You need something to go with that sandwich," he said. "Orange soda okay?"

She looked pleased. "How did you know I liked orange soda?"

Steve made a mental note to send flowers to the receptionist. "Just a hunch," he lied.

When he came back with two sodas, he pulled the tab off one of the cans and handed it to Edith.

"Thank you." After a short hesitation, she offered him half of her lunch, but Steve shook his head.

"I never eat while I'm working," he said. "Too distracting."

Edith nodded as if she knew exactly what he meant, and bit into what looked like a plain cheese sandwich.

Suspecting blunt questions would put her on the defensive, he eased into the interview gently. "Councilman

Bradshaw's death must have left a big void." He watched as city employees began walking out of the building. "I understand he was well liked."

"Paul was one of the kindest, most considerate people I knew." For a moment, her gaze fastened on the building entrance as if she half expected to see her late boss walk through it. "I can't imagine why anyone would want to kill him."

"He had no enemies that you knew of?"

Pulling her gaze away, she took another bite of her sandwich. "His ex-wife didn't like him very much."

The barely veiled accusation took Steve by surprise. "You think Julia Bradshaw killed him?"

Her eyes glinted with resentment. "She's hot tempered. Everyone knows that."

The bitterness in her voice was a tad more than what he expected from a secretary—even a devoted one. Or was there more to her feelings than plain devotion? "I take it you liked Paul Bradshaw a lot."

"We all did." She chewed slowly with her mouth tightly closed.

"And you worked for him for a long time?"

"Seven years."

"Then you, more than anyone, must know his habits, the people he saw, who he didn't like. Or trust."

Edith finished the first half of her lunch, washed it down with a few sips of soda and started on the second half. Her movements were unhurried and precise. "He saw a lot of people. All the councilmen do."

"You wouldn't happen to still have his appointment book, would you?" he asked hopefully.

"The police took it, but I always memorized his schedule." She paused and looked at Steve, as if trying to make up her mind. Her expression gave nothing away. "I could tell you who he saw during the last three weeks or so before he died," she said after a while.

"I'd really appreciate that, Edith."

She seemed pleased that he had used her first name. In a monotonous voice, she named all the people Paul had had contact with in the last twenty days. Those included the mayor, with whom Paul had daily briefings; the other three councilmen; his campaign manager, who took a huge chunk of his time; half a dozen of his most generous supporters; and a number of local reporters.

Steve wrote them all down. "He didn't get a call from a stranger? Or someone you thought sounded suspicious or dangerous?"

Edith shook her head. "Vinnie Cardinale is the only person who falls into that category, but he never came to see Paul. Whatever contact they had with each other was via the telephone or Cardinale's attorneys."

"Was Paul worried about him?"

"If you mean was he afraid Cardinale would kill him—" she shook her head "—no, he wasn't. And in spite of Cardinale's reputation, I never considered him a threat, either. A man like that doesn't care if he's turned down in one town. He just moves on to the next."

Steve had come to the same conclusion, which was the reason he wasn't planning on interviewing the mobster. Not yet, anyway.

At last he asked the question he had been burning to ask. "What about *Gleic Éire?* I heard Paul was thinking of reopening his sister's case."

Edith waited until she had swallowed her last bite before answering him. "That's true. A couple of months ago he asked me to compile all the information that was available on the Manhattan bombing and on *Gleic Éire.*"

"Do you think *Gleic Éire* was the reason he scheduled a news conference?"

"I don't know. It could be." Head bowed, Edith crumpled the plastic wrapper into a tight ball and held it for a while before dropping it into the brown bag. "I teased him about it," she said, with a sad smile that instantly softened her features. "I accused him of keeping secrets from me, his most faithful employee."

"What did he say?"

"That I should bear with him a little longer, that all the secrecy would soon make sense."

She stopped abruptly, as if realizing she had said much more than she had intended. When she glanced at her watch, he knew the conversation was over.

"Thanks for talking to me, Edith."

"You're welcome." She stood up. "I'd better go. I don't want to be late."

He doubted Edith Donnovan had ever been late or absent a day in her life. Standing by the bench, he watched her walk away. When she neared a trash container, she threw the crumpled brown bag into it and soon disappeared into the building.

Steve stood staring at the door for a moment, then, glancing at his watch, he realized he had just enough time to walk over to the police station for the daily briefing. After that he'd try to get hold of Jennifer Seavers and see if he could take a look at her uncle's house.

That might hold the answers to many of his questions.

Thirteen

Wearing her yellow slicker, a matching rain hat and black rubber boots, Julia ignored the driving rain and slowly made her way down the hill to check on possible water damage to her property. Fifty feet below, the sea, barely visible through the downpour, pounded savagely against the rocks.

Thanks to El Niño, this spring had produced some of the fiercest storms in the history of central California. Today was no exception. After three days of balmy weather, the rains had returned a little before two o'clock in the afternoon, lashing at the shore and the surrounding hills with renewed fury.

Residents up and down the coast had tried desperately to keep their homes from sliding into the sea by piling sandbag over sandbag, building a virtual wall between the rain and the foundation. Some structures had managed to hold, but others had succumbed, carried down the hills by the force of an engulfing mud slide.

With the tip of her boot, Julia tested the earth beneath her feet and winced as she felt the spongy surface give slightly. Because of her meager budget, flood insurance had been the last thing on her mind. Now, watching the rain carve a small river into the hillside, she wished she had made the expense a priority.

Trying to remain optimistic, she thought of Sandi Garcia's comments about the house the first time she had come to look at it.

"They don't make 'em like this anymore," the old man had said proudly. "She may be old and she may be tarnished, but she is strong as a rock."

I hope you're right, Sandi.

Julia looked up toward Cliffside, where a dozen or so guests chatted happily as they lunched on the glass-covered veranda. The luxury complex had been built on a higher hill, far enough from the precipitous edge for the owners not to have to worry about mud slides.

Before she could feel too sorry for herself, thunder cracked and lightning slashed, dangerously close. Turning around, Julia carefully made her way back toward The Hacienda.

From the parlor window where he had been standing for the past fifteen minutes, Steve watched Julia as she climbed the steep grade.

He had caught the look of worry on her face as she watched the rain run down the hill. Yet at the same time, he had sensed a remarkable strength about her, a determination that, no matter what Mother Nature chose to dish out, she would fight back.

Moments later, Julia walked into the parlor and gave a little start when she saw him and the crackling fire. She had shed her yellow slicker and looked sexy as hell in brown jeans, thick black socks pushed down around her ankles and a cream turtleneck he tried not to examine too closely.

"I hope you don't mind." Steve gestured toward the fire. "You did say to make myself at home."

"I'm glad you did." She rubbed her arms as if to warm

them. "The temperature dropped fifteen degrees since yesterday and that front shows no sign of moving away."

Steve glanced out the window. "Andrew will be disappointed."

"Oh, don't worry about him." She came to stand by the fire, extending her hands toward the shifting flames. "He and his friend Jimmy are never short of things to do, even on a rainy day."

"Here." Steve took a mug from the small round table by the window and handed it to her. "I thought you might enjoy something hot."

Her startled gaze told him she wasn't used to being waited on. "I see you're also good at reading minds."

"Occasionally."

Julia sat down at one end of the sofa and took a sip. "Mmm. Excellent coffee."

"It'd better be or my mother would most likely disown me. I'm Cuban born," he explained. "In our family, making good coffee is a rite of passage."

"In that case your parents would be proud."

Steve tried to ignore the way she curled up on the sofa, like a contented cat. Pulling his gaze away, he picked up thc poker and gave a few quick jabs at the logs. One, burned down halfway, collapsed with a gentle hiss, sending blue and pink sparks shooting up.

"How bad is it out there?" he asked.

"Bad enough. Thank God I had the foresight to order more sandbags earlier this week. They're going to come in handy." She wrapped her hands around the fat blue mug and took another sip. "I've seen all kind of disasters in the last thirty-four years—fires, earthquakes, droughts." She shook her head. "But nothing as fierce as this. Or as relentless."

Steve hung the poker back in its stand. "I took a walk

around The Hacienda earlier. The grounds around the foundation seem solid. Still, the additional sandbags are a good idea."

He walked back to his chair and picked up his mug. "I'd be glad to put them down for you, since I doubt Andrew and I will be playing catch this afternoon."

She tilted her head to the side, a gesture that made the resemblance between her and Andrew even more striking. "And here I thought you'd be bailing out and seeking shelter somewhere safer."

"I'm not the bailing out type. Besides, I've seen worse storms than this."

"Really? Where?"

"Indonesia, during my foreign-correspondent days. You don't know the meaning of heavy rains until you've been in a monsoon."

She sank deeper into the cushions. "What made you switch to investigative reporting?"

"Fate." This time he couldn't pull his gaze away, so he just sat back and enjoyed. "A high-profile Manhattan plastic surgeon had just been accused of killing his wife. The regular reporter wasn't available. I was. My editor, the man you talked to last week, gave me the assignment. When I was done with the story, I found out I liked searching for clues, putting them together, solving the puzzle." He shrugged. "I talked to my editor about a permanent position and the next thing I knew, I was in."

"Was he guilty?"

"I beg your pardon?"

"The plastic surgeon. Did he kill his wife?"

"Oh." He smiled. "No. The wife's sister did. When she realized I was on to her, she tried to kill me, too. Fortunately, I was one step ahead of her."

Julia continued to sip her coffee. "Your job sounds a little dangerous."

"Only if you're not careful." He grinned. "I'm very careful."

"Good. I wouldn't want anything to happen to my only guest. Especially one that makes such good coffee."

He let his gaze skim over her graceful body. "That's quite a statement coming from someone who slammed the door in my face less than twenty-four hours ago."

A soft, embarrassed flush rose to her cheeks. "That's not one of my proudest moments, but I was still fuming from a rather unpleasant run-in with another reporter the day before."

Steve felt a sudden, inexplicable need to protect her. "Really? Who was he? I may know him."

"His name is Ron Kendricks."

"Never heard of him."

"He works for the *L.A. News,* a daily tabloid, distributed mostly in southern California and the Southwest."

"What did he want?"

She shrugged. "To write my story, highly sensationalized of course, and then sell it to Hollywood. He was even going to use Andrew for a more dramatic slant."

That bastard. No wonder Julia had been wary of reporters. "If he shows up again," Steve said, "let me know. There are ways to deal with scum like him."

The remark made her smile. "Like you dealt with Larry at the hardware store?"

Steve laughed, remembering his conversation with the hardware man. There had been no violence, not even a harsh word, but Larry had gotten the point very quickly. "Whatever works."

"Oh, it worked. Larry stopped by while you were out and measured the window. I should have the stained glass in about three weeks." She chuckled. "He said he'd put a rush on it."

Steve nodded, pleased. "I'll have to buy him a beer." Suddenly serious, he leaned forward, hands around the mug. "I talked to Edith Donnovan today."

Julia threw him a quick, startled look. "Paul's secretary? How did you manage that?"

"I found out she has lunch in the park every day at noon, so I went and joined her. We had a nice chat."

"I'm surprised. Edith doesn't take kindly to strangers."

"I guessed that much. What do you know about her?"

Julia studied the fire for a moment. "Not a whole lot. She's quiet, efficient, loyal."

"And she was in love with your ex-husband."

Julia gaped at him. "She told you that?"

"No, but it wasn't too hard to figure out. I take it you knew?"

"She was never obvious, at least not in front of me, but yes, I knew Edith was attracted to Paul."

"It didn't bother you?"

Her gaze, a shade cooler now, locked with his. "If you mean was I jealous, the answer is no. In fact, at first I thought her infatuation was rather...cute. Paul and I often joked about it. When he and I started drifting apart, however, I stopped paying attention."

"Watch out for her, will you? She could be dangerous. Perhaps not physically, but verbally."

"You mean she could spread rumors about me?"

"She may already have."

At those words, Julia looked mildly uncomfortable. "You're wrong. Edith may not like me, but she wouldn't do me any harm."

Yet, Steve thought, a few nights before, someone with

that same kind of hatred had hurled a brick through her window.

"How did you find out about Edith in the first place?" Julia asked.

"Detective Hammond gave me a list of the people he had questioned."

Looking surprised, Julia slowly shook her head. "I'm impressed. Except for the daily briefings, which I'm told are torture for him, Detective Hammond makes it a point never to talk to reporters."

Steve grinned. "That's because he never met one whose passion for hockey equaled his own."

"Passion, huh?" She smiled. "I didn't think Hammond was capable of *any* kind of passion."

"Those quiet types can fool you."

Watching her stretch her legs on the red sofa, he wondered what it would take to awaken passion in her. It was there, just beneath the surface. He had caught a glimpse of it when she had slammed the door in his face the other day, and again when she had talked so proudly about The Hacienda. He had a sudden urge to reach out and touch her, just to see if he could get a reaction.

He was about to give in to the temptation when she spoke again. "Did Edith say anything about *Gleic Éire?*"

He gave her a complete account of what the efficient Miss Donnovan had told him. When he mentioned he would probably be talking to Jennifer Seavers next, she looked surprised.

"Jennifer? Why?"

"I'd like to take a look at her uncle's house, if that's possible. I understand Eli left it to her in his will."

"That's right, but the FBI already searched it, quite thoroughly from what Jennifer told me. They didn't find much of anything."

He shrugged. "They may have missed something. It wouldn't be the first time."

"I'd be glad to call her for you," she said unexpectedly. "And let her know that you're staying here. I believe she left a set of keys with Eli's elderly neighbor, a woman by the name of Esther Hathaway."

The offer, which would make his job considerably easier, touched him. "That would be very helpful. Thank you, Julia."

Outside the window, the downpour had tapered to a thin drizzle. Steve put his cup down and stood up. "A favor deserves another," he said briskly. "Why don't you show me where you keep those sandbags? Now seems as good a time as any to get started."

"You don't have—"

"I know." He held out his hand. "Come on. Show me where they are."

He saw her hesitate, then without a word, she put her hand in his and let him pull her out of her chair.

"Julia!" Penny exclaimed as she burst into Julia's kitchen. "There's a Greek god sandbagging the inn."

Julia looked up from her checkbook, where she had been trying to make the numbers add up. "Down, girl. You're married, remember?"

Penny pressed her nose against the window so she could take a better look. "Who is he?"

"My new guest."

"You don't say." Penny turned around, her eyes bright with mischief. "Your new guest is quite a hunk."

"You would think that."

"Oh, come on. Don't tell me you didn't notice."

"I noticed and that's all I did, so don't start reading

anything into it. And for God's sake, get away from that window. He'll see you."

Penny came to perch on the edge of Julia's desk. "How long is he staying? What does he do? Is he married?"

Julia let out an impatient sigh and flipped her checkbook shut. There was no use trying to get her finances in order with Penny giving her the third degree. "His name is Steve Reyes. He's an investigative reporter for the *New York Sun,* he lives on a houseboat in Florida, I don't know how long he'll be staying and no, he's not married." She exhaled. "There. Is your curiosity satisfied now, Miss Must-Know-It-All?"

"Well." Penny's expression turned smug. "Now I know you did more than notice his good looks."

"And why is that?"

"The man is a *reporter?* And you let him in? Better yet, you gave him a *room?*"

"I needed the money."

"Uh-huh." Penny's mouth opened as if she was about to say something more, but the back door swung open and Steve came in, his hair matted down from the rain, his broad chest heaving from the exertion.

"All done," he said, wiping his feet on the mat. Then he saw Penny. "Sorry. I didn't know you had company."

"Oh, I'm not company." Beaming, Penny rushed forward, hand extended. "I'm Julia's friend, Penny Walsh. And you must be Steve."

Steve shook the young woman's hand. "Did you say Walsh? As in *Frank* Walsh?"

"You know my Frankie?"

"Only through Andrew."

"In that case, you'll have to meet him soon." She threw Julia a sly look. "Maybe we could double-date some evening. Do you like seafood, Steve? I know a great place down on Cannery Row that serves the best *chioppino*—''

''You must excuse my friend.'' Smiling apologetically, Julia placed her hands on Penny's shoulders, spun her away from Steve and gently pushed her across the room. ''She is very nice but tends to blabber.''

With that, Julia shoved Penny through the door.

''Put it right here, slugger.'' Standing in the doorway of The Hacienda, Julia watched as Steve hit his fist into the pocket of his new baseball glove. ''Give it all you got.''

With a form that was quite remarkable for a boy his age, Andrew slowly raised his knee, drew back his pitching arm and fired the ball. It hit Steve's glove with a solid thump.

''Good pitch!'' Steve tossed the ball back to Andrew, who caught it easily.

Taking advantage of a break in the weather, they had come out the moment the rain had let up and had been playing steadily for over an hour. Julia hadn't had the heart to stop them. In spite of the fact that Andrew's spirits had lifted considerably, this was the first time in over a week that he had shown any interest in outside activities. It felt good to see him being a kid again.

As Andrew prepared for another pitch, Julia approached them. ''Aren't you two tired yet? You've been playing since three o'clock.''

Steve rotated his shoulder. ''Is that all?''

Julia threw him an amused glance. ''I keep a tube of Ben Gay in every guest's bathroom should you need it.'' She waved at Andrew. ''Come on, sport. I have to take Grandma to the doctor, remember? And you're going to Aunt Penny's.''

''Aw, Mom,'' Andrew cried plaintively. ''Can't I stay

here instead? Steve and I didn't get to play yesterday because of the rain."

"That's no reason to impose on Steve today."

It was the first time she had referred to Steve by his first name. She had done so unconsciously and was surprised at how easily the name rolled off her tongue. "I'm sure he has better things to do than to baby-sit a little troublemaker like you."

"As a matter of fact I don't," Steve said. He jammed a fist into the glove pocket and winked at Andrew. "Besides, I was just getting warmed up."

Julia hesitated. She had never left Andrew with a stranger before. Somehow between her mother, Penny and Frank, there never seemed to be a shortage of baby-sitters.

At the same time, she couldn't bring herself to think of Steve Reyes as a stranger. Not anymore. In three short days the reporter had broken down the last of her defenses and managed to make himself indispensable. More surprising was the discovery that she liked having him around. She liked the sound of his footsteps each morning as he ran down the stairs and went for his morning jog, rain or shine. And she liked the way his woodsy aftershave lingered in the foyer long after he was gone. She even liked the way he looked at her at times, with a mixture of amusement and admiration.

"Mom, please." Andrew's eyes were imploring. "I won't give Steve any trouble. I swear."

"Penny was supposed to help you with your homework later."

"Steve can help me. Can't you, Steve?"

"As long as you don't ask me to spell. I was tossed out of the spelling bee contest six times in six years."

"Well..." Julia felt herself waver. Andrew seemed to be having such a good time. Did she really want to take him away? "All right," she said after a while. "I guess I can trust you to stay out of trouble for a couple of hours." She turned to Steve. "But he must do his homework."

"Got ya."

"You can reach me either on my car phone or at my mother's house or at Dr. Cantrell's office. The first two numbers are on speed dial. Dr. Cantrell's is in the little red book on my desk."

Steve gave her a two-finger salute. "Yes, Commander."

As Andrew burst out laughing, Julia rolled her eyes and strode toward the Volvo.

"Do you want to come in, honey?" Grace asked when Julia pulled into the driveway. "I've got some of that pound cake you like."

Julia shook her head. "Another time, Mom. I've been gone over an hour and I don't know how much more Steve can last. You know how merciless Andrew can be."

"Oh, I wouldn't worry. From what you told me about your Mr. Reyes, he sounds like a capable and responsible young man."

"He's not *my* Mr. Reyes, Mom."

"Whatever." Grace fished in her purse for her keys. "It was very sweet of him to offer to stay with Andrew."

"Andrew left him no choice."

Grace sneaked a sideways glance at her daughter. "I think I'd like to meet him."

Julia was instantly suspicious. "Why?"

"Because he sounds charming. And because I want to take a look at the man who is affecting my daughter in such a way."

Julia felt a hot flush rise to her cheeks. "*Affecting me?* What are you talking about? He's not affecting me at all. Have you been talking to Penny?"

Grace's hand came out of her purse holding her keys. "Well, yes, now that you mention it. She did stop by the house briefly yesterday."

"What did she say?"

"That Steve Reyes was handsome and very helpful around the inn, which is rather unusual, don't you think?" Her green eyes twinkled with humor. "You don't normally let your guests work, do you? Or invite them to have breakfast with you and Andrew?"

"How did Penny know Steve had breakfast with us?"

"She didn't. Andrew told me. Your new guest seems to have made quite an impression on him."

Knowing any further denial would be pointless, especially when Grace and Penny, and now Andrew, had joined forces, Julia shook her head in frustration. "I've got to go."

Grace leaned over and kissed Julia on the cheek. "Thanks for coming with me today, honey. I'm such a baby when it comes to doctors."

Julia's irritation dissipated instantly. "And you had nothing to worry about. Dr. Cantrell gave you a clean bill of health, as always."

"I know. And I always feel guilty afterward for dragging you with me." Grace opened the passenger door. "Hurry home, dear. Your two men are probably waiting for you."

Julia started to snap a reply, but Grace was already out the door.

Steve, Andrew and a man Julia didn't know sat at the kitchen table when Julia returned to The Hacienda.

A new guest? she wondered, feeling suddenly hopeful. Or a friend of Steve's?

As the stranger turned to look at her, Julia dropped her purse on the desk and took a quick inventory of the man. She judged him to be in his early to mid-sixties. He had blue eyes that had inexplicably gone misty, deep lines around his mouth, graying hair and a broad chest. He wore neatly creased dark green trousers and a red polo shirt.

Without knowing quite why, Julia didn't come forward to introduce herself. Instead, she stayed rooted where she was, her eyes riveted on the man.

Pushing back his chair, the stranger rose.

"Hello, princess," he said.

Fourteen

Julia stood stock-still. As recognition dawned, a pain stabbed through her chest, as raw as that terrible morning twenty-three years ago. She tried to speak and found herself incapable of uttering a single word. If it hadn't been for the desk beside her, which she gripped blindly, she might have fallen.

"Mom, look who's here!" Unaware of the battle that raged within her, Andrew jumped out of his chair. "It's my grandpa."

Anger, so bitter she could taste it, snapped her out of her trance. "What are you doing here?" she asked, barely recognizing her own voice.

Coop took a couple of steps toward her. "I wanted to see you, find out how..."

As his voice trailed off, she stared at the father she had adored, the man she had defended time after time, to her brother, to her classmates, even to her mother. "He'll be back," she had told them. "You'll see."

To claim she hadn't thought of him in all that time would be a lie. The year following his disappearance, she had thought of him every night as she fell asleep and every morning as she woke up. When she had graduated from high school, she had hoped, foolishly, that he would suddenly appear and share this proud moment with her.

She had thought of him on her wedding day, and when

Andrew was born, and then again when her brother, Jordan, was killed. But by then the adoration had waned, replaced by a deep, debilitating resentment.

"You thought what?" she asked, blinking away hot, angry tears. "That you would waltz back into my life as if nothing had happened? As if you'd just stepped out to buy the morning paper?"

"Julia—"

"Stop." She raised a warning hand. "I don't want to hear your lies. You're not welcome here, so just go."

"Mom!"

With a sinking feeling in her stomach, Julia saw Andrew take Coop's hand. His eyes were filled with a mixture of shock and reproach as he looked at her. "He's my grandpa. He came a long way to see me. I don't want him to go."

"Andrew, go to your room." She hadn't meant to sound so harsh but the words just blurted out. "Please," she added in a whisper as Andrew started to protest.

Steve, who had remained silent and watchful, rose. "Come on, slugger," he said, wrapping an arm around Andrew's shoulder. "What do you say we give your mom and your grandpa some time together? Maybe you could show me that fancy robot of yours. What's his name again, Zokor?"

Pouting, Andrew allowed Steve to gently steer him toward his room.

Julia waited until they had disappeared, then, because she was afraid Andrew would hear them, she said curtly, "Outside."

In the courtyard, the late afternoon fog was already drifting in from the ocean, wrapping The Hacienda in a damp mist that chilled her to the bone.

She turned to Coop, her fury unleashing so quickly she couldn't have held it back if she had tried. "How dare you come here?'' she snapped. ''Invade my home and disrupt my son's life? Haven't you done enough harm? Must you hurt us all over again?''

''I don't want to hurt you, Julia.'' His voice was the same low baritone she remembered. ''I've missed you so much. Not a day has gone by without me thinking of the three of you, praying you were all right, wishing things could be different.''

''They could have been if you hadn't chosen booze over us.''

''I tried.''

She let out a dry, sarcastic laugh. ''Oh, spare me the bull. I've heard it all before, remember? I may have been young but I wasn't deaf. Or blind. Or stupid.''

''I'm sorry.''

She wrapped her arms around herself in an effort to ward off the chill, though she doubted anything could chase away the coldness inside her. ''Why now?'' she asked, suddenly bone tired. ''After all this time?''

''I heard about your husband's death, how you were being questioned by the police. I...saw you and Andrew on the news,'' Coop added, his voice almost breaking.

''So?''

''So I thought maybe, if I came...I could make things easier for you, help you...somehow.'' His eyes were almost pleading. ''And I wanted to meet my grandson.''

Still reeling from the shock of seeing him, she let out a shuddering breath. ''How did you find me?''

''I kept in touch with an old friend of mine. You know him—Spike Sorensen.''

She wondered if Spike had told Coop about Jordan. She wanted to throw her brother's death in his face. She wanted to hurt him, the way he had hurt her. She couldn't get the words out. ''Does Mom know you're in town?''

"No. I checked into the Monterey Arms and came straight here."

She took a deep breath and looked into the fog, wishing she could disappear into it, pretend none of this was happening. "I want you to leave and never come back."

"Julia—"

"I don't need your help. None of us need your help."

"I want to get to know my grandson. Surely you can't deny me that."

"Deny you?" she scoffed. "What about what you denied *us?* A normal childhood free of fear and embarrassment. Birthdays and Christmases spent together, like normal children, a father to love and to look up to."

"I know I made mistakes."

"Do you? Do you have any idea how difficult it was for Jordan and me all those years? Watching our friends with their fathers, wondering where ours was, if he'd ever come back?"

"I do." His voice was just a whisper now. "And I know that forgiveness is a lot to ask. But I never wanted to hurt you. You've got to believe that. The only reason I left was because I knew that you'd all be better off without me."

She laughed, and for a frightening moment, she thought she'd burst into tears. "Is that how you justify what you did? By convincing yourself you did us a *favor?*"

"I may have, at first," he admitted. "Because it made everything easier. But I know better now. What I did was wrong and I hate myself for it, for having been so weak. It hasn't been easy for me, either. When I heard about Jordan..." This time his voice did break, and his face contorted with pain.

"You know about Jordan?" Julia asked in a muffled voice.

Coop nodded.

"And you still didn't come home? For your own son's funeral?" Her voice shook with indignation and disbelief. "My God, what kind of monster are you?"

"I tried to come." He looked away. "It just...didn't work out that way."

"Meaning you were drunk."

"Yes." He met her hard, unforgiving gaze. "But those days are over, Julia. I don't drink anymore. And I go to AA every day, no matter where I am."

"You're twenty-three years too late," she said, refusing to feel any kind of compassion. "So if you expect me to be impressed, you're wasting your time. I don't want you here," she added, when he continued to look at her with that ravaged expression. "And I don't want you near my son."

Coop's eyes filled with tears. "You don't mean that."

"Yes, I do." Feeling a sob rise to her throat, she ran back into the house.

Steve had never been good with crying women. Too often they cried over a man, and the fact that he was a man made him feel as if he was part of the problem.

Julia's tears touched a part of him he'd thought could never be affected again. She sat in one of the big easy chairs in the kitchen-living area, her head buried in a pillow. Her muffled sobs ripped through her, convulsing her shoulders. He felt a sudden driving need to take her in his arms and rock her until she fell asleep.

Feeling helpless, Steve closed the door that separated the kitchen from the bedrooms and just stood there, watching her. He decided to let the tears run their course. Such despair needed to be let out.

Only when the sobs quieted did he walk over to the sink,

fill a glass with water and take it to her. "Here. You probably can use this."

Julia looked up, her eyes red and swollen. "Thanks." She took the glass and drank from it. "I suppose you think I'm a horrible person."

"No, I don't. And I'm sorry if I contributed to whatever problem you and your father have. Andrew and I were still playing ball when Coop arrived and introduced himself. I didn't let him in until he showed me an ID. He said he had been away and thought it was time to meet his grandson."

"And you didn't think there was something wrong with that?"

There was an edge to her voice, but Steve ignored it. "It wasn't my place to judge him, Julia. Or to deny him a visit with his grandson. And it's not as if I left them alone. I was there the whole time."

"What kind of lies did he tell you?" she asked sarcastically.

"All he said was that he had made mistakes and he wanted to rectify them, if it wasn't too late. Andrew took to him right away."

"I saw that," she said bitterly.

A wisp of blond hair clung to her wet cheek. He pushed it away before she could. "Want to talk about it?"

"No." She took another sip of water. "Yes."

She waited for another minute, then memories she must have pushed into a far corner of her mind suddenly gushed out. "I was eleven when he left," she began in a voice that still shook. "One moment he was there, the next he was gone. I was devastated. I didn't know how to cope. My mother wasn't much better and my younger brother cried for an entire week."

"Why did he leave?"

She kept staring at the glass in her hands. "He drank.

Heavily. He'd go on week-long binges, forgetting to come home. He had been kicked out of the army a few years earlier and went through a series of menial jobs after that, none of which he could keep for very long.

"I'd go to sleep every night listening to the sounds of my mother crying in the next room. And then there were the fights we weren't supposed to hear, the accusations, the slammed doors, the neighbors who avoided us and the kids who called us names."

"I'm sorry," he said quietly.

"We survived. It wasn't easy, but we survived. After he left, my mother had to take a second job in order to make ends meet. I remember her being so tired when she got home at night she could barely stand. But she always had time for us, time to listen to our problems, time to comfort us. We never once felt neglected."

Julia laughed, a sad little laugh that nearly ended in a sob. "I kept waiting for him. Every night after dinner, I'd sit at my bedroom window and wait for his old Chevy to turn the corner. Every time a set of headlights appeared, my heart would leap in my throat at the thought that he had finally come home."

"Where is your brother now?"

Her eyes squeezed shut and fresh tears spilled out. "He died. He was a narcotics detective for the Monterey PD He was killed during a drug raid a year ago."

Steve didn't say anything. At times like these, words just weren't enough.

He saw her small fists clench. For a moment, the only sound in the room was an occasional dry sob as it escaped her throat.

"Jordan expressed his grief differently," she continued. "After he finally stopped crying, he went on a rampage and destroyed everything that reminded him of my father, every toy Coop had ever given him, every picture he had taken, every piece of clothing he'd left behind. We couldn't stop him."

She looked at Steve, her eyes flat. "Tonight I found out that Coop knew about Jordan's death, but was too drunk to come to the funeral." A tear ran down her cheek and she took a vicious swipe at it. "Can you believe it? He was too drunk to come to his son's funeral."

"Alcoholism is a terrible disease, Julia. It can turn the kindest, most dependable people into—"

"Stop taking his side! You don't know him. And you don't know how it was for us." Pressing the back of her head against the cushion, she stared at a point in the ceiling. "I loved him so much. And he threw that love away."

"No, he didn't. If he had, he wouldn't have come back here and faced your rage. And your rejection.

"I think I understand what you went through," Steve went on when she didn't reply. "I know how it feels to lose a father."

Julia blinked away her tears. "Your father abandoned you, too?"

"No. He died."

"Oh." She raked her hair back. "I'm sorry."

"I was in college at the time, and my sister was still in high school. My father owned a small charter airline in Miami. He also belonged to an organization called Brothers to the Rescue."

"I've heard of them." With a tissue she blotted her eyes. "They fly missions to rescue other Cubans who want to leave their country."

Steve stared into space. "That's one of the things they do. And my father did it very well. He had flown dozens of such missions, each one of them successful. One night he took off for Havana, this time to rescue my uncle who had stayed behind when Castro came to power. Dad had it all planned—the route, the low altitude to avoid being detected, the landing strip on a deserted beach where my uncle and his family would be waiting."

Her pain momentarily forgotten, Julia leaned forward. "What happened?"

"He misjudged Castro's new technology and his capabilities to detect low-flying aircrafts. Two miles off the coast of Cuba, my father's plane was shot down by two Migs. The Cuban air force didn't even bother to issue a warning, and they didn't send a plane to escort my father to the nearest air base. They just started firing. My father never had a chance. His plane exploded and plunged into the sea. Only a few body parts were recovered."

"Oh, Steve, how awful." Julia moved her hand to his arm and kept it there. "For you and for your family."

"We were never truly a family after that. The three of us are very close, and now we have my sister's children, but with my father gone, it's just not the same."

"He died for a cause he believed in."

"I know, but he and I often argued about those missions. I told him they were getting too dangerous, that he should stop and find another way to help his people. He just laughed. 'There is no other way for me to help my people, *hijo*,' he told me. 'This is what I do.' I never said anything more after that, but we both knew he hadn't convinced me.

"I envy you, Julia, having your father here." He returned his gaze to her. "I would have done anything to see mine one more time, to tell him that I loved him, that I understood why he had to do what he did."

With an abrupt gesture, Julia withdrew her hand. "I hope you're not comparing your father to mine."

"No. I'm merely saying that regret for something we

could have done and didn't do can often be more painful than the loss itself."

Behind him, Steve heard the door open. Turning around, he saw Andrew standing in the doorway. "Where's Grandpa?" His voice was flat, his expression cool as he glanced around the room.

"He left—" Julia began.

The boy's gaze settled on her. "Did you tell him to?"

"I know this is hard for you to understand, Andrew—" She started to go to him, but he took a step back.

"You did, didn't you?" he cried. "You sent him away. He drove hundreds of miles to be with us and you sent him away."

"Andrew, you don't know anything about him."

Tears that seemed to make Julia's own pain even more acute spilled down Andrew's cheeks. "I know he did some bad things, but he's sorry. That's why he came back—to apologize."

"I can't talk about this now," Julia said, looking as if she was on the verge of tears again herself. "Why don't you go wash your hands. Dinner—"

"I don't want any dinner!"

He stalked off, slamming the kitchen door behind him.

Fifteen

Coop took a can of Coke from the six-pack he had bought on the way back from The Hacienda and popped the lid open, wishing it was a beer.

He had felt so damned low after Julia's rejection that, for a frightening moment, he had been tempted to buy a six-pack of beer instead of the Coke. It had taken all of his willpower, and some he had in reserve, to walk away from the enticing display.

Shoulders slightly hunched, he went to stand by the window of his motel room and watched an eighteen-wheeler pull into the parking lot.

His attempt to reconcile with his daughter had failed miserably. She had told him, in no uncertain terms, that she had written him off long ago and had no intention of forgiving him.

What the hell had he expected? A hero's welcome?

With a disgusted grunt, he walked back into the room, his gaze stopping on the nightstand, where a letter was propped up against the table lamp. It was to Julia. He would mail it in the morning. One last apology to the daughter he loved and then he'd be on his way and would never bother her again.

In spite of the pain deep in his heart, he was glad he'd had a chance to meet Andrew, even briefly. What a great kid. Just seeing him there, pitching balls to that nice reporter, had shaken the hell out of him. And now Andrew, too, was lost.

You deserve nothing more than what you got, old man.

A knock at the door spared him from sinking further into self-pity. "Who is it?" he asked, one hand on the knob. If there was one thing he remembered from his days as a drunk, it was to be wary of muggers.

There was a short silence. Then the voice he thought he'd never hear again spoke softly. "It's me, Julia."

They sat in the parlor at either end of the large red sofa. After thanking Steve, who had stayed with Andrew until he had fallen asleep, Julia had settled down with her father for a heart-to-heart talk.

She had battled with her feelings for nearly an hour after her conversation with Steve. For the better part of that hour, all she had wanted was to wallow in her fury and not have to feel guilty about it. Her anger was the only thing that brought her comfort, and dammit, no one was going to take it away from her.

It wasn't until Andrew, still sulking, had refused to come out of his room that she had realized how deeply her decision was affecting him. The boy was still grieving for his father and here she was, taking away the grandfather he had just met.

And oddly enough, she had felt just as guilty toward her father. Coming here had taken a great deal of courage on his part. If she hadn't been so preoccupied with her anger, she would have seen that. And she would have seen that beneath that anger was a much more powerful emotion—love.

The realization that she still loved him had staggered her. A few minutes later, shaky but certain of what she had to do, she had gone to the Monterey Arms to get her dad.

Her dad. She had said that word over and over, in her mind at first, then out loud, as if she needed to reacquaint herself with the sound of it before she could actually use it.

Now, with the anger gone, she wanted to hear everything, from the daily binges and occasional trips to a shelter to that awful moment a month ago when Coop had awakened in jail with no recollection of how he had gotten there.

She didn't interrupt. And she didn't comment. Not even after he was finished.

"Now it's your turn," Coop said, picking up his coffee cup.

She told him everything he wanted to know, waiting for his questions, answering them as best as she could. She didn't tell him about Paul's abuse. And she didn't bring up Jordan. Coop would have to do that.

They were on their third cup of coffee when he finally said, "Tell me about Jordan. What was he like?"

Julia took a moment to collect herself. "Handsome, gentle, funny. He loved helping people. That's why he became a cop." Julia smiled. "I bet Spike didn't tell you Jordan graduated from the police academy with honors."

Coop shook his head.

"After he made detective, he was assigned to the narcotics division and was teamed up with Frank Walsh."

"His idol."

"That's because Frank was always there—for both of us. Like a big brother."

Coop pressed the tip of a finger to the corner of his eyes as if to stop a tear. "I'm glad you kids had someone to look up to."

"Frank taught Jordan a lot during those first few years. He had even predicted that Jordan would make sergeant before Frank did. He might have, too, if..."

She bit her lip, struggling not to cry.

"What happened? How did he die?"

"Didn't Spike tell you?"

"He gave me the newspapers' accounts. I want to hear it from you."

Julia wished she didn't have to relive that terrible day but understood why Coop had to know. "Jordan and I had an argument that day."

Coop frowned. "What about?"

She stared at her hands clasped on her lap. "For days, something had been troubling him. I asked him what it was, but he wouldn't tell me. When I pressed him and asked if he and Cassie were having problems, he told me to mind my own business, and stormed out."

"Who's Cassie?"

"His fiancée. They were to be married that following June."

"She lives around here?"

"Not anymore. She moved to L.A. shortly after Jordan died. She still comes to visit every couple of months."

Julia paused, feeling the weight of her grief all over again. "After Jordan left, I tried to call him at the station to apologize, but the desk sergeant told me he and Frank were responding to a call. They had been investigating a drug ring right here in Monterey. That night, someone phoned in to say that something was going down in a warehouse near the wharf. Frank and Jordan didn't realize they were outnumbered until they were inside the building."

"Didn't they call for backup?"

"Three squad cars were on the way, but Jordan and Frank got there first. Frank wanted to wait, but Jordan wouldn't listen. He was itching to go in, to surprise whoever was there. Instead, the surprise was on them. A lookout positioned on the roof saw them coming. Gunfire broke out and Jordan was hit in the chest. Frank immediately rushed to his side, but it was too late. Jordan died in his arms.''

Tears rolled down Coop's weathered face.

''Frank was devastated,'' Julia continued, struggling not to give in to her own tears. ''He was convinced Jordan's death was his fault, that he shouldn't have let him go in until backup had arrived. But Jordan as a grown-up wasn't any different than the Jordan you knew as a boy. He was impulsive and fearless. It used to drive Frank crazy.''

''Frank should have stopped him,'' Coop said. ''He was Jordan's superior.''

''No one knows that better than Frank. For a while, he actually contemplated leaving the force. It took Mom, Cassie and me weeks to convince him that he would be doing more good in the force than out—especially since the scum who killed Jordan managed to get away.''

Coop's jaw clenched. ''You mean they never caught them?''

Julia shook her head. ''They vanished without a trace. Frank thinks they moved their operation to another state, maybe even to Mexico.

''I miss him so much,'' Julia murmured. ''He was my pal, my best friend. And he loved Andrew.''

''Andrew.'' Coop shook his head. ''How did he handle losing an uncle and a father in the space of a year?''

''Not well. He had never experienced death before Jordan passed away, and I had to explain it to him. Thank God for Frank and his wife, and Mom, of course. I don't know what I would have done without them.''

''You would have found a way to help your son. I have no doubt about that.'' Coop's look was tender. ''You were always such a strong little girl, and so wise for your young age, always giving advice to others, comforting, mothering."

She looked at him, surprised. "You remember that?"

"I remember everything about my kids."

Slowly, almost timidly, Coop slid his big callused hand across the cushions, then turned it over, palm up.

After a short hesitation, Julia took it.

"Wake up, sleepyhead." Sitting on Andrew's bed, Julia shook him gently.

Andrew groaned something unintelligible. Bending over him, Julia kissed his forehead. He had never gone to bed without dinner before, and he would be famished.

"Andrew?" She shook him again, a little harder this time. "There's someone here who wants to say hello."

He was suddenly wide-awake, as if his kid radar, which seemed more acute than ever these days, had tipped him off. When he saw Coop framed in the doorway, he let out a yelp of joy, jumped out of bed and ran into his grandfather's arms.

"You're staying?" His big blue eyes were bright as he gazed up.

"Looks that way."

Watching them, Julia felt a pinch in her heart and hoped she had made the right decision in letting Coop stay. Andrew was such a trusting soul. He gave his love totally and unconditionally. But could she trust her father? What if he started drinking again? And pulled another of his disappearing acts and broke Andrew's heart in the process?

One arm wrapped around Coop's waist, Andrew turned to Julia. "Thanks, Mom."

"You're welcome." She ruffled his hair. "Grandpa will be staying with us until he finds a place of his own, so you'll have plenty of time to spend together. Right now, you've got to get ready for school, okay?"

"'Kay."

As Andrew sprinted toward the bathroom, Coop squeezed Julia's arm, then walked back to the kitchen, where he and Steve had been arguing about which National League baseball team would go to the play-offs.

As she took eggs and milk out of the refrigerator, Julia thought about the next hurdle she had to face.

Telling her mother that Coop had returned.

"He's here?" Horrified, Grace stared at Julia. "In Monterey?"

Sitting in her mother's living room, surrounded by familiar furniture and old mementos, Julia nodded.

"Oh, my God." As if afraid her legs wouldn't support her, Grace sat down in one of the dark blue easy chairs.

"How did he find you?" Grace asked. "Where has he been? What does he want?"

"He's been traveling, getting by. Then one day last week, he heard about Paul, and came to see if he could help."

"Help?" Grace jumped out of her chair. "Is he out of his mind? Did we ask for his help? Has he ever offered it in twenty-three years?"

"He also wanted to meet Andrew."

Grace's voice rose as she began to pace. "This is so typical. Not a word from him in all this time—not even a phone call—and then he reappears just like that." Stopping in front of the sofa, she fluffed a pillow, then another. "He has some nerve."

"He's changed, Mom."

"Oh, please." She turned around, her smile so bitter it

looked more like a grimace. "You didn't fall for that tired old line, did you? Or let him anywhere near Andrew?"

"Actually, I didn't have much choice," Julia replied. "Andrew was there when he arrived. I wasn't. I was with you."

Grace drew in a long breath and took her time blowing it out. "All right. I suppose that couldn't be helped. Where's Coop now?"

Julia braced herself. "At The Hacienda."

"What do you mean, at The Hacienda? You said..." Her eyes went wide with disbelief. *"He is staying with you?"*

"Until he finds his own place."

"Oh, Julia." Grace sank back in her chair. "What have you done?"

"What else *could* I do, Mom?"

"You could have told him to go back to wherever he came from."

"I did. At first I was just as angry as you are now. I yelled at him, I called him names and I told him to leave us alone. But Andrew was devastated. I couldn't make him understand, Mom." She paused before adding, "Nor did I want to. Not after all he's been through."

"And in typical fashion," Grace said pointedly, "Coop took full advantage of the situation."

Bound to her father by a loyalty she couldn't explain, Julia shook her head. "No, he didn't. After I lashed out at him, he left and went back to his motel room. It wasn't until Steve told me about his father that—"

Grace's brows knitted. "What does Steve's father have to do with all this?"

"He died. Before Steve could resolve his own differences with him. I started to wonder, what if Coop died? Right here, in a motel room half a mile from my house. How would I feel? How would I explain it to my son?"

"And now Coop is at your house, no doubt raiding your liquor cabinet or stealing your money. Or both."

"He won't. Not as long as he's around Andrew. Besides, he's sober now. He goes to AA."

Grace made a sarcastic sound with her tongue. "How long is *that* going to last?"

"I don't know, Mom, but he made it through an entire month. It may not seem like much, but it's something, and maybe this time, with a little help, he's going to make it all the way."

"He's going to hurt you, that's what he's going to do," Grace snapped. "And he's going to hurt Andrew. Not voluntarily maybe, but he'll hurt him. Don't say I didn't warn you. And don't bring him here." Her face took on that pinched look Julia knew so well. "I don't want to see him."

The sound of a car pulling into the driveway interrupted them. Grace walked over to the window and pulled the white café curtain to one side. "I'll go see who that is."

Julia's gaze followed her mother until she disappeared, then swept slowly across the room. Except for the absence of her parents' wedding picture, which had been removed long ago, the house was the same now as it had always been. Grace hadn't changed a thing, not even the placement of furniture. She had wanted to, many times—as a way of erasing the past—but whenever Julia or Jordan had offered to help her, she would always find an excuse to postpone the task.

It was a good house, Julia thought as her gaze touched all the familiar places. The smell, a mixture of chocolate cookies and Pledge, was still there and brought back sweet memories. There had been happiness in this house. And there had been despair.

Her thoughts were interrupted by the sound of the front

door closing. Then Grace was walking back into the living room, carrying a shoe box.

"What's that?" Julia asked.

"Jordan's audiotapes. You remember I told you Paul borrowed them last month, hoping they'd help him with his crime commission work." She put the box on the coffee table in front of them. "Detective Hammond found them in Paul's house and took them to the station as potential evidence."

"Did he find anything?"

"Apparently not. That was one of his men. He told me Detective Hammond was finished and I could have the tapes back."

Julia remembered only too well Jordan's passion for unsolved crimes. Meticulous as well as stubborn, he would spend days, sometimes weeks, going through police records, studying each piece of evidence, rereading statements made by various witnesses, before recording his findings into a tape recorder. Once or twice, his patience had paid off and an old case was solved, but most of the time, he did it for the sheer joy of investigating.

Leaning over the table, she read each label handwritten in Jordan's familiar scroll. Suddenly, she frowned. "Wait a minute. Didn't you tell me you gave Paul eight tapes?"

"That's right."

Julia's fingers moved quickly, flipping each cassette. "There are only seven here."

"How can that be?" Grace counted the tapes, then met Julia's gaze. "Do you suppose Detective Hammond found something after all and didn't tell me?"

Julia was already reaching for the blue princess phone on the end table. "That's what I intend to find out."

When the detective answered his phone, Julia was brief and to the point. "Detective, this is Julia Bradshaw. I'm calling about my brother's tapes. The ones you just sent back."

"What about them?"

"Do you remember how many cassettes you found in Paul's house?"

"Seven. Why?"

"My mother says there were eight cassettes when she gave the box to Paul last month."

There was a short silence. "Is she certain?"

Julia glanced at Grace, who was watching her intently. "She's positive. She gave Paul eight tapes."

At the other end of the line, the detective was silent. She could hear him shuffling through a file. "We only signed for seven tapes," he said after a while. "I've got the form right here."

"Then one is missing."

"I'll go back to the house and take another look. It could still be there, though I doubt it. My team doesn't usually miss that kind of stuff."

Julia felt a leap of excitement. "Will you call me when you get back?"

She heard him sigh. "Mrs. Bradshaw, I'm a busy man—"

But Julia wasn't about to be pushed around. "I'm aware of that. But I have a big stake in this investigation, Detective, so if there's even the slightest possibility that Paul found something incriminating, something that might clear me, I have a right to know, don't you think?"

"I'll call you," he said gruffly, and hung up.

"What now?" Grace asked after Julia put the receiver down.

"I have to get back, but I'll call you as soon as I hear from Hammond."

Sixteen

"I'm afraid you're not going to like this." Luther Aldridge scanned through the file in front of him. "In a nutshell, Charles, you don't have a case."

Charles glared at the man who had been his attorney for more than three decades, wondering why he kept him. "Then you'd better come up with a case, Luther. I'm not paying you five hundred dollars an hour to twiddle your thumbs."

Seemingly impervious to the remark, Luther leaned back in his chair. "I know that's not what you wanted to hear, but I have to lay it on the line for you. Your chances of being awarded custody of Andrew are just about nil. The police have not charged Julia with Paul's murder, and frankly, I doubt they will. Unless they come up with some hard evidence."

"Then forget about hard evidence and concentrate on the fact that Julia's father is back in town and living under the same roof as my grandson."

"Your point?" Luther asked coolly.

"My point, dammit, is that Coop is a drunk, a man who abandoned his family and came back to freeload off his daughter. What kind of example is that for a six-year-old?"

"I'm afraid you've got that scenario all wrong, Charles. First of all, Cooper Reid no longer drinks. He's been sober for over a month, goes to AA meetings and helps out around the inn. As for Andrew, according to Joe and Vera Martinez, whose son is Andrew's best friend, the boy adores his grandfather. If that upsets you," he added, when Charles made an impatient sound with his tongue, "I'm sorry."

"Sorry won't cut it," Charles said in a sour tone. "You were supposed to unearth damning information on Coop, not give me a glowing report."

"That's what I'm trying to tell you. There's nothing damning about Coop. He's a reformed man."

"Okay, okay," Charles said impatiently. "Forget about Saint Coop. What about The Hacienda? How's it doing?"

Luther shook his head. "The inn's situation is pretty much status quo at the moment. Julia has only one guest. However, she's devised a rather ingenious way of making money."

"I'm afraid to ask," Charles said sarcastically.

Luther ignored the comment. "She's starting a series of gourmet cooking classes, and, from what I've been hearing, the new venture looks like it's going to take off. So if you were counting on The Hacienda going belly-up anytime soon, you're in for another disappointment."

Charles digested the news. Much as he hated to admit it, Julia was a resourceful woman and perhaps a better businesswoman than he had given her credit for. But dammit, he wasn't going to give up on Andrew. Not without a fight. "What do you suggest we do?" he asked.

Luther shrugged. "Right now, nothing. If Julia *is* arrested, and that's a big if, you may have a chance to get the boy, but I wouldn't count on it. Julia will most likely give temporary custody to her mother, and there's no reason why the court wouldn't grant it. Grace Reid is above reproach and perfectly capable of caring for her grandchild."

After volleying back and forth for another ten minutes, Charles left his attorney's office on Alvarez Street, wishing he had stayed home. As he stepped onto the sidewalk, he was immediately surrounded by an army of reporters, many of whom he knew well.

Glad for the opportunity to express his feelings, he stopped on the threshold as Syd Rimer, a columnist for the *San Francisco Star,* elbowed his way to a front row spot.

"Mr. Bradshaw, how do you feel about the possibility that *Gleic Éire,* the same group that killed your daughter, may also have killed your son?"

"That's a ridiculous assumption," Charles snapped. "Totally unfounded."

"Are you saying that the police are wasting their time in pursuing that lead then?"

Charles put up a hand. "I'm not saying that. The police have a job to do and that job is to examine every possibility. But as far as *I'm* concerned, the evidence that *Gleic Éire* is involved just isn't there."

"Yet you feel there's enough evidence against Julia Bradshaw?" someone else asked.

Charles glanced at the reporter who had just spoken and saw a tall man in sunglasses and a Boston Red Sox hat. He couldn't make him out, but knew he wasn't a local. No Monterey reporter would dare address him in that tone of voice.

"Yes, I do," he replied, watching as the man shouldered his way through the crowd. "And so do the good people of Monterey. Julia Bradshaw killed my son and I want her punished for it. Now if you don't mind, I'm in a hurry." He started to leave and found his path blocked by the same smart-ass reporter.

"What evidence do you have that Julia Bradshaw killed Paul?" The man's tone was downright challenging. "Or are you just trying to discredit her so you can get custody of her son?''

At the undisguised attack, Charles almost choked. Squaring his shoulders, he gave the heckler, certainly not the first he had dealt with in his lifetime, a glacial look.

''What's your name, young man?'' he asked. ''And what publication do you represent?''

''Why don't you just answer the question?''

Charles gave him a look charged with venom. ''I'm not trying to discredit anyone. I'm simply expressing an opinion, based on what I know.''

''And what exactly *do* you know, Mr. Bradshaw?'' Taking another step, the reporter came to stand directly in front of Charles.

Charles's heart slammed in his chest.

Even with the sunglasses, he would have recognized that face anywhere. It belonged to Steve Reyes, a man he hated almost as much as he hated the men who had killed his daughter.

Aware that cameras all around him were snapping, Charles willed himself to stay calm. He would not let that bastard draw him into a public confrontation.

''If you don't know,'' he said with all the self-restraint he could muster, ''you have no business being a reporter.''

Then, his stride a little stiffer than usual, Charles walked past him and headed for his Eldorado, parked across the street.

It had taken Charles exactly four-and-a-half minutes to find out when Steve Reyes had arrived in town and where he was staying. When he heard that the *New York Sun*'s reporter had booked a room at The Hacienda, his anger turned into full-blown rage.

Because Garrett was the only person who knew about

Sheila's affair with Steve Reyes, Charles went directly to his friend's office. "Did you know that Steve Reyes was in town?" he asked the chief of police without any ceremonies.

"I did," Garrett replied calmly.

"Why didn't you tell me?"

"Because I didn't want any trouble, Charles. I have enough to worry about right now, or haven't you noticed?"

Charles leaned across the chief's desk. "I want him out of town."

Garrett's mouth twitched. "Before sundown I presume?"

"Don't patronize me, Garrett."

"Then stop acting like a four-year-old. Steve Reyes hasn't done anything wrong. I went along when you wanted to keep him away from Sheila's funeral because I felt you had a right to bury your daughter in private, but I can't, and won't, order him out of town. The man is only doing his job."

"He's screwing with me."

"Then take that up with him. But do it calmly, for God's sake. You're not going to solve anything by having a heart attack." Swinging back in his chair, Garrett glanced out his window and chuckled. "Well, what do you know? Here's your chance."

Charles followed Garrett's gaze. Reyes had just come out of the police building and was walking toward the far end of the parking lot. "What the hell is he doing here?" he mumbled.

"Probably checking in with Hammond. Hank seems to have developed a liking for the guy."

Charles was already out the door.

"Reyes!"

Recognizing Charles's voice, Steve turned around. "I

was wondering how long it would take you to track me down."

For a moment the two men measured each other, two old enemies trying to gage their respective strengths. And weaknesses.

"How dare you show your face in this town again?" Charles asked, as he marched toward Steve. "I thought I made myself clear the first time. You were never to come back."

Steve leaned against the Land Rover and folded his arms. "Last I heard, this was a free country."

"What do you want?"

Steve shrugged. "What I've wanted for eight years—to find Sheila's killers and bring them to justice."

"You won't find them here."

"That's for me to decide. If you have a problem with that—"

"I have a problem with *you*, Reyes. I want you out of my town."

Charles's condescending tone made Steve ache to teach this ornery old goat a lesson. Remembering he couldn't do much behind bars, which was exactly where he'd end up if he hit the former governor, Steve slowly unclenched his fists.

"Your days of ordering me around are over, Bradshaw." Steve's voice ripped through the air like a blade, and for an instant, he had the satisfaction of seeing Charles flinch.

"However," he continued, "since I know how much you hate the thought of some low-life exile being connected to your family, you can relax. I have no intention of telling anyone that Sheila and I were engaged to be married. Or," he added, enjoying the look of sheer rage on Charles's face, "that you ordered her to have an abortion so the precious

Bradshaw name wouldn't be soiled. That *is* how you put it, isn't it, Charles? Those were your exact words."

Charles's eyes narrowed into dangerous slits. "She was only a child and you took advantage of her innocence. If it hadn't been for you, for the lies you fed her, she would have done as I said. She would have come home."

"And if she hadn't been so eager to escape your tyranny, she wouldn't have left home in the first place. Did you ever think of that?"

The remark seemed to strike a cord. Charles's face turned beet-red and a small vein began to pulse at his right temple. "You bastard."

Steve's lips pulled into a tight smile. "Takes one to know one, Charles."

The former governor glared at him for a long minute, his eyes as hard and implacable as they had been the first day the two men had met. Steve had always been a strong believer that time and grief mellowed people. They hadn't mellowed Charles Bradshaw. He was still the same mean, arrogant son of a bitch he'd been all his life.

When Charles finally turned around and started to walk away, Steve watched him for a few seconds, feeling suddenly sorry for the guy. He'd had so much at one time. Now he had nothing. He would have to spend the rest of his life in that big, fancy house of his, all alone.

With a small sigh, Steve opened the door of the Land Rover, slid behind the wheel and headed for Salinas, where he had an appointment with Eli Seavers's neighbor.

Thanks to Jennifer Seavers, who had made all the necessary arrangements, Esther Hathaway had agreed to answer Steve's questions and to take him to Eli's house afterward.

"Though I don't know what you think you'll find there,"

the woman had told Steve on the phone. "Those FBI agents tore the place apart in search of God knows what, and left it in shambles. Jennifer and I spent two hours tidying up after they left."

Steve could tell from the tone of her voice that neither the feds nor the Monterey police had made a favorable impression on her. Maybe he could make that work in his favor.

Esther's house was a ten minute drive from the center of Salinas. It stood at the end of a long road that cut through several miles of fertile farmland, a small yellow ranch house with white shutters and an old-fashioned white picket fence. Eli's house, similar though smaller, was directly across the yard. A For Sale sign stood in the front yard.

He found Esther in her garden, clipping dead daisies from a thick rambling patch and dropping them in a paper bag at her feet. She was a tiny, white-haired woman with a gentle smile and intelligent eyes.

"Oh!" she exclaimed when Steve handed her a stunning fern he had bought in a Monterey flower shop earlier. "How sweet of you, Mr. Reyes."

"Jennifer told me you liked ferns."

She held the plant lovingly against her chest as she led the way inside the house. "I *adore* ferns. They can be such a challenge, can't they?"

"I wouldn't know." Following her lead, Steve wiped his feet several times on the thick outdoor mat. "I'm afraid I don't have much of a green thumb."

"Oh, nonsense. Plants are living things, and like all living things they need a little tender loving care, that's all."

The inside of the house was tidy and spotless, with a tweed sofa and matching chairs in the living room and gold shag carpeting everywhere. At the sound of their voices, a small calico cat ran in from a back room, looked at Steve for a moment, then, as a sign of approval, came to rub against his leg.

"Leave my guest alone, Houdini." Esther put the fern on the broad, sunny windowsill. "Now," she said, turning around. "May I offer you some lemonade? I always keep a pitcher handy, in case my daughter comes to visit."

Sensing that a refusal would offend her, Steve nodded. "That would be lovely, Mrs. Hathaway. Thank you."

Moments later, she was back with a tray that held two tall glasses of lemonade and a silver plate heaped high with gingersnaps. After taking her glass, Esther sat in one of the tweed chairs. Houdini, who had been waiting patiently for her to do just that, immediately jumped on her lap, turned around a couple of times, then settled down for a nap.

"You're different from the others," Esther said as she started to stroke the cat.

"The others?"

"The police and those FBI people. They came here like a rush of wind, barely said hello and started snapping questions at me like I was a machine."

Steve chuckled inwardly at the mental image of stiff, dark-suited G-men sitting uncomfortably in Esther's living room and glancing at their watches, while a lonely little old lady with a cat on her lap tried to be social. He would have bet the farm they had turned down the lemonade.

"This is very good," he said, taking an unhurried sip. As Esther smiled approvingly, he glanced at the house across the street. Eli's garden, though not as lush as Esther's, was well cared for. Steve could even see a sprinkler pulsing and turning, misting every inch of the small front yard.

"I couldn't let his flowers die," Esther said, following his gaze. "Gardening was one of Eli's rare joys."

"Jennifer told me you used to look after Eli's house when he went away."

"Only his garden," she corrected. "And that was before he became ill. He never went away again after that." She gestured toward the plate. "Have a cookie."

Steve hated gingersnaps but helped himself to one, anyway. "I understand you also looked in on him when he started getting ill."

"Oh, he didn't need much looking in on at the beginning. He would get a little confused every now and then, and he would forget my name, but for the most part, he was getting on just fine. I would stop by two or three times a week to make sure he didn't need anything.

"It was no bother," she continued. "And he had always been so nice to me in the past, so thoughtful. Do you know that he never forgot to bring me a little something from his travels—expensive soaps from Germany, chocolate from Switzerland." She nodded toward the plate that held the cookies. "He brought me this from France once."

Steve put his glass down and took a closer look at the plate. It was small but lovely, with an engraved floral pattern and a scalloped border.

"Very nice." He looked up. "And you said Eli bought this in France?"

Esther nodded. "At a little antiques shop on rue Jacob. That's in Paris," she added rather proudly.

"When was that, do you remember?"

She was thoughtful for a moment. "Summer of 1987, I believe. Or was it the fall?" She shrugged. "I can't recall, but it was around that time."

Steve acknowledged her reply with a nod. When and where the object had been bought could easily be verified. What might be a little more difficult was to convince Mrs. Hathaway to part with it for a couple of days.

"Did you show this plate to the FBI agents when they were here?" he asked.

"Why...no." Looking suddenly distraught, she stopped stroking the cat. "I never even thought of it. They weren't here more than a few minutes, you see. All they were interested in was Eli's house."

"It's all right, Mrs. Hathaway. You didn't do anything wrong." He waited until her hand was once again moving along Houdini's fur before adding, "Would you mind terribly if I showed this plate to an antiques dealer?"

Her face expressed mild dismay. "What on earth for?"

"I need to know where Eli bought it."

"I told you where," she said a little irritably. "In a gallery on rue Jacob."

"I know that's what he told you, but I'd like to make sure."

"You think he lied." Her tone turned reproachful.

"He may have." Steve leaned forward. "Will you trust me, Mrs. Hathaway?"

She squared her shoulders. "I don't know you, Mr. Reyes."

A veteran reporter with two Pulitzers had once told him that, in order to get people to cooperate, a reporter either had to lie or tell the truth. The trick was to know what to tell to whom.

After nearly fifteen minutes in Esther Hathaway's company, Steve decided she was too shrewd to be told a lie. "Do you read the papers, Mrs. Hathaway?" he asked.

"Of course I do." She raised her chin. "And I watch CNN."

Steve held back a smile. "Then you know that Eli Seavers might have known something about that Irish extremist group we've all been hearing so much about lately. *Gleic Éire?*"

She gave a curt nod. "That's why the FBI was so interested in his house. They thought they'd find something about those horrible people."

"Exactly."

"But they didn't."

"No." Stoically, Steve took another cookie and bit into it. "This plate might help us find out where Eli was traveling to when he went away."

She let out an impatient sigh. "I told you that, too. Aren't you listening? He went to France, and to Germany and sometimes to Switzerland. And I wish you people would stop acting as if he was some kind of criminal. Eli was a sweet and generous man, who kept to himself and expected others to do the same. So why don't you let him rest in peace? You and everyone else."

Her excitement had caused her to stroke the cat a little too energetically and Houdini let out a loud meow, jumped down and ran off.

"I admire your loyalty, Mrs. Hathaway," Steve said quietly, wondering how many gingersnaps he'd have to consume before she decided he could be trusted. "But the truth is, Eli may have been traveling elsewhere, and the only way we're going to know that is by exploring all the avenues."

He tapped the edge of the plate. "And this may be our most significant clue yet. I promise I won't keep it for more than a couple of days, and I'll make sure to hire only the most reputable antiques dealer on the Monterey Peninsula."

"Well..." She was slowly warming to the idea. "Since you trusted me enough to tell me the truth instead of making up some silly story, I suppose I can trust you, too. And Jennifer did say to cooperate with you in any way I could."

"Thank you, Mrs. Hathaway." He glanced across the

road again. "And now if you don't mind, I'd like to take a look at Eli's house."

She stood up. "I'll get the keys. Meanwhile, why don't you have another cookie? You hardly touched them."

Seventeen

Her eyes glued to the television set, Julia watched in disbelief as Charles faced the cameras and called her a murderer. Until now his accusations had been made at random and to a limited group of people, and while he had made his feelings clear on the day of Paul's funeral, he had never attacked her so publicly, or so viciously.

No wonder everyone in this town treated her as though she had the plague. With words like those, and from a man who was so loved, why would they act any differently?

When she realized the reporter who had antagonized Charles was Steve Reyes, her first reaction was one of anger. If he hadn't goaded Charles with his inflammatory remarks, there might not have been a public accusation. But her anger was short-lived. She knew Charles too well not to know this informal press gathering was an opportunity he hadn't intended to let pass.

What he hadn't counted on was one reporter's determination to openly discredit and embarrass him. And judging from the way Charles abruptly ended the discussion and cut through the crowd, Steve had accomplished exactly that.

Watching the former governor stalk off, Julia wished she could feel at least a morsel of satisfaction for this small victory. She couldn't. Charles's harsh words hurt too much. And by this evening, they'd be heard by millions of Californians. What hope did she have to save her business after such an attack?

A massive weariness tugged at her. At times like these, she didn't even feel like fighting anymore. Suddenly, she wished she could take Andrew, leave everything else behind and move to another town—far away from Monterey.

For an instant, the thought was almost appealing. She could start a new life, without suspicion or cruel remarks or the constant fear that her son could be taken away from her.

The realization that she'd be a fugitive and would have to look over her shoulder every minute of her life stopped her cold. What was she doing? She was no quitter. She had roots here, people who loved her, and that included her father who had become such a vital part of her family. How could she leave them all behind and not feel as though she was deserting them?

Pushing aside her fears, she stood, took her plate with the untouched sandwich to the sink and tried to put Charles out of her mind.

Still fuming from his verbal match with Steve Reyes, Charles slammed the front door of his house, threw his keys on a table in the foyer and went into his drawing room for a well-deserved drink.

That smug, arrogant bastard. Who the hell did he think he was, talking to a Bradshaw that way? Defying his orders? And what the hell was he doing at The Hacienda? Probably conspiring with Julia, trying to find ways of embarrassing him.

"Good, you're home," his housekeeper said behind him. "I want to talk to you."

Charles let out a sigh of irritation. He knew that tone. It meant that Pilar was on the warpath.

He waved an impatient hand. "Not now, Pilar."

"*Sí, señor,* now." She came to plant herself in front of him, small fists on her hips. "I have to say something and it can't wait."

"You always have something to say," Charles muttered. Knowing any further protest would be useless, he walked over to the bar and poured himself a Scotch. A stiff one. "All right then, get it over with. What atrocity have I committed now?" He turned and met Pilar's hot gaze. "Did I leave my dirty shirts all over the bathroom floor? Wet towels on the bed? What?"

"You put your big foot in your mouth, that's what you did."

Charles took a sip of his Scotch. "Don't know what you're talking about."

"Then I'll tell you." She folded her arms across her chest and scowled at him. "What were you thinking when you stood in front of a camera and accused Julia of killing your son? You know what that's going to do to Andrew when he finds out?"

"If you're talking about my statement to the press earlier, there were no television cameras there, Pilar, only reporters—*newspaper* reporters."

"Wrong, Mr. B. WKYS was there and they put you on the twelve o'clock news. I saw it." Her dark eyes smoldered with anger. "How can you claim to love that child and do this to him? You know how much he loves his mother."

"I didn't see a camera," Charles said stubbornly. But deep down he wasn't sure it would have made a difference even if he had. After Reyes had so blatantly attacked him, he hadn't given a damn who heard him.

"You didn't see the camera because you were too busy

bad-mouthing Julia,'' Pilar continued. ''That's all that matters to you these days.''

''All right, Pilar, that's enough. You said what you had to say, now—''

''I'm not finished.'' She lay her hands on the back of a green damask chair. ''I have worked in this house for thirty years. I helped you and Mrs. B. raise your children, and God is my witness, I loved them as if they were my own.''

''I know that—''

She raised an accusing finger and pointed it at him. ''But there are things I never approved of. One of them is how you've always treated Julia, as if she wasn't good enough for your son, or the Bradshaws.''

Charles opened his mouth, took a look at his housekeeper and shut it again.

''The poor girl did her best to fit in,'' Pilar continued. ''And to please Paul. If he had tried half as hard to make the marriage work, maybe they would have stayed married. But they didn't, and of course, you blamed her. You never once asked yourself if maybe Paul had done something to make Julia walk out. And now you want her to go to prison for something she didn't do? And you want to take her boy from her?'' She shook her head. ''Oh, Mr. B., that's wrong. That's very wrong.''

''Are you finished?'' Charles asked calmly.

''Yes.'' She gave a nod. ''I'm finished.''

''Okay. My turn. First of all, Andrew will be better off with me. He'll have stability here and the kind of upbringing he deserves. And second, Paul didn't do anything to make Julia walk out. He may have had his faults, but he was a good husband—''

''He was a lousy husband,'' Pilar retorted.

''How can you say that? Julia is the one who let him down when she left him.''

"And you don't know why she left?"

"Of course I know why. She couldn't put up with the stress of being a politician's wife. She said so herself." He shook his head in disgust. "I don't know what's wrong with women today, always doing their own thing, never having time or interest for their husband's career. You'd think loyalty had become a dirty word."

"Julia was loyal to Paul," Pilar said, her voice suddenly very quiet. "More than you know. That's why she never said anything."

Charles lowered his glass. "Never said anything about what?"

Pilar's expression turned skeptical. "You really don't know? Or are you too embarrassed to talk about it?"

"I just told you—"

She gestured impatiently. "Not that cockamamie story about stress. *La verdad, señor.* The truth."

"What truth, for God's sake?"

Pilar held Charles's gaze without flinching. "Paul was beating her."

If the house had fallen down on him at that very instant, Charles couldn't have been more shocked. He looked at his housekeeper, wondering if the years had finally caught up with her and rendered her senile.

"Don't look at me like that," Pilar said sternly. "I'm not *loca.*"

"Then how did you come up with a crazy story like that?"

"I didn't come up with anything. I have eyes. I can see. Oh, Julia tried to hide the pain, inside and outside." She shook her head. "But she couldn't fool me."

"You're making this up."

"No, Mr. B., I'm not. I tried to get her to talk to me, you know, woman to woman. But she would just smile and say she was fine, just tired. But tired people don't make faces when they get up from a chair. And they don't walk like they have a broom handle stuck in their back.''

Charles felt something cold settle in the pit of his stomach. ''Paul would never strike a woman,'' he said. ''Least of all his wife.''

''Paul was an angry man. I could see it in his eyes, hear it in his voice. Why didn't you?''

Charles sat down. ''I don't believe you.''

''Then why don't you ask Julia?''

Charles was silent. What Pilar had told him made no sense. Paul had never been the violent type. And he would never, absolutely never, hit Julia. He had loved her too much.

Then why was Charles feeling as though he had just aged ten years? And why was he suddenly filled with such doubts?

He gulped his drink. Maybe the booze would make it all go away.

''You want some lunch now?'' Pilar's voice had softened. It always did after a good fight.

''I'm not hungry.'' He handed her his empty glass. ''I'll take another one of these, though.''

''At one o'clock in the afternoon? On an empty stomach?'' She snapped her tongue in disapproval. ''I don't think so.''

''Dammit, Pilar, who the hell is boss in this house?''

She didn't bother to answer. ''I'll be in the kitchen if you change your mind about lunch.''

Then she turned around and walked out.

Contrary to what Julia had feared, Charles's accusations didn't affect her plans for a cooking class. Minutes after the news segment had been broadcast, her phone had begun to ring. To her surprise, the callers weren't reporters, or crank cases, but people responding to her flyers. Within an hour, nineteen men and women, some from as far as Pebble Beach, had signed up for the course, making it necessary for her to schedule two back-to-back cooking series. The first would start in a few days and the next one sometime in July. And if her good luck held, the publicity might bring her a few overnight guests, as well.

With Steve in Salinas, searching Eli's house, and Coop on his way to baseball practice with Andrew, the inn was quiet, allowing her to spend the next hour preparing menus and jotting down a list of ingredients she would need for her first class.

She would set the table in the parlor, she decided, and drape it in that antique cloth her grandmother had given her years ago. Then she would top it with her best china and fresh flowers from her garden. Hopefully, the meal itself would be a memorable experience and would generate conversations from here to Sand City for days to come. Word of mouth, she knew, was everything.

She was going over her recipe for *poulet Normand* when she heard a knock at the door. It was Detective Hammond. He had traded his brown suit for a navy one that was a little less rumpled. But it was the quiet, almost regretful way he looked at her that brought a sigh from her throat.

Her shoulders sagged. "You didn't find the tape, did you?"

"No." He jammed his hands in his pockets and followed her into the kitchen. "Three of us searched every inch of your ex-husband's house. We found nothing. I'm sorry," he added, as though he sincerely meant it.

Julia leaned against the island, hands braced behind her. The brief burst of hope she had experienced at her mother's house had waned. "Are you sure you looked everywhere?"

Even as she spoke the words, she knew that was a stupid question. Hammond was nothing if not thorough.

His gaze rested on the tray of chocolate chips cookies she had set out to cool. "I'm sure."

"Then it has to be somewhere else."

"Or the killer found it and destroyed it."

Julia didn't miss the implication of that statement. "Does that mean you no longer think of me as a suspect?"

She thought she heard a light chuckle. "Don't go putting words in my mouth, Mrs. Bradshaw. I'm just keeping my options open, that's all."

When she saw him glance at the tray again, she took a dessert plate from the hutch and arranged three cookies on it. "I hope this won't be considered a bribe," she said lightly. "I wouldn't want to aggravate my situation."

"It'll be our secret." Hammond picked up a cookie and took a healthy bite. "Mmm." He bobbed his head in approval. "Excellent. Where did you learn to bake like that?"

"In my mother's kitchen, then later at the French Culinary Institute in San Francisco."

"My wife can't cook," he said, his mouth full. "She burns everything."

Julia took a flyer from a stack on the island and handed it to him. "In that case, why don't you give her this?"

Hammond read as he ate. "Cooking classes, huh? When did you decide to do that?"

Pulling a glass jar toward her, she began dropping the cooled cookies into it. "When I realized I wouldn't be able to pay my bills." She glanced at him sideways. "You see, Detective, one doesn't have to resort to murder to get out of a tight spot. There's always a way."

Hammond didn't comment. Still chewing, he folded the flyer in three, lengthwise, and slid it into his breast pocket. "I'll tell my wife."

He devoured the third cookie, passed on a fourth. "Thanks, but I've got to go. I want to search Charles Bradshaw's house before I go off duty, just in case the councilman hid the tape there."

"Charles?" She couldn't quite picture her former father-in-law lending a hand to help clear her name. "Will he let you do that?"

Hammond brushed the crumbs off his lapels. "He won't have a choice. A warrant should be waiting for me by the time I get back to the station."

Eighteen

Dressed in loose chinos and one of his colorful Hawaiian shirts, Ian McDermott bent over an exquisite pink dendrobium and felt totally content. Few things in life brought him as much pleasure and satisfaction as his award-winning orchids.

Hundreds of them, of every size, color and variety, were displayed in his state-of-the-art, climate-controlled greenhouse. Two stone paths cut through the maze of potted plants and climbing vines, while small fans, strategically placed, whirred gently, circulating the air and humidity that were so crucial to the survival of orchids.

An intricate misting system provided just the right amount of water each week, though at times, McDermott preferred to water his "beauties," as he called them, the old-fashioned way—with a watering can.

He visited the greenhouse each morning at precisely ten-fifteen and walked slowly from plant to plant, talking to each one, studying their progress and tending to their daily care. Most plants bloomed fairly quickly—in ninety to a hundred and twenty days. Others took as much as seven years to produce the first bloom. Many gardeners lacked the patience to wait such a long time. Not McDermott.

McDermott was a very patient man.

The intercom near the greenhouse door buzzed. Annoyed

at the interruption, he let out an audible sigh and walked over to answer it. "What is it, Eanu?" he asked irritably.

His butler's voice remained unruffled. "Mr. Briggs is on the phone, sir. He says it's urgent."

Aaron never called unless he had something important to discuss. "Very well," McDermott said. "Put him through."

The newspaper publisher didn't bother with a greeting. "We have problems, Ian. You remember that young cop who died in a drug bust about a year ago?"

"Julia Bradshaw's brother. What about him?"

"He left some tapes behind."

"What kind of tapes?"

"Detective Reid had a habit of investigating old, unsolved cases and recording his findings in a tape recorder. The police found the tapes in Paul Bradshaw's house. They're harmless. However, one is missing."

"Why is that significant?"

"Because according to Paul Bradshaw's secretary, the councilman had been investigating *Gleic Éire,* therefore the police are now assuming the missing tape contains information about us."

McDermott inhaled deeply. That was something he hadn't expected. "We have to find that tape, Aaron."

"How? The police looked everywhere, including Charles Bradshaw's house. They didn't find anything."

"Did they search The Hacienda?"

There was a short silence. "Why The Hacienda?" Briggs asked at last. "Julia and her ex-husband were barely speaking."

"All the more reason Paul Bradshaw would have considered the inn a safe place."

"Hmm. I hadn't thought of that."

McDermott drew his lips into a sarcastic smile but said nothing.

"What do you want to do?" Briggs asked.

"Let me think about it. I'll call you back."

McDermott hung up, started to get back to his orchids, then changed his mind. He was no longer in the mood for gardening. Briggs's news had disturbed him. As much as he enjoyed the hunt, he didn't like it when the hunter got too close. And he didn't like loose ends.

They had to find that tape.

He pushed the intercom button again. "Eanu, get my nephew on the phone."

"Well, aren't you full of surprises," Julia said after Steve told her about his visit with his new friend, Mrs. Hathaway.

In spite of Steve's hopes that he might find something the FBI had missed, Julia hadn't shared his optimism, not after hearing how thoroughly they had searched the place.

The thought that she was now looking at a potential piece of evidence lifted her spirits to new heights.

"How could the FBI have missed this?" she asked, holding the lovely silver plate.

"By concentrating too much on the obvious," Steve replied. "In this case, Eli's house."

"But what if Eli bought the plate exactly where he said he did—in Paris?"

"Then we'll follow that lead and see where it takes us. Maybe the antiques shop on rue Jacob has the name of the hotel where Eli stayed, and if we're lucky, the hotel clerk will remember a visitor, or a caller."

Some of Julia's excitement waned. "Oh, Steve, isn't that an awful long shot? It's been eleven years. Do you really think anyone will remember him after all this time?"

Steve's optimism was unflappable. ''Have a little faith, Julia.''

She sighed. ''I'd like nothing better. It's just that every time I get hopeful, someone dumps a bucket of ice on my head.''

Steve shot her a quick concerned look. ''Did something happen?''

She told him about Jordan's missing tape and Hammond's unsuccessful search. ''Which means that I'm still a suspect,'' she said when she was finished. ''Hammond is no longer treating me like one and that's a huge relief, but I'm not out of the woods yet.''

''Then all the more reason to have this checked,'' Steve said as he rewrapped the silver piece. ''And see if we can put our fearless detective on someone else's track. Do you know a reputable antiques dealer?''

''Several, but the one I would recommend is Maurice Garnier. He owns a shop in Carmel and is an expert on just about anything. He's a little formal, but he gets the job done. He located those for me some years ago.'' She waved at the hutch where her antique Spanish plates were displayed.

Steve tucked the plate under his arm. ''Then what are we waiting for?''

The owner of Belvedere Antiques on Carmel's Dolores Street was a small, dapper man with an unctuous smile, impeccable manners and an obvious appreciation of beautiful women.

''Madame Bradshaw,'' he said, barely noticing Steve. ''How delightful to see you again. What can I do for you today?'' His gaze was a tad cooler as it rested on Steve.

''Mr. Reyes is a friend of mine, Mr. Garnier,'' Julia explained. "I brought him here because he needs your expertise with a piece of silver."

As she talked, Steve laid his package on the glass counter and unwrapped it.

Without a change in expression, the dealer took a round, short-handled loupe from under the counter and bent over the plate, inspecting it closely. "Hmm." Turning it over, he repeated the process, this time studying the small engraved crest in the center.

"Very nice," he said at last as he put the loupe down. "It's a Sheraton, circa 1795, and is part of a set of twenty-four such plates that were cast that year. This particular one happens to be in pristine condition. I should be able to get you a good price—"

"I'm not interested in selling it," Steve said.

The dealer's features cooled another notch. "Oh. Then you only want it appraised?"

Steve smiled apologetically as he shook his head. "Sorry. I only want to know where it was last purchased." He looked at the Frenchman. "Can you do that?"

As though the question had insulted him, Maurice Garnier drew himself erect. "But of course, *monsieur.* The inquiry might take a day or two, perhaps three, but I will have an answer for you."

"Merci, Monsieur Garnier."

The dealer allowed the suggestion of a smile to cross his lips. *"Le plaisir est à moi."*

All-business again, he took a small pad from a drawer, quickly wrote a receipt, jotting down the necessary information, and handed the bottom copy to Steve. "I will call you as soon as I hear something." He bowed to Julia. "My regards to your mother, Mrs. Bradshaw."

"Thank you, Mr. Garnier."

"Well," Julia said once they were outside. "What do you think of him?"

"I think," Steve said, taking her arm and hurrying her across the busy street, "that I may have inadvertently wounded his Gallic pride and as a result he'll move heaven and earth to get me the information I need."

Julia laughed. "Inadvertently, my foot."

"I beg your pardon?"

Her eyes twinkled with mirth. "You did it on purpose. You sensed that he wasn't exactly thrilled about the menial little job you gave him, so you found his button, and you pushed it."

On the sidewalk, Steve took Julia's chin between two fingers and dropped a quick kiss on her luscious lips. "And you, beautiful lady, are beginning to know me much too well."

Sitting at the desk in front of his bedroom window, Steve booted his laptop and began typing the first in a series of investigative reports for the *New York Sun*.

> Last week, the peaceful coastal town of Monterey in California was rocked by the murder of city councilman Paul Bradshaw. Nine days later, the police, who have been working around the clock on the investigation, are no closer to finding his killer than they were on the night of the shooting.
>
> But there are clues. One, as puzzling as it is chilling, comes in the form of a second death—that of a man who may have known the identity of Paul Bradshaw's killer.
>
> By all appearances, Eli Seavers was a simple man who led a simple life. A former professor of economics at UCLA, then later at the American University in

Beirut, he had retired in the quiet, fertile valley of Salinas, where he lived a frugal, solitary life for seventeen years. In 1996, he was diagnosed with Alzheimer's disease and was eventually put in a nursing home, where he died.

What makes his death suspicious is that Eli Seavers died only two days after telling the former Mrs. Bradshaw, in a brief, single moment of lucidity, '*Gleic Éire* did it,' meaning that *Gleic Éire* had killed Paul Bradshaw.

Gleic Éire, we know, is a group of ruthless Irish extremists who are determined to perpetuate violence and destroy the peace process between Northern Ireland and England. They want freedom for Ireland, but offer no compromise. They want peace, but won't sit down at the bargaining table. They want the rest of the world to sympathize with them, but they'll do nothing to stop the bloodshed.

Why would a man like Eli Seavers, a man of no apparent connection with *Gleic Éire,* make such an accusation? Why would he become agitated at the mere sound of the Bradshaw name? And why did he, an apparently quiet, passive man, walk out of his room in the middle of the night and jump off a cliff?

Was his death accidental? The police think so. And so does the hospital staff. They say Eli was a delusional, confused, paranoid man, a victim of his own fears.

But what if he didn't wander off the grounds accidentally? What if, by speaking those few words, *Gleic Éire did it,* he suddenly made himself a threat? And had to be silenced?

Those are questions that must be answered—

A gentle knock at the door stopped him from finishing the sentence. "Come in." In one quick motion, he hit the save key, pushed his chair back and stood up.

His bedroom door opened just enough for Julia to poke her head through. "Is this a bad time?"

"Not at all. As a matter of fact, I was looking for an excuse to take a break."

"Good. Because there's someone downstairs who wants to meet you."

"Really? Who?"

"Frank Walsh." She smiled. "Don't you know that you've become the talk of the town?"

"Me?"

Her eyes gleamed briefly. "Yes, you. That little one-on-one with Charles Bradshaw yesterday made every headline between here and San Francisco."

"Oh, that." He laughed. "The guy had it coming."

"So you told me."

As they entered the kitchen, a handsome man in his late thirties set a can of 7UP on the counter and climbed down from his stool, hand extended.

"Hi. I'm Frank Walsh."

"Steve Reyes." Steve shook the detective's hand. "I understand you throw a mean baseball."

"And you know Gary Sheffield." Frank's face broke into a grin. "Talk about a tough act to follow."

Steve leaned a hip on the corner of the island. "I don't think you have anything to worry about in the popularity department. Andrew can't speak a sentence without mentioning his uncle Frank."

Julia patted her friend's shoulder. "Frank trained him well."

The detective gave Steve a long approving look. "I caught a rebroadcast of the twelve o'clock news at the station.'' He chuckled. ''Some job you did on our ex-governor. I've never seen Charles so rattled. If I didn't know better, I'd swear the two of you were archenemies settling an old score.''

Steve gave Frank Walsh extra points for perceptiveness, but didn't let the remark faze him. ''I'm just a reporter doing his job,'' he said lightly. ''Though I admit that in this case, it was a little more than that.''

''The old goat pissed you off by attacking Julia?''

Steve laughed. ''That's close enough.''

Frank's expression turned serious. ''Be careful, Steve. The man's got more contacts than a motherboard. He could make trouble for you.''

That wasn't something Steve was worried about. Charles was too determined to keep his daughter's brief relationship with a Cuban under wraps to make trouble for him. But he couldn't tell Frank that. ''Thanks for the warning,'' he said simply.

''Don't mention it. I appreciate you looking after my little pal here.'' Frank wrapped an arm around Julia's shoulders and pulled her to him. ''She's kind of special to me.''

Steve's gaze lingered on Julia for a moment. ''Yes, I can see that.''

Frank glanced at his watch and brushed his lips over Julia's cheek. ''I'd better go. The chief is on the rampage again. Anyone more than five minutes late gets to pull an extra hour at the end of his shift.''

He took one last gulp of his soda before putting the can down. ''Nice to have met you, Steve. Let's get together sometime, when I'm not so rushed.''

''I'd like that.''

Steve watched Julia walk him to the door. ''Nice guy,'' he said when she came back. ''You two seem to have a very special bond.''

"Frank and I go back a long way."

He felt a small but noticeable pang he refused to identify. "How long?"

"We went to elementary school together. One day, shortly after my father left us, a classmate said something about Coop that made me cry. Frank decked him in front of a hundred gawking kids. Then he pulled him up and made him apologize."

Steve kept watching her, wondering if Frank was more than a good friend. "Pretty heroic stuff. I'm surprised you didn't end up married to him yourself."

"Many thought we would, but the truth is we were just good friends." She tossed the empty 7UP can in the trash under the sink. "Even better friends after I introduced him to Penny."

Steve felt himself relax. "You enjoy playing matchmaker?"

"Not nearly as much as Penny does. She's been trying to fix me up with Mr. Irresistible for months—a different one each time. I lost count, but we may have reached number twenty-five by now."

Another pang. Not so small this time. "Hit the jackpot yet?"

Julia shrugged. "I wouldn't know. At the last minute I always chicken out and cancel the date." She made a face. "I hate blind dates. I hate dates period."

"Isn't that odd," he said, grinning. "So do I." He kept his tone casual. "Maybe we could get together some evening and trade horror stories."

Julia tossed him a quick, startled glance. "Are you asking me on a date?"

"Oh, no." He raised his hands in mock protest. "Nothing as distasteful as that. Just dinner...between friends. How about tonight?"

Looking suddenly flustered, she shook her head. "I'm sorry. I—"

"You pick the place. Something casual." He grinned again. "A nondate kind of place."

"Really, Steve, I'd be a terrible dinner companion."

"I'll chance it. Seven o'clock?"

Before she could turn him down, her phone rang and she went to answer it.

Grateful for the interruption, Steve walked quietly back to his room.

Nineteen

Charles stood at The Hacienda's front door, wondering for the hundredth time what he was going to say to Julia when he was finally face-to-face with her.

His decision to come here and talk to his ex-daughter-in-law had been made hours before dawn, as he paced his bedroom, unable to sleep. As much as he trusted Pilar's instincts, he still couldn't believe Paul had abused his wife. He wouldn't believe it until he heard it from Julia herself.

Squaring his shoulders, he rang the bell.

Julia answered it within moments and just stood there, looking at him, her expression one of total shock.

"Hello, Julia."

She would have been justified in slamming the door in his face. Instead, she gave a curt nod. "Charles."

"May I come in? Please." He kept his voice low, his tone almost humble.

Without a word, she pulled the door open. As he stepped in, he glanced toward the parlor and saw the elegant table set for ten. He looked back at her. "Are you entertaining?"

She laughed. "Hardly. I will, however, be dining with my students." As he frowned, she added, "I'll be giving cooking classes, Charles. The first one starts tomorrow."

"Oh." He remembered his conversation with Luther the other day. "That's right."

"You know about that?"

He nodded. "My attorney told me."

She raised her chin. "I see. You've been keeping tabs on me."

Instead of replying, he followed her into the parlor. As he did, he couldn't help but admire what she had done with that old relic. The place glowed, and even with the extensive renovations he knew she had done, she had managed to retain the beauty and character that had once been the very essence of this famous landmark.

"You don't mind if I keep working while we talk, do you?" she asked over her shoulder.

"No." He watched her place the silver beside each place, wondering where he should begin. And how. He had never been very good in the apology department. Especially when the apology had to be made to someone he had always considered his enemy.

"Would you like something to drink?" Julia asked. "Coffee? A soda?"

"Why didn't you tell me?"

Looking startled, Julia met his gaze. "Tell you what?"

"I know everything."

She gave a slow, perplexed shake of her head. "I'm sorry, Charles. I don't have the vaguest notion what you're talking about."

"Dammit, are you going to make me say it? Isn't it enough that I'm here?"

"Charles, will you please stop talking in riddles and—"

"I know Paul was beating you, all right?"

She drew a sharp breath. For a moment, her mouth tightened, as though she was preparing a denial. Then, as she continued to stare at him, she sighed and lay the remaining forks on the table. "Who told you?"

"Pilar."

"I don't understand. I never—"

"She knew anyway." He made an impatient gesture. "Women's intuition, or something like that."

Because he had never been a man who could stand still for long, he walked around the room, stopping every now and then to look at a watercolor, a book, an antique candleholder.

"She said she tried to talk to you about it several times," he continued, his back to her. "She hoped you'd confide in her, I guess. But you always made one excuse or another."

He could feel her eyes following him as he moved across the room. "It was my problem," she said in a low voice.

He whipped around and gave her a long look. "You should have come to me."

Julia let out a harsh laugh. "Oh, come on, Charles. You never would have believed me. Any more than you believed me when I swore to you that I didn't kill Paul."

Hands behind his back, he came to stand on the other side of the table. "When did the abuse begin?"

She hesitated, as if she couldn't quite bring herself to share that part of her life with him. "The first time was on Andrew's first birthday," she said at last. "The afternoon you and I had that argument regarding his schooling."

Unable to think of a suitable response, Charles said nothing.

"Paul was furious at me for standing up to you, for not realizing how fortunate I was that you took such an interest in Andrew's education."

"I love that boy as if he were my own child."

She didn't flinch. "But he isn't."

A few uncomfortable seconds passed. "Paul hurt you that night?"

Julia looked away. "Yes. But the bruises went away—the physical ones, anyway."

"And there were other...situations?"

She smiled. "Yes, Charles, there were other situations. Lots of them."

"No apologies?"

"Oh, there were lots of those, too. Along with the promise he'd never hit me again, promises he could never keep. Then a few weeks later something else would set him off and the cycle would begin all over again."

"What exactly *did* set him off?"

"Exactly?" She pursed her lips. "Let's see. There were his allegations that I was unfaithful." As Charles raised a brow, she bristled visibly. "I wasn't. But of course I couldn't convince him of that. If we went out and someone paid a little too much attention to me that night, he would blame me, blame the way I dressed, or walked, or smiled. He also felt I wasn't doing enough for his career, that I was too focused on Andrew, spoiling him, turning him into a mama's boy."

"And you never mentioned any of this to anyone? Never thought of seeking counseling?"

"Counseling?" She gave a mirthless laugh. "Paul wouldn't hear of it. He was afraid the news would leak out and would damage his career. The only person who knows the truth is my mother, and the only reason I told her was because she didn't believe my flimsy excuses."

"Why didn't he try to stop you from leaving? Or fight for custody of Andrew?"

She picked up the forks again and began walking around the table. "Paul and I had a deal. He wouldn't contest the divorce, or the custody, and I wouldn't go to the newspapers."

"The newspapers?" Charles's lips curved. "I doubt they would have believed you, Julia."

"I know that. That's why the morning following that last

beating, I took Polaroid pictures of myself. And I went to see a doctor in Santa Cruz."

So that's how she had done it, he mused—by using her head. No wonder Paul hadn't pushed for custody. She had scared the pants off him.

His hands still behind his back, his head bowed, Charles started to pace in front of the table, in slow, measured steps. "Would you believe me if I told you I never knew what was going on?"

"I never thought of you as a liar, Charles," Julia said. "Stubborn, yes. A bully, certainly. But not a liar."

He started to smile, then stopped himself. "Pilar said Paul was an angry man. I...wasn't aware of that."

"He didn't want you to know. He would rather have died than let you see his failings."

"Why the anger?" he asked. "Paul had everything he wanted. He was going places."

She shook her head. "He didn't have the one thing he wanted most."

"What was that?"

"To be like you, as good as you, so you would be proud of him. He wanted that more than anything in the world, and he knew he couldn't have it."

Charles went to stand by the window. His chest felt as if a hundred-pound weight was pressing against it. He remembered Paul's last words to him.

"You're going to be proud of the kid, Dad."

Is that all he had ever wanted? For his father to be proud of him? Had Paul scheduled that news conference not so much to impress Julia but to impress his father?

Then Charles had a thought that brought an acute, almost debilitating pain.

Had he inadvertently killed his own son?

"I'm sorry, Charles."

He felt Julia's hand on his shoulder, but didn't turn around. "You did nothing wrong."

"I'm not apologizing. The sorrow I feel is for you, for your suffering."

"I'm not sure I deserve your sympathy."

"Right now you do." She patted his shoulder before withdrawing her hand. "And in case you haven't already guessed, I appreciate your coming here. It couldn't have been easy for you."

"Easier than to face Pilar if I hadn't."

His attempt at humor made Julia smile. "I hope you won't wait another twelve months to come back."

Their eyes met and held. "I won't."

He stood there for a moment, feeling awkward. "How's Andrew?" he asked, ending the silence.

"Getting better every day."

"That's good." He nodded. "I'll be in touch."

He walked toward the Eldorado, his head bent as he fought the demons he knew would haunt him for the rest of his life.

Twenty

"Mom, are you going on a date?"

Lying on his stomach on Julia's bed, Andrew cupped his chin in his hands and watched her with great interest.

"It's not a date." Julia took a black blazer from the closet and held it in front of her as she studied her reflection in the cheval mirror. "Steve and I are just going out to dinner."

"Grandma says it's a date."

She would, Julia thought. Late yesterday afternoon, after making sure Coop wasn't there, Grace had stopped by The Hacienda to meet Steve. It had been obvious, from the first delightful appraisal, that she was very pleased with Julia's new guest. Even more so when she learned Steve and Julia were going out.

"If it's not a date," Andrew persisted, "then why did you put that stuff on your eyes? Jimmy's sister puts on tons of it when she's going out with her boyfriend."

Alarmed she may have overdone the eye shadow, Julia glanced in the mirror. She didn't think she had, but she moistened her finger with her tongue, anyway, and rubbed it lightly over her eyelids, leaving only a dusting of green.

"There," she said, turning and making a funny face. "Is that better?"

Andrew grinned.

Julia turned back to the mirror. Thank God she didn't

have to worry too much about what to wear, she thought as she pulled another jacket from the closet and subjected it to the same rigorous inspection. Raging Bull on Cannery Row was the embodiment of casual, with sawdust on the floor, loud conversation and great steaks. Anything she wore would be fine.

"Do you like him?" Andrew asked suddenly.

"Who?" She gave him an innocent look, pretending not to know who he was talking about.

Andrew rolled his eyes. "You know who. Steve."

She wasn't surprised at the question. Andrew had hinted, more than once, how much he wished Steve could stay in Monterey. Permanently. His attachment to the reporter worried her, for only one reason. Steve would eventually have to leave, and when he did, Andrew would be hurt.

She tossed the jacket on a chair with the other three and came to sit next to him on the bed. "Yes, I suppose I do like him," she said in answer to his question. "What about you?"

"I like him a lot," Andrew said earnestly. "He's cool. He tells me stories about his houseboat in Florida and how it almost sank one time, and how he and his friend Jesus had to jump overboard." He laughed. "He's funny."

In one quick movement, he sat up on the edge of the bed and started banging his sneakered feet against the box spring. "Aunt Penny says he's a hunk." There was a mischievous gleam in his eyes. "Do you think he's a hunk?"

Julia couldn't hold back a small laugh. "Do you even know what the word means?"

"Sure I do. Jimmy's sister says it all the time. She says she only dates hunks."

Because Andrew looked so adorable, Julia stole a quick kiss. "I guess some women would think of Steve as a hunk. I don't really look at him that way."

The thought that she had just delivered a bold-faced lie, and to her six-year-old son of all people, sent a flush to Julia's cheeks.

Before the conversation had a chance to get stickier, she gave Andrew a friendly pat on the bottom. "What do you say you go down and wait for Grandma? She should be here any second."

"'Kay." He sprinted out the door.

After he was gone, Julia changed from her tailored black slacks, which looked too dressy, to a pair of faded jeans that were more Raging Bull's style. Opting to keep the same blue-striped blouse, she slipped into the black blazer and pushed the sleeves up for a more casual look.

For someone who's not worried about her looks, you're sure going through a lot of trouble, girl.

No, she wasn't, she reasoned as she ran a brush through her hair. Not really. After all, tonight was the first time she'd gone out with a man since her divorce from Paul, and she was a little indecisive, nothing more.

But if that's all it was, then how did she explain those confusing feelings she was experiencing every time she thought of Steve Reyes? Annoyance one moment, giddiness and anticipation the next.

Not to mention this sudden obsession with her clothes.

Thank God they were going to Raging Bull and not to some romantic, candlelit hideaway as Penny had suggested. Then Julia might have had reason to worry.

As for Steve, if he had any ideas other than sharing a good meal and some pleasant conversation, she would quickly steer him back in the right direction.

She wasn't some dewy-eyed teenager, after all. Even while married to Paul, she had met more than her share of Romeos. She had always known how to handle them.

That point settled, she checked the contents of her purse,

threw her lipstick into it and zipped the black tote shut. On impulse, she picked up the bottle of Joy Penny had given her for Christmas and sprayed a quick mist of the expensive fragrance behind her ears.

Then, refusing to analyze that last gesture, she turned off the light and left the room.

As always, Raging Bull was packed with a lively crowd when Steve and Julia arrived a little after seven. Thanks to a waitress Julia knew, they were quickly escorted to a table for two in the back. Taking her pencil from behind her ear, the gum-chewing blonde pointed at a blackboard where the daily specials were written in green chalk, took their drink orders and disappeared.

Eyeing the crowded bar and the constant stream of people coming through the door, Steve gave an approving nod. "You seem to have made a good choice."

"If you like steaks and can get past the noise, this is the place to be."

His hunger forgotten, Steve leaned back in his chair and watched Julia as she studied the blackboard. She had been beautiful in daylight, but here, with a background of dark wood and in the subdued lighting, her eyes took on an even brighter sparkle, her skin a new creaminess.

It wasn't just her beauty that attracted him to her, he realized, it was the woman beneath that beauty. In spite of her admission to the contrary, Julia Bradshaw was a gutsy, courageous woman. But by far, her most appealing attribute was her love for her son. Something happened to her when Andrew entered a room, something so wonderful and touching, Steve never tired of watching it. At the same time, it made him realize, with an aching clarity, how much he had missed by not having a family of his own.

The waitress was back within moments with two Heinekens—no glasses—and a bowl of peanuts.

After they had both ordered New York strips, medium rare, Steve picked up his bottle, tapped it to hers. "To tomorrow—and your first class, which I predict will be a huge success."

"Thank you."

"Nervous?"

"A little." She sipped. "This is a new venture for me, something I hadn't planned on doing until I was established."

"You're going to be a hit. We're all rooting for you, you know—Penny, Frank, your mother. Not to mention Coop. He's so proud of you, he could split a seam."

Julia took a peanut from the straw basket and cracked it open. "He's being a typical dad, but I appreciate the vote of confidence, from all of you."

Steve took another sip of his beer. "I saw Charles at The Hacienda earlier," he said casually. "I was going to come down in case he started blaming you for the way I antagonized him. But he didn't look like a man about to pick a fight, so I kept to myself."

She popped the shelled peanut into her mouth. "Charles was on his best behavior for a change."

"How come?"

Her shoulders stiffened slightly. If Steve hadn't been so keenly aware of her, he might have missed the movement altogether. As she looked off in the distance, he decided not to rush her. She had a right to her secrets. Just as he had a right to his.

"He came to apologize," she said after a while.

"Really? What for?"

When she didn't answer, he realized there was more to Charles's visit than he had thought. Curious, and because he sensed she needed to talk, he pushed, just a little. "If you feel like talking, I'm a pretty good listener."

Julia smiled. "He didn't apologize for his public accusations," she said, after making sure no one was eavesdropping. "Or for threatening to take Andrew from me, though I sensed he did that, too, in a more subtle way." She took a deep breath. "He came to apologize for what his son did to me while we were married."

Steve's eyes narrowed. "Was Paul unfaithful?"

She laughed. "I wish it had been that simple." When he continued to look at her, she said quietly, "Paul beat me."

Steve's jaw clenched. "On a regular basis?"

She nodded.

"That son of a bitch."

"That's why I left him. I couldn't take the abuse anymore."

"And Charles wasn't aware of anything?"

"No one was—except my mother."

"Then how did Charles find out?"

"His housekeeper told him." Julia took another peanut from the basket, but only played with it. "I knew Pilar was intuitive but I never imagined she had guessed our ugly little secret. She told Charles the truth after seeing the twelve o'clock news the other day." She looked at him across the table, a light smile on her lips. "I would have loved to hear that conversation. Pilar is not one to mince her words—even to her boss."

Though he didn't say anything, Steve remembered Pilar well, not because he knew her but because Sheila had talked about her with great affection.

"Charles took Paul's weakness very hard," Julia continued, as their food arrived. "And he took it as a personal failure. All his life, he tried to give his children what he thought they should have—a good education, good breeding, a sense of pride. In the process he forgot to give them what they needed the most—the freedom to be themselves. His daughter, Sheila, left home when she was only twenty because her father was stifling her. Sadly, she died three months later.''

She looked up from her plate. ''But surely you know all this. If you researched *Gleic Éire,* and I'm sure you did, you know that Charles's daughter was killed by a bomb in New York City and that *Gleic Éire* claimed responsibility for it.''

Steve didn't meet her gaze. He hated lying to her, but it was too late now to tell her the truth about him and Sheila. Julia would think he had been using her. Initially, he had kept quiet simply because his past was no one's business. Now, because his feelings for Julia were changing, his lie lay heavily on his conscience.

For an instant, he was tempted to confess everything and accept her anger. After a moment of reflection, he decided not to. Why stir up memories he had worked so hard to forget? What purpose would it serve?

''I do know about Charles's daughter.'' He busied himself with his steak so he wouldn't have to look at Julia. ''Unlike you, however, I don't feel much sympathy for him. He's a hard man to like.''

She smiled. ''That from a man who, less than four days ago, was preaching the virtues of forgiveness?''

He laughed. ''Touché.''

Steve wasn't sure when the conversation drifted away from the Bradshaws and focused on solely Julia. Suddenly, she was talking about her three months at the culinary institute, which had included two weeks in Provence, and making him laugh with her recollection of her adventures in a temperamental French chef's kitchen.

They talked for more than an hour, lingering over coffee

as they exchanged amusing anecdotes of their respective families. In the course of their conversation, they found out they both had a passion for 1940s movies, Agatha Christie mysteries and strawberry ice cream.

"Come," he said, after he had paid the bill. "It's a beautiful night. Show me around."

In a gesture that was as natural as if they had known each other intimately for years, he took her hand and tucked it under his arm as they walked out of the restaurant.

The air had turned brisk and, because the sidewalk was crowded, Julia snuggled closer to Steve and held on to his arm, another gesture that, at this very moment, seemed perfectly natural.

She felt surprisingly relaxed. Either innocently or by design, Steve had managed to make her forget, at least for tonight, that she was still a suspect in her ex-husband's murder.

"You love it here, don't you?" Steve asked as they walked through the throng of tourists and locals that came here every night.

"I do. Few places in Monterey are more colorful or elicit more controversy than Cannery Row. It began as a small Chinese fishing village in the mid-1800s. You see those white rocks over there?" She pressed closer to him as she pointed toward the sea. "They were markers for Chinese fishing families who sailed north from Canton, came through the Bering Strait, down the West Coast and eventually into Monterey Bay."

"Amazing. What's the controversy about?"

"A developer wants to use the site of a famous art gallery, which has closed its doors, to build a shopping mall. Merchants along Cannery Row are furious. They feel a shopping mall will destroy the historical integrity of the area."

"Doesn't the city protect historical buildings?"

"That's the problem. Everyone was under the impression that all of Cannery Row had historical value and was therefore protected, but now the city is claiming that only one building falls into that category."

In the light of the full moon, Julia saw Steve's eyes spark. "I don't have to ask what side you're on."

She smiled a little. "Monterey is where I was born and raised. I would like to see not only Cannery Row, but the entire town retain its unique characteristics. I have nothing against shopping malls, mind you. They just don't belong on this waterfront."

"Do you go to public meetings? Express your opinion?"

"Not anymore. Not since I divorced Paul. Maybe when all this is over and I'm no longer under suspicion, I'll start attending again, get more involved."

She pointed at a yellow stucco building. "Over there is La Ida Café. Steinbeck immortalized it in his novel *Cannery Row* in the forties. The second story used to be a brothel." She chuckled. "It was one of the most popular places on the entire peninsula."

A gust of wind, raw from its journey over the ocean, made her shiver. Untangling his arm from hers, Steve wrapped it around her shoulders and brought her close to him as they continued their walk.

Julia's body stiffened, then relaxed. It had been a long time since she had been in such close physical contact with a man. The realization that she enjoyed it much more than she had expected made her wonder if she, too, was getting too attached to the handsome reporter.

Spotting the Land Rover, she almost heaved a sigh of relief.

"Thanks for the tour," Steve said, walking her to the passenger side. "I couldn't have asked for a better or lovelier guide."

"My mother used to work for the Chamber of Commerce. I've had good training—"

Unexpectedly, his hand reached for her hair, gently fingering a curl before sliding behind her neck, pulling her to him.

With a small, catchy sigh, Julia went to him, powerless to do otherwise. The kiss was gentle at first, a teasing of lips, a darting of tongues. She stood very still, absorbing every sensation, allowing the heat to build, layer by layer. His tongue, arousing, probing, was warm and soft as satin. Suddenly, standing still was no longer an option, not with those strong hands moving up and down her back, pulling her closer, as though he wanted her inside of him.

As the kiss changed to one rough with need, a moan escaped her throat. She couldn't remember ever feeling this way. She couldn't remember such sweet, aching wanting, the liquid warmth, the slipping away of her control, this control she had sworn to hold on to.

Oh, God, what was she doing? What was she getting herself into?

It took all her willpower to finally push him away. She drew a long, shuddering breath and held on to him for a moment, testing her balance.

"If you expect me to say I'm sorry," Steve said in a husky voice, "I won't. I've been wanting to do that since the day I first saw you."

She smiled, feeling inexplicably brazen. "I hope I didn't disappoint you. I'm a little rusty."

He brought her fingers to his lips and kissed the tips gently, one by one. "You didn't disappoint me. As for being rusty, you know what they say—practice makes perfect."

Another sigh caught in her throat. Whatever he was doing to her fingertips had her body responding in ways that left her breathless. She felt herself staring at his mouth, wanting to explore it again, wanting to touch him.

Quickly, before she could weaken again, she pulled her hand away. What was happening to her? One kiss and she was turning into a sex-crazed teenager, ignoring all the rules she had set, throwing caution to the wind.

"It's late," she said, barely able to get the words out. "We should go."

She waited, almost hoping for another suggestion.

Steve simply opened the passenger door and helped her up.

Twenty-One

The sound of voices and laughter could be heard all the way from the courtyard. Smiling, Steve got out of the Land Rover, walked along the brick path and let himself into The Hacienda.

Julia held court to seven women and two men who were assembled around the cooking island. A white apron with the caricature of a tipsy chef on the bib was wrapped around her slender waist. Not a movement was wasted as she chopped, tossed and sautéed.

She was truly in her element, Steve thought as he listened to her happy chatter and watched the glow on her cheeks. Ignoring the recipes she had so diligently prepared, she went through her instructions and answered questions with flair and self-confidence, spicing them with just the right amount of humor.

As he continued to observe her, she said something he couldn't hear and drew a ripple of laughter from the small audience.

Quietly, though no one was paying attention to him, he headed for his room.

Monsieur Garnier's call came the following morning as Steve was having his first cup of coffee in Julia's kitchen.

"It's for you, Monsieur Reyes." Julia handed him the phone with a flourish.

The dealer's smooth voice was filled with self-satisfaction. "I have the information you requested, *monsieur.*"

"I'm listening."

"The plate in question was purchased on August 3, 1987, at Malamoud Antiques in Cairo."

Steve glanced at Julia, who was listening intently. "Did you say Cairo, as in Cairo, Egypt?"

"That's correct."

Steve exhaled slowly. Seavers had lied, after all. Why? What had he been doing in Egypt? "Do they have a record of the person who bought it?" he asked.

"No, *monsieur*. The purchase was paid for in cash."

"Thank you, Monsieur Garnier. I'll be by shortly to pay what I owe you and to pick up the plate."

"That will be fine."

Steve hung up, then immediately dialed Tim in New York. "Get into the *Sun*'s archives," he said when the editor answered. "And check if any terrorist activities occurred either in England or in Ireland on or about August 3, 1987."

"Why? What happened on August 3, 1987?"

Steve told him. As Tim hit his computer keys, Julia put down her coffee cup. "Eli bought that plate in Cairo?" she asked.

Steve covered the mouthpiece with his hand. "The past life of our innocent little professor is getting more suspicious by the minute."

"What was he doing in Cairo?"

"I don't know. But whatever it was, he didn't want anyone to know about it."

"Steve?" Tim was back.

Steve removed his hand from the mouthpiece. "You got something?"

"There were a couple of bombings in France and one in

Rome, but the Shiites took responsibility for those, not *Gleic Éire*. I did find something else, however. The dates aren't the same, but there could be a connection."

"What is it?"

"On September 13 of that year, Scotland Yard received a tip that a large shipment of arms had just been delivered to Northern Ireland, presumably to *Gleic Éire*."

Steve could hear Tim's fingers flying across the keys. "A few days later," the editor continued, "*Gleic Éire* launched a series of deadly attacks both in Northern Ireland and England. World War II excluded, the month of September 1987 will go down in history as being one of England's bloodiest periods."

"I remember. There was also a rumor that an American man with ties to the Middle East had arranged the deal, but nothing was ever proven."

Tim's voice was tight. "Are you thinking what I'm thinking?"

"Seavers could have been that man?"

"He had the right background—twenty years in Beirut. He spoke the language fluently. And he had lots of well-connected Libyan friends." The clicking of keys could be heard again. "There's only one problem."

"What's that?"

"How could he have been in Egypt when the passport the FBI recovered from his house only showed travels to and from Libya during his teaching years in Beirut?"

"Phony documents, my dear Watson. If he was an arms negotiator, he would know exactly where to go for something like that." Steve's blood was pumping rapidly. "Maybe I should take another look at his house."

"Maybe you should." Steve heard a phone ring. "I have another call," Tim said. "Keep me informed."

Julia was watching as Steve hung up. "An arms negotiator? That frail, helpless old man?" She shook her head. "I can't believe it."

"It's those we suspect the least who are often the most undetectable. That's why they're so successful." Every nerve tingling, Steve was pacing, going over everything he had done at Eli's house, the places he had searched so thoroughly, both inside the house and in the shed. Seventeen years of the man's life were hidden somewhere. And he had found nothing.

"What could I have missed?" he said, wondering if he was rustier than he had realized. "I thought I looked everywhere."

"Did you see any keys laying around?" Julia asked. "Maybe he had a safe deposit box."

"There was a safe deposit box, but when the FBI opened it, it only had a copy of his will, in which, as we know, he left everything he owned, namely the house, to his niece."

"Maybe in another bank? One we don't know about?"

Steve shook his head. "They checked that out, too. He only had one bank, one checking account, no savings."

"Did he have an attic?"

He shook his head again. "No attic, no basement, no garage. Just that tiny house and a shed full of garden tools, herbicide and other stuff."

"I don't know what to tell you," Julia said with a disappointed sigh. "Mrs. Hathaway seems to know him better than anyone else. What did she tell you about him? Maybe she gave you a clue and you didn't realize it. What did Eli like to do?"

"Nothing much. She said he puttered in his garden a lot. That seemed to be the only place that brought him true pleasure..."

He stopped, spun around. "That's it! The garden!" He slapped the kitchen counter. "Why didn't I think of it?

What a dummy.'' Taking Julia's face in his hand, he kissed her full on the mouth. ''You're a genius. Thank you.''

She laughed. ''I didn't do anything.''

But he was already flying out the door.

This time Briggs's call came from Monterey, where he had attended the daily police briefing himself. ''I'm afraid I've got more bad news,'' he told McDermott on the phone.

McDermott blew out his breath. ''You're beginning to bore me, Aaron. What is it now?''

''Steve Reyes is in town. And he's staying at The Hacienda.''

As he heard the name of the man who had so relentlessly pursued him eight years ago, McDermott stiffened. ''You saw him?''

''Yes. He was at the briefing.''

''He's been in town all this time,'' McDermott bellowed, ''and this is the first I hear about it?''

''He hasn't been in town all this time,'' Briggs replied testily. ''He got in a week ago. And I just found out.''

A week ago. McDermott did a quick calculation. That would be just after Julia Bradshaw's visit to Pine Hill Nursing Home. ''If he came this late,'' he told Briggs, ''it can only mean one thing. He didn't come to Monterey to solve Paul Bradshaw's murder. He came for us.''

''I figured that much. What are we going to do about him?''

McDermott allowed himself a smile. Steve Reyes had proved to be a formidable enemy. He was bright, resourceful and above all unforgiving, which had given him, at least for a time, the stamina of a young bull.

When McDermott had learned that Reyes had given up the hunt and resigned from the *New York Sun,* he had been both relieved and disappointed. It wasn't every day that he met with a man whose intelligence and energy equaled his own. For a while, he had been tempted to throw the reporter a bone, a small clue for the sole purpose of keeping him on the trail.

The others had voted him down.

And now Reyes was back. How thrilling. How utterly thrilling.

"Ian," Briggs said impatiently, "did you hear me? What are we going to do about Reyes?"

"Nothing." Maybe the resourceful reporter would get close enough to allow McDermott to play a harmless little game of cat and mouse. For old times' sake.

"What do you mean we'll do nothing? Didn't you hear me? He's staying at The Hacienda. How can we send one of Flynn's men to look for that tape if Reyes is there?"

From the front door came the sound of voices and greetings. McDermott smiled. "We won't have to send one of Flynn's men, Aaron. I have someone better."

"What are you talking about? Who..." At the other end of the line, McDermott heard Briggs groan. "Oh, no. You didn't send for Ben, did you? Not without consulting us."

"What have you got against my nephew?"

"The kid is immature, impulsive and unpredictable. How's that for a start?"

"He's changed, Aaron. And more important, the job is right up his alley."

"I don't care. We agreed one of Flynn's operatives would do it."

McDermott shook his head. "Too risky. We need someone we can trust implicitly."

"Flynn hires only people he can trust."

"But they're still strangers, Aaron. They could talk."

"Do the others know you sent for Ben?"

"I was waiting to talk to him before I called them. Don't

worry," he added. "If I feel he's not ready, I won't send him."

McDermott was hanging up when his nephew walked in, a duffel bag slung over his shoulder and a cocky smile on his lips. At twenty-six, Ben Rosenthal was well over six feet and strong as an ox. In contrast with his impressive physique, he had fine blond hair cut almost as short as McDermott's, blue eyes as innocent as those of a newborn babe and a smile few women could resist.

McDermott had inherited his sister's only child twelve years ago when Lizzy and her husband had died in a plane crash. He hadn't been prepared for fatherhood, or for the mouthy, thrill-seeking fourteen-year-old whose favorite hobby was to hang around malls and rob unsuspecting shoppers.

Worried the youth would be a hindrance, McDermott had put him in a boarding school, allowing him to come home only on holidays and during summer breaks. Over the years, the boy's rebellious attitude had improved considerably. His affinity for stealing, however, had not.

Ben had just graduated from high school when he found out—after eavesdropping on his uncle's conversations—that McDermott and his four rich friends were members of *Gleic Éire.* To McDermott's surprise, Ben already knew a great deal about the Irish people's struggle for independence and was a strong sympathizer of the cause.

"Mom hated the Brits for what they did to her parents," he had told McDermott. "I hate them, too, Uncle Ian. Your secret is safe with me."

Ben had kept his word. Shortly after that conversation, he had embarked on a backpacking tour of Europe. There, he had used his good looks and his talents as a con man to seduce rich, lonely women and rob them of their jewels while they slept.

The European press had dubbed him the Gentleman Thief because of his trademark, a red rose he always left on the pillow of the women he robbed.

When, during a brief visit home, McDermott had asked Ben why he took such risks when his parents had left him so much money, the intrepid boy had replied, "Why, Uncle Ian, for the thrill, of course. What else is there?"

Except for a close call a few years ago over a ruby necklace that had belonged to a Saudi princess, he had never been caught. Last year, bored with Europe, Ben had returned to the U.S. and enrolled at Santa Barbara College.

His inspection of his nephew finished, McDermott nodded. "You're looking well."

"Thanks." Dropping his bag on the floor, Ben sat comfortably in the chair opposite his uncle's and gave him a wolfish grin. "So, what was so urgent that had I had to leave a hot babe behind?" He bent forward, his expression eager. "You and your *compadres* need me to steal something? Jewels? A painting?" The blue eyes gleamed. "Bearer bonds?"

"Nothing quite so thrilling, I'm afraid. I just want you to find something for me."

"What's that?"

"An audiotape."

Ben looked disappointed. "That's it?"

"That's it."

"Sounds boring." His eyes narrowed. "Wait a minute. That wouldn't happen to be the mysterious tape the Monterey PD has been looking for and can't find, would it? The one they think is tied to Councilman Bradshaw's death?"

McDermott was pleasantly surprised. Except for the *Irish Voice,* which he read faithfully, Ben had never been much of a newshound. "How do you know about Councilman Bradshaw's death?"

Ben's smile was smug. "I make it a point to know a little about everything, Uncle Ian. Isn't that what you taught me?"

"I didn't know you listened."

"I always listen to you." Stretching his long legs in front of him, Ben hooked his fingers behind his head and leaned back. It was his turn to scrutinize. "Why do you want the tape? Did you kill the guy?"

"No, I didn't, but the tape may contain information about my partners and me—information I don't want to fall into the wrong hands."

Ben grinned. "Then I'm your man."

"Not so fast, Ben. We have a few things to square away first."

As if readying himself for a scolding, Ben crossed his arms across his broad torso. "Okay, shoot."

"This job, if I decide to give it to you, isn't some pleasure trip into one of your lovers' boudoirs. There will be no roses, no little poem left behind, no theatrics. Is that understood?"

Ben rolled his eyes as if he had heard the lecture a hundred times before. "Yeah, yeah."

"Don't get smart with me, boy," McDermott snapped. "You screw up and I could be facing a two-hundred-year prison sentence."

Ben sobered instantly. "I won't screw up, Uncle Ian."

"Did you tell anyone you were coming here?"

"Not a soul."

"Good. You'll have to stay in a hotel somewhere, not in Monterey, though. Pick something discreet. And pay cash."

"I always do."

McDermott studied his nephew in silence for a few seconds. Though still cocky, Ben was anxious to please, and above all, he could be trusted.

When Eanu suddenly appeared in the doorway and gave a signal, McDermott rose. "Let's continue our talk over lunch. Eanu has prepared that Moroccan dish you like so much." One arm draped around the boy's broad shoulders, McDermott led him onto the sun-drenched terrace.

The fragrant *tagine* in its cone-shaped clay pot was already waiting, centered on the stone table. Tall glasses of hot mint tea, the traditional Moroccan drink, and a round loaf of dark bread completed the meal. Beside each plate was a small bowl of lemon water for their fingers.

Eanu served them each a generous portion of the *tagine* then disappeared.

A stickler for authenticity, Ben dug into the lamb stew with his fingers and ate with great gusto. "Mmm. I see Eanu hasn't lost his touch. This is terrific."

Preferring the more conventional method of eating, McDermott picked up his fork. "The house I'd like you to search is actually an inn."

Ben chewed another mouthful. "Secluded?"

"Somewhat. The Hacienda is on the upper part of Via del Rey, past Veterans Memorial Park. I believe you're familiar with the area."

Ben nodded as he chewed. "Quiet neighborhood. Mostly residential."

"Mrs. Bradshaw has two immediate neighbors—an elderly woman who lives on the east side of the inn and a doctor and his family on the west side. Both properties are about a hundred feet from The Hacienda."

"Is the inn filled up?"

"Not at the moment. Julia Bradshaw, who happens to be the dead man's ex-wife, has only two guests—her father and a reporter by the name of Steve Reyes."

"Reyes, Reyes," Ben said as he chewed. "Isn't he that reporter who was hot on your trail some years ago and almost caught up with you once?"

McDermott made an effort to hide his irritation. "He didn't even come close," he snapped. He took a sip of his mint tea, which was just the way he liked it, hot and strong. "Getting back to Julia Bradshaw. She and her young son live on the premises. I would guess in the downstairs area."

"Not a problem."

"But Reyes could be."

Ben propped an elbow on the table and flexed an impressive biceps. "I can handle Reyes."

"I don't want a physical confrontation, Ben," McDermott said sharply. "I just want the tape."

"If it's there, you'll have it." He dipped his fingers into the thick meat-and-vegetable mixture again. "Did Julia Bradshaw hide the tape herself?"

"No. The councilman would have done that. I doubt it has even occurred to Julia, or to anyone else, for that matter, that the tape or a backup copy could be there."

"Will I need to search the entire house?"

"I hope not. If we're lucky, it'll be somewhere in Julia's living quarters. If not, be prepared to search the upstairs, as well."

"Okay."

"You can't be spotted while doing your reconnaissance work. You understand that."

Ben's face took on a pained expression. "Please, Uncle Ian. I'm not an amateur."

"This is a small town. People notice strangers. They remember."

"Don't worry." He grinned. "If there's one thing I know how to do, besides stealing," he added with a grin, "it's how to blend. No one will even give me a second look."

Ben seemed totally unconcerned, and that worried McDermott a little. He had learned early on never to take any job, no matter how trivial, for granted. And he expected others to do the same.

"How long will the preliminary preparations take you?" he asked.

"If all goes well, a couple of days. Three at the most."

"I had hoped sooner."

Ben shook his head. "No can do, Uncle Ian. If the place was empty, it'd be different. But with all those people inside, I need to study their habits, see who goes out, who stays in, what time they go to bed, if the place is wired." He grinned. "If anyone sleepwalks. All those details take time."

After another long minute of reflection, McDermott nodded. "All right, then, three days." He watched Ben pile his plate with another helping of *tagine*. "But not a minute more."

Esther Hathaway was delighted to see Steve again, and to have her plate back.

"Mr. Garnier took the liberty of appraising the piece, Mrs. Hathaway," Steve said as she set it almost reverently back on a shelf in the dining room breakfront.

She turned around. "But I didn't ask—"

"I know. But considering the value of the item, Mr. Garnier thought you should know."

She blinked a few times. "How...how much is it worth?"

Steve thought of his own shock when the dealer had given him the appraisal, and wondered if Mrs. Hathaway's seventy-five-year-old heart would be able to handle it.

Taking a gamble it would, he decided to tell her. Besides, after taking care of Eli and his garden all this time, she deserved a little reward. "The entire set of twenty-four dishes once belonged to the Archbishop of York," he explained, repeating the name Garnier had so proudly enunciated. "In today's market, this particular plate is valued at eleven thousand dollars."

For a moment, he thought she was going to faint. "Oh, dear." Mrs. Hathaway's hand went to her breast. "Eleven thousand dollars." She looked around her. "The contents of this entire house don't amount to that much."

"Now they do, Mrs. Hathaway." From his pocket, he took a card and handed it to her. "This is the name and address of the dealer. He said to tell you that if you were ever interested in selling the plate, you should give him a call."

As she tucked the card under a flower vase on the dining room table, he added, "And now if you don't mind, I'll go take another look across the street."

"Another look?" Then, as Steve was already moving toward the door, she sighed and went in to get her keys before he could tell her he didn't need them.

"Why are you walking around Eli's backyard?" she asked when she joined him there a few minutes later.

He decided to answer her question with one of his own. "You did tell me he loved his garden, didn't you? That he spent a lot of time here?"

"That he did." She walked with him, the keys rattling in her pocket. "He even knew the Latin name of every plant and flower. And he loved to weed, plant and replant. Even that wild patch over there brought him pleasure." She pointed to an overgrown area behind the shed. "He called it his 'untamed garden,' and he didn't want me to weed it or disturb it when he was away. He said he liked it just as it was.''

Steve's heart skipped a beat. ''Did he really.''

He walked to the overgrowth, encompassing about four hundred square feet. Thick vines and weeds, some almost four feet tall, covered the entire area. Stepping over a low dividing wall made of gray stones, Steve crouched down and started to pull back some of the vines.

''What are you doing?'' Esther sounded alarmed. ''That area is crawling with poison ivy.''

Steve threw another casual glance around him. He saw no sign of poison ivy. But letting an overzealous neighbor believe the poisonous plant grew in great profusion was a sure way of keeping the curious at bay. ''I'll be careful.''

Moving a few feet at a time, he continued his search. After World War II, fortunes in jewels, artwork and gold coins had been found buried in the French countryside by owners who hadn't wanted their treasures to fall into enemy hands.

Maybe Eli had been thinking along those lines when he had needed a hiding place.

After working tirelessly for almost fifteen minutes, Steve suddenly bumped into something solid. Looking down, he saw a rock similar to those used on the dividing wall. It could have been left there by mistake, while the wall was being built.

Or Eli could have used it as a marker.

While Esther looked on, a scowl of disapproval on her face, Steve rolled the rock out of the way. Then, using his bare hands, he started to dig in the dirt. When he realized he wasn't progressing fast enough, he ran to the shed and came back with a shovel.

''What are you doing now?'' Esther demanded. ''Jennifer didn't say anything about you digging up her uncle's yard."

"I'll take full responsibility, Mrs. Hathaway," Steve promised as he started digging. "Just trust me."

After a few more strokes, the shovel hit something hard. Dropping to his hands and knees, Steve swept the rest of the dirt aside and reached inside the hole.

"Bingo," he said under his breath.

"What did you find?" Still apprehensive about the poison ivy, Esther came as close as she dared and craned her neck, trying to get a better look.

"I don't know yet." Steve's fingers found a handle. Grasping it, he pulled out a metal box, held closed by a simple latch.

His throat dry with anticipation, he flipped the lid open. "I'll be damned," he said under his breath.

Inside the rusted container, wrapped in several sheets of clear plastic, were a half-dozen passports. Except for one, which was a U.S. passport, the others had been issued by various foreign countries.

"What's in the box?" Esther's voice shook with curiosity. He couldn't really blame her. This clandestine operation in her neighbor's garden was probably the most exciting thing that had ever happened to her.

"Passports, Mrs. Hathaway." Steve took out the American passport first. It had been issued in 1983 and bore an earlier photograph of Eli Seavers. But the name beside the photograph was not Eli Seavers. It was John C. Spivak.

Steve quickly flipped through the pages of what was, more likely, a false document. They showed entries into Spain, Italy, Tunisia and Egypt.

Another passport, this one issued by the Iranian government, identified the unsmiling bearded man in the picture as Ahmed Jamoul. Only by looking closely at the eyes and the eyebrows could one detect a resemblance between the Iranian and J. C. Spivak.

Judging from the many stamps inside that particular passport, Ahmed had been a frequent traveler to Libya between 1985 and 1991. One date in particular drew Steve's attention—August 4, 1987. One day after Eli's visit to Malamoud Antiques in Cairo.

It didn't take a genius to figure out Eli's clever scheme. Using his phony American passport, he would first travel to Europe or Egypt, then he would switch to the Iranian document, or any of the other four passports at his disposal, and fly to Libya.

Libya. The country where Eli had taught all those years.

The country where the shipment of arms to Northern Ireland had originated.

"I think I'd better call the police, Mrs. Hathaway. This..." He stopped in midsentence as his gaze drifted back to the hole in the ground. Buried deeper was a bag, also secured in plastic.

Kneeling, Steve pulled out the bundle, tore the protective wrapping and unzipped the bulging bag.

He let out a slow whistle.

Inside the musty canvas were stacks of hundred dollar bills. Thumbing through the thick piles, he made a rough count.

The stash amounted to about half a million dollars.

Twenty-Two

"Half a million dollars!" Julia let her mouth hang open for a second or two. "That's unreal. How did Eli accumulate that kind of money?"

"I doubt he did it teaching economics."

"But...I don't understand. Jennifer said he didn't even have enough money in the bank to cover his burial. She had to pay for that."

"He probably lived better than anyone realized, taking what he wanted from that bag as he needed it, and no more. Then, when his illness worsened and his memory began to fade, he must have forgotten where he had put the money, or that he even had it."

"Where is the money now?"

"I gave it to Hammond, who gave it to the FBI. They're trying to trace it."

She couldn't get the image of Eli sitting in that rocking chair out of her mind. "He seemed like such a harmless man, almost endearing, actually. I felt sorry for him, for all the internal agony he was going through, the fear, the confusion."

"Your compassion wasn't deserved." Once again, Steve's face showed no emotion. "If my suspicions are correct, Eli Seavers, alias Ahmed Jamoul, alias three other names I can't remember, may have contributed to the death of more than four hundred innocent people over the last eleven years."

Julia let out a long breath. "How could he do something so hideous for so long and not get caught?"

"Some people are very good at leading double lives. It gives them a sense of power. And, of course, let's not forget the monetary rewards. Considering what Eli had been making as a professor, the money had to be a great motivator."

"You think he was working for others besides *Gleic Éire?*"

"Most likely. The traffic of arms has always been a huge market, not just in Europe but in Africa and South America, as well."

"That lucrative pastime of his must be the reason he never contacted his niece," Julia said. "Even though he knew where she lived. He didn't want to be found." Julia remembered that afternoon at Pine Hill, how sweetly attentive Jennifer had been to her uncle. "Poor Jennifer," she murmured. "If all this turns out to be true, she'll be devastated. She loved her uncle very much."

As another thought crossed her mind, she looked up at Steve. "Will she be able to inherit the money?"

"Not until the feds find out where it came from. If it's in any way tied to drug trafficking, extortion, terrorism or crime of any kind, she'll never see a penny of it."

"She wouldn't want it, anyway. Not if it came from the suffering of others."

From the next room, where Andrew, Jimmy and Coop were playing Monopoly, came a whoop of victory. "I won!" Andrew shouted.

Steve smiled and pulled Julia out of her chair. "Come on," he said. "Let's put all that stuff aside for an evening and go join that happy little group out there." He winked at her. "Maybe Andrew will use his winnings to take us all out to dinner."

Julia wasn't sure what woke her up a few nights later. One moment she was sleeping peacefully, the next, she was wide-awake.

A quarter moon filtered through the white sheers. Outside her window, the branches of a pine tree swung in the night breeze, casting oddly shaped shadows on the wall opposite her bed.

Julia lay frozen, with all her senses alert. There it was again, a rustle so faint she could have imagined it. The noise had come from the kitchen. Had Steve come down for something? And not turned on the light?

As she read the time on the clock dial, she rejected the thought. He would never come into her kitchen at one o'clock in the morning.

Which meant only one thing.

A prowler was in the house.

She considered calling 911, then thought better of it. People didn't make emergency calls unless there *was* an emergency.

Pushing the covers to one side, she swung one leg out, then the other and walked soundlessly across the room, then down the hallway.

She passed Andrew's empty room, grateful that he was spending the night at Jimmy's house. A nervous mother was the last thing he needed right now.

Except for the green light of the digital microwave clock, which she could see from where she stood, the kitchen was in darkness. And now, silent as a tomb.

She breathed a sigh of relief. *You've been reading too many Miss Marple mysteries, old girl.* Unfortunately, she was now wide-awake and wouldn't be able to sleep, so she decided to make some tea. She started to reach for the light switch.

A gloved hand clamped over her mouth.

Julia went numb with shock.

"Don't make a sound," a male voice whispered in her ear. "If you do, I'll kill you."

She couldn't have uttered a word even if she had wanted to. Her vocal cords had tightened and she seemed incapable of a single coherent thought.

And then she felt it. The hard barrel of a gun pressed against her side.

Raw fear shot through her body. Oh, God. This couldn't be happening. It was a dream. A horrible nightmare.

When the arm around her waist tightened, jerking her back against her assailant, she knew it was no nightmare but a terrifying reality.

Tumbling thoughts rushed through her head. A burglary? Rape? She tried to remember what she had learned in a rape prevention class she had taken years ago.

Her mind was a blur.

Warm lips pressed against her ear. "Did you hear me?"

She nodded, slowly and carefully, terrified that the slightest motion might make the gun go off. Fear had turned her legs rubbery. Only through sheer willpower was she able to keep them from folding under her.

"I hadn't counted on you waking up," the man whispered in her ear. "But since you did, I might as well take advantage of it." He tightened his grip around her middle. "Where is it?"

Money? Was that what he wanted? At that thought, hysterical laughter bubbled at the base of her throat and died there as he gave another vicious squeeze. "Answer me."

"In the desk drawer," she whispered as his hand pulled

away from her mouth just enough for her to let out the words. "You won't find much—"

The gun dug a little deeper, bringing out a muffled whimper from her throat. "Don't play games with me, Julia. You know what I'm talking about."

He knew her. And he didn't want money. Or sex. Then what?

"The tape, Julia," he said impatiently. "Your brother's tape. Your husband hid it. And you're going to tell me where."

Jordan's tape. He thought *she* had it. The demand was so ridiculous that for an instant the fear was gone, replaced once again by an absurd desire to laugh. Didn't he think that if she had it she would have turned it in so she could clear her name?

Tears burned behind her lids. "I don't have it," she said in a muffled voice. "Paul would never—"

"Think, Julia, think. You knew him. You knew how he thought. If he had wanted to hide something in this house, where would he put it?" The gun barrel buried itself a little deeper. "Help me, Julia, or I swear, I'll kill you right here and now.

"Or maybe..." His voice turned nasty. "I could start with the kid. How would you like that, Julia? Should I go get Andrew? I know where he is. I've been watching him for a couple of days now." He sang the last four words, as if he was preparing to play some game of hide-and-seek.

Terror clawed at her throat. "N-no," she begged. "Don't hurt him, please."

He chuckled. "Will you cooperate?"

"Y-yes."

She fought the fear back, taking short, shallow breaths, trying to stay calm and think rationally. He wouldn't kill her, not as long as he thought she knew where the tape was. Time. She needed to buy some time.

Her eyes adjusting to the darkness, she glanced toward the foyer, praying Steve was a light sleeper. If she could send some sort of signal upstairs, without putting herself in too much danger, she might be able to survive this.

"I'm beginning to lose my patience, Julia."

"I'm—I'm thinking. Trying to—"

"You're stalling." He yanked her back toward him again and in doing so, bumped into one of the stools. In the still night, the scraping of wood against tile sounded like an explosion.

She felt him go rigid. The gloved hand pressed against her mouth, hard. For a chilling moment, she thought she was going to suffocate. Then his hand relaxed and she was able to breathe again. Her eyes shot toward the ceiling. *Please, Steve, Dad. Wake up.*

When, after several seconds, nothing happened, the man gave a short, nervous laugh. "I guess your two guests aren't as restless as you are, huh?"

He knew Steve and her father were upstairs? And he had come in spite of it? Was he that fearless? she wondered as a new wave of panic washed over her. Or just insane?

She never had a chance to wonder any further. With no warning, a tremendous force suddenly blindsided them, sending them crashing into the island. A copper pot that had been left on the stove clanged to the floor. Dropping to all fours, Julia picked it up and scrambled to her feet.

She heard the sound of a struggle, of a fist hitting bone, then a solid thump followed by a curse.

"Steve!" she cried. "Are you all right?"

"I'm fine. Stay out of the way."

Feet hit the floor at a gallop as the intruder made a run for the front door.

Holding the pot's handle with both hands, as she would a baseball bat, Julia swung it with all the strength she could muster and hit him on the back of the head just as he went by.

She might as well have swatted a fly. Without missing a beat, the man flew past her.

Steve took off after him, heedless of the pain in his side where the attacker had sunk a vicious kick. But by the time he reached the sidewalk, the man was gone.

Not bothering to catch his breath, he ran back the short distance to The Hacienda. Julia, pale and disheveled, was standing in the middle of the kitchen, holding a copper pan in her hand. She wore a pale blue nightshirt that barely covered her thighs. It had the name of some alma mater scrawled on the front and skimmed her curves in a distracting way.

"Did he get away?" With her free hand, she held on to the island.

"He should be dead with that blow you gave him. Unfortunately, he did get away. I'm sorry."

Realizing she was shaking, he took the pan from her hands, lay it on the island and wrapped his arms around her, bringing her close. "Easy, baby. It's all right. He's gone."

Julia stayed against him for a moment, her face buried in his shoulder. Then, as if suddenly aware that neither of them was wearing very much—she a thin nightshirt and he a pair of boxer shorts—she gently disengaged herself. "I'm sorry…I didn't mean to fall apart on you."

"Are you all right?" Steve asked gently. "Did he hurt you?"

"No." She rubbed her elbow.

"You *are* hurt." He took her arm, turned it gently and checked her elbow with his thumb.

She tried to make light of the situation, but the pallor in her cheeks told a different story. "What do you expect when you come charging down like a bull?" she teased.

"I'm sorry. I reacted without thinking."

"I'm glad you did."

Steve walked over to the freezer, took out a handful of ice cubes from the bin and wrapped them in a dish towel. "Here. Hold this against your elbow. It'll keep the swelling down."

The sound of running footsteps made them both look up.

"What the hell..." Coop, wearing blue-striped pajamas, looked from Steve to Julia. It took him only a second or two to assess the situation. "Julia? What happened?"

Just as Steve released her, Coop gripped Julia's shoulders. "You okay, baby?"

She bobbed her head. "There was a break-in. A man..."

"Did he hurt you?"

"No." She shivered. "He...was looking for the tape, Jordan's tape."

"He thought *you* had it?"

"Yes." She pressed a hand to her breast. "He... threatened Andrew."

Coop uttered a short, harsh oath. "I'll kill him," he said between clenched teeth. "I'm going to find him and then I'll kill him."

Unable to stay on her feet, Julia sank into the nearest chair. "He said he knew where Andrew was," she murmured, starting to shake all over again. "He's been watching him." She let out a moan. "What if Andrew had been here?"

"He was only trying to scare you," Steve said.

She stood up. "I have to know he's all right—"

"Julia, it's one o'clock in the morning—"

"I don't care! I want to know if my son is all right!"

"Okay. Shh, relax." Gently, Steve pushed her back into the chair. "I'll take care of it. I'll call Joe Martinez."

Her eyes, wide with fear, followed him as he picked up the phone, ran his finger down the phone list and pushed a button. When Jimmy's father answered, Steve was brief.

"I'm sure the boys are fine," Joe Martinez said. "But I'll go check."

He was back within moments. "They're sound asleep, Steve. The burglar alarm is on, but I'll be staying up, just in case."

After thanking him, Steve hung up and relayed the message to Julia. Only then did she seem to relax.

Picking up the phone again, Steve called Detective Hammond.

Twenty-Three

Hammond and a crime scene team arrived quickly and gave The Hacienda a thorough check.

While one of his men dusted for fingerprints, Hammond took Julia's statement, then Steve's, getting as many details as they could remember.

Julia, who had slipped into a yellow terry-cloth bathrobe, went to sit in one of the easy chairs. As the anxiety clung stubbornly to her, she watched Steve brief Hammond. The reporter was the picture of calm and self-control. He spoke in a neutral, unhurried tone, as if he had been in this situation dozens of times. She, on the other hand, felt as though she was on a roller coaster—up one moment, down the next. With no way of knowing when the crazy ride would end.

Unable to chase away the chill, Julia hugged herself and sank deeper into the chair, anxious for something familiar to surround her.

"Mrs. Bradshaw?"

She jumped. Realizing Detective Hammond had been talking to her, she looked up. "I'm sorry. Did you say something?"

"Yes. You said the intruder called you by your name. Did you recognize his voice?"

Julia thought for a moment. So many people in this town resented her, yet she couldn't think of a single person who would be hateful enough and vicious enough to hold her at gunpoint and threaten Andrew. "No. He never raised his voice above a whisper."

She gave a tired laugh and glanced at the copper pot on the counter. "He had a hard head, if that's any help."

Hammond gave Julia a rare smile. "I'll make note of that. And I'll take the pan with me, if you don't mind." He nodded to one of the lab technicians, who immediately picked up the pan with gloved hands and dropped it into a plastic bag. "It might have a hair or two stuck to it, and if we're lucky, some blood residue.

"By the way," he continued. "Not that I'd want to alarm you unnecessarily, but the perp didn't get what he was after, so there's a chance he could come back, though probably not tonight. I wish I could put a uniform outside your door, but as usual, we're shorthanded."

"That's all right, Detective." Steve pointed at the other chair. "I intend to stay right here tonight."

"Good." He looked around, saw that his men were packing up. "I guess we're done here. Call me if there's any further disturbances." He looked at Steve. "You have my home phone, don't you?"

"Yes, Hank. Thanks. For everything."

Steve and Coop walked him to the door. Then Julia heard the door close. The dead bolt clicked shut.

When the two men came back, Coop went to the stove to boil some water and Steve came to sit in the other chair. "We're going to find this guy," he said quietly. "Whatever it takes."

Still feeling numb, Julia nodded and watched his hands as they took hers.

"Your hands are cold." He rubbed them briskly.

"I'm scared. Not for myself, but for Andrew. He could have been killed. It could still happen."

"I won't let it."

"Oh, Steve," she said impatiently. "You can't watch him twenty-four hours a day. No one can."

Coop walked over and handed her a mug of steaming chamomile tea. "I can."

She blinked as she accepted the mug. "What? How?"

"I can take him away from here. To Spike's cabin in the mountains. He'll be safe there. And you'll have peace of mind."

Julia remembered Spike's cabin, the fun she'd had there as a child, fishing, hiking, bird-watching. She also remembered the dark, forbidding forest, the howl of wild animals at night, the many signs warning hikers not to venture into certain areas.

"It's too dangerous," she said, her motherly instincts immediately kicking in. "I'd be a nervous wreck the whole time he was there."

"I won't let anything happen to him." Coop took her chin between two fingers and forced her to look at him. "And if you're worried that I'll start drinking again, don't. I made you a promise and I intend to keep it."

"I wasn't worried about that," she said honestly. "I trust you, Dad. It's just that...Andrew is a little boy. He needs me."

Coop smiled. "You were five the first time I took you to the cabin. I didn't hear any complaints from you that entire week. In fact, if memory serves, you didn't want to go home."

"This is different," she protested. "He just lost his father. He needs stability. He needs to know that I'm here for him."

But even as she talked, images of what had just happened, what *could* have happened if Andrew had been here, kept playing in her head. She had to protect her son.

Coop lay a hand on her shoulder. "Let me do this for you, Julia. I came here to help and so far I haven't done anything worthwhile."

"That's not true!" she protested. "You've been wonderful."

"Coop is right," Steve interjected. "With that maniac at large, Andrew will be safer if he's away."

"What about school?" she asked, grabbing the first tangible excuse.

"There's only three days left before the summer break," Steve pointed out. "I'm sure if you explained the situation to Andrew's teacher, she'd understand. Especially since the news of the break-in will be all over town by morning."

He was right, Julia thought as her assailant's threats once again echoed in her head. At home, at school, or at his friend's house, Andrew would be a target. The only other alternative was to keep him inside, under twenty-four-hour guard. And even that was no guarantee he'd be safe.

But he could be safe with Coop. She pressed her fingers to her eyes, already missing him, already wondering how long it would be until the police found her attacker. Days? Weeks?

Think of Andrew. She kept repeating those words to herself, over and over, like a mantra, until she felt strong enough to do what had to be done.

"All right," she said, looking up to meet her father's eyes. "You take him to the cabin, Dad."

"Good." Coop stood up. "Now that we've got that settled, what do you say we all go back to bed and get some shut-eye? Morning will be here before you know it."

After he was gone, Julia pushed herself to the edge of her chair. "About the sleeping arrangements," she said as Steve rose. "You don't have to stay down here and stand guard. You heard what Hammond said. Whoever broke in won't be back. Not tonight."

"I'm staying, Julia. So don't give me a hard time."

He was interrupted by a sudden flash from the window. Startled, Julia jumped. "What was that?"

"A camera flash. Stay here."

For the second time in less than an hour, Steve found himself chasing an intruder. But this time, anger gave him wings. And this time, dammit, he wouldn't let the bastard get away.

Just as the man turned right on Via del Rey, Steve leaped, arms extended. Both men fell to the ground and rolled down the steep incline. When they finally stopped, the man, trapped under Steve's body, shouted a warning.

"You lay a finger on me and I swear I'll sue you!"

"Sue me?" Steve flipped him over and straddled him. "Buddy, you ain't gonna live that long." Taking a fistful of the man's shirt, he gave him a hard shake. "Who the hell are you?"

"My name is Ron Kendricks." Shaky fingers searched inside his breast pocket, produced a press ID. "I'm a reporter."

"Well, what do you know." Steve's grip tightened. "You're the piece of slime who's been harassing Julia Bradshaw."

"I'm just doing my job, Reyes."

"Are you now?" Spotting the camera lying in the gutter, Steve let go of Kendricks and walked over to pick it up.

"Hey!" Kendricks scrambled to his feet just as Steve flipped open the film compartment. "What the hell do you think you're doing?"

Steve didn't answer. He pulled out the film and crumpled it in his hand.

"Why, you son of a bitch. That's my livelihood you're tampering with, dammit."

"And this is private property you're trespassing on, so get the hell out of here."

Kendricks started to make a move to retrieve his film, then thought better of it. "You'll pay for this, Reyes."

Steve tossed him the camera. "Scram."

He stood on the sidewalk until Kendricks had disappeared down the street. Only then did he walk back toward The Hacienda.

From the doorway where she had been waiting, Julia moved aside to let Steve in. "It was Kendricks, wasn't it?"

"Spineless little bastard," he muttered.

Concerned because she had seen the quick flash of fury in Steve's eyes, Julia watched him as he flipped the dead bolt. "What did you do to him?"

"Not enough." Steve dropped the useless film on the coffee table. The hint of a smile skimmed across his mouth. "What did you *think* I did to him?"

"Oh, I don't know. The way you looked when you took off, I thought at the very least you'd beat him to a pulp."

"The thought crossed my mind."

She let out a nervous laugh, but felt some of the tension that had built up over the last hour ease off a little. "I'm sure he deserved nothing less. I just hope he learned his lesson and won't be back."

"Oh, he'll come back," Steve said, drawing a startled look from her. "That type always does. He won't do it tonight, though, or when I'm around, but he'll find a way to worm his way back here."

"Great."

"Don't worry." Steve glanced out the window, where once again, all was quiet. "I'll talk to Hammond in the morning about a restraining order. Right now, let's take your father's advice and get some sleep. You look like you need it."

She doubted she'd be able to sleep, but didn't tell him that. "Is there any way I can convince you to spend the night in your bed?"

"Nope, so don't even try."

Julia fought back a smile. "Did anyone ever tell you that you're incredibly stubborn?"

"My sister, all the time."

She stifled a yawn. "You'll need bedding."

"I'll get it from my room. Go to bed, Julia."

She was too tired to argue.

He couldn't sleep. Not that he had expected to. Surprisingly, though, it wasn't the night's events that kept him awake but the mental image of Julia in that skimpy little nightshirt.

He had pushed the two easy chairs together and was stretched out fairly comfortably in the makeshift bed, staring at the shadows on the wall. It had begun so innocently, he thought. A simple awareness of a beautiful woman, followed by a little harmless flirting. How often had he indulged in that timeless pastime and experienced nothing more complicated than pure enjoyment?

Somehow, Julia had affected him differently. And tonight, when he had abruptly awakened and realized someone was down here, possibly hurting her, something inside him had snapped. In that second it had taken him to slip quietly out of bed, he had known that if that person so much as touched one hair on her head, he'd be a dead man.

Steve glanced toward the long, dark hallway that led to the bedrooms. Knowing she was there, sleeping peacefully, perhaps feeling safe, filled him with a mushy feeling he hadn't experienced in years.

Christ. He ran a hand through his hair. He had always been in such control of his emotions, never allowing anyone to get under his skin. What the hell was happening to him?

You're falling for her, old man.

And he was damned if he knew what to do about it.

Because she didn't want to frighten Andrew unnecessarily, Julia hadn't mentioned the previous night's attack when she went to pick him up at the Martinez house the following morning. At Steve's suggestion, she had explained that a nosy reporter had been lurking around The Hacienda, trying to take photographs, and she wanted Andrew out of the way.

He hadn't put up much of a fuss, not after finding out where he was going and with whom.

Now, with tears threatening to spill, Julia watched him as he came out of the house, his fishing pole in one hand, his robot in the other. Tucked under his arm were a half dozen of his favorite videos.

Julia smiled bravely. "One more trip to your bedroom and we'll have to rent a U-Haul."

"Nah." Andrew lay his rod in the trunk of Coop's Buick Regal. "I'm done."

Hugging him fiercely, she reminded him to call her every day and to mind his grandfather. "I love you, sport," she said, swallowing past the knot in her throat.

"I love you, too, Mom." Looking at Steve, he started to put his hand out, then, with a small shrug, he hugged him, too.

Julia could tell by the expression on Steve's face that the spontaneous show of affection had staggered him. But not for long. Scooping Andrew off the ground, Steve hugged him back. "Have a good time, slugger."

"I will."

Within moments Andrew and Coop were buckled up, honking the horn and waving through the open windows.

Her teeth clamped hard over her bottom lip so she wouldn't cry, Julia watched the car go down the driveway. When Steve's arm wrapped around her shoulder, she leaned into him, glad for the support, physical as well as moral. "I know he's not going far," she said. "And I know he's in good hands, but..."

"But you're his mom and you'll always worry." He kissed her cheek. "Come on," he said, turning her around. "I'll make you my instant cure-all."

She looked up at him, not sure what to expect. "What's that?"

"*Café Cubano.* Guaranteed to lift your spirits."

She worked up a smile. "And raise your heart rate?"

"Oh." He nudged her a little closer. "I was hoping to do that without the help of artificial stimulants."

With a chuckle, she followed him inside the house.

"Coop?" Grace stared at Julia as though she had suddenly gone mad. "You entrusted your son, your most precious possession, to your *father?* A man who couldn't have protected his own children from a stray cat?"

"Dad will take good care of Andrew, Mom. I know you're concerned about his drinking, but he swore he would never touch another drink and I believe him."

Relentless when she put her mind to it, her mother gave her a stern look. "If you wanted Andrew to be safe, why didn't you leave him with Charles? His house is a fortress. And say what you want about the man, he loves Andrew and would have taken good care of him."

"I won't argue about that. And I would have no problem with Charles taking care of Andrew, especially now that... things are different between us."

"So why didn't you?"

"Because Andrew would be bored to tears at Charles's house. If he's going to be away from home for an extended period of time, he might as well have fun."

Grace gave a resigned shrug and for the third time started to rearrange the stack of *Good Housekeeping* magazines on the coffee table. "You're the boy's mother, so I suppose I have to trust your instincts, but for the record, I don't like it."

Giving up on the magazines, she turned to Julia. "Is Andrew all right? Have you heard from him?"

"He's fine. I talked to him just before I came here." She smiled. "He said to tell you hi, and that you should come up and spend some time with him and Coop."

Grace's cheeks colored slightly. "He didn't say that."

"I swear he did. He had a lot of questions about you and Dad. I tried to answer them as best as I could, but maybe the rest should come from you."

Grace's expression turned sour. "There's nothing for me to say."

"Mom—"

Grace waved an impatient hand. "Not now, Julia, please. I'm too upset over what happened to you last night to discuss my worthless husband."

Julia felt instantly guilty. "I don't want you to worry about me, Mom. I'm fine. And I'll stay fine. Steve is making sure of that."

Grace's irritation vanished quickly. "That's good, but what about the police? Are they even trying to catch that man who attacked you?"

"Of course they are. Detective Hammond is going door

to door on Via del Rey, hoping someone saw something. So is Steve, but so far, no one has.''

Or if they had, Julia thought, they weren't talking, which wasn't too surprising considering how this town felt about her.

Sitting across from Julia on the sunny patio of the Clock Garden on Abrego Street, Penny ignored her lobster salad and propped both elbows on the table. ''I can't believe that bastard pulled a gun on you,'' she said, her voice trembling with indignation. ''I wish Steve had strangled him while he had the chance.''

Julia smiled. ''Why, Penny, I wasn't aware you had such sadistic tendencies.''

''How can you joke about something like that?''

''Because if I don't, I'll go insane.'' As Penny finally started to eat, so did Julia, cutting through her broiled flounder. ''I'm perfectly fine,'' she added. ''And more important, Andrew is fine.''

''Yes.'' Penny speared a chunk of lobster with her fork. ''Thank God for that.'' She chewed in silence for a few seconds before looking across the table again. ''Frank wants you to move in with us until they catch the guy.''

Julia shook her head. ''I can't do that, Penny. I have a business to run.'' She smiled. ''Besides, Steve is there, and believe me, since last night, we're practically joined at the hip.''

''Hmm.'' Penny did her Groucho Marx imitation, flipping her eyebrows up and down in a suggestive manner. ''Not a bad place to be, if you ask me.''

Julia looked down at her plate. ''Any other time, I would have agreed with you. Steve *is* charming, and distracting, but right now I'm too worried about this maniac and the possibility that he might come back to think about romance."

"Then stop worrying." Penny picked up the bottle of Evian and refilled their glasses. "Frank was fairly sure you'd turn down our invitation to stay with us, so he asked a couple of rookies he knows to patrol your street at regular intervals, night *and* day. It's not the same as having a uniform outside your door, but it should help."

Dismayed, Julia leaned back in her chair. "Oh, Penny, he shouldn't have done that. He could get in trouble."

"No, he won't. He just called in a couple of favors, that's all. Those guys do that all the time."

Julia shook her head. "All I seem to be doing is inconveniencing a lot of people—my father, who was thrown into a stressful situation practically overnight, Steve, who now feels he has to guard me every second of the day, Frank, you, my mother."

"Will you stop it?" Penny said, leaning across the table. "We love you. We don't look at what's been happening to you as an inconvenience, for God's sake."

"I know. I was just indulging in a moment of self-pity. I seem to be doing that a lot lately." Knowing she wouldn't be able to swallow another bite, she pushed her food out of the way. "I want my life back, Penny, my simple, peaceful life with Andrew, just the way it used to be."

"*Exactly* as it used to be?" Penny asked with a twinkle in her eye. "Are you sure you wouldn't want to make one small addition?"

Julia's sinking spirits began to lift a little. "Well, now that you mention it," she said, deciding to have a little fun at Penny's expense, "I could use another downstairs bathroom."

Penny gave Julia's hand a playful slap. "Oh, you."

* * *

"Eleanor, what a pleasant surprise."

Julia opened the door to let her former neighbor in. Eleanor Bailey was one of the few people in Monterey who hadn't snubbed her after her divorce from Paul. Julia even suspected that the older woman knew exactly what had been going on behind the closed doors of the beautiful Tudor she had lived in with Paul. Discreet to a fault, however, she had never uttered a word.

Julia hadn't seen her since the funeral, and even then, for only a brief moment. But today, rather than the pleasant, familiar smile Julia had expected, Eleanor's expression remained somber, and she didn't come in.

"I wanted to return that chocolate cookbook I borrowed from you a couple of months ago," she said, averting her eyes.

Julia glanced at the book Eleanor handed her, a little startled by the woman's cool behavior. "There was no rush," she replied. "But I'm glad you stopped by." Reaching out, she pulled Eleanor inside. "Come in. Let's catch up. I'll make some coffee. I might even have a few oatmeal cook—"

"I can't stay."

Julia let her go. "Is something wrong?"

"No, I'm just in a hurry, that's all."

But that wasn't all, Julia thought, troubled by this sudden change in her old friend. "Are you upset with me?" she pressed. "Have I done something to offend you?"

When the older woman's eyes finally met Julia's, they were filled with a mixture of sadness and disappointment.

Julia's heart sank. "Oh, Eleanor, you haven't been listening to those silly rumors that I killed Paul, have you? You know they aren't true."

Looking even more distressed, Eleanor started for the

door. "I shouldn't have come," she said, waving Julia away.

Deciding that a bold approach was the only way to clear the air between them, Julia positioned herself in front of the door, which was still open. "You and I have known each other for a long time, Eleanor, and we always had a good relationship, always felt comfortable with one another. But you're not comfortable now and I want to know why."

"Certain things are better left unsaid," Eleanor said stubbornly. She stole a quick glance in Julia's direction, but couldn't quite meet her eyes. "That's why I didn't say anything to the police."

Perplexed, Julia shook her head. "Didn't say anything to the police? About what?"

"About seeing you on the night Paul died." She took a white handkerchief from her purse and dabbed her eyes. "I didn't want to get you in trouble."

"Oh." Julia let out a small sigh of relief. "There was no need to keep that a secret, Eleanor. I told the police that I was parked outside Paul's house myself. It was in the papers."

Eleanor dabbed her other eye. "I saw more than that, Julia."

Startled, Julia stared at her. "What are you talking about? What did you see?"

Holding her handkerchief in a tight ball, Eleanor gave her an agonized look. "Oh, Julia, don't you know?"

"No, I don't!"

"I saw you, Julia! I saw you going into Paul's house."

Twenty-Four

Staggered by what she'd just heard, Julia took a step back. "You couldn't have," she said after a few stunned seconds. "I never went in. I stayed in my car the whole time I was there."

Eleanor gave a stubborn shake of her head. "I looked out my window twice that night. The first time I saw you, you were sitting in your car. I couldn't imagine what you were doing there at that hour. In fact, I even wondered if it *was* you or someone who looked like you. Then I recognized the car, and when the driver's door opened, I saw you very clearly."

"But I closed the door almost right away, *without* getting out. Didn't you see that?"

Eleanor shook her head again. "I pulled away from the window because I was afraid you'd see me and think I was being nosy. But I admit I was curious, and a little while later, I took another peek." She looked down at the handkerchief she had wound even tighter. "That's when I saw you get out of the car and walk toward the house."

"It wasn't me!" Julia cried in frustration. "You must have seen someone else."

"It was you, Julia. The following morning when the police knocked at my door and told me Paul was dead, I...didn't know what to think. But when they asked if I had seen anyone the previous night, or heard anything, I couldn't bring myself to tell them that I had seen you."

Her eyes were still moist as she looked at Julia. "In all my seventy-one years, I have never told a lie, Julia. The only reason I did that morning was because I couldn't bear seeing you go to prison, not after all you've been through with that man."

In frustration, Julia gripped the woman's shoulders. "Eleanor, listen to me. Whoever you saw that night wasn't me. Do you hear me? You said it yourself—it could have been someone who looked like me. Or maybe in the rain—"

"What's going on in here?"

At the sound of the familiar voice, Julia let go of Eleanor's shoulders and whipped around. Framed in the doorway, Detective Hammond stood looking at them, his calm gaze shifting from Eleanor to Julia before finally resting on Eleanor again.

"What was it you saw and didn't tell me, Mrs. Bailey?" He walked into the foyer and closed the door behind him.

Under his steady gaze, the older woman's face turned crimson. "Nothing...I—I told you everything I know."

"Not everything, Mrs. Bailey." He glanced at Julia. "And apparently neither have you."

"It wasn't me." Julia didn't seem capable of saying anything but those three little words. And from the look on Hammond's face, he didn't believe them any more than Eleanor had.

"Mrs. Bailey." Hammond spoke slowly, patiently. "Did you or did you not see Mrs. Bradshaw go into Councilman Bradshaw's house on the night of May 26?"

Eleanor shot a desperate look at Julia.

"Don't look at Julia, Mrs. Bailey. Look at me. And answer the question, please."

"I don't know...I mean...I'm not sure."

"Then let me help you. Your house sits directly across from Paul Bradshaw's house, is that right?" He waited until she had nodded before continuing. "And you saw Mrs. Bradshaw clearly—that was your word, *clearly*—when she opened the driver's door that night. Am I correct?"

"Yes." Eleanor's voice was barely audible.

"And when you looked again some time later, you saw Mrs. Bradshaw walking toward the councilman's house. That is what you said."

Mrs. Bailey tugged at the corner of her handkerchief. "I saw someone in a raincoat and hood come out of a car."

"Can you identify the car?"

Her face turned white with panic. "It was...black."

"Was it a Volvo?"

"I don't know cars very well." Her voice was tight with fear and Julia felt sorry for her. She was trying to help and in the process was making things worse.

"Did it look like Mrs. Bradshaw's car?" Hammond insisted.

"I...I suppose it did."

Hammond turned to Julia. "What were you wearing that night, Mrs. Bradshaw?"

Cold sweat trickled down between Julia's breasts. "A raincoat."

"Did it have a hood?"

"Yes, but that doesn't prove a thing. Anyone who went out that evening had to have had some kind of rain gear on them."

Hammond sighed, as though the task he was about to do wasn't something he looked forward to. "You'd better come with me to the station," he said. "I need to ask you a few more questions. You, too, Mrs. Bailey."

"Are you arresting me?" Julia asked in a trembling voice.

Hammond's eyes softened somewhat. "No, but I'd call a lawyer if I were you. You may need one before the day is over."

Nervous because he hadn't yet heard from Ben, McDermott was in his greenhouse, anxiously waiting for his nephew's call, when the door opened.

One look at the shiner that partially closed Ben's right eye and he knew the mission hadn't gone as planned.

"What the hell happened to you?" he barked.

"Ah..." His embarrassment evident, Ben shifted from one foot to the other. "There were complications."

McDermott didn't move. "What sort of complications?"

"Julia woke up." His hand moved up to the back of his head, which he touched gingerly. "That bitch almost cracked my head open. I probably need stitches."

McDermott made a stoic effort to remain calm. "Do you have the tape?"

"No."

He drew a sharp breath and didn't exhale for several seconds. When he was certain he'd be able to hold his temper in check, he let his breath out, slowly. "From the beginning, Ben."

Ben spoke slowly, apologetically, swearing it wasn't his fault. He hadn't done anything wrong. He had been quiet as a mouse. How was he to know Julia Bradshaw was a light sleeper? And that Reyes would come down without a sound and rush him like a linebacker?

After a while, McDermott tuned him out. What difference did it make why or how the fiasco had happened? What mattered was the damned tape was still out there. And that he would have to suffer the wrath of his four colleagues, all of whom had been skeptical about Ben's abilities to carry out this mission.

"I'm sorry, Uncle Ian," Ben said when he was finished.

"You ought to be. I trusted you, Ben. I even defended you when my partners expressed reservations about you. And what do you do? You screw up, making me look like a fool. That's something I don't take lightly."

"Let me explain it to them, Uncle Ian. They'll understand."

McDermott gave him a condescending smile. The naiveté of the young, he thought, to think they could repair their mistakes with words. It never failed to amaze him.

His disappointment temporarily overshadowing his other problems, he opened the drawer where he kept some of his smaller garden tools and stared pensively at the contents for a moment. "I had great hopes for you, Ben," he said wistfully. "Hopes that you could someday become my second-in-command. I would have enjoyed that, working side by side with you, teaching you all I know."

"And I want that more than anything, Uncle Ian," Ben said earnestly. "You know that. The others know that."

"But you see, that's no longer possible."

"Yes, it is. I'll...I'll find the tape. I'll comb the entire town if I have to, but I'll find the tape."

"I'm afraid that's not good enough."

"Why not?"

Having located what he was looking for, McDermott's hand slid inside the drawer and came out holding a Glock 17.

When Ben saw the gun pointed at him, he began to blabber incomprehensibly—another disappointing trait, McDermott thought in disgust. Every man and woman in the McDermott family who had faced death had always done so with courage and dignity. It pained him that the nephew on whom he had placed so much hope was nothing but a hopeless coward.

"Uncle Ian... Wh-what are you doing?" Ben made a pitiful sound, something between a sob and a laugh. "You can't kill me...we're family."

Raising the pistol, McDermott aimed it at Ben's heart and fired three quick shots.

Twenty-Five

Confident that the truth, no matter how incriminating, was on her side, Julia had declined her rights to have an attorney present during questioning. Where would she find a criminal attorney, anyway? And more importantly, how would she pay his retainer?

In the stifling, windowless room where Hammond and another detective had taped her statement, she had stuck to her story. She had driven to Paul's house with the intention of confronting him about the loan, then had changed her mind and gone back home.

When she was finished, they made her repeat it, asking questions at random, as if to trick her into giving a different answer. She didn't. Despite the fact that she was terrified, her second summary was as detailed and concise as the first, her voice weary but calm. It wasn't an easy task. Everything about Detective Hammond, from his sharp, watchful eye to his rapid-fire questioning, was meant to throw her off. He was a far cry from the man who had stood in her kitchen eating her chocolate chip cookies.

Prior to leaving The Hacienda, she had called Penny. Always calm and collected in times of crisis, her friend had told her that Frank was off duty, playing golf somewhere, but she would find him.

The two of them arrived twenty minutes later, just as Julia was being led back to Hammond's desk. Steve, his face a mask of concern, was with them, and so was a short, portly man Julia had never seen before.

While Frank talked to Hammond, Steve rushed to her, the stranger in tow. "Are you okay?" He cupped her face in his hands and searched her face.

How could she be okay? she thought, on the verge of tears. Outside the police station, reporters had jostled her, throwing questions at her, shoving microphones into her face. Inside, the climate hadn't been much better. She had been questioned like a common criminal and had been looked at as if she were the star attraction in some freak show. Not since the days she had suffered Paul's abuse had she felt so low and so unworthy. "I'm fine," she said flatly.

She could tell from the protective way he wrapped his arm around her shoulders that he didn't believe her. "Julia," he said, as he waved the stranger over. "This is Michael Rumson. He's a criminal attorney and, from what Frank tells me, a very good one."

Panic flowed. "Steve, I can't afford an att—"

"Shh." He laid a finger on her lips. "That's been taken care of."

"By whom?"

"By me. Now stop giving me a hard time. You can pay me back later if that makes you feel better. Right now I want to get you out of here."

"I'm afraid that's out of the question."

The man who had just spoken was Tanner Brooks, one of the toughest and most ambitious district attorneys Monterey had ever had. Undoubtedly because this was an election year and a high-profile murder trial would do wonders for his career, he had taken a personal interest in the case from the very beginning.

"Why?" Michael Rumson demanded, immediately stepping into his defender's role. "My client has done nothing wrong. She has come here willingly and answered all your questions. Furthermore, you have nothing but circumstantial evidence against her, therefore I ask that she be released immediately."

"We have an eyewitness," Brooks said flatly. "Mrs. Bailey, who lives across the street from Paul Bradshaw, has identified Julia Bradshaw as the person who went into Paul's house the night he died."

"That's not true!" Julia protested. "She made a mistake—"

Rumson laid a hand on her forearm to silence her. "Come on, Tanner," he said with a familiarity that was meant to be reassuring. "You have no grounds here. Mrs. Bailey is an old woman whose sight—"

"You'll have plenty of time to plead your client's case, Counselor." Brooks started buttoning his suit jacket, then, turning to Hammond, gave him a curt nod and left.

Hammond pressed his lips and turned to Julia. "I'm sorry, Julia. I have no choice but to place you under arrest for the murder of Paul Bradshaw."

The rest of the morning was like a scene from a bad movie. Walking stiffly, Julia followed a uniformed policewoman into another room, where she was photographed, fingerprinted and officially charged with second-degree murder.

In spite of Mike Rumson's diligent efforts to get her a reduced bail, the judge set it at two hundred thousand dollars, a sum so outrageously high it might as well have been two million.

The preliminary hearing, which would determine whether or not the case would go to trial, had been scheduled for June 30. She had stared at the judge in quiet shock, her mind focused on only one person. Andrew. How would she explain to her little boy that she had been charged with murder? And what would happen to him if she was found guilty?

"You'll be out of here before the end of the day," Steve promised before a police matron took her back to her jail cell. "Just hang in there for a little while longer."

Julia didn't answer. She didn't even say anything about the bail, which she knew he planned to pay. As she was led out of the courtroom, all she could think of was that she had told the truth and no one had believed her. She had never realized what a fragile commodity freedom was until the cell's door clanged shut behind her.

She glanced around her, her gaze slowly sweeping over the grimy walls, the cracked, smelly toilet bowl, the cot with its dark brown blanket and pillow stacked on one end.

After a while, she sat down in the single wooden chair. They had taken her watch so she had no way of tracking the time. She kept thinking of Andrew. God, please, don't let him hear about this.

Steve had sworn he wouldn't. He would call Coop and tell him to keep Andrew away from the television set.

Somewhere down the hall, a woman was rattling her door and cursing loudly as she demanded to be released. Before long, a man who sounded more intoxicated than angry joined her. Someone yelled, "Shut up down there!" The rebellion only got louder.

An eternity later, the same policewoman, a large buxom brunette with a swagger, was back, keys clinking around her belt. "Looks like this is your lucky day, Goldilocks." She unlocked the door. "You made bail."

Steve was waiting in the front room. He stood by her as she collected her belongings, signed a form. She went through each motion like a robot that had lost most of its powers.

"Did you get ahold of my father?" she asked, when they were finally walking out.

"Yes. He said not to worry. Spike never bothered to install cable so there's no TV up there. Andrew is fine."

She breathed a sigh of relief. Once outside, she couldn't walk away from the station fast enough. "About the bail," she said, as they crossed the street. "I'm going to pay it back, even if I have to—"

"I didn't pay your bail."

She stopped walking. "You didn't?"

He shook his head.

"Then who did?"

"Charles."

"Hello, Pilar."

"Señora Bradshaw!" Pilar's face broke into a huge welcoming grin. "It's so good to see you." She glanced at the Land Rover, where Steve, who had refused to let Julia take a cab, sat waiting. "Will...the gentleman be coming in?"

Julia almost chuckled. "I don't think so, Pilar."

The housekeeper closed the door. "Are you okay?" she asked worriedly. "They didn't mistreat you in that awful jail cell, did they?"

Julia smiled. "It wasn't the Ritz, but no, they didn't mistreat me."

"And you're not mad at me?" She looked suddenly embarrassed. "You know...for telling Mr. B. about some of the things that...happened?"

Julia squeezed the housekeeper's hand. "Actually, I'm thankful. You were able to accomplish what I never could—to make Charles look at me with something other than contempt."

"Mr. B. is a good man," Pilar said, her loyalty to her boss evident. "He's just stubborn, that's all."

"He's also lucky to have you, Pilar. Is he in?"

"In his study."

"No need to announce me," Julia said. "I'll just surprise him, okay?"

Pilar nodded and disappeared.

Julia found Charles doing what he did every afternoon at this time, sitting in his favorite leather chair and reading the *Wall Street Journal.*

Though the door was open, Julia gave two soft knocks.

He looked up, folded the paper and stood up. "Julia." He gave her a quick up-and-down look. "Rough morning?"

Again, his attempt at humor made her smile. "The afternoon is shaping up much better—thanks to you."

"Ah." He made a gesture of dismissal.

But his generosity wasn't something Julia could easily dismiss. "I'm grateful for what you did, Charles. But I didn't come here just to thank you."

Charles tossed the newspaper aside. "You want to talk about Eleanor Bailey and what she told the D.A."

Was there anything the man didn't know? "Yes, I do."

Charles pointed to a chair and she took it, too nervous to lean back comfortably, the way he did. "I'm not going to sit here and call Eleanor a liar," she began as he calmly observed her. "I like her. She and I have been friends for a long time."

"She must like you, too, or she wouldn't have withheld such important information from the police."

"I did not go into Paul's house that night, Charles," she said earnestly. She didn't know why, but suddenly it was terribly important that he believe her. "I don't know who Eleanor saw, but it wasn't me."

"Then who was it?"

"I don't know! At first she swore it was me, but then

she wasn't so sure. When Detective Hammond questioned her at The Hacienda, she said she had seen someone in a raincoat coming out of a car that *looked* like mine. Then at the station, she made a complete turnaround."

To her surprise, Charles nodded. "I know all about that. Apparently the D.A. leaned on Eleanor so hard the poor woman was totally overwhelmed. Not to worry," he added. "Once on the stand, a good defense attorney will blow her testimony all to hell. And that's what you need, Julia. A first-rate defense attorney."

"I have an attorney. A very competent one."

Charles made another impatient gesture. "Competent won't cut it. You need a gutter rat, someone not afraid of fighting with the likes of Tanner Brooks. And I have just the man for you."

The phone on his desk rang, and he picked it up right away. "That will be him now," he said as he lifted the receiver.

Other than a brief hello, Charles remained perfectly silent for nearly a minute as he listened and studied the pattern of his Aubusson carpet. When the caller was apparently finished, he thanked him and hung up.

He turned to Julia. "Well, it looks like you won't need an attorney, after all."

"What do you mean?"

"That was the chief of police. The charges against you have been dropped. They've arrested Edith Donnovan for Paul's murder. They found the Beretta buried in her backyard."

Twenty-Six

"Edith?" Steve gave a bewildered shake of his head as Julia told him what she had just learned. "That's ridiculous. She doesn't fit the profile of a killer any more than you do."

"I thought you said she was dangerous."

Anxious to leave the Bradshaw grounds, Steve put the car in gear and started down the long, oak-lined driveway. "She's not dangerous in that sense of the word," he replied. "Even if she were capable of murder, which she's not, *you* would have been her target. Not Paul."

Julia drew back in mock shock. "Thanks a lot."

"You know what I mean. And anyway, your attacker was a man."

The traffic grew heavier as they neared the popular wharf area, forcing Steve to slow down. Julia turned around in her seat. "If you don't think Edith is guilty, then what's *your* theory of what happened?"

"Actually, I have two theories. The first is that, while going through your brother's tapes, Paul discovered damaging information about *Gleic Éire,* perhaps the names of their leaders, or their base of operations, or maybe both. Whatever he learned was important enough for him to schedule a news conference. When the leaders of *Gleic Éire* found out what he was about to do, they killed him."

Julia took a second or two to consider. "Then why are

they looking for the tape? Wouldn't they have made sure they had it before killing Paul?"

"Maybe Paul wouldn't give it up, but because silencing him was paramount, the killer shot him, planning to look for the tape later."

"But you don't think he found it," Julia said when he stopped for a red light.

"I'm beginning to wonder about that."

"You said you had two theories. What's the other?"

As the light turned green, Steve started driving again. "I've never really believed *Gleic Éire* killed Paul, though I believe they killed Eli. Just as I believe that the man who broke into The Hacienda the other night was either a member of the group, or someone they hired."

"Either way, he wasn't very good," Julia remarked.

He smiled. "I agree. And that baffles me, too. Asking you where the tape was hidden was a dumb move, not at all something those clever bastards would do."

Once again she had the vague, unsettling feeling that he knew much more about *Gleic Éire* than he was letting on. "You talk as if you knew them intimately," she said quietly.

He shrugged. "They're not that hard to figure out. They're driven by hatred and a diabolical need for power. They won't stop killing until they have what they want. Or until someone stops them."

"Someone?" Her voice was just a whisper. "Meaning...you?"

He laughed, a laugh so genuine she was almost convinced her suspicions were totally unfounded. "I was speaking figuratively. Anyway, enough about *Gleic Éire.* Tonight we celebrate your freedom." He swung the Land Rover onto Via del Rey. "What do you say we have a nice little dinner someplace special and break out a bottle of champagne? We'll even drink a toast to Charles."

His enthusiasm was contagious. "Considering what he did," she teased, "don't you think we should invite him to join us?"

"Don't push it. His feelings toward you may have changed, but he still hates my guts for embarrassing him the other morning. About dinner?"

"You're a persistent guy, you know that?"

His lips curved. "Is that a yes?"

"On one condition," she said, remembering the crowd that had been waiting for her outside the police station earlier. "That we have the celebration at home. I'm not up to being around a lot of gawking people. I also need a shower," she added, rubbing a dark smudge from her blouse. "After three hours in jail I feel as if the stench of that cell is embedded into my skin."

"Then home it is."

By the time they arrived at The Hacienda, the news of Edith Donnovan's arrest was the topic of every radio broadcast. According to a statement made by Detective Hammond, the police had received an anonymous phone call. The "concerned citizen" had told the police that he had seen Edith bury something in her backyard late on the night of May 26. When asked why he hadn't come forward sooner, the informant had simply said he had been afraid to, and had hung up.

Ten minutes later, a police team had found the weapon buried in Edith's rosebushes. Despite Edith's repeated protests that she was being framed, she had been arrested and charged with second-degree murder.

While Julia was showering, Steve helped himself to a Bud from her refrigerator and went out in the courtyard, his mind still on Edith. How could he have been that wrong about her?

He was still thinking about her when he heard the sound of footsteps crunching the gravel. Looking up, he saw little Jimmy Martinez coming up the driveway.

He was a short, chunky boy with hair as black as Andrew's was blond. Tucked under his arm was what looked like a case of Hot Wheels. A car buff, Jimmy had a collection of miniature cars that numbered in the hundreds.

Seeing the forlorn expression on the boy's face, Steve guessed he was missing his friend. "How's it going, Jimmy?"

The eight-year-old shrugged. "Okay."

"You miss your buddy, huh?"

"Kinda."

Steve smiled. Jimmy was a boy of few words, except when he was with Andrew. Then you couldn't shut him up. "What you got there?" He pointed at the case under the boy's arm.

"My new set of Hot Wheels."

Steve waved him over. "Let me take a look."

Jimmy's face brightened instantly. Coming to sit on the step beside Steve, he opened the case and laid it between them. Without prompting, he began naming all twenty-four cars, stopping every now and then to point at a favorite.

When he was finished, he looked up. "When is Andrew coming back?"

"Oh, in a week or two." Steve hoped he wasn't being overly optimistic. Judging from the number of phone calls Julia had already made to the cabin, she wouldn't last much longer than that.

"You understand why he had to go, don't you?" Steve asked.

As restless as Andrew, Jimmy started to fidget with some

of the cars. "My mom said it's because of a nosy reporter, but I know it's not."

Steve pulled his head back in surprise. "You do?"

His Hot Wheels case still open, Jimmy began to toy with one of the cars. "I heard my mom and dad talking. I know that a man with a gun came into The Hacienda and scared Mrs. Bradshaw. That's why you and that policeman are going around to all the houses asking questions."

"You're a pretty bright kid, Jimmy."

Big brown eyes watched him intently. "Are you going to find the man who did it?" he asked.

"I'm trying to. But it's not easy. No one saw anything." Always keenly aware of people's moods and expressions, Steve caught the sudden spark in the boy's eyes and kicked himself for not having thought of questioning him sooner. "Did *you* see anything unusual, Jimmy?"

The boy didn't look up, but kept playing with his miniature car. "Sorta."

Steve's heart gave a single, solid thump. "What did you see?"

"A car."

That in itself wasn't unusual. Several homes on Via del Rey and surrounding streets were without garages, making it necessary for residents and their visitors to park on the street. But Jimmy knew that. "You mean, you saw a car you never saw before?"

Jimmy nodded.

"When was that?"

"Wednesday and Thursday. It was parked way down the street. Across from Mr. Obermill's house."

"And you didn't see it on Friday? Or today?"

Jimmy shook his head.

"Did you see anyone in the car?"

"A man," Jimmy replied without hesitation. "But I

couldn't see him too good. He had a beard and a hat over his eyes."

Could have been a disguise, Steve thought. "What about the car? Can you describe it?"

The boy took the tan sedan he had been fondling out of its slot and handed it to Steve. "It looked like this one."

Steve inspected the small, nondescript car—the kind no one would ever notice, except a car aficionado like Jimmy. "Why didn't you mention any of this before?" Steve asked gently.

Jimmy shrugged. "Nobody asked me."

Steve held back a smile and swore he'd never take another kid for granted. "Did you happen to notice the numbers on the license plates?" He probably hadn't, but it was worth a shot.

"No." Jimmy paused. "But I saw the sticker on the windshield."

Steve felt another thump. "What kind of sticker?"

"The kind you get for parking. My dad has one."

"Could you read what it said?"

Jimmy was instantly defensive. "I'm eight years old. I know how to read."

"I'm sorry, Jimmy. Of course you do." Steve waited a beat, hoping he hadn't destroyed his chances with that stupid question. "What did the sticker say?"

"Santa Barbara College. Student No. 117."

"You were close enough to the car to read all that?"

Jimmy nodded. "My school bus drops me off at the corner and I had to walk right by it."

Steve handed the miniature car back to Jimmy. "Did the man inside the car see you read the sticker?"

"He wasn't in the car on Thursday. That was the day I saw the sticker."

Steve slowly let his breath out and tried not to get overly

optimistic. What Jimmy had told him didn't prove a thing. The driver of the car could have been a student visiting his parents. Or the car could have been bought secondhand and the new owner hadn't bothered to remove the sticker.

The problem with those two suppositions, Steve thought as Jimmy started to close his case, was that he wasn't buying either one of them.

The vision in front of him as Steve walked back into The Hacienda's kitchen took his mind miles away from the mystery car and its occupant. Julia had changed into a T-shirt the same green as her eyes and had tucked it into white, pleated silk pants. She wore no makeup, nor did she need any, and her hair, still wet from the shower, had been left to dry on its own.

"Wow."

She laughed, the first truly genuine laugh he'd heard since he had arrived at The Hacienda. "I take it you approve."

"Oh, I approve."

She looked down at her slacks. "You don't think this is too dressy for an at-home dinner?"

"It's perfect," he said, unable to take his eyes off her. "I feel as if I should change into a tux."

"Let's not get carried away." She wrapped the apron with the tipsy chef around her waist. "Was that Jimmy I heard talking?"

The question brought him back to reality. "It was. He and I had an interesting conversation."

She took a bottle of chardonnay from the refrigerator and handed it to him along with a corkscrew. "Really? What about?"

As he told her what Jimmy had seen, she took two long-stemmed glasses from a cabinet. "You think the driver of that car was the man who broke into The Hacienda?"

"There's only one way to find out." Steve touched his glass to hers. "How would you like to take a ride to Santa Barbara first thing in the morning?"

They had spent the evening quietly, in the parlor, eating and discussing Jimmy's intriguing revelation. Steve had lit a fire and the huge room felt warm and cozy. On the coffee table were the remains of a light dinner—a mushroom omelette, a salad and the nearly empty bottle of chardonnay they had started earlier.

For the first time in three weeks, Julia felt relaxed and content, not quite free of worry, but close.

That the reason for her happy mood was sitting next to her wasn't something she could easily overlook. In a few short weeks, Steve Reyes had become as indispensable as the air she breathed—to the point that she wondered how she would manage once he was gone.

She hadn't wanted to fall in love with him. After being let down first by her father, then by Paul, trusting a third man, much less falling for him, wasn't on the charts. But from the moment she had seen him standing on her doorstep, charm oozing from every pore, she hadn't stood a chance.

"What's this?" He leaned close to look into her eyes. "Brooding? On a night like this?"

"I don't brood."

"Whatever it is, we'll have to get rid of it." He tipped her head back. "Maybe this will help."

He kissed the corner of her mouth, then with deliberate slowness, moved his lips to cover hers. She responded instantly, sighing softly. "Steve..." His name caught in her throat. She closed her eyes, thrilling at the feel of his hands stroking her shoulders, cupping her breasts, skimming her nipples. Whatever control she had claimed to want to hang on to slipped away.

"You're beautiful, Julia." He was kissing her eyes, her mouth, the hollow of her throat. "So beautiful."

"Is that the chardonnay talking?" she teased.

"Oh, hardly."

Coiling her arms around his neck, she strained against him, shamelessly arching her body, demanding to be touched, oblivious to everything but the heat that consumed her, a heat that had nothing to do with the blazing fire that burned in the hearth.

With fingers that trembled, she worked the buttons of his shirt, undoing them quickly, awkwardly. She laughed at her own clumsiness when she almost ripped the last one off. Then, with a little sigh of victory, she peeled the shirt wide, baring his chest.

Straddling him, she pushed him against the cushions and bent over to flick the tip of her tongue over his nipples.

"You're stealing all my moves," Steve said hoarsely.

She glanced at him from beneath lowered lashes. "Complaining?"

"No."

Steve grasped the hem of her T-shirt and gently pulled it over her head. Dextrous fingers moved to her back, unhooked the white lacy bra and tossed the garment aside. With his hot gaze fixed on her bare breasts, he started to pull her to him, but she stopped him.

With a teasing, throaty laugh, she slipped out of his grip, stood up and slowly wiggled out of her pants. All there was left covering her now was a wisp of white lace between her legs.

His gaze riveted to that lacy white triangle, Steve hooked

his thumbs on each side of the elastic band and slowly began to lower her panties until they, too, were gone.

With a small groan, he wrapped his hands around her buttocks and drew her to him, pressing his mouth against her.

Eyes closed, Julia threw her head back. It was as if she was being lifted and held under a hot burning light. More, she thought as his mouth did delicious things to her. She wanted more.

"I'll give you all you want," Steve murmured. "All you can take."

She hadn't realized that she had spoken aloud, but she didn't care. She wanted him to know everything about her, every thought, every longing, every need.

She wasn't sure how they ended up on the thick white rug in front of the fireplace, or how Steve managed to shed the rest of his clothes. Suddenly they were tangled in each other's arms, exploring each other's bodies with a hunger they could no longer hold back.

"I want you, Julia," he murmured against her mouth. "God, how I want you."

The words made her hot, and wet. Deep in her belly, the pressure built to a pitch, demanding to be released. "Then why don't you take me? Right now."

He slid into her, rock hard, and caught her gasp of pleasure in his mouth. She wrapped her legs high around him and began to move with him, finding his rhythm, slow at first, then increasing in speed and power. With a passion that no longer astonished her, she matched his frenzy. Her hips, powered by a will of their own, pounded against his, relentlessly, again and again.

Her body was slick with sweat now, her breath hot and ragged. The climax came almost without warning, slamming into her with a force that had her crying out. In that moment, as she hurtled over the edge, she knew, with absolute certainty, that she could never belong to anyone but this man.

Twenty-Seven

Heavy clouds had once again begun to gather when Steve and Julia drove into the beautiful beach town of Santa Barbara, two hundred and forty miles south of Monterey.

The college was a sprawling pink stucco building with an ocean view and palm trees swaying gently in the breeze. Because the last semester had just ended, the parking lot was nearly deserted. And slot number 117 was empty.

A cleaning crew directed them to a room at the end of a long hall, where a pretty secretary, answering to the name of Sophie Mathers, sat behind a desk piled high with files.

Holding Julia by the hand, Steve smiled at the suddenly attentive brunette. "Good morning, Miss Mathers," he said pleasantly. "My name is Steve Reyes. And this is my sister, Anita Delgado."

Julia threw him a brief, startled look, but he ignored it. "Her husband disappeared six months ago," he continued. "And we think he may be attending SBC, possibly under an assumed name."

The brunette, looking somewhat sympathetic, glanced at Julia. "Shouldn't you be talking to the police, Mrs. Delgado?"

Before Julia could think of an appropriate answer, Steve smiled apologetically. "Ah...I'm afraid my sister doesn't speak English."

"Oh." Sophie Mathers seemed quite content to focus her

attention solely on Steve. "I'd like to help you, Mr. Reyes, but I don't think I can. We don't get involved in..." her gaze shifted briefly to Julia again "...domestic quarrels."

Letting go of Julia, Steve braced his hands on the secretary's desk and leaned forward so his face was a scant five inches from hers. Whatever act he was putting on, Julia thought, mildly annoyed, was thick enough to cut. But it was working.

"To tell you the truth, Miss Mathers," he said, lowering his voice, "my sister doesn't want to involve the police, or do anything that might embarrass the college. And she certainly doesn't want a quarrel. She just wants to talk to her husband."

Miss Mathers gave an understanding nod. "What exactly do you want me to do?"

"An address would be helpful."

"School ended two days ago, Mr. Reyes. Most of our students have already gone home."

"I realize that." He flashed her another smile.

Still reluctant, the secretary hesitated. "We don't want any trouble."

"There won't be any." Steve wrapped a brotherly arm around Julia's shoulders and drew her close. "Anita is a sweet, peaceful girl. She just wants to talk. If the marriage can be saved, then fine. If not..." he gave a resigned shrug "...she'll get on with her life."

He grinned at Julia, who, right on cue, gave him a hopeful, rather vacuous smile.

Miss Mathers turned to her computer and punched a key. "All right. What's his name?"

"Antonio Delgado," Steve said.

The girl scrolled down the screen, stopped at the *D*s, read up and down. As expected, she shook her head. "No one in our files under that name."

"Is there any way you could cross-reference through his student parking permit?" Steve asked sweetly. "His number is 117."

"One seventeen. Let's see." Once again, the secretary keyed a function, waited for the screen to come up, scrolled down again. "One seventeen. I have a Ben Rosenthal?"

She looked up just as Steve gave Julia a discreet nudge in the ribs. Julia jumped and, assuming she was expected to improvise, nodded vigorously. *"Si, es possible,"* she said in what she hoped was fairly good Spanish. *"Antonio tio...se llama Benito. Benito Delgado."*

"Antonio's uncle is named Benito," Steve translated. "We may have found him."

The secretary was already jotting down the address on a square of paper she had torn from a pink cube on her desk. "He lives off campus," she said, handing the address to Steve. "You shouldn't have any trouble finding it. Chapala Street isn't far. Turn left at the light, then left again."

"Thank you, Miss Mathers. You've been most helpful."

The girl blushed. "I'm glad I could help." She glanced at Julia, then, as if remembering she spoke no English, looked at Steve. "I hope your sister finds her husband."

"So do I." Steve tucked the address in his jeans pocket. Then, taking Julia's hand again, he led her out of the office.

Once out in the hall, Julia yanked her hand free. *"Anita Delgado?"* she asked.

Steve chuckled. "What's the matter? Don't you like the name?"

"It's not a matter of likes or dislikes. How could you do this to me? You took me completely by surprise."

"You were wonderful. Where did you learn to speak such good Spanish?"

"Oh, stop it. It was awful and you know it. I can't believe I fooled her. You could have at least warned me."

"How? I had no idea what I was going to say until I walked into Miss Mathers's office." He pushed one of the double glass doors open to let Julia through.

"You mean you made up that ridiculous story about a lost husband on the spur of the moment?" Julia asked incredulously.

"What can I tell you? I'm an impulsive kind of guy. And may I remind you that ridiculous story got us the information we wanted."

"No wonder," she sniffed. "With all that charm you shoveled at that girl, it's a wonder she didn't volunteer to go look for Ben Rosenthal herself."

"In my business we call that seizing an opportunity."

Julia gave another sniff. "I call it disgusting."

Steve's tone turned playful. "Jealous, sweetheart?"

Julia rolled her eyes. "I don't have a jealous bone in my body. And don't call me sweetheart."

As they reached the Land Rover, he opened the passenger door and held it for her. "Can I call you Anita?"

Because his good humor was impossible to resist, she laughed. "Okay, you win. The little scene we just played *was* effective. And funny."

"And you enjoyed it."

"A *part* of me enjoyed it," she conceded. She waited until they were both settled inside the vehicle before asking, "I'm puzzled, though. What are you going to tell this Ben Rosenthal if you find him? We don't know if he was the man who broke into The Hacienda. All we know is that Jimmy saw a car that may or may not be Ben's."

Steve put the key into the ignition. "It depends on how defensive he gets. We'll play it by ear."

Julia couldn't resist one last dig. "Are you going to put the move on him, too?"

His eyes shimmered with laughter. "The only one I want

to put the move on at the moment,'' he said, cupping her face in his hand, ''is you.''

The taste of him as he kissed her was intoxicating enough to make Julia forget they were in a parking lot. Eyes closed, she lost herself in the sheer pleasure of having his mouth on hers. It wasn't until a group of young girls in very short skirts passed by, giggling, that she pulled away. ''Why don't we check on Benito first and neck later?'' she suggested.

''Mmm. I like the sound of that—the necking part, I mean.'' He let her go, then, with a wave at the girls, who were still nudging each other, he put the truck in gear and backed out of the parking space.

They found the door of Apartment B2 open. Inside, a pretty redhead in tight blue jeans was carrying household goods from the galley kitchen to the front door. Two bulging suitcases, a CD player and a TV set were already waiting there, apparently ready to be carted back home for the summer break.

Julia gave the door a gentle knock. ''Good morning.''

The redhead spun around. ''What the hell do *you* want?'' She looked ready to pounce on them.

Taken aback, Julia glanced at Steve.

Fists on her hips, the redhead showed no sign of getting any friendlier as she glanced from Julia to Steve. ''What's the matter with you two? Are you deaf?''

Protectively, Steve pushed Julia behind him. ''We're looking for Ben Rosenthal. We were told—''

The girl never gave him a chance to finish. Picking up a framed photograph from an end table, she hurled it against the wall, missing Steve's head by inches. ''There,'' she said. ''You found him.''

The act seemed to appease her. ''I'm looking for the son

of a bitch myself,'' she said. ''So if you do find him, you give him to me, you hear?''

Steve looked at the debris on the floor. ''I take it he, ah, left?''

''Crawled out of here like a snake while I was in the middle of finals,'' she spat. ''No goodbye, no so long, no it's been nice knowing you. Nothing. Not a word. *Nada.* He packed everything he owned and left me with the bills.'' She gave the easy chair next to her a vicious kick. ''That creep.''

Sensing the girl might need a woman's sympathy, Julia stepped forward again. ''Men can be such sleazes,'' she offered.

In lieu of an answer, the girl took a carry-on bag from the dining room table and brought it to the door, where she dropped it next to the others. As she did, she bumped lightly into Julia, but offered no apology.

Glancing at Steve, Julia shrugged and motioned for him to take over. He was a lot better at improvising than she was.

Steve cleared his throat. ''Do you know where he went?'' he asked.

The girl looked at him as if he had just landed from the moon. ''He cut out on me, mister. You know? Gave me the old ditcharooney. So why would he leave me a forwarding address, huh? So I can drop by and carve out his cheating heart?''

Casually, Steve started walking around the room, checking the empty bookshelves, opening drawers.

''What do you think you're doing?'' the girl asked testily.

''Checking to see if Ben left something behind.''

''He didn't. I already looked. The bastard wiped the place clean.''

Julia nudged Steve's arm and handed him the picture she had taken from the floor. It showed the redhead, in a more amiable mood, hanging on to the arm of a tanned, handsome Apollo type. No beard.

Steve held out the photograph. "Is that him?"

The girl frowned, instantly suspicious. "I thought you knew him."

"Not personally. He owes some money to a friend of mine."

The girl folded her arms against her slender chest, looked from Steve to Julia. "You two are in the collection business or something?"

"You could say that," Steve replied.

"Well, when and if you find him, you have my permission to break his legs, push pins under his fingernails or do whatever it is you guys do to delinquent accounts. But remember, *I* get him first."

Holding back a smile, Julia looked around the room. Except for that one photograph, there was nothing left of Ben Rosenthal in the apartment. "Can you tell us anything about him?" she asked. "Where—"

"He's a dirty, rotten, backstabbing, lying son of a bitch. How's that?"

From the chuckle behind her, Julia assumed Steve was enjoying himself immensely. "I mean...did he have a family? Friends? A favorite place where he liked to hang out?"

"His parents are dead." The girl inspected a frying pan, decided it wasn't worth taking along and tossed it in a trash can. "He didn't talk about them." She was calming down, taking deep breaths between sentences. "He has an uncle, but he doesn't talk about him, either. The guy's got to be loaded, though, because Ben spends money like it's water."

Julia and Steve exchanged a glance. "Does this uncle have a name?" Steve asked.

"Ian McDermott. But he hasn't seen or heard from Ben since the Easter break."

Hands in his pockets, Steve leaned against the dinette table. "Would you happen to have an address for Mr. McDermott?" He took some money from his pocket, selected a hundred-dollar bill and laid it on the table. "A small token of my appreciation," he said.

The girl looked at the money but didn't touch it. "All I have is a phone number."

"That'll do."

"I took it from the phone bill," she explained as she searched through an old, battered leather purse. "Ben doesn't even know I have it."

She handed Steve a small address book opened to the letter *M*. Steve wrote down the number on one of his business cards. "Okay if I keep the picture?" he asked.

"Be my guest. It would have ended up in the trash, anyway."

Carefully, Steve removed the photograph from the frame, tossed the twisted remains into the trash and tucked the snapshot in his breast pocket.

"I meant what I said about having my say with Ben first." The girl took the hundred, folded it and slid it into her leather purse. From the address book, she took out one of her own business cards. "This is where I'll be this summer. Call me when you find him."

Julia glanced at the card. It identified the fiery redhead as Kelly Sanders of Scottsdale, Arizona.

"I'll do that," Steve promised.

Without a change of expression, she pointed at the pile by the door. "And since you two owe me, you can help me load that stuff into my car."

"My pleasure." Winking at Julia, Steve picked up the TV set. "Lead the way."

Behind him, Julia hooked the strap of a garment bag around her shoulder and followed him.

Ten minutes later, her little blue Camry packed tighter than a sardine can, Kelly Sanders pulled out of the parking lot, gave a single honk of the horn and was gone.

"Interesting girl." Julia watched the Camry disappear.

Steve chuckled. "Not someone *I'd* want to cross."

Julia's eyes flashed. "This is not funny, Steve. What Ben did to her was rotten. Any woman would have reacted exactly the same way."

"Hmm." He took her hand and pressed his mouth to her palm. The kiss had an immediate soothing effect. "Remind me to never cross *you.*"

The wind had picked up and the air was suddenly fragrant with the smell of orange blossoms from the trees nearby. "What do we do now?" Julia asked as they walked toward the Land Rover.

Steve was already taking his cell phone from his pocket. "That part is easy. We call Tim in New York and wait for his extensive information network to come up with the data on Ian McDermott and Ben Rosenthal."

"Can he do that?"

He punched in the editor's number. "Never underestimate the powers of a big city newspaper." He waited for Tim's secretary to put him through. "And while we wait, we can check into one of those little beach cabanas we saw on the way in, maybe have a picnic on the beach. How does that sound?"

She smiled. "Very romantic."

The cabana came complete with a covered terrace, a hot tub and a small private beach. Julia sat on a blanket Steve had spread over the warm sand, and stared in delight as he took out little containers from a picnic basket.

"When did you have time to do all this?"

"I didn't. I just talked to the desk clerk, told her to call the best caterer in town, and she did the rest."

He started to removed the lids. "We have *paté de campagne,*" he said in nearly flawless French, "a cucumber and mint salad, cold salmon in *ravigote* sauce, grilled zucchini blossoms, a fresh baguette, and for the grand finale, strawberries Benedictine."

She gave a startled laugh. "That's my favorite dessert."

"I know. Penny told me."

"You called Penny?"

He inserted the corkscrew in a bottle of Sancerre and began twisting. "When one wants to impress, one has to pull out all the stops."

"No one has ever done that for me."

The cork came out with a light pop. "Then I'm thrilled to be the first." He took a very ripe, very red strawberry and fed it to her, licking the juice from the corner of her mouth. "I love it when you smile," he said.

She laughed. "You keep this up and I'll be smiling a lot."

"I could get used to that."

While soft R & B music filtered through the terrace speakers, they ate and laughed, and for a while, Julia was able to forget that a killer was still out there, maybe waiting for her.

They were attacking the strawberries when they heard the first rumble of thunder.

"You want to go in before we get soaked?" Steve asked.

Julia shook her head and looked out toward the sea. "Let's wait awhile. It's so beautiful out here. And I love to watch the ocean when a storm is approaching. There's something both frightening and magnetic about an angry sea."

"True." Steve stared at the vast expanse of water in front of them. "That's why I chose to live on the water. I feel the same pull to it."

She sipped her wine. "Don't you miss New York?"

He looked away. "No." Before she could question him further, thunder cracked and Julia jumped. Almost instantly, fat drops began to fall, making little craters in the sand.

"Uh-oh." Steve stood up and pulled her to her feet. "We're going to have to make a run for it now."

Moving quickly, they threw the rest of their feast into the picnic basket, grabbed the blanket and broke into a dead run just as an overhead cloud burst, releasing a downpour.

Once on the terrace, Julia dropped the blanket on the floor and fell back against the wall, panting and laughing as she tried to catch her breath. "Another second and we would have had to swim back."

As Steve turned toward her, Julia watched him, enjoying the way his white cotton shirt clung to him. Through the soaked fabric she could see his skin and the thick mat of hair she knew ran all the way down to his belly button.

He was all man and all heat, and she wanted him, right here and right now. As his gaze met hers, she saw the same need in his eyes and only had to move forward to see that need turn into raw passion.

She touched his wet face, her fingers skimming his cheeks, his chin, his lips.

"Are you thinking what I'm thinking?" he asked in a husky voice.

"Hmm. It depends. What are you thinking?"

"How much I want to make love to you."

Giddy from the wine, she grabbed his shirt and yanked him to her. "So what are you waiting for?"

Then, before he had a chance to answer her, she crushed

her mouth to his. Her head spinning a little, she dug her fingers into his shoulders, the nails biting through the fabric and into his flesh. "I want you, too," she murmured against his mouth. "Can you tell?" Laughing, she unbuckled his belt, fumbled with the zipper and pushed his jeans over his lean hips.

He responded instantly, pushing her dress up, stroking her wet thighs. "You make me crazy, Julia."

She took fistfuls of his hair. "I like men who go crazy over me."

As if sensing her urgency, Steve slid his hands under her buttocks and lifted her, wrapping her legs around him.

This time it was she who set the pace, pounding her body against his, urging him on, calling out his name as she clung to his shoulders.

And then she felt it, a heat so intense, so explosive that it rocked her from head to toe and blurred her vision. Her head buried in his shoulder, she cried out his name one more time, then stayed there, spent, waiting for the throbbing inside her to ease and her breathing to return to normal.

Twenty-Eight

It astounded him that after spending half the night making love to her, the mere sight of Julia sleeping could still arouse him. Knowing it wouldn't take much to wake her, Steve ran a finger between her breasts, smiling as he saw her stir.

She opened one eye and grinned. "You wouldn't."

"Try me."

He was already flipping her over when the phone rang. When he ignored it, Julia shook him gently. "Steve, the phone."

"Let it ring." He took a nipple into his mouth.

Julia sighed, closed her eyes. "It could be Tim."

He let his head drop on her chest. "The guy always did have lousy timing."

Reaching toward the nightstand, he picked up the receiver. "Yeah?"

"What's the matter with you?" Malloy said from three thousand miles away. "You sound like you just ran the New York Marathon."

Steve winked at Julia, who responded by cuddling into his arms. "Nothing so uninspiring, I assure you." He switched the phone to his other ear and wrapped his free arm around Julia's shoulders. "What have you got?"

"Quite a bit. According to my sources, Ian McDermott is, or rather was, a well-known, wealthy boatbuilder. Thirteen years ago, he sold his business and retired to Point Cobra, ten miles or so from Monterey, where he raises orchids.''

''Any connection to *Gleic Éire?*''

''None that we found, but my people are still checking. From all appearances, the guy seems to be okay, upstanding citizen and all that.''

Steve twirled a blond curl around his finger. ''Is that doubt I hear?''

''Oh, you know me, I don't like it when the pieces fall neatly into place. But like I said, we're still checking. I should know more about the guy in a few days.''

''What about the nephew?''

''The nephew,'' Malloy said with a trace of satisfaction in his voice, ''has somewhat of a checkered past.''

Steve stopped playing with Julia's hair. ''How's that?''

''He has a record. Mostly B and E and theft, all before the age of sixteen. His uncle managed to keep him out of juvy courts by returning the stolen goods and paying the victims a hefty settlement. Seven years ago, he was arrested again, but the charges were later dropped.''

''How come?''

''The woman he was supposed to have robbed, a Saudi princess, came forward and claimed her ruby necklace was in her safe all along, buried under a stack of cash.''

''Lucky break for Ben. Anything else?''

''Nope. He seems to have been on his best behavior ever since that incident.''

''Thanks, Tim. I'll be in touch.''

After he hung up, Julia looked at him. ''Well? What did he say?''

''Later.'' He lowered his mouth over Julia's breast. ''Now, where were we?''

* * *

It took Steve and Julia nearly two hours to get the information they were after. Ben's photograph in hand, they had begun with the many inns and hotels in and around Monterey, then had expanded their search to Pacific Grove, Carmel and Sand City.

They had already checked eleven establishments when the desk clerk at the Hidden Oak Inn in Sand City remembered Ben. "He paid cash for an entire week," she said, checking her computer screen. "But only stayed three nights."

"When did he check in?" Steve asked.

"On the afternoon of June 15."

"Did he make any phone calls?"

Again she checked her computer screen. "No."

"Did he receive any?"

She shook her head.

"Well," Steve said as he and Julia left the secluded inn, "we now know that Ben Rosenthal was definitely in the area at the time of the break-in."

"I don't understand. Why wouldn't he stay with his uncle?"

Steve gave her a lopsided grin. "Why don't we go and ask him?"

Feeling unusually restless, McDermott filled a flowerpot with dark, rich soil and thought his frazzled nerves would have been better served with a long, hot soak in his hot tub.

Steve Reyes's phone call and request to talk to him about Ben had shaken him badly. How had the reporter tracked Ben down? And just what kind of information did he want?

Those were questions Reyes had promised to answer, face-to-face, provided McDermott agreed to see him.

As if he had a choice, McDermott thought, slamming a

handful of dirt on the workbench. To turn him down, no matter what excuse he chose, would have been regarded as highly suspicious. He couldn't afford that.

He waited for the frustration to ease. It wouldn't do to have Steve Reyes sense he was worried. It was crucial that he be in complete control of his emotions by the time the reporter and Julia Bradshaw arrived.

When he felt calmer, he walked over to the wall, unhooked the Dustbuster and began sweeping up the mess he had made.

Though obviously troubled by Steve's request for an interview, Ian McDermott had graciously invited Steve and Julia to his home in Point Cobra.

The luxurious Mediterranean villa was situated high atop a majestic, twelve-acre knoll framed by the Gabiland Mountains in the east, the Pacific Ocean in the west and a thick cypress grove to the south, directly behind the greenhouse.

A polite but unsmiling butler in a white Nehru jacket and black pants answered the door. The small man's sandaled feet made no sound on the terrace floor as he led Julia and Steve to the greenhouse, where Ian McDermott was waiting for them.

As they walked, Steve's practiced eye noted two sets of tire tracks left in the rain-soaked ground. Both led from the front of the house to the garage area. A third set led farther south, into the cypress grove.

"Ah, Mrs. Bradshaw," Ian McDermott said, as they walked in. "And Mr. Reyes. Please, come in."

Their host was shorter than Steve had imagined, but what he lacked in height he more than made up for in muscles. The thought that McDermott could have been Julia's assailant vanished quickly; the intruder had been well built, but also much taller.

"You don't mind if we talk in here, do you?" McDermott said, gesturing behind him. "One of my plants developed a virus and I want to make sure the disease doesn't spread to the others."

"Not at all," Steve replied. "It was very kind of you to see us, Mr. McDermott." He looked at the profusion of plants, all orchids, and wished they had met elsewhere. In the heavy humid surroundings, the cloying scent was almost sickening.

McDermott's gaze rested briefly on Julia before returning to Steve. "You said on the phone that you were looking for my nephew. May I ask why?"

"He may have some information regarding a recent attack on Mrs. Bradshaw."

Looking perplexed, McDermott dragged his eyes back to Julia. "What kind of information?"

"Ben's car was seen parked on my street for two whole days before the break-in," Julia said. "Then it vanished." As McDermott kept studying her, she asked, "You did hear about the break-in, didn't you? And that I was held at gunpoint?"

"I did hear. And I'm very sorry." He shook his head, as if he couldn't quite understand what she was driving at. "And you think Ben...is the one who broke into your inn and attacked you? Is that what you're trying to tell me?"

"We're not accusing him of anything," Steve interjected. "But his car *was* seen on Via del Rey." He tried to sound as unthreatening as possible. "That's why we would like to talk to him, get his side of the story. He may have noticed something. Or someone."

"I see." McDermott's clear blue eyes rested on Steve

before returning to the plant he had been inspecting. "Are you sure it was Ben's car you saw?"

"We didn't see the car," Steve replied. "A neighbor did." He leaned casually against the workbench and watched McDermott as he examined the underside of a leaf. "We traced it back to SBC through the parking sticker on the windshield," he explained. "Administration gave us Ben's off campus address and we found out from his girlfriend that he had left school early, for destination unknown."

McDermott moved to another plant, repeating the examination process with each leaf. "He could have lent his car to a friend. He often does that, you know."

"That's why I visited several hotels in and around Monterey. Ben checked in at the Hidden Oak Inn in Sand City on the afternoon of June 15 and was never seen again after June 18, even though he had paid for the entire week—in cash."

As McDermott turned his head, Steve thought he saw a trace of admiration in the man's eyes, but couldn't be sure.

"You're quite resourceful, Mr. Reyes," he said, straightening up. "And apparently very thorough. But I'm almost certain the desk clerk at the Hidden Oak Inn made a mistake. First of all, Ben wouldn't come to the area without letting me know, and second, he has no reason to break into anyone's home. His parents left him a substantial inheritance—"

"He didn't want money," Julia interrupted.

"Oh?" A thin eyebrow went up. "What *did* he want then?"

"A tape." Steve bent over a flower as if to smell it. "An audiotape Mrs. Bradshaw's ex-husband left behind. He even threatened to kill her if she didn't tell him where the tape was hidden."

At those words, McDermott, his plants forgotten, looked quite stricken. "You *have* to be mistaken, Mr. Reyes. Why would Ben want that tape?"

Steve shrugged. "Money? Fame? You know him better than we do. What do you think?"

McDermott squared his broad shoulders and immediately came to his nephew's defense. "I think someone is trying to frame him, that's what I think."

It was as good a time as any to be a little more direct. "Did your nephew ever discuss Irish politics with you, Mr. McDermott?"

"Irish politics?" This time, McDermott's face registered pure, undiluted shock. "Dear God, man, are you suggesting my nephew has some sort of connection to that Irish group everyone is talking about...*Gleic Éire?*" He seemed barely able to get the name out.

Steve gave him a long, probing look. Either the guy was telling the truth or he was one hell of an actor. He decided to push a little harder. "I'm going to level with you, Mr. McDermott. Before coming here I took the liberty of running a background check on Ben. I understand he's been in trouble before? While attending boarding school?"

McDermott let out a regretful sigh. "That's not something either one of us is proud of, Mr. Reyes. And it happened a long time ago."

"But the charges *were* breaking and entering, weren't they?" Steve insisted. "On two occasions, both of which you succeeded in hushing up by returning the stolen goods and paying a generous settlement to the victims."

McDermott nodded sadly. "I admit I did intervene." Looking at Julia, as if only she could understand, he added, "That's what parents do, isn't it? Help and protect their children? And I assure you," he added, turning back to

Steve, "Ben is as much my son as if he had been born to me."

"Sometimes," Steve pointed out, "by protecting our children instead of disciplining them, we do them more harm than good."

The remark earned Steve a cynical smile. "Do you have children, Mr. Reyes?"

It was stupid, Steve knew, but he had the uneasy feeling that McDermott already knew the answer to that question. "No, I don't."

"But you do." Once again, McDermott fixed his gaze on Julia. "Therefore you understand." Picking up a towel from the workbench, he began to wipe his hands, slowly, one finger at a time. "I'm not trying to condone what Ben did in school," he said quietly. "But there are extenuating circumstances for his behavior. Ben's parents died when he was fourteen years old, you see, and up to that time, the only discipline the boy had came from his nannies, who, quite frankly, didn't give a damn. After Lizzy died and Ben was left to me, I tried to teach him good values, but..." He shook his head and left the sentence unfinished.

As McDermott talked, Steve glanced out the window. That third set of tire tracks bothered him. It almost seemed as if a car had been driven into the grove. Unless, of course, McDermott had a boat he kept there for some reason.

His eyes cut back to McDermott. "I understand you're a boatbuilder, Mr. McDermott."

The abrupt change of subject didn't seem to bother their host. "Was," McDermott corrected. "I sold my business some years ago so I could spend more time with my orchids." He smiled. "Are you a boating enthusiast, Mr. Reyes?"

Steve felt it again—that same odd sensation that the man was playing with him. "Very much. I live on a houseboat."

McDermott's interest was instantly evident. "What do you have? A Gibson? Or a Sunstar, perhaps?" He gave Steve a quick appraising glance. "You look like the Sunstar type."

"I have a Kingscraft."

"Ah, an excellent vessel. Where do you keep it?"

"Florida." Steve resisted the urge to glance out the window again. "What about you? What did you keep from your impressive fleet?"

"Nothing. I sold my last Sea Ray several years ago when I realized I no longer had time to enjoy it."

The suspicion that a car could be hidden in those trees was getting stronger by the minute. Afraid he'd give himself away by constantly glancing in that direction, Steve turned from the window. "To get back to your nephew," he said pleasantly, "I was hoping you could tell us where we could find him."

"I'm afraid I don't have the vaguest idea where Ben is. As I told his girlfriend when she called yesterday, I haven't seen him or heard from him since Easter, when he stopped by for a few days."

"Doesn't he come home for the summer?" Julia asked.

McDermott's sigh was filled with regret. "Hardly ever anymore. Like his father, Ben is quite an adventurer. He likes to backpack through Europe, explore remote islands, climb the Himalayas."

"And he never calls?"

"Only when he needs something." That same indulgent smile returned to his lips. "That's kids for you, I suppose."

He dropped the towel on the bench and glanced at his watch, giving them an unmistakable signal that the visit was over. "I wish I could be more helpful," he said in a regretful tone. "If only to prove to you that my nephew had nothing to do with that break-in."

Walking unhurriedly, McDermott escorted them out of the greenhouse.

"Will you let me know if you do hear from Ben?" Steve asked. "I'm staying at The Hacienda."

"Certainly. Goodbye, Mr. Reyes." Turning to Julia, he bowed at the waist. "Mrs. Bradshaw."

"Goodbye, Mr. McDermott. And thank you."

His hands behind his back, their host stood in the driveway, watching them as they drove away.

"That poor man," Julia said as she buckled up. "It must be awful for him finding out from two total strangers that his nephew may have been involved in some sordid foreign intrigue."

Steve threw her a quick glance. "You're feeling sorry for this guy?"

"A little, I suppose."

"Why?"

"Because he obviously loves his nephew very much. And he's right, you know—I do understand why a parent would want to protect his child."

"The man is a phony."

"And you're so suspicious." Julia stretched her legs and wiggled her toes, which had been confined in her loafers since leaving Santa Barbara this morning. "Can't you see that under that cool composure, the man is scared that Ben really did break into The Hacienda?"

Steve rolled his eyes. "Boy, has he sold you a bill of goods. I can't believe you're that gullible."

Offended, she turned to look at him. "Why am I gullible?"

"Because the man is lying. He's hiding Ben, Julia."

"What makes you say that?"

"Just a feeling I have." He slowed to allow a buzzard,

which had been feeding on the carcass of a dead bird, to fly away. "And then there are those damned tire tracks."

"Now you've lost me. What tire tracks?"

Steve negotiated a sharp curve, then another. "There are two sets of tire tracks leading to and from the garage area and a third set leading into the wooded area behind the greenhouse. That's why I asked him if he had a boat. I thought maybe he kept it in the grove, out of the sun."

"And since he no longer has a boat, you think Ben's car is there?"

"I'm certain of it. And I'm certain that one way or another, the kid is connected to *Gleic Éire*. I'm not sure in what capacity, but he's connected."

Julia studied Steve's profile, the tight clamp of his jaw she now knew so well, the knitted brows. What was it about that group that ate at him so much? Was it just a matter of simply doing a good job? A burning desire to solve a case no one else could? Or was it something else? Looking at him now, his obsession with *Gleic Éire* seemed almost...personal.

"Are you going to talk to Hammond about this?" She half expected him to say no, that he was going to handle the matter himself as he had others, but he surprised her.

"You bet I am. What we found out about Ben plus those tire tracks should be enough to justify a search warrant."

"And if it's not?"

Steve merged smoothly onto the highway, leaving the villa at the top of the canyon far behind. "Then I'll go search that cypress grove myself."

From the edge of his terrace, where he had an unobstructed view of the winding access road, McDermott watched the Land Rover make its way down the barren canyon.

It excited him that he had finally come face-to-face with Steve Reyes, though it was clear now that he had grossly underestimated the reporter. Seven years out of the newspaper business had not impaired the man's investigative talents in any way. Not that it made any difference. Reyes's visit had no reason to cause any alarm. Even if the intrepid reporter went to the police with his suspicions, what could they do? Reyes had nothing to tie McDermott to the break-in. And now that Ben was out of the picture, not even a reporter of Steve Reyes's caliber would be able to unearth the truth.

Killing Ben had been an unfortunate necessity. For an instant, only an instant, McDermott had considered sending him away to some remote Caribbean island, instead. The boy was, after all, family. But McDermott hated leaving loose ends behind, especially one as volatile as Ben.

Fortunately, disposing of the body hadn't been a problem. After making sure Eanu had left for his morning errands, McDermott had attached two old rusted anchors to the corpse and wrapped it in a blanket. Then, and that had been the most extraneous part, he had dragged the heavy bundle to the edge of the cliff and rolled it into the churning sea.

Because this area was known for its strong, dangerous undertow, boats never ventured near Point Cobra, and he hadn't had to worry about nosy fishermen. Ben's body, if it hadn't already been devoured by hungry fish and other scavengers, soon would be.

As for the car, that shouldn't be a problem, either. For the moment, it was safely hidden in the grove. In a day or two he would begin taking it apart, piece by piece, burning what he could and burying the rest.

The only possible concern was Eanu. The trusted Pakistani, who had been in McDermott's employ for thirteen years, had developed a deep affection for Ben over the years. Usually quiet and self-effacing, he had been reluctant to accept McDermott's explanation that Ben had left abruptly, without saying goodbye.

McDermott was thoughtful for a moment. Maybe in a week or two, he should start worrying out loud to Eanu. Maybe even call the police and express his concern about Ben. A risky move, perhaps, but he was up to the challenge. And it would detract suspicion from him later, if foul play was suspected.

At the moment, the only immediate danger was still that missing tape. The search for the damn thing had been so fraught with mishaps that he was beginning to wonder if it even existed.

A minute later the Land Rover had disappeared. Satisfied that Reyes would not bother him again, McDermott went back into the greenhouse.

Twenty-Nine

Hammond was shaking his head before Steve was even finished. ''I know what you're going to ask and you might as well save your breath. A judge will never issue a warrant based on such flimsy evidence. Ian McDermott is a respected member of the community. He's not quite in the same league as Charles Bradshaw, but he comes pretty damn close.''

''Those tracks—''

''Could have been made by anyone—the gardener, delivery people or some houseguest who backed his car a little too far. And just in case you're about to ask me to barge in there *without* a search warrant,'' he added, ''forget it. I like you but I don't like you enough to risk my badge.''

Steve tilted a can of Pepsi to his mouth and took a long swallow. ''Your badge wouldn't be at risk if you found Ben's car, *and* Ben Rosenthal.''

''That's a gamble I'm not willing to take. Sorry.'' Hammond took a pack of Sweet'n Low from his desk drawer, tore off the top and poured the contents into his coffee. ''What's with you and *Gleic Éire,* anyway? Why are you so damned determined to find those people? I thought that once Paul Bradshaw's murder was solved, you'd be anxious to get back home.'' There was a sudden twinkle in his eyes. ''Or is there something, or should I say someone, in our fair town with whom you can't bear to part?''

Steve let the remark pass and tried a question of his own. ''Do you really believe Edith Donnovan killed Paul?''

''The gun was found buried in her backyard. And it *is* the murder weapon. Ballistics confirmed it.''

''You didn't answer my question.''

Hammond took a noisy slurp of his coffee. ''What I believe is irrelevant. We have strong, concrete evidence. We even have a motive.''

''What's that?''

Hammond shrugged. ''It'll be out soon enough so I might as well tell you. Edith was in love with her boss. She denies it as emphatically as she denies killing him, but two of her co-workers claim she had it bad for the councilman and he knew it. That he didn't take her seriously—again, according to the co-workers—made Edith a brooding nightmare. My bet is that, after all those years of selfless devotion, she felt Paul owed her a little more than a perfunctory 'Good morning, Edith' each morning. One day, she made her move, he turned her down and she lost it.''

Steve wondered if that was Hammond talking or that ambitious D.A. ''Just like that?'' he said. ''She walked into his house late one night, found his gun and shot the man she loved.''

Hammond shrugged. ''It happens. That's why they call it temporary insanity.''

Steve still wasn't convinced. ''How would she know where he kept the Beretta?''

''Come on, Steve. She knew everything about the man, including what he had for breakfast every morning. But even if she didn't know about the gun, and even if the co-workers' statements are nothing more than office gossip, the fact remains that the murder weapon was found in her backyard.''

And that, Steve reflected, was exactly what the district attorney was going to drive home during the trial.

As Steve slowly unfolded his legs, Hammond eyed him through narrowed lids. "I wouldn't do anything stupid if I were you," he said sharply.

Steve gave him an innocent look. "Like what?"

"Like going to McDermott's house in the dead of night and checking out those suspicions of yours. Because if you do, if I have one single call from that man reporting an intruder, I'll throw the book at you."

Steve crushed his empty can, tossed it in the trash next to Hammond's desk and rose. "Thanks for the soda, Detective. Next time the drinks are on me."

Julia tossed Steve a smile and hung up the phone. "Andrew says hi."

Looking as though he was miles away, Steve nodded. "How is he doing?"

"Wonderful. He caught a fish, but it wasn't big enough so Coop made him throw it back." She turned around in her chair. "Hammond didn't go for it, huh?"

"No. Apparently McDermott is another highly valued citizen who should be handled with kid gloves."

Julia listened as he told her about his conversation with the detective. Because she had begun to know Steve so well, she could almost guess what he would do next. He had already hinted at it.

"We just need a little more evidence, that's all," she said, hoping the suggestion would appease him. "Tim said he should know something more about McDermott in a couple of days, didn't he?"

"I'm not going to wait a couple of days."

"Steve."

Leaning against the island, he folded his arms across his

chest. "I'm going back there, Julia. I'm going to find that damn car."

Julia jumped out of her chair. "Are you insane?" she demanded. "Search McDermott's house when Hammond specifically warned you not to?"

"Not his house," he corrected. "His yard. More specifically, the grove behind the greenhouse."

"It's still insane. What if the property is wired? What if McDermott has two-hundred-pound rottweilers guarding it?"

"I'll bring a couple of bones."

Julia slapped the palm of her hand against the counter. "Stop joking, dammit! This is serious. And dangerous. Not to mention illegal. He could shoot you, for God's sake. And he'd be perfectly justified."

"Why would he shoot me if he has nothing to hide?" Steve smiled, took a blond curl between his fingers and crushed it gently. "Or aren't you so sure about that, anymore?"

She slapped his hand away. "Don't try to confuse me. The bottom line is going there is dangerous and I won't let you do it."

His eyes gleamed with that amused look she had come to know so well, the one that won her over every time. Bracing his hands against the island on each side of her, he caged her there, as the last of her resistance melted away.

"Not even if I let you help me?"

"Oh, great," she said only halfheartedly. "Now you're asking me to be an accomplice to a crime. As if I haven't been in enough trouble with the police."

"Oh, come on. You're dying to do it. Admit it."

Exasperated by this reckless side of him, she tried to push him away. The effort was futile. "I could go to Hammond,'' she threatened. ''Tell him what you're up to. He'll stop you.''

Steve smiled. ''You could but you won't.''

A last speck of defiance had her raising her chin. ''How do you know?''

He held her challenging gaze. ''Because you know this is important to me. And you know I wouldn't go looking unless I was damned sure I'd find something. The way I did with Mrs. Hathaway.''

''Mrs. Hathaway wasn't dangerous. McDermott could be.''

''I'll be careful.'' He nudged her nose with his. ''Come on. What do you say? We could pretend to be Bonnie and Clyde. Without the machine guns.''

''Well...'' She was staring at his mouth as it moved closer to hers. ''I suppose if I can't stop you, I might as well join you. And hope I'll keep you out of trouble.''

Her last thought as she lost herself in his kiss was that there wasn't a woman who could keep such a man out of trouble.

Thanks to a heavy cloud cover that hovered over the entire peninsula, McDermott's house lay in shadows when Steve stopped the Land Rover a hundred feet from the property.

Sitting next to him, dressed in black from head to toe, Julia looked nervous but did her best to conceal it.

Steve glanced around him, glad he didn't have to worry about a lone motorist or two. ''This is it,'' he said, turning back to Julia. ''Wish me luck.''

''You mean wish us both luck, don't you?''

As she started to get out of the car, he clamped his hand on her wrist. ''Hold it, Bonnie. This is as far as you go.''

She was instantly rebellious. "Now, wait a minute. You said I could help."

"And you are. By staying in the car and timing me."

In the glow of the interior lights, her eyes flashed. "*Timing* you? What am I? Your running coach?"

He held back a smile. "Don't underestimate the small jobs, darling. Watching the clock could save my life." As she calmed down, he looked up at the house again. "I shouldn't be there more than thirty minutes. Hopefully there's no perimeter security system to worry about—"

"What if there is?"

He didn't bother to tell her that an alarm would complicate matters considerably and he'd cross that bridge when he came to it. "I'll run like the devil. Just keep the engine running."

Julia leaned against her seat. "This is madness. Why did I agree to it?"

"Because you know I'm right about this guy."

"I should have handcuffed you to the bed."

One corner of his mouth pulled up. "Mmm," he said, leaning toward her. "Why don't you hold that thought? It could be my reward for a job well done."

She glared at him. "What if you're not back in thirty minutes?"

Steve kissed her mouth. "Call Hammond," he said, one hand on the door handle. "His number is in the glove compartment."

It took him a little under five minutes to reach the entrance to McDermott's property. Praying he was right in assuming there was no perimeter security, he walked in and waited another five minutes in case his arrival had activated a silent alarm and somebody came running.

When all remained quiet, he let out a sigh of relief and

moved quickly across the terrace toward the cypress grove, following the tire tracks he had seen earlier.

"Hold it right there!"

The commanding tone followed by the cocking of a trigger brought Steve to a standstill.

"Your arms above your head."

Steve did as he was told.

"Turn around!"

As the area was suddenly inundated with light, Steve once again obeyed the order.

McDermott, fully dressed, stood in front of him, a twelve-gauge shotgun aimed at Steve's midriff.

Thirty

"Mr. Reyes." The shotgun remained steady as a rock. "Did you forget something?"

Steve took a moment to study his adversary. There was no doubt in his mind that McDermott would use the gun if he had to. The politeness he had displayed earlier was gone, replaced by a well-controlled but unmistakable anger.

"No," he said, trying not to sound concerned. "I was just curious about something."

"And what's that?"

Figuring there wasn't much point in lying, not with the barrel of a twelve-gauge staring back at him, Steve pointed his forehead toward the tracks in the ground. "I wanted to see where those led to."

McDermott gave the tracks a quick glance. "Why didn't you say something when you were here?"

"I didn't think you'd give me a guided tour."

"So you came back for a little reconnaissance work, is that it?" There was a deadly calm to McDermott's voice now. "You are either very brave or very stupid, Mr. Reyes."

"I'm just an ordinary man doing his job."

"And your job includes trespassing on other people's property in the middle of the night?"

Steve started to relax. Apparently there *had* been a silent alarm and the police were probably already on their way, which meant McDermott wouldn't shoot him. Maybe.

"Are you worried I'll find something incriminating?" he asked.

"You're the one who should be worried, Mr. Reyes. You're on *my* property, which means I can claim you threatened my life and shoot you in self-defense."

"Oh, come on, McDermott, stop the melodrama and put down the gun. As you can see, I'm not armed." Steve spread his arms wide. "You can frisk me if you like."

"Shut up and keep your hands up." McDermott glanced beyond Steve's shoulder, toward the cypress grove. "What exactly are you looking for, Mr. Reyes?"

"Your nephew."

The man's smile was scornful. "And you think you're going to find him over there? Hiding in the trees?"

"All I need to find is his car, and I'll know he's here."

McDermott gave a short laugh. "You reporters, you're all the same. You have a great imagination but very little common sense." As he spoke, he kept the shotgun trained on Steve. "If you had said something earlier, you could have saved yourself a trip." McDermott smiled, but the eyes remained cold. "Not to mention a lot of embarrassment."

Steve took a chance and lowered his hands, making sure he kept them in plain sight. "You mean you have an explanation for that third set of tracks?"

"Indeed I do. They belong to my butler's car. I sent Eanu downtown to buy several bags of fertilizer a couple of days ago and he unloaded them behind the greenhouse, by the back door."

Steve gave the guy credit. He was quick on his feet. "Then why do the tracks go all the way into the grove?"

McDermott's smile was more tolerant than annoyed.

"Eanu isn't the best driver in the world, Mr. Reyes. It's possible that in the fog, or the rain—I can't remember what the weather was like that day—he backed up a little too far. That's all. If—"

"Mr. McDermott?" Eanu, wearing a navy robe, stopped under the porch light and gave a slight start when he saw the shotgun. "I heard voices. Is everything all right?"

"Just fine, Eanu. Mr. Reyes was just leaving."

"Eanu," Steve said quickly, before McDermott could stop him. "Those bags of fertilizer you bought a couple of days ago—do you remember what day that was, exactly?"

Eanu's startled expression as he glanced at his employer was so brief Steve almost missed it. With a poise and sang-froid typical of well-trained butlers, however, he recovered quickly and gave a slight shake of his head. "No, sir, I don't."

They were lying, Steve thought. Both of them.

"Are you satisfied now, Mr. Reyes?" McDermott's tone was mildly condescending. "If you are, perhaps we could all get some sleep?"

Steve found himself glancing at the villa again, wondering if Ben was in there, watching him from a window. Or had his earlier visit prompted a hasty departure?

Maybe that's why McDermott was so damned smug. He knew Ben and the car were no longer here.

"The police will be arriving soon, Mr. Reyes. I'm being generous and letting you go, but if you'd rather stay and have me press charges, I will. It's entirely up to you."

Steve would have liked nothing more than to call his bluff. Hammond's threat, still fresh in his mind, was enough to make him reconsider, though. "I'm leaving."

"Thank you."

As he walked away, he could almost feel the gun barrel boring a hole into his back.

* * *

McDermott waited until Steve had disappeared from sight before lowering the shotgun and turning to his butler. "Eanu, we have to get rid of Ben's car."

Eanu's expression registered instant alarm. "Ben's car? He didn't take it with him?"

"No." Tucking the shotgun under his arm, Ian searched his pockets for Ben's keys.

"What happened to Ben?" Eanu insisted. "Where is he?"

"He's in trouble, and he's asked me to drive his car back to the college and leave it there."

"What kind of trouble?"

McDermott held back a curse. Eanu's persistence was beginning to get on his nerves, but he could hardly brush him off. It would only arouse more suspicions.

"A girl at the college claims Ben got her pregnant," he improvised quickly. "Ben denies it, but I think he's lying, so I thought it best to send him away for a while, to Italy, until things cool down. He's fine," he added when Eanu's frown deepened. "In fact," McDermott said with a laugh, "our boy is probably on Via Veneto right now, sipping a cappuccino and checking out the women."

At last, that seemed to make sense to the butler. Eanu smiled. "When do you want me to leave, sir?"

A cloud drifted across the sky, revealing a crescent moon. If Eanu left now it would still be dark when he arrived in Santa Barbara, and he wouldn't be noticed driving the car onto the college parking lot.

"As soon as we're finished with the police." He glanced at his watch. "They should be here shortly. From Santa Barbara you'll take a flight back to Monterey Airport. I prefer not to pick you up there, however, so take a bus to the market and call me from there. I'll come get you." He tossed him Ben's keys.

Eanu contemplated them for a moment, then, seemingly satisfied, he bowed. "Yes, Mr. McDermott."

"Oh," McDermott said casually. "And afterward wipe all fingerprints from the car, will you?" As Eanu began to show signs of alarm again, he added, "I wouldn't want either one of us being accused of helping Ben avoid his responsibilities to that girl should she be pregnant, after all." He gave Eanu a conspiratorial smile. "Even if that's exactly what we're doing."

Eanu bowed again and disappeared inside the house.

The wait was excruciating. Anxiety gnawed at Julia, slowly changing to cold fear as the minutes ticked away. She had seen the lights go on in the house and the yard and was imagining the worst.

The thought that Steve may have been caught had her chewing on her fingernails, something she had never done before. For a moment she had considered going to his rescue. But everything was so quiet up there, what if she fouled things up for him?

So she had decided to follow Steve's instructions and stay put.

Now, as she waited, she kept her eyes on the dash clock. When the thirty-minute mark was past, she cast another anxious glance up the hill.

Her hand was already on the phone when she saw him jog down the road. Within moments he was seated beside her. "It's about time," she said, her heart flooding with relief. "Another second and I was calling the cavalry."

Then, giddy at the thought that he was all right, she took his face between her hands and kissed him passionately. He returned the kiss instantly, and though his heart was definitely in it, the expression on his face told her that the little raid hadn't gone as hoped. "What happened?"

"I struck out."

"The car wasn't there?"

"I never had a chance to find out. There was a security system, after all. McDermott stopped me before I could reach the grove." Turning on the ignition, he glanced in the rearview mirror. "The bastard was gloating. He said he wouldn't tell the police about my visit and let me leave."

"Maybe he's telling the truth, Steve," she suggested gently. "I know you don't like to hear that, but—"

"He's not." Steve banged an angry fist against the steering wheel. "And that creepy butler of his is lying through his teeth, as well. They're both protecting Ben. Aw, shit."

"What?"

"The cops." He pointed toward a flashing red light down the road.

"I thought you said McDermott wouldn't tell them anything as long as you left."

"That won't stop the police from interrogating me if they see me on this road." Spinning the steering wheel, he turned onto a dirt road that led toward a dune. The mound wasn't quite high enough to completely hide the Land Rover, but in the dark, no one would notice.

No more than two minutes later, a police car sped by. Steve waited another minute before getting back onto the main road.

Julia heaved a sigh of relief. "That was close."

"Too close."

She sent him an uneasy glance. "What do we do now?"

"I've got to prove that McDermott is lying. Maybe Ben's girlfriend—ex-girlfriend, I should say—can help me do that."

"How?"

"She said she took McDermott's name from the phone bill. If she has that bill with her, she should be able to tell me the last time Ben called his uncle." He threw one last look in the rearview mirror. "I bet you anything it was a lot more recent than Easter."

After two calls to Kelly Sanders's home the following morning and getting only the Sanderses' answering machine, Julia suggested they put that task aside and forget about the case for a while. Her next cooking class was coming up and she needed a few supplies. Steve agreed to accompany her to the open-air market.

Rather than try to find a downtown parking space, they left the Land Rover at the museum lot and took a shortcut through the Presidio, which, at this early hour, was deserted.

"Well, I'll be damned," Steve said under his breath as they neared Artillery Street.

"What?" Julia followed his gaze. In a quiet section of adjoining Larkin Park, a tall man in a light gray suit and a Panama hat was talking to another, much smaller man. The tall man was so broad, not much could be seen of his companion except his hands, which kept moving excitedly as he talked. "You saw someone you know?" she asked.

Steve nodded toward the man in the Panama. "Not personally, but I know *of* him. His name is Aaron Briggs. He's the owner and publisher of the *San Francisco Star* and one of the most respected newsmen in the country. I heard he was covering Paul's murder himself, but I haven't seen him until now."

Julia slanted Steve an amused glance. He sounded almost as excited as Andrew had been when Steve had casually announced that he was a friend of Gary Sheffield. "You sound like quite a fan."

"I'm a *huge* fan. When I graduated from college, all I wanted to do was write for the *Star*."

"Why didn't you?"

Steve shrugged. "The *Star* wasn't as eager to hire me as I was to be hired, so I ended up at the *New York Sun* instead."

"Not too shabby."

"No." He continued to observe the man in the Panama. "I wonder why he's covering this story, though. He hasn't done that in years, not since Reagan was shot."

"Why don't you go and ask him?" Julia suggested, glad that for once, he had something else on his mind besides *Gleic Éire*. "Introduce yourself. Invite him to stop at The Hacienda for a drink if you want." She took the shopping basket from him and gave him a gentle push. "Go ahead. I can take care of the marketing by myself."

Steve didn't seem to have heard her. "Something about that man he's talking to is familiar, but I can't see enough of him to..."

He stopped in midsentence. As the famous publisher moved to the side and his companion was suddenly exposed, Steve jerked back. "Son of a bitch."

Thirty-One

"What is it?" Julia's head snapped around. "You look like you've seen a ghost."

"Don't you recognize the other man?"

Shielding her eyes with her hand, Julia squinted. "I can't see him. Briggs is in the way. Wait...now I..." She gasped. "Oh, my God, it's McDermott's butler!"

Steve's mind, usually so quick at grasping clues, was blank as his eyes remained fastened on the two men. There was no conceivable reason why a man like Aaron Briggs should be talking to McDermott's butler.

Unless...

Unless Briggs and McDermott were friends.

His mind shot into action. Bits and pieces of what he had learned eight years ago came back with vivid clarity. He remembered one particular night in Belfast. He had come to a pub where an old Irishman, a former member of the Irish Republican Army, had told him what he knew about *Gleic Éire.*

"The organization has been attracting new blood," the Irishman had told him over a pint of dark ale. "*Rich* new blood. The word in the street is that a small group of wealthy Irish Americans living in the United States is financing *Gleic Éire*'s reign of terror."

For a while, speculation as to the identity of those men had run rampant. Names like Curtiss O'Rourke, head of the

Irish American Cultural Society in New York City, had been mentioned. And so had the names of John Mahonney, a respected Chicago judge and Sean Clark, the owner of Clark Department Stores. All three men were immensely wealthy and outspoken about their political beliefs. They had also kept strong ties with their native country.

The rumors regarding their possible involvement with the extremist group had ended when Judge Mahonney threatened to sue every newspaper and television station that ever mentioned his name and *Gleic Éire* in the same sentence again.

McDermott and Briggs. Why not? Steve thought as Julia pressed him for answers. There was enough money between those two to feed a third world nation for several decades. Both were of Irish descent. And while that in itself didn't prove anything, there was the nagging little fact that Briggs, who never covered stories anymore, had come to Monterey not when Paul Bradshaw was murdered but immediately following Eli Seavers's death.

Julia tugged impatiently at his sleeve. "Steve, for God's sake, talk to me. Why is Eanu so upset? And what is he doing talking to the publisher of the *San Francisco Star?*"

Realizing they were in plain sight, Steve pulled her back behind a tree. "That's what I'd like to know."

He glanced at the two men again. Whatever Eanu was saying was having a profound effect on the publisher, who kept his head bowed and his index finger curled around his mouth as he listened.

Finally, Briggs nodded, said a few words that seemed to appease Eanu, and walked away in the direction of the conference center.

Looking calmer now, Eanu reached into his pants pocket, pulled out a handful of change and headed for a public phone a short distance away.

Steve took Julia's hand. "Come on. Let's go say hello."

Eanu was getting ready to insert the first quarter into the slot when Steve lay a hand on his shoulder. "Hello, Eanu."

The butler's first reaction when he saw Steve was one of utter shock, then fear. For a second or two, he seemed unable to move, as stunned as Steve had been a moment ago. Suddenly, he bolted.

Expecting him to do just that, Steve wasn't surprised. He took off after him and caught him easily. "You're not being very neighborly, Eanu. What's the matter? Am I catching you at a bad time?"

"Yes, you are. Please let me go, Mr. Reyes." Eanu struggled to release his arm from Steve's hold. "I have errands to run."

"Why are you trying to avoid me?"

"I'm not...I'm in a hurry."

Steve glanced in the distance, but Briggs had long since disappeared. "You didn't seem in such a hurry a few minutes ago, when you were talking to Aaron Briggs. That *was* him, wasn't it?"

Eanu shook his head. "I don't know what you're talking about."

As Eanu continued to struggle, a narrow folder that had been sticking out of the man's shirt pocket fell to the ground. Before the butler could bend down to retrieve it, Steve had already picked it up.

It was the stub from an airline ticket.

Without formalities, Steve thumbed through it. "Santa Barbara," he said, watching the butler become even more agitated. "What could you possibly have been doing in Santa Barbara, Eanu?"

"That's none of your business."

"And why only a return ticket?" Steve added relentlessly. "How did you get to Santa Barbara? With Ben's car, maybe?"

Steve felt Julia's hand on his arm. "Steve, take it easy. He's frightened."

As if spurred by Julia's words of compassion, Eanu suddenly turned hostile. "I don't have to talk to you," he said, glaring at Steve. "You're not my employer."

Certain the little man would try to slip away again if he gave him the chance, Steve didn't release his hold. "Would you prefer to talk to the police, Eanu? Or perhaps the FBI?"

The terrified look in Eanu's eyes was the only answer Steve needed. The man had the word *guilty* written all over his face. Making him talk would be a cinch, but this was a public place and anytime now someone was bound to intervene.

Without loosening his grip, Steve took out his cell phone and dialed the police station.

"Detective Hammond, please," he said to the desk sergeant who answered. When the detective came on the line, Steve was brisk and to the point. "I'm on Eddie Burns Street," he said briskly. "Right by Larkin Park. And I have someone here you'll want to question."

"What the hell are you up to now, Reyes?" Hammond's voice simmered with anger.

"I ran into McDermott's butler—"

Hammond let out an oath.

Steve let it fly over his head. "Trust me on this, Hank, okay? I promise you won't regret it."

Breaking Eanu hadn't been as easy as Julia had expected. But once again, Detective Hammond, who had allowed her and Steve to listen to the questioning from another room, turned out to be a superb interrogator, playing the butler like a violin, confusing him by being sympathetic one moment, quick and sharp the next.

But it wasn't until an hour later, when Hammond had promised the immigrant immunity instead of deportation, that Eanu finally cracked.

Watching and listening from behind a double-sided mirror, Julia and Steve heard Eanu tell Hammond how, at his boss's request, he had driven Ben's car from McDermott's house, where it had been hidden in the cypress grove, to SBC. Also at McDermott's request, Eanu had wiped all fingerprints from the car.

"What do you know," Steve muttered under his breath. "I was wrong, after all. McDermott wasn't hiding Ben. The bastard killed him."

At the question, "Do you know where Ben Rosenthal is?" Eanu only shook his head, but it was obvious by his worried expression that he, too, feared the worst.

With a little more coaxing, Eanu also admitted that Aaron Briggs and McDermott had been friends for a long time and that the publisher was a frequent visitor at the Point Cobra house. Sometimes he came alone and sometimes he came with the others.

"What were you doing with Aaron Briggs?" Hammond asked.

"I was worried about Ben," Eanu answered. "So when I returned from Santa Barbara, I called Mr. Briggs at his hotel and asked him to meet me at Larkin Park. I was hoping he could talk to Mr. McDermott and find out where Ben was."

"Why were you worried? Don't you believe Ben is in Italy?"

Eanu lowered his gaze, as if doubting his employer pained him. "No," he whispered.

Hammond bobbed his head a few times. "Tell me about the others," he said. "Who are they?"

The three people Eanu named were some of the wealthiest, most prominent men in the country. The moment Eanu had named them, Hammond turned to the officer who stood by the door and snapped his fingers.

"Gardner, I want you and Brown to go to Point Cobra and arrest Ian McDermott. Take backup and be careful. The man is armed and dangerous."

"Yes, sir."

From the front room where he and Julia had returned, Steve watched Gardner and four other officers take off at a dead run. This was it, he thought, his chest so tight it hurt to breathe. This was the moment he had been waiting for, the moment he had imagined and replayed in his mind a hundred times during that first year following Sheila's death.

And now that it was finally here, he felt nothing other than a deep satisfaction. The rage and need to kill that had lived with him all those years were gone. All he wanted now was for McDermott and his nasty little group to stand trial.

A jury would do the rest.

Hammond came out of the interrogation room, looking no less rumpled or tired than he had an hour earlier. "You know who Spencer Flynn is, don't you?" Steve asked.

Hammond nodded. "The head of the security firm hired to protect Patrick O'Donnell when he visits Chicago next month."

Julia looked from one man to the other. "Who is Patrick O'Donnell?"

"The leader of the Ulster Unionist Party," Steve explained. "He's the man responsible for bringing Great Britain and Northern Ireland to the bargaining table. *Gleic Éire* hates him with a passion. They've had a death sentence on him ever since he came up with his peace agreement, but he's so well guarded, no one has been able to get near him."

"How did Spencer Flynn get hired to protect him?"

Hammond gave a short laugh. "Easy. Flynn International is the best security company in existence. Over the last twenty years, they have guarded some of the world's most controversial heads of state and never had a mishap."

Walking over to his desk, Hammond picked up the phone. "Gary," he said when the desk sergeant answered. "Get me Scotland Yard on the phone, will you?"

After hanging up, he turned to Steve. "You want to stick around until McDermott arrives?" One of his rare smiles worked its way to his mouth. "After the hard time I gave you, you've earned a little gloating."

Watching a defeated McDermott walk into a police station was something Steve couldn't quite pass up. He looked at Julia. "You mind?"

Wrapping her arm around his waist, she shook her head. "Not at all. And I agree with Detective Hammond. You deserve a little gloating."

No one was sure who leaked the story to the press. Moments after the two squad cars sped away, a mob of reporters and people from nearby towns had descended on the police station, clamoring for details.

His famous composure intact, the chief of police himself came and tried to calm the crowd. It was no use. The moment they heard he couldn't say anything until he'd had a chance to talk to McDermott, the cacophony began again, louder than before.

As the public waited for the five officers and their infamous prisoner to return, barricades were erected to contain the crowd, and armed officers were positioned at various points to provide McDermott safe entry into the building.

Thirty-five minutes later, the wait was over. When the first squad car pulled up to the curb and McDermott stepped out, the crowd went wild, booing and throwing insults at him from every direction.

As cameras flashed, McDermott remained the picture of calm. His hands cuffed in front of him, he paused for a long second and gazed at the crowd in a slow sweeping motion that had some people stepping back. Then, as one of the officers who was escorting him gave him a nudge, he resumed walking.

At the top of the stairs, where Steve and Julia stood next to Hammond and Chief Browning, McDermott stopped again, this time in front of Steve.

Steve returned the man's expressionless stare without flinching. "You should have killed me when you had the chance, McDermott."

The Irishman didn't answer, yet there was an unmistakable tension in the air, one that everyone seemed to sense. In the sudden silence only the constant whirr of cameras could be heard.

As if aware that this scene would be played and replayed dozens of times by the media, McDermott made the most of it, taking his time studying his enemy's features with a composure that was mind-boggling.

Suddenly, McDermott leaned forward, his bottomless eyes gleaming briefly. "We're not finished yet, Reyes," he whispered.

Then, as quickly as it had appeared, the flame was gone and McDermott's eyes went flat again.

"All right," the chief said tersely. "Get him inside."

As the captured terrorist was led into the station, pandemonium broke once again. One reporter, a little more aggressive than the others, forced his way through the barricades and was immediately followed by a wave of people.

Taking advantage of the confusion, Steve took Julia's arm and quickly led her away.

They hadn't been able to extract one small morsel of information from McDermott. Not with threats, not by playing back Eanu's taped confession and not with promises of a plea bargain.

Aaron Briggs, on the other hand, hadn't been so stoic. When he was arrested in his hotel suite at the Monterey Plaza Hotel, the publisher's first words, "I want to see my attorney," had brought a sigh of relief from everyone, including FBI Agents Braddock and Norfield.

As Briggs and McDermott were being questioned, field agents in Chicago, New Orleans and Minneapolis were arresting the other three men. Spencer Flynn, apparently tipped off, was apprehended at O'Hare Airport as he prepared to board a plane for Zurich.

Except for McDermott, who still wasn't talking, all four men vehemently denied having killed Paul Bradshaw. Or knowing the whereabouts of Ben Rosenthal, whose flight to Rome had never taken place. They did admit, however, that McDermott had sent Ben to The Hacienda to look for the missing tape. The college student had disappeared shortly after that.

Briggs, who was, by his own admission, second in command to McDermott, had also told them that the decision to kill Eli Seavers, whom they knew as J. C. Spivak, had been unanimous. When asked if they had also been planning to kill the head of the Ulster Unionist Party during his U.S. visit, all four men remained as closemouthed as their leader.

Several hours after the multiple arrests, Julia and Steve were cuddled on the sofa, watching the latest developments on television. An FBI forensic team had been sent to McDermott's house where they'd found traces of blood on the recently scrubbed greenhouse floor. Though it was suspected the blood belonged to Ben Rosenthal, it would be several days before DNA tests could be completed.

The bureau had also discovered an underground vault with enough explosives hidden in it to blow up the entire Monterey peninsula. Tucked in a folder was a detailed map of the Barclay Hotel in Chicago, where Patrick O'Donnell and his entourage were scheduled to stay.

Written in a small notebook, FBI agents had found the name J. C. Spivak and a phone number that had been disconnected long ago. According to an entry in the book, Spivak had not only acted as *Gleic Éire*'s arms negotiator, but had also masterminded several bombings for the terrorist group. One of them was the 1990 incident that had killed Sheila Bradshaw.

"Now I know why Eli reacted the way he did when he heard the name Bradshaw on television," Julia said as she kept watching the broadcast. "Somehow, in spite of his illness, the name awakened memories of what he had done." She paused. "Perhaps even regrets."

Steve nodded. "That would explain his warning to you."

She turned to look at Steve. "What about Ben? Will we ever know what happened to him?"

"Not unless McDermott decides to talk," Steve replied. "And it doesn't appear as if he'll be doing that anytime soon."

Julia wrapped her arms around him and held on tight. "He threatened you, didn't he?"

Steve kissed the top of her head. "He's in no position to threaten me."

"Being behind bars doesn't make him any less of a threat. He has a huge network, Steve—people who must be itching to get back at you. The lack of funds alone could put an end to *Gleic Éire*'s activities. They can't be too happy about that."

He gave her a gentle shake. "Will you stop worrying? This is a joyful day. I want no brooding."

She studied his strong, tanned hands, those hands that had driven her to the brink of ecstasy and then beyond. She tried not to think of what her life would be like after he was gone. She didn't want him to leave, but she had to be realistic. His job here was finished. In a few days, he would pack his bag and return to his life, and she would return to hers.

On the screen, the news had turned to another local event—Edith Donnovan's bail hearing.

Behind her, Steve made a disapproving sound with his tongue. Julia knew why he was annoyed. He had never believed that Edith Donnovan killed Paul. He still didn't. And since finding Paul's killer was the reason he had come to Monterey, was it possible, she wondered, that he might stay a little while longer? Until he *had* found the real killer?

"You still don't think Edith killed Paul, do you?" she asked.

"Nope. And I'm not leaving here until I find out who did."

Julia smiled and sank deeper into his arms.

Thirty-Two

The announcement that the alleged leaders of *Gleic Éire* had been arrested and that a reporter by the name of Steve Reyes was responsible for their capture was the lead story of every television newscast in the country.

Suddenly, everyone wanted to know who Steve was, what he had been doing before coming to Monterey and if he was available for interviews. Tim had already called with requests to appear on "60 Minutes," "20/20" and "Good Morning America."

The thought of so much publicity made Steve cringe. If it hadn't been for Julia, he would have returned to Florida with as little fanfare as possible and tried to put the whole mess behind him. But Julia was very much on his mind these days, even more so now that his reason for coming to Monterey was behind bars.

And so, on this warm, breezy day, as the sun rose over the mountains, he had gone to the only place that could guarantee him a few minutes' peace—Sheila's grave.

His flowers, probably long wilted by now, had been replaced by an elaborate arrangement of calla lilies that was as formal and stiff as the man he knew had put them there.

He crouched down and let his hands hang between his knees. "I got him, Shel. You and the baby can rest in peace now." Even though he had never believed in supernatural experiences, he looked up toward the heavens as if seeking a sign from her. When none came, he returned his gaze to the headstone. In the bright sunlight, Sheila's name seemed to glimmer.

"I met someone, Shel," he said softly. "I never thought I would. And I sure never believed I'd ever fall in love again, but I did." He swallowed. "I thought you should know. Or maybe...I just needed to hear myself say it."

The only answer came from fifty feet below, where the raging waves met the centuries-old rocks.

"I was thinking of asking her to marry me, but I'm not sure it's the right thing to do. It's a big step. For me and for her. I don't even know if she'd accept."

As a gust of wind rustled through the almond tree, a blossom fluttered down and came to rest on the grave, inches from Steve. He picked it up and looked toward the sky again. Then, smiling, he brought the blossom to his mouth before laying it back on the stone.

After a while, he stood up and said a silent farewell to Sheila.

This time he knew he wouldn't be back.

"You again!"

Exasperated to find Ron Kendricks standing on her doorstep, Julia tried to slam the door shut, but the annoying reporter had already wedged his foot in the opening.

"Hello, Mrs. Bradshaw."

"What is it going to take for you to understand you're not welcome here?"

Unfazed, he glanced over her shoulder. "Where's your watchdog?"

"I'm alone," she snapped. "But don't let that go to your head, Kendricks. I'm not defenseless, you know. Even you should know that by now."

He didn't seem to have heard her. Or if he did, he didn't

care. "Collecting his laurels, is he?" he said sarcastically. "The man of the hour. Everybody's hero." He made a face. "What bullshit."

As Julia tried to push his foot out of the way, he leaned against the door and gave a hard shove. "Aren't you going to invite me in?"

Disgusted, Julia threw her hands up in the air. "That's it. I'm calling the police."

But before she could even take one step, Kendricks grabbed her arm and pulled her back. "Not so fast, blondie. I haven't told you why I'm here yet."

At the stench of booze on his breath, Julia winced. "You're drunk."

"Yeah, well, not much else for me to do now that I've been fired."

She hadn't heard about that and immediately felt sorry for him, which she knew was stupid. He hadn't felt sorry for her a few days ago, or for Andrew. All he'd been interested in was money. "Knowing you, I'm sure you brought that on yourself," she said, trying to sound detached.

He hiccuped. "Is that all the sympathy I get? No 'gee I'm sorry, Ronny'?"

Her compassion was quickly evaporating. "I had nothing to do with you getting fired, Kendricks."

"Don't you want to know who did?"

"No. Now let me go or—"

"Charles Bradshaw. Yeah, that's right, your ex-daddy-in-law-turned-Sir Galahad heard I tried to take your picture the other night and called my publisher." He finally let go of her arm, swaying a little as he started to lose his balance. "Can you believe the nerve of some people, thinking they can play God?"

"I didn't tell him about the photo, if that's what you're thinking."

"Then who did?"

"Not Steve," she said quickly, afraid he'd go after him next. "The two of them don't even talk."

"I know." His gaze was heavy with an innuendo she didn't understand. "You want to know why they don't talk?"

"I know why."

"Wrong, blondie. You *think* you know." His laugh sounded like a cackle. "The truth is those two have a looong history together." He dragged out the word as if it held some special meaning.

"You're babbling, Kendricks," she said irritably. "Do yourself a favor and go sleep it off somewhere."

He cocked his head to the side. "What? And miss the chance to get back at Reyes for what he did to me the other night?" He shook his head drunkenly. "No way, José."

He leaned forward, squinting a little as he tried to focus. "You see, I did a little checking on your knight in shining armor. And I found out that he's a little tarnished around the edges."

"I'm not interested in hearing your lies."

"Really?" He waited a beat. "Not even if I told you Steve Reyes was once engaged to Sheila Bradshaw? And that she was expecting his child when she died?"

Julia grabbed at the wall in shock. It wasn't true, she told herself. A vicious lie. Kendricks was a small, petty man who would do anything to get back at Steve for humiliating him. He had said so himself.

"You're lying." But her voice was suddenly weak, betraying her doubts.

He hiccuped again. "I wouldn't make up something like that. Not when it can be so easily verified."

"By whom?" she scoffed. "The same phony sources you use for the garbage you write?"

"My sources are as legitimate as any," Kendricks replied, sounding mildly offended. "You can check this one yourself by calling Sergeant Bruno Cavalieri of the NYPD."

"Your sergeant Cavalieri is misinformed. Steve never met any of the Bradshaws until he arrived in Monterey three weeks ago."

The reporter gave her a long knowing look. "You're the one who's misinformed, Julia. Reyes knew them all—Charles, Sheila, even Paul."

She shook her head, slowly, repeatedly. Steve would have told her, she thought. He wouldn't have lied about something as important as this.

"The reason you or anyone else in this town never heard a word about it," Kendricks continued as if he had read her thoughts, "is because old man Bradshaw immediately put a lid on the story, pregnancy included."

"How would they even know Sheila was pregnant? There was no autopsy."

Kendricks's smile turned smug. "That's true, but Sheila went to see a doctor the week before she died, and the doctor confirmed the pregnancy."

"I don't believe a word of it." But Julia knew from the sick feeling inside her stomach that the seeds of doubt had already been planted.

All of a sudden, she remembered that morning outside Luther's office when Steve and Charles had exchanged those harsh words in front of a television camera. Even Frank had wondered if the two men had known each other, which, of course, Steve had denied. She hadn't thought anything of it at the time, but now…

As Kendricks continued to watch her, his eyes filled with

mirth. ''Believe it, sweetheart. Wonder boy is a big fat liar.''

He burst into wild laughter as though he found the remark hysterically funny. ''Bet he also didn't tell you he hasn't worked for the *Sun* in seven years, that he agreed to come to Monterey for only one reason—to catch the men who had killed his precious Sheila.''

''You're lying.'' But this time Julia couldn't muster any kind of conviction as she murmured the words.

''He used you, Julia,'' Kendricks said, his eyes gleaming with malice. ''He never gave a damn if you were guilty or innocent. All he wanted was to avenge the death of the woman he loved. And the child he lost. That's why he came to Monterey. And that's why he booked a room at The Hacienda. So he could be close to you and pump you for information—about Paul, about Eli Seavers, about whomever would lead him to Sheila's killer.''

He cackled again, looking pleased with himself. ''But don't take my word for it. Talk to Charles the Great. He'll set you straight, especially once you tell him you're screwing the guy.''

The words hit her like a slap in the face, which was exactly what Kendricks, even drunk as he was, had intended.

''Well, I guess I've done my good deed for the day.'' Kendricks pulled himself erect. ''I think I'll go and celebrate. You call if you change your mind about the two of us doing that book, okay? That new romantic chapter in your life should be worth at least another mil.''

Moving with the exaggerated slowness of the drunk, the reporter walked away.

Slowly, Julia closed the door and immediately leaned her forehead against it. He was lying. Or if he wasn't, someone else was lying.

She didn't move until she heard Kendricks's car leave. Then, pushing back the tears that threatened to erupt, she walked into the kitchen and scooped up her keys from the desk.

Only one man could put her mind at rest.

His face paler than usual, his eyes fastened to hers, Charles listened as Julia told him, word for word, what she had learned from Ron Kendricks.

When she was finished, he pressed the back of his head against the chair's rich brown leather and closed his eyes.

Julia's stomach took a nosedive. He should have been angry, outraged. He should have threatened to strangle the bastard who was spreading such ridiculous rumors about his dead daughter. Instead, he just sat there, his jaw set, while Julia's heart broke.

"Charles...did you hear me?"

Slowly, he reopened his eyes, rested them on her. "Are you in love with Steve Reyes?" he asked.

The unexpected question startled her. For a moment she was tempted to tell him her answer was of no importance and was her business only. But under his sudden scrutiny, she could only offer a small sigh of surrender. "Yes."

The admission astounded her, not so much because she had finally admitted it to herself, but because she had admitted it to a man she still wasn't sure knew what true love really was.

"Ah." Charles rested his elbows on the armrests and propped his fingers in a steeple, tapping them gently against his chin. "That complicates things."

Julia's stomach churned. "Then it's true," she said with another sinking feeling in her stomach. "Everything I said."

"It's true." He frowned. "Reyes didn't tell you?"

"No." She pressed her hand against her chest as if to stop the pounding of her heart. The wild beating continued. "How...how long had they known each other?" she managed to ask.

"Not long. Three months."

"Kendricks said you didn't want anyone to know about their relationship." The reasoning behind that escaped her totally. "Is that true?"

"Yes."

"But why? What difference—"

"Because I was angry!" His hands came down to slap the armrests and he jumped out of his chair like a shot. "Angry that she would throw her life away over the first man she met, a man she hardly knew." He took a deep breath, as if readying himself to say something he knew would be unpleasant. "A Cuban," he said at last.

Julia sat in stunned silence. Discrimination wasn't a flaw she would have associated with the popular ex-governor. Charles Bradshaw had spent the last forty years donating money so the less privileged, many of whom were immigrants from Central America, could have a better life. In office, he had campaigned for higher wages and better living conditions, and in return the Hispanic population had supported him wholeheartedly, chanting his name at political rallies, pushing and shoving for the chance to touch his hand and thank him personally. But sincere though he had been, Charles had apparently drawn the line at a Cuban exile marrying his daughter.

He moved over to the window and was silent for a moment. Behind him, his interlaced fingers, as restless as the rest of him, kept closing and opening.

When he spoke again, his voice was calmer. "When Sheila called me from New York to say she had met a man and planned to marry him, I thought it was just a case of a young girl's infatuation. It'll pass, I told myself. When I realized she was serious, I tried to reason with her. I told her she was too young, too impulsive.

"She only laughed at me and reminded me she was twenty-one and knew what she was doing. Because I didn't want to hear any more, the conversation ended right there. A few weeks later, she called back with more shocking news. She was pregnant. This time I was furious. I told her she knew nothing about Steve Reyes other than he was some hotshot reporter. For all she knew he could be after her money."

"Steve doesn't care about money," Julia snapped, then shut up. Why was she defending him? A man who had betrayed her, used her?

"I know that now." Charles gave a short, sad laugh and turned around to face her. "Believe me, I've crammed a lifetime of learning into a few short days.

"I gave her an ultimatum," he continued in that flat, monotonous tone that was so uncharacteristic of him. "I told her to come home or I would disown her."

"Oh, Charles." The thought that a parent could turn away from his child, for any reason, was beyond Julia's comprehension.

At the disapproving tone of her voice, Charles bobbed his head a few times. "I know, it was the wrong thing to say. And I paid dearly for it." He looked off in the distance. "A few days later, she was dead."

His pain was so evident that Julia felt an involuntary tightening of her chest. "I'm sorry, Charles."

"Don't be. I brought every agonizing minute of my grief on myself. I should have never attacked the man she loved. In doing so, I alienated her completely." His head high, he met Julia's gaze. "I may have been a successful politician, but as a father, I was a total failure. I loved my children but didn't know how to show it, at least not in the way they expected. I wanted them to succeed, but instead I stifled them, forcing one to leave home and making it impossible for the other to be anything but what *I* wanted him to be."

Walking over to the mantel, he raised his fingers to touch a framed photograph of a beautiful, happy, smiling Sheila. "I couldn't even do the right thing at her funeral."

"What do you mean?" Julia asked in a whisper.

"Steve came to the cemetery, as I knew he would. So I asked Garrett to put a couple of uniforms at the gates. When Steve showed up, they escorted him out."

Somehow Julia couldn't quite conjure up the image of Steve being quietly led away. "And he let them do it?"

"He did it for Sheila, so her burial wouldn't turn into a circus. I knew that, too, and took advantage of it." He continued to look at his daughter's picture. "He loved her better than I ever did," he murmured.

And still does, Julia thought, feeling miserable. Otherwise he would have told her the truth. Her vision blurred as tears welled up in her eyes.

Letting go of Sheila's picture at last, Charles turned around. "What is it about that man that two Bradshaw women should fall so hopelessly in love with him?"

Julia realized, not without a certain jolt, that this was the first time he had ever thought of her as a Bradshaw.

He must have realized it, too, because his gaze suddenly softened. "Perhaps," he said gently, "if you talked to him, tried to square things away..."

"Oh, I'll talk to him, Charles. You can count on that."

She wasn't looking forward to going home. She wasn't even sure what she would say to Steve when she got there, or what his reaction would be. Would he admit the truth? Or would he lie? He would choose the latter, she decided. For some people, lying was always the easiest road to take.

And Steve was so good at it.

Thirty-Three

At the angry pounding on his bedroom door, Steve rose from his desk and went to answer it. Julia, her eyes blazing, stormed past him.

"When were you going to tell me?"

He didn't need to ask what she was talking about. One look at her face, a livid contrast with the red-hot anger in her eyes, and he knew the truth had finally found its way home. Somehow. "How did you hear?"

"Does it matter?"

"No, but I would have preferred to tell you myself."

She snorted in disdain. "Then why didn't you?"

"I wasn't ready," he said lamely.

"So you lied." Coming to stand in front of him, she gave him the full brunt of her anger. "You led me to believe that the only reason you came to Monterey was to investigate my ex-husband's murder—"

"I did."

"Oh, stop it. I'm not stupid. A little gullible maybe, as you pointed out not too long ago, but not stupid. You came here for only one reason—to look for the men who killed Sheila. You came to seek revenge on McDermott and his little group of fanatics." She was nearly out of breath but managed to fire one more shot. "And you used me to do it."

Beneath the rage he saw the pain, and it ripped him apart

to see her suffer like that, all because of him. Hoping to soothe her, at least long enough to explain, he reached out to her. When his fingertips touched her arm, she jerked back as if she had been burned.

"Don't touch me!"

He withdrew his hand. "I never meant to hurt you, Julia." Suddenly, he was terrified of losing her.

"Really?" She raised a defiant chin. "Is that why you went to McDermott's house the other night, unarmed, knowing damned well he could kill you? Did you take a moment to think of what it would do to me if something happened to you?" The green eyes, so fiery a second ago, turned to frost. "Did it even matter?

"You don't have an answer, do you?" she asked when he remained silent. "And you know why?" She walked slowly toward him, stopping only inches from where he stood. "Because at that moment, nothing mattered but Sheila."

"Sheila is dead."

"No, she's not. You proved it the other night when you risked your life to avenge her death."

"I wanted a killer to get his dues."

"You wanted *Sheila's* killer to get his dues!"

"Stop throwing Sheila in my face!" As Julia started to turn away, he gripped her shoulders and whipped her around. "It's you I love, dammit." Then, in a lower voice, he stated, "Only you. If you've ever believed anything, you must believe this."

She squirmed to get free. "I stopped believing in fairy tales a long time ago." The bitterness in her voice took another nip out of his heart. "These days I only believe in facts. Fact number one, and by far the most difficult to get past, is that you lied to me."

"I was going to tell you, in time, in my own way."

"Fact number two, you used me. You took advantage of my feelings for you and pumped me for information, and I was too stupid to see it."

"I was trying to clear you of a murder charge."

"Fact number three," she continued relentlessly, "you suspected me of having killed my ex-husband." Her tone turned sarcastic. "Did you also think that perhaps *I* was the leader of *Gleic Éire?* That wouldn't be such a ridiculous assumption, would it, Steve? Not when you already thought of me as a killer."

"I never thought of you as a killer. Yes, I was suspicious at first, and I suppose that doesn't make me any better than the rest of the people in this town, except they should have known better. They knew you, I didn't."

Looking suddenly bone tired, Julia took a step back. "I'm not going to be swayed by your lies," she said. "Or charmed. Ever again." She took a deep breath. "I want you to pack your things and leave."

"Julia, listen to me." He gripped her shoulders and held her still. "I'm sorry I didn't tell you the truth. I didn't know how, but you're right, that's no excuse. I didn't mean to deceive you, darling. I kept silent because what happened to Sheila was part of my past, just as Paul's abuse was part of your past."

"I told you all about that! I bared my soul to you."

"Because the time was right." He shook her gently so she would meet his eyes. "How many people know what Paul did to you? How many did you tell? And I'm not counting that doctor you saw in Santa Cruz."

Stubbornly, she looked away.

Another shake. "How many?"

She sighed. "My mother," she said reluctantly. "You, and now Charles."

"Not Penny? Or Frank?"

She shook her head and refused to meet his gaze.

"Why was that?" he persisted.

She didn't answer.

"I'll tell you why," he said quietly. "Because that period of your life was so painful and so private that you couldn't bring yourself to talk about it, not even to your two closest friends. Am I right?"

"Let me go," was the only reply she could manage.

"You know I'm right, Julia, so why is it so difficult for you to understand I would feel the same way?"

"Because withholding the truth about what Paul did to me didn't hurt anyone, but withholding the truth about you and Sheila hurt me."

His right hand let go of her shoulder and came up to cup her cheek. "I'm sorry I hurt you. That's the last thing I wanted." When the silence between them became too painful, he added, "I love you, Julia. Just give me a chance to prove it."

The words seemed to have the effect of an ice-cold shower. She pulled back. "That's what Paul used to say," she murmured. "I made the mistake of believing him, but I won't make that mistake again."

"Dammit, Julia, I'm not Paul!" he shouted. "Can't you get that through your head?"

"You had your chance," she said, walking over to the door and opening it. "You blew it." One hand on the knob, she turned around. "I'm going to Penny's. Please be gone by the time I get back."

Then, without another look, she left.

"I am the law! You are under arrest!"

At the sound of the deep, commanding voice, Coop almost dropped his coffee cup. "What the heck—" he began as he whipped around.

Andrew threw his head back and laughed hysterically as he jabbed his finger at his twelve-inch toy robot. "That was Mighty Zokor talking, Grandpa. Scared you, huh?"

Coop puffed up his chest. "Nothing scares a green beret, kiddo. We're too tough."

Coffee cup in hand, Coop approached the card table where Zokor, complete with a space weapon firmly anchored in his hand, a red iridescent light in his helmet and a missile launcher strapped to his back, stood, looking invincible and fearless. Scattered over the table were a half-dozen microcassettes, each no larger than a pat of butter.

"Zokor is tougher than anyone, Grandpa," Andrew said proudly. "He can shoot a grenade by just touching his belt buckle." Eager to demonstrate, he pressed a button and a grenade the size of a small olive shot across the room.

"And he can walk through fire, bullets and enemy missiles." Andrew pushed another button and Zokor began walking in slow, rigid steps, issuing a series of commands.

"Hmm," Coop murmured. "No wonder they call him mighty." He pointed at the cassettes. "And what are those?"

"Six of Zokor's adventures." He opened a small flap in the robot's back, took one of the cassettes from the table and inserted it into a slot. "Each tape is ten minutes long and tells a different story," Andrew explained. "This one is called 'Zokor Fights the Invaders.' It's my favorite."

He lowered his head, looking suddenly sad.

"What is it, kiddo?" Coop asked gently.

Andrew started pushing the cassettes around and around on the table in a random pattern. "My dad gave me Zokor, and he had promised we would listen to some of the tapes together, but then he died."

Coop's heart lodged in his throat. This ache in Andrew's heart must have been what Jordan had experienced when

Coop had left him. "I tell you what," he said, his voice hoarse with emotion. "Why don't you and I listen to your favorite tape? Right now."

Andrew's face brightened. "You mean it, Grandpa?"

Coop laughed. "Only if you promise to hit the sack right after that."

"I promise."

"I feel so stupid," Julia said, wiping her eyes with the back of her hands. "Crying over a man. I can't even remember the last time I did that."

"That's because few men in this world are worth crying over," Penny said wisely. Removing a copy of the Monterey *Herald* from Frank's chair, she sat down, facing Julia. "But Steve is different, and in my opinion, worth crying over." She lowered her head in an attempt to look at Julia's eyes. "And maybe worth forgiving?"

Julia sniffed. "You always did have a soft heart."

"Oh, and you don't?" Penny scoffed. "Come on, now. Who are you kidding? Forgiveness is your middle name."

"Not this time."

"Why not?"

"He lied to me, Penny. Repeatedly. One lie after another, without as much as batting an eyelid. How can I ever trust him again?"

"You could start by putting yourself in his place, seeing his side and understanding why he did what he did. Sheila is his past," she continued gently. "You're his future. Why can't you focus on that instead of letting a creep like Kendricks destroy the best thing that ever happened to you?"

The ringing of Julia's cellular gave her a little start. Reaching inside her purse, she pulled out the phone and unfolded it. "Hello?"

"Hi, Mom!"

Andrew's cheery voice nearly brought another flood of tears. How was she going to tell him that Steve had moved out of The Hacienda and would probably be returning to Florida in the morning?

"How are you doing, sport?"

"Great," Andrew said excitedly. "I saw a condor, Mom! He flew right over me. And tonight, we cooked hamburgers outside."

"We?" Julia teased. "Meaning you helped with the cooking? That's a first."

"Grandpa says a good soldier has to learn to do everything."

"Did he also tell you that good soldiers go to bed when they're supposed to and it's well past *your* bedtime?"

She heard him giggle. "That's because we listened to some of Zokor's tapes. We even found another tape," he said excitedly. "It was stuck way under the battery pack."

"Another tape? That's funny. I thought Zokor came with only six tapes. What is this one about?"

"I don't know. We tried to play it but it wouldn't fit into the slot like the others."

"Have your grandfather take a look at it," Julia said, remembering how Coop loved to tinker with things. "I'm sure he can figure out what's wrong."

"He already tried, but it won't work. He says it's a smidgen too big."

Julia heard Andrew yawn. "Okay, sweetie, that's it for you. Blow me a kiss and go to bed. Tomorrow is a big day. You're coming home, you know."

"Yeah. Grandpa told me about Steve catching all those bad guys." His voice filled with pride. "He's cool, huh?"

"Yes, darling," she said, unable to spoil his happiness by giving him the bad news. "He's very cool."

After Julia hung up, she folded the phone and dropped

it back into her purse. "I didn't have the heart to tell him about Steve," she said.

"You did the right thing." Penny picked up her coffee cup. "He sounds like he's having a great time with Coop."

Julia laughed. "He's got his grandfather completely wrapped around his little finger. He even got him listening to Zokor's tapes."

"I heard." Penny took a sip of her coffee. "What was that about an extra cassette?"

"I have no idea. He and Coop found it hidden under the battery pack, but when they tried to play it, it wouldn't fit. That's very strange." She shrugged. "Oh, well. It's probably some kind of factory snafu. We'll get it straightened out, provided I can remember where Paul bought the robot."

From the back of the house, Julia heard the sound of an alarm clock and looked up.

"Frank has the night shift again this week," Penny said with a sigh. "The poor darling has been working so hard, I can barely wait for the end of the month. The captain promised him four consecutive days off." Her eyes turned dreamy. "Maybe we'll go someplace romantic—like San Francisco, or one of those extravagantly expensive spas where you eat rabbit food and prance around naked all day long."

For the first time since Julia had known Penny, she envied her friend's happiness. For a brief moment, the same kind of bliss had been just within Julia's reach. But the moment had passed. Once again, she was alone.

"I'd better go," she said before she started feeling sorry for herself. "I have a cooking class tomorrow afternoon and I haven't set the table yet."

"Why don't you wait a second? Frank will probably come out and say hello."

After a few minutes, when he didn't appear, Julia kissed Penny's cheek. "He's probably running late. Give him a hug for me."

Penny walked her to the door. "Will you at least think about what I said?"

There was nothing to think about, Julia mused. All that needed to be said had been said. Her beautiful romance was over. "Thanks for the shoulder," she said, choosing to remain noncommittal. "It was just what I needed."

Then, with a wave, she walked out the door.

After making sure Andrew was asleep, Coop tiptoed back to the living room, walked straight to the phone and called Steve on his cell phone.

"Sorry to bother you this late," he said when the reporter answered. "But is there a chance you could come up to the cabin? And bring a tape recorder with you?"

"A tape recorder? What for?"

"It may be nothing to get excited about," Coop said, his eyes on Andrew's robot. "But earlier this evening, Andrew and I were listening to a couple of his Mighty Zokor tapes and we found an extra one hidden inside, under the battery pack."

Steve's voice sharpened. "What kind of tape?"

"I don't know. At first glance, it looked just like the others. But then I realized it was bigger. And when I tried to play it, it wouldn't fit into the slot. Spike has a tape recorder here but it's the wrong kind. I need one that will take microcassettes."

"You think it could be Jordan's tape?"

"Everything is starting to add up, Steve. Paul gave Zokor and the six cassettes to Andrew a couple of days before he died. It would have been easy enough for him to make a copy of the original tape and hide it inside the robot. That sucker was put in there so good it was practically invisible.''

''I shouldn't have any problem finding a recorder,'' Steve said, ''provided the shopping center is still open.''

Coop heard him tear a piece of paper.

''Give me directions to the cabin.''

Sitting on the front porch in Spike's old, squeaky rocker, Coop inhaled the cold, crisp air and looked up at the stars. Every now and then the shrill cry of a bobcat pierced the night, reminding him that, though the cabin was only forty-five minutes from Monterey, this was wild-animal territory.

Instinctively, his hand went to his pants pocket, where he had put the tape after Andrew had gone to bed, and felt the small bulge through the fabric. Was he being overly optimistic in thinking he had found Jordan's tape? Or was his hunch right?

The thought that Paul, the boy's own father, had bought Zokor for the sole purpose of hiding incriminating evidence, thus endangering Andrew's life, made Coop wish he had killed the bastard himself.

A small crunching sound, the kind one made when walking on dry leaves, made him tense. It couldn't be Steve. It was much too soon. What then? An animal? So close to the cabin?

All his senses alert, he stood up, letting the rocker bang against the wall. His eyes peered into the darkness. ''Spike,'' he called out. ''That you, buddy?''

Then, as he heard the sound again, he realized it had come from behind him. But before he could turn around, something hit him in the back of the head.

With a curse that died in his throat, Coop crumpled to the ground.

Thirty-Four

Back home, surrounded by all the things she loved, Julia found the house was suddenly too big, too cold, too silent.

Against her better judgment, she walked up to Steve's bedroom. He had left the door open, and the moment she stepped in, the familiar smell of his aftershave brought a quick twist of pain.

The room was as neat and clean as the first day she had showed it to him. Except for the scent, not a single personal item had been left behind. It was as if he had never been here.

On the bedside table, the telephone was like a magnet. If she wanted to, she could easily find out where he was. He would have checked into the Monterey Arms, a large, fairly comfortable motel on the edge of town, or into any of the picturesque inns and hotels along Cannery Row.

If she wanted to. Which she didn't.

As she kept staring at the desk where he had sat so many times writing his articles, the words he had said to her during their confrontation played in her head. *"I love you, Julia. Only you. If you've ever believed anything, believe this."*

Had she been too hard on him? Too unforgiving? Yes, she hated lies, hated them even more when they came from someone she loved. A lie was a betrayal. Pure and simple.

Or was it?

"Put yourself in his place." That's what Penny had said. But Julia hadn't been able to do that. She had been too angry, too devastated by the certainty he still loved Sheila.

Feeling the prickle of tears behind her lids again, she shook the disturbing thoughts from her head, closed the door and went back downstairs.

On the kitchen counter, the special homecoming treat she had baked for Andrew—a cherry pie—awaited the happy occasion. That's all that mattered now—Andrew's return.

Her eyes, still misty, stopped on the little yellow slicker that hung by the back door. She smiled. God, how she had missed her boy, missed their nightly battles over his bed-time, missed the gap in his teeth when he grinned, the way his voice rose to a pitch when he was excited, the way he had been earlier when he had told her about that mysterious tape he and Coop had found.

Suddenly, she stiffened. *Mysterious tape.* Until now those two words had only been used to describe Jordan's missing tape.

As a staggering thought exploded in her head, Julia gasped. No, it couldn't be. Not in Andrew's robot. Paul would never…

Oh, God.

Sudden panic shot through her. Paul had given the robot and the six tapes to Andrew as a peace offering for missing his last parental visit. That was May 23, only three days before Paul was killed.

Struggling to stay calm, she picked up the cordless phone from the desk and punched in the numbers of Spike's cabin. At the first sound of a busy signal, she let out a cry of frustration. Who could Coop be talking to at this time of night?

Worried she may have misdialed, she tried again, slowly

this time, then hung up when she heard the busy signal. She would wait five minutes and try again.

An uneasy feeling fluttered briefly in her stomach. Her eyes on the wall clock above a cabinet, she counted as the hand ticked off the seconds. After three excruciatingly slow minutes, she picked up the phone again.

The line was still busy.

This made no sense. Only she and Steve had that number. And Steve would never call this late. Maybe Coop had called him first. Or he had taken the phone off the hook for the night.

A sudden thought, one that brought an instant chill, crept reluctantly into her mind.

What if Coop was drinking?

Ashamed at her lack of faith in her father, she tried to dismiss the intrusive thought but couldn't. Spike had always been a two-fisted drinker, and because of that, his cabin was well stocked. What if Coop, all alone and without the support of AA, had succumbed to the temptation?

Without another moment's hesitation, Julia grabbed her bag from the desk, along with her keys, and flew out the door.

Steve had arrived at the Del Monte Shopping Center just in time. Another few minutes and the electronics store would have been closed.

Now, sitting in the Land Rover with the tape recorder next to him, he picked up his phone and dialed The Hacienda. Angry or not, Julia would want to be in on this. And maybe the forty-five minute drive to Spike's cabin would give them a chance to talk some more and, hopefully, to straighten things out. One thing was certain, he wasn't about to give up on her.

But instead of Julia's hello, it was her recorded message

he heard. Glancing at the luminous dial on the dashboard clock, he frowned. Ten o'clock. Would she go to bed that early? Or was she screening her calls so she didn't have to talk to him?

Cursing under his breath, he pressed on the accelerator and headed for Via del Rey.

Except for the landscape lights in the courtyard, the inn was dark when Steve arrived. And the carport where Julia kept her Volvo was empty. *Where the hell could she be at this hour?*

Not bothering to speculate, Steve ran up the steps and rang the bell. As silence stretched, he rang again, then banged the wrought-iron bull horns. "Julia!"

After waiting a full minute and getting no answer, he returned to his car.

His teeth clamped over his bottom lip, he drummed his fingers impatiently on the steering wheel and tried not to worry. There could be a half-dozen reasons why she wasn't here. She could be at her mother's, or at Penny's.

Penny. Of course. Why hadn't he thought of that sooner? Julia had told him that's where she would be. Picking up the cellular again, he called information for the number.

Penny answered on the third ring, her voice thick with sleep. "'Lo?"

"Penny, it's Steve," he said, barely able to conceal his worry. "I'm looking for Julia. Have you seen her?"

At the other end, Penny was suddenly wide-awake. "She was here earlier but went home about an hour ago. She wanted to prepare for tomorrow's class."

He felt a stirring of alarm. "She's not here. And her car is not here. Could she be at her mother's?"

"I doubt that very much." The concern in Penny's voice did nothing for his own nerves. "She knows Grace goes to bed early. Have you tried her cell phone?"

He kicked himself for not having written the number down. "Give me the number, Penny."

He jotted it down on the back of a gas receipt, promised to call Penny back the moment he located Julia, and hung up. His eyes on the inn's dark silhouette, he dialed and let out a sigh of relief when Julia answered.

"Where the hell are you?" was all he could manage to get out.

"What business is that of yours?"

Her sharp tone stung, but now wasn't the time to feel sorry for himself. "Your father called," he said. "He thinks he found Jordan's missing tape and—"

"In Andrew's robot?" All signs of anger were gone from her voice. "Oh, God, then it's true."

"How do you know?"

"Andrew called earlier. He told me that he and Coop had found a tape hidden under the battery pack. I didn't put two and two together until a little while ago when I remembered that Zokor and the six cassettes were a gift from Paul. He gave them to Andrew just three days before he died." She paused. When she spoke again, her voice had a worried edge to it. "I tried to call my father several times since then but the line has been busy. I'm on my way up there, now."

Cradling the phone between his cheek and his shoulder, Steve switched on the interior light and opened the map he had bought when he'd first arrived in Monterey. "Give me your location, Julia."

He half expected her to tell him to go to hell, but she didn't. "I just left 101 and turned west on Route 18," she said after a short hesitation. "I figure I'm about thirty minutes from the cabin."

With his finger, Steve traced the route. "Okay, I'm leaving right now." He swung the Land Rover around. "The traffic is light, so I should make good time."

"Steve?" Her voice shook. "You don't think...something happened, do you? I mean...I must have called four times since leaving the house and Coop still doesn't answer."

That worried him, too. Coop wouldn't take the phone off the hook knowing Steve was on his way and might need further directions. He couldn't tell her that, not in the shape she was in already. "He probably took the phone off the hook," he said with as much conviction as he could muster. Then, realizing what she was truly fearing, he added, "He wasn't drinking, Julia. He called me just a few minutes ago, completely sober."

He heard her sigh. "Thanks, Steve."

As soon as she hung up, he called Hammond at home.

"You're getting to be a royal pain, Reyes, you know that," the detective muttered. "What the hell is it now?"

Steve had grown used to Hank's bad humor in the last three weeks, and he ignored it. In clear, succinct sentences, he briefed him on what Coop had told him, adding, "Julia has been trying to reach her father for half an hour, and the line is busy. She's worried and so am I. Coop wouldn't take the phone off the hook, Hank. Not when he knows I'm on my way and might need directions."

At the other end of the line, Steve heard an audible sigh. "Okay, okay. Where's that damn cabin?"

Coop came to slowly and painfully, his face pressed against a bed of pine needles. Gingerly, he touched the back of his head and winced as a sharp pain shot through.

Fortunately, the blow had glanced off the side of his skull and, though it had been hard enough to knock him out for a while, it hadn't done any serious damage.

When he was sure he could stand on his feet, he grabbed the edge of the porch railing and pulled himself up.

From where he stood, he could see the inside of the cabin, the brick fireplace with the embers glowing, the wood-paneled walls, the brown sofas and chairs.

Zokor stood on the card table where Andrew had left it. Scattered around the robot, in a disorderly fashion, were the six tapes.

A man in dark pants and a black parka was quietly, methodically searching every piece of furniture in the room. Though his right hand was partially hidden, Coop could see a gun.

The intruder started to turn around. But even before his face was in full view, Coop shot back from the window, in shock.

The man was Frank Walsh.

Thirty-Five

Motionless except for the pounding in his chest, Coop stood frozen in place, unable to make sense of what he was seeing. If the tape everyone was looking for contained information on *Gleic Éire,* and if McDermott's nephew was the man who had attacked Julia, then what the hell was Frank doing here?

There was only one answer.

The tape did *not* contain information on *Gleic Éire,* as everyone thought, but some sort of incriminating evidence against Frank. Somehow he had found out that the tape was hidden in Andrew's robot and he had come for it.

The realization sank in slowly, almost reluctantly.

Frank was Paul's killer.

And he had let Julia take the fall.

"Son of a bitch." Coop started to go inside, ready to pound the hell out of the younger man, or at least give it a good try.

A wave of dizziness stopped him. Leaning against the railing, he waited for the spinning to pass. When it did, he was forced to rethink his options. In his condition, he could hardly charge into the cabin like Dirty Harry and hope to take on a man thirty years younger who had a gun in his hand.

And no matter how hot the rage, at the moment his priority was Andrew. He had to get the kid out of here. Once

Frank realized the tape wasn't in the cabin, he'd know Coop had it on him and would come looking for it.

Coop could play it two ways. Pretend to still be unconscious, let Frank find the tape and allow him to escape. Or Coop could keep the tape, grab Andrew and make a run for it.

The first option would guarantee that he and Andrew would stay alive, unless Andrew woke up—like he'd been doing for the last three nights—and saw Frank. In which case, the detective would have no choice but to kill them both. That was no good.

The second option was iffy. A lot depended on how quickly Coop could slip into Andrew's bedroom and get him out of there. Patting his pockets, he muttered a curse. His car keys were inside the cabin. Scratch the quick escape in the Buick. He and Andrew would have to head for the forest, on foot. And hope Frank wouldn't come after them.

Still, considering that Andrew had been waking up regularly at about this time every night, the latter option was the least risky.

All right, Sarge. Enough talk. Let's go.

His old army survival training springing into action, Coop kept his body low so he wouldn't be seen from the window. He moved quickly and soundlessly as he ran along the path that led to the back of the cabin. The window to Andrew's room was closed, he knew, but not locked.

Hooking his fingertips under the frame, he tried to push the window up and cursed when he realized that time and rain had warped the old wood. After a short struggle, the panel finally gave, and he was able to raise the window just enough to slip through.

Andrew had kicked off the blankets and was tossing around restlessly, which convinced Coop he had chosen the right option.

Knowing there was no time to lose, he grabbed Andrew's duffel bag, stuffed it with the boy's quilted jacket and the socks and sneakers he had left by the side of his bed. Then, after hooking the strap over his shoulder, he took the boy, bedding and all, in his arms, and left the same way he had come.

As Coop stepped over the windowsill, Andrew stirred. "Grandpa?"

"Shh. Be quiet." Coop's voice was just a whisper as he ran toward the dense forest only a few feet from the cabin. "We're playing a little game, okay?"

Andrew stuck an arm out of the blanket and rubbed his eyes. "What kind of game? Why are you carrying me?"

"So we can go faster."

The back door to the cabin was suddenly flung open and Frank's broad frame appeared in the doorway. Coop swore silently. The detective must have heard them, then realized they were both gone.

"Hey!" Andrew exclaimed. "It's Uncle F—"

Coop clamped a hand on Andrew's mouth. They were out of sight, but not necessarily out of earshot. "Shh," he said again, sinking deeper into the trees. "We don't want him to hear us."

From the relative safety of the dense forest, Coop watched as Frank, the .38 in his hand, whipped around from side to side. "Coop!" he bellowed. "I know you're there, man. Don't make me come looking for you."

Andrew, fully awake now, squirmed until Coop had to put him down. "What's the matter with Uncle Frank?" he asked, squinting at Coop. "Why is he mad? And why aren't you answering him?"

Coop didn't think the kid would swallow that game-playing bull much longer. He was too smart for that. "I'll tell you later," he said, stalling for time. "Right now I want you to put your jacket and your shoes on so you're ready to go."

"Where are we going?"

"Home." He waved at the clothes he had taken out of the duffel bag. "Come on, Andrew, hurry."

They would take the hiking trail, Coop decided, the only one this side of the mountain. Steep and narrow, it climbed a few hundred feet, wound around the Hekeneke Pass and then began to dip down again, toward the lake.

Whether or not Frank would follow them was debatable. Though he had come here a few times with Jordan when he was a kid, he didn't know the terrain as well as Coop did. On the other hand, he couldn't very well afford to let Coop and Andrew go, not now that he had exposed himself.

Coop kept his eyes on the clearing below. The detective kept walking around in circles, looking up in their direction from time to time. As long as that's all he did, Coop thought, they'd stay put. If he started coming after them, they would have to head for the pass.

He didn't want to think about Steve, who should be arriving soon, and what would happen if the reporter suddenly found himself facing Frank's gun. Andrew was the one he had to worry about now. No one else.

Suddenly, Frank cupped his hands around his mouth. "It's no use running, Coop! You'll die in those mountains. Is that what you want? For you and Andrew to die?"

"Yeah," Coop mumbled under his breath. "Like we've got a better chance with you."

Andrew stopped lacing his sneaker. His eyes were huge as he looked up at Coop. "Are we going to die, Grandpa?"

"No way, kiddo."

Andrew stood up. "I want to go back to the cabin," he said in a plaintive tone. "I want to be with Uncle Frank."

Coop couldn't blame him. Andrew had known Frank all

his life. He trusted him. And right now, anything looked better than this cold, dark forest.

Coop zipped the duffel bag shut and glanced toward the clearing again. Frank hadn't budged. "We can't go back to the cabin, Andrew."

"Why not?"

Coop thought of all the ways he could break the truth to him. In the end, he rejected them all. The thought of looking into those innocent eyes and telling him that the man Andrew loved and trusted had killed his father and wouldn't hesitate to kill him as well made him sick to his stomach. He would as soon face a pack of wild animals than do that to his grandson.

"Andrew, listen to me," he said gently. "I know you have questions. And I know you're scared—"

"I'm not scared."

Coop smiled. "Good, because you shouldn't be. I'm going to get you back home safe and sound, and you'll have one heck of a story to tell all your friends at camp this summer."

As Andrew continued to look at him, he added, "I wish I could tell you more, kiddo, but it's complicated and I'd rather let your mother explain it to you. For now, you'll just have to trust me. Can you do that?"

Andrew nodded—not with a whole lot of conviction, but he nodded.

"That's good. Now zip up. It's getting cold."

"How long will it take us to get home?" Andrew asked as he bundled up.

Coop wished to God he knew. They had no food, no water, no medical supplies and no weapons to protect themselves. Fortunately, the moon was out tonight and there wasn't a cloud in the sky. At least he'd be able to tell where they were going. "Not too long," he said, wishing he could believe his own words.

Suddenly, a long, tortured howl pierced the night.

Down in the clearing, Frank jumped about two feet. At the same time, Andrew grabbed Coop's waist and held him tight.

"What was that, Grandpa?"

"Just a bobcat. Don't worry," he added, resting his hand on Andrew's head. "He's more scared of you than you are of him."

He glanced toward the house again. Frank had apparently made a decision. With a resolute step, he began heading for the trail.

He was coming after them.

Trying to keep the anxiety from his voice, Coop took the boy's hand again and in a playful tone said, "Ready, soldier?"

Andrew sighed. "I guess so."

"Then let's go."

Though Julia hadn't wanted to admit it, knowing that Steve was on his way took some of her anxieties away. She hadn't passed a soul since she had taken the steep mountain pass, and the landscape looked dark and desolate. Thank God it was a clear night and the road signs and landmarks she remembered from her childhood were still there. Otherwise, God knows where she would have ended up.

She cursed the twisting road that prohibited her from driving any faster than thirty-five miles an hour. Gripping the steering wheel tightly, she forced herself to stay calm. She wouldn't be much use to anyone if she cracked now. But, in spite of the pep talk, every now and then the taste of fear would rise in her throat, almost choking her. Let him be safe, she prayed.

In the glare of the high beams, the sign for Ridge Lane suddenly appeared. She gave a sharp turn of the wheel, started skidding, then quickly brought the powerful car under control. *Steady, old girl.*

As the brightly lit cabin came into view, she said another silent prayer. Please, dear God, let Andrew be all right.

Her heart pounding, she brought the Volvo to a jolting halt next to Coop's Buick and jumped out of the car. "Dad!" she cried as she ran inside. "Andrew!"

She stopped dead in her tracks and went cold. The place had been ransacked. Cushions lay on the floor and Andrew's robot and the six cassettes were scattered over the card table. In the kitchen, cabinets had been emptied of their contents. So had Coop's tackle box.

A sick feeling began to churn in her stomach. "Oh, my God! Andrew!"

She ran into the first bedroom, took one look at the stripped bed and the open window and felt faint. With legs that barely supported her, she ran into the second bedroom. That bed hadn't been slept in.

The sound of a door slamming made her whip around. "Dad!" She ran to meet him, tears of relief already running down her cheeks.

It wasn't Coop she collided into but Steve.

She hardly missed a beat. "They're gone!" she cried, grabbing his leather bomber jacket and holding on to it as she would a lifeline.

Steve glanced back at Coop's car. "What do you mean, gone?"

"Someone was here! They searched the cabin and now Coop and Andrew are gone. His bed is completely stripped and Coop's hasn't been slept in." She pressed her head against his chest. "Something's happened to them."

With his arm wrapped tightly around her shoulders,

Steve walked into the cabin and quickly took in the scene, first in the living room, then in each bedroom. "Take it easy," he said quietly, still holding her. But his voice sounded flat and worried. "Coop won't let anything happen to Andrew."

"Who are you calling?" she asked when he took the phone from his pocket.

"Hammond. He's on his way up here. Hank," he said, holding the phone so Julia could hear the conversation. "Coop's car is here, but he and Andrew are gone. And the place has been searched. There's also a car parked fifty feet or so down the road, but I didn't recognize it."

Julia's gaze shot up.

"Go and check it out," Hammond instructed. "Break in if you have to, but find out who owns it. Then call me back."

"What car?" Julia asked when Steve hung up. "I didn't see a car."

"You weren't looking for one." He took her hand. "Come on. Let's go take a look."

It took them only a few minutes to reach the black sedan. Julia stopped in her tracks and grabbed Steve's arm. "That's Frank's Lexus," she said in a whisper.

"Are you sure?" But even as she was nodding, Steve was already opening the passenger door, which wasn't locked. He opened the glove compartment and took out a small leather folder.

"I'll be damned." Looking stunned, Steve turned to Julia. "What the hell is he doing here? And why would he hide his car?"

"I don't know. He's supposed to be on duty."

"Did he know about the tape Andrew found?"

"I don't see how...." She pressed her hands to her chest, refusing to believe the maddening thought that was trying to snake its way into her head. "I told Penny. Frank wasn't there. He...he was in the back, getting ready for his late shift."

He could have heard her, she realized. That's why he hadn't come out to say hello.

She looked at the car, pushed deep into the brush. He knew the location of the cabin as well as she did. He had come here often as a kid, with her and Jordan.

No. She kept shaking her head in denial. Not Frank. Not her best friend in the whole world. Not the man she had trusted with her life.

"It was him all along," she whispered. "It was Frank." Then, refusing to think the worst, she looked at Steve. "He wouldn't hurt Andrew. Whatever he did, whatever his reasons, he...he won't hurt Andrew."

Steve looked up toward the dark, forbidding mountains. "He may not even have Andrew," he said.

"Why do you say that?"

"Because his car is here. And Coop's car is here. And the bedding on Andrew's bed is gone."

She couldn't follow him. Her mind was too muddled. "So?"

"So I think Coop got Andrew out of the cabin before Frank realized they were gone."

"Then where is Frank?"

"Maybe he took off after them." His gaze sweeping around, Steve studied the darkness. "The three of them could be up there somewhere, Coop and Andrew trying to get away and Frank hoping to catch up with them." He looked back at Julia. "Is there a hiking trail nearby?"

She nodded, pointing upward. "Just beyond that sign. It goes up and then down toward Crystal Lake."

Steve flipped his cell phone open and dialed again.

Standing close to him, Julia heard Hammond as he answered on the first ring. "Hammond."

"You're not going to like this, Hank," Steve said. "The car belongs to Frank Walsh."

"Aw, shit."

"We need a helicopter," Steve continued. "All three of them are on foot, and by now they could be anywhere."

"I've already called for one, but we'll have to wait awhile. Every chopper in the area is being sent to San Luis Obispo to rescue flood victims."

Steve hung up. "Does Charles have a helicopter?" he asked Julia.

She shook her head. "I don't think so." She was thoughtful for a moment. "But a couple of his friends do."

He handed her the phone.

While Julia made the call, Steve ran back into the cabin. A locked gun cabinet with a glass front was mounted on the wall. Inside were half a dozen hunting rifles and several boxes of ammunition.

There was no time to look for a key, or to even try to force the lock open. Without a moment's hesitation, Steve grabbed the fireplace poker and broke the glass.

As the window shattered, Julia ran in, her expression haggard. "What—?"

She stopped as Steve selected a Remington. "What are you doing?"

He tore open a box of bullets. "I'm going after them. Find me a flashlight, will you?"

Julia ran to the kitchen and returned seconds later with one. She flicked the switch on and off. "It works."

"Good." Steve tucked the flashlight into his waistband, then slid the rifle under his arm. "You wait here for Hammond," he instructed. "He's bringing an officer with him along with a search and rescue team. Just direct them to the trail.''

Her eyes filled with worry. She gripped his arm. ''Be careful.''

''I will. Did you get hold of Charles?''

She nodded. ''He said he'd find a helicopter even if he had to steal one.''

The remark brought a smile to Steve's lips. Leaning toward Julia, he kissed her lightly on the lips and headed for the trail.

Thirty-Six

"Andrew, watch out!"

Coop's warning came too late. Barely avoiding hitting his head on a low-hanging branch, Andrew lost his footing and fell. As he cushioned his fall with his hands, he let out a yelp.

Coop rushed to help him up. "You okay, kiddo?"

"I think I cut myself."

He had, Coop noted grimly. His palm had a two-inch gash in it, caused by a shard of glass some careless hiker had left behind. Coop let out a small sigh of relief when he saw the steady flow of dark red blood oozing out of the wound. Venous bleeding was serious but easier to control than arterial bleeding.

He glanced behind him, but couldn't see Frank. The trick had worked. A few minutes ago, as the policeman was beginning to gain ground on them, Coop had veered off to the left, taking a steeper, less traveled trail that led to the same place but bypassed the falls. To make sure Frank would stick to the larger trail, Coop had covered their tracks with dried leaves and kept his fingers crossed.

"Sit down," he said. "I'll have you fixed up in no time."

Pale, but calm, Andrew did as he was told. Moving quickly, Coop took the bedsheet from the duffel bag and ripped off a corner. Folding it over several times, he applied the thick square directly onto the wound, pressing it firmly, listening for sounds as he worked.

"That should stop the bleeding," he told Andrew. He shoved the duffel bag under the boy's elbow for support. "Here, rest your arm on this."

"What if the bleeding won't stop?"

The kid always had a question, Coop thought with a chuckle. Just like his mother. "Then we'll have to do something else."

"Like a tourniquet?"

Coop's mouth twitched at the corners. "How do you know about tourniquets?"

"My friend Jimmy cut his leg at camp last summer and the doctor had to put a tourniquet right here." With his good hand, he pointed at a spot above his knee.

"Did the bleeding stop?"

Andrew nodded.

"See? Your old grandpa knows what he's doing." As he talked, he looked up, trying to gauge the distance they still had to climb before reaching the pass. A mile? Two? Andrew would never make it.

Coop stuffed the sheet back into the duffel bag. Maybe they could spend the night here. There were enough trees with low, thick branches to provide adequate cover. Dry leaves and evergreen boughs could be made into a mattress and would insulate them from the cold ground.

When he looked down again, Andrew was asleep, his head resting on the duffel bag.

The choice had been made.

Steve had been gone for a little over fifteen minutes when Julia heard the unmistakable rumble of a helicopter. Almost immediately, her cell phone rang. It was Charles.

"We're here, Julia," he shouted above the noise. "We

can't see much but I'm hoping Coop will find a clearing and signal us."

Julia looked up. The chopper was right above her, its powerful beams illuminating the entire area. "You've got to find them, Charles," she shouted back.

"We will. Did the police show up yet?"

"No, but Steve didn't wait for them. He went looking for Coop and Andrew."

The helicopter rose higher, to clear the trees, and Charles's reply was lost in a blast of static.

Steve continued to climb, glad that he had kept up with his jogging all those years. The regular exercise had built up the muscles in his legs and gave him the stamina he needed to tackle the mountains. He wasn't so sure about Coop and Andrew, though. Or Frank, for that matter. The man was in good enough shape but was beginning to show signs of softness around the middle.

Maybe that would slow him down.

After another five minutes, Steve stopped abruptly. Up ahead, a shadow was moving. Then he saw him—a lone figure in dark clothing, climbing laboriously, stopping every few seconds to catch his breath.

Trying to make as little sound as possible, Steve stepped up his pace. When he was only twenty feet or so from the man in black, he stopped.

"Frank!"

As the man whipped around, Steve shone the flashlight on him. In the white glare, Frank looked as scared as a trapped animal. "Give it up, Frank. You're cornered."

From a distance, but approaching rapidly, came the sound of a helicopter. A voice, coming through a loudspeaker, called out Coop and Andrew's names. Then a shout. "There they are!"

Steve heaved a sigh of relief. Coop and Andrew had been found.

As Frank started running again, Steve took off after him. In spite of the cold air, the steep climb had him panting and sweating. Up ahead, the helicopter continued to hover.

"No use running anymore, Frank," he called out. "You're only making it harder on yourself."

Without stopping, Frank turned around and started firing.

As a bullet passed Steve's head, making a sharp, cracking sound, he let out an oath. The bastard had just missed him. His jaw set, Steve raised the rifle, focused the sight on the running man and, as Frank fired another shot, pressed the trigger.

The policeman screamed and fell to the ground, holding his leg. Steve ran to him, scooped up the handgun and tucked it into his waistband. "You stupid son of a bitch," he muttered, kneeling beside the fallen man. "Don't you know when you're licked?"

Frank closed his eyes and leaned his head against a tree. "Fuck off."

"Oh, I will, my friend. But first I'm handing you over to the police. Where are you hit?"

"The thigh," Frank groaned.

Steve pushed the pant leg up and quickly inspected the wound. The bullet had grazed the fleshiest part of the policeman's thigh. It was bleeding, but not heavily. "The bullet just knicked you," he said, finding it difficult to show any kind of sympathy. "Come on. On your feet."

Getting no response from him, Steve bent over, hooked an arm around the man's waist and pulled him up. "Either you cooperate," he snapped as Frank started to fight him, "or I'll drag you all the way to the cabin. Your choice, buddy."

Muttering under his breath, Frank started limping his way down.

Hammond and his search and rescue team arrived just as Charles's second call came through.

This time he was jubilant. "We found them, Julia! Andrew is fine. So is Coop."

"Thank God. Are you sure Andrew is okay?" she asked anxiously. "He's not hurt?"

"We don't have him yet. The copilot is going down right now to pick him up...but he appears to be okay. He and Coop are waving." With the roar from the helicopter engine, she could only make out half of what Charles was saying. "...then we'll take them to Memorial...make sure..."

"I want to talk to Andrew, Charles."

"Hold on. Here he comes now."

She heard a series of grinding noises, shouts. Seconds ticked by, excruciatingly slow. Around her, the five men, each holding a shotgun, had fallen silent and were watching the sky. The helicopter had disappeared but they could still hear it.

Then the voice she had been waiting to hear burst through the noise. "Mommy!"

The relief was so intense, she wasn't sure how she managed to stay on her feet. "Andrew! Oh, baby. Are you all right?"

"Yeah. We heard the helicopter. Then Grandpa had to look for a place that didn't have so many trees. And when we did, we started waving." She heard him laugh. "Just like in the movies."

Tears poured down her cheeks but she didn't bother to wipe them off. "Where's Grandpa?"

"He's coming up now. It was so neat, Mom. That man

came down on a *cable!* And then he grabbed me, hooked me to his belt and up we went."

She let out a trembling sigh. For Andrew the ordeal had been nothing more than one big, exciting adventure. And maybe that was just as well. "You're sure you're okay?" she asked again.

"Yeah, I'm fine." He sounded so tough, she thought, so grown-up all of a sudden. "I got cut a little but Grandpa fixed it. We've got to go now, Mom. Grandpa Charles is taking us to the hospital."

"I know, darling. I'll be there as soon as possible, okay?"

"Okay."

Julia hung up and turned to Hammond and the others. "They're both fine."

Emotions too powerful to control finally got the best of her. Feeling herself going down, she reached for a tree. In two leaps, Hammond was by her side, holding on to her.

"Easy now," he said in his gruff voice. "Everything is going to be all right."

"Steve," she murmured. "He's up there, with Frank."

Hammond was already snapping orders. Three of the men were getting their first-aid kits from the trunk of the car when Steve, his arm around Frank, suddenly appeared.

"Hey, Detective," he called out. "Look what I caught."

Five stunned men looked up at the odd-looking duo approaching them.

"He's got a bullet wound in the thigh." Steve let Frank slide to a sitting position. "Nothing serious, but he's bleeding."

As one of the rescue men knelt beside Frank and started tending to his wound, Julia rushed into Steve's arms. She had never loved him more, never been more grateful. And never felt more stupid for having pushed him away. He had risked his life for her son. What better proof of love was there? "Are you all right?" she asked in a small voice.

He nodded. "Andrew?"

"He and Coop have been rescued. They're fine, and on their way to Memorial for a checkup."

Sitting on the ground, Frank was being cleaned and bandaged. There was a tortured expression on his handsome features as he looked at Julia. "I wouldn't have hurt him, Jules," he said in a broken voice. "I swear I wouldn't have hurt him."

When Frank was pulled up to his feet again, Hammond snapped a pair of handcuffs on him. "Tell it to the judge," he said gruffly.

"No." Julia raised her hand. "If you don't mind, Detective, I'd like to hear what he has to say. Now." She looked at the man she had always considered her best friend and felt nothing but contempt. "You went after Andrew and my father with a gun. You would have killed them both and you know it."

Frank didn't answer.

"Why did you do it, Frank?" She walked slowly toward him, aware that part of her still didn't want to believe he was a killer. "What is on that tape that would make you kill for it?"

Frank took a deep breath. "Paul found out I was working for Vinnie Cardinale."

"You dirty scum," Hammond muttered under his breath. He gave a yank on the cuffs, making Frank wince.

"How did you know Paul had figured that out?" Steve asked.

"He told me. The son of a bitch asked me to come to his house, said he had something to tell me. When I got there, he had a gun on me and was holding Jordan's tape. I begged him not to turn me in. I told him that Vinnie would give him money, would even guarantee his election. All he had to do was hand over the evidence and keep his mouth shut.

"Paul just laughed at me," he continued. "He told me that after the announcement he was about to make at the news conference, his election was in the bag, anyway. He didn't need Vinnie." He hopped on his good leg. "And he wanted to impress you, Julia. He thought that exposing your brother's killers would change your feelings toward him."

Frank made a derisive sound. "He was so busy being smug, he never saw me coming at him."

Julia felt Steve's hands on her shoulders. The contact seemed to give her a new strength. "How did Paul find out you worked for Cardinale?" she asked.

A long second passed, then another. When Frank spoke again, his voice was just a whisper. "He found out from Jordan's tape."

Julia gaped. *"Jordan knew?"*

"Yeah, he knew. He found out while he was investigating an old drug case."

"And he never said anything?" Hammond asked incredulously.

"He was going to." Frank looked at Julia. "He was too good a cop not to. I begged him to keep quiet. I offered him money, anything he wanted. He turned me down. He was ready to throw away a twenty-five-year friendship."

As if someone had suddenly yanked a cord, Julia's back went rigid. "My God," she said under her breath. "If you knew he was going to turn you in, then..."

Her eyes, filled with horror, fastened on Frank. "You killed Jordan!" Her hands flew to her mouth.

"I didn't pull the trigger, Jules. Vinnie's men did that."

"Vinnie?" Steve repeated. "I thought you and Jordan were investigating a local drug ring."

"Vinnie made that up. To lure Jordan to the warehouse." Tears ran freely down his cheeks now, forming dark streaks on his dirt-stained face. "I didn't want to do it, Jules. I loved him like a brother."

"You had him ambushed," she said dully. "You knew Vinnie's men were waiting for him, and you led him to that warehouse, knowing they were going to kill him."

"He was going to turn me in, Julia. My career would have been over. Nineteen years down the drain."

"You bastard!" She flew out of Steve's grip and lunged at Frank. Steve caught her just as her first blows landed on the detective's chest, and pulled her back.

"Let it go, Julia. He'll get what's coming to him."

"That I can promise." Hammond's tone was scathing. He nodded at the uniformed officer. "We've heard enough. Read him his rights and take him to the car. I'll be right there."

But even as Frank was being pulled away, he kept talking to Julia. "Don't hate me, Julia! I was always there for you, wasn't I? I'm the one who planted the gun in Edith's backyard so they'd let you go. I wouldn't have let you go to prison, Jules, I swear."

"You framed Edith?"

"I did it for you, Julia!"

Julia buried her head against Steve's chest. She didn't want to hear any more. She just wanted to go home. She wanted to hold her son in her arms and forget this entire nightmare.

She leaned against the man who had worked so hard to make that happen. "Take me to Memorial, Steve. Please. I...I don't think I can drive."

Steve glanced at Hammond, who nodded. "Go ahead. I'll have one of the men drive Julia's car back. I won't be far behind you. I've got one man to book for murder and an innocent woman to release from jail.'' He shook his head. ''Two wrongful arrests in this case. Not the kind of record a homicide detective ought to be proud of.'' He shrugged. ''Maybe it's time I retired.''

A few minutes later, Julia sat in the Land Rover, staring silently out the window, barely aware of Steve's hand on hers.

''What is it, Julia?''

''Penny,'' she said in a whisper. ''She's going to be devastated. She loves Frank so much.''

Steve squeezed her hand. ''You'll be there for her. You'll help her get through this.''

Julia shook her head. ''I'm not sure I'll be able to. They couldn't have children, you see, and Frank was her entire focus, the only man she has ever loved. This is going to hit her terribly hard.''

''Do you want to call her?''

''I already tried. The machine answered. She must have gone to the station.''

Steve brought her hand to his lips and kissed it. ''Just tell me what I can do and I'll do it, okay?''

The words, spoken with such sweet sincerity, warmed her heart. ''Okay.''

Thirty-Seven

Except for a mild concussion and the doctor's recommendation to stay in the hospital overnight for observation, Coop had been given a clean bill of health.

In the emergency room of Monterey County Memorial, Julia watched the same doctor, a young intern with a winning smile, put a last strip of adhesive tape on Andrew's clean dressing.

"Your grandfather did a fine job on that cut," he told Andrew. "It'll be healed in no time." He looked up at Charles, who hadn't left Andrew's side. "In fact, I'd say you're pretty lucky to have two such terrific grandfathers."

"Yeah, I know." Andrew beamed at Charles. "That helicopter ride was cool, Grandpa. Can your friend take me up again sometime?"

Charles chuckled. "I'm sure that could be arranged." He glanced at Julia. "But only if it's all right with your mother."

Julia gave a short nod and smiled. He *had* done a lot of learning in the last few days.

Andrew's attention returned to the doctor. "Can my grandpa Coop come home with us?"

"Not until tomorrow, Andrew. But since you're done here, why don't you go and see him before he gets transferred to a regular room? I'm sure he'd love to see you."

Grace, who had arrived at the hospital moments ago,

wrapped a protective arm around her grandson's shoulders. "Maybe it would be best if Andrew went home," she said pointedly. "He needs to rest."

Julia took her mother by the arm and pulled her aside. "I don't think another few minutes will make much difference, Mom. In fact, I was hoping *you* would go in to see Coop before Andrew did."

"Me?" Grace's eyes widened in shock. "What on earth for?"

"Don't you want to thank him for saving Andrew's life?" She lowered her voice. "Aren't you the least bit remorseful to have doubted him?"

When Grace didn't reply, Julia gently pushed her toward the door. "Go on, Mom. You know you want to."

"I do not." A deep flush colored Grace's cheeks. "Well...I suppose I could...for a minute."

Smiling, Julia watched her mother walk out of the room.

From the gurney where he had been lying since arriving at Memorial, Coop held his breath and watched Grace as she slowly approached his bed.

She was still a beautiful woman, he thought, his throat tight with emotion. Almost as beautiful as the day he had married her. Oh, there were lines on that beloved face, and her hair was already showing signs of gray, but those green eyes that had turned his head so many years ago were still as dazzling as he remembered.

"Hello, Gracie." He was so choked up he was surprised he could talk. And even more surprised that she answered him.

"Hello, Coop." There was no anger in her voice, just sadness—a sadness *he* had put there. "How do you feel?"

"Better now that you're here." He knew it wasn't what

she wanted to hear, but that's how he felt and he needed to say it. "How's Andrew?"

"He'll be fine. The doctor..." She paused, as if unsure she ought to continue. "The doctor said his cut would have been a lot worse if it hadn't been for your quick intervention."

"Andrew was a real trooper."

Grace looked at her hands. "Frank would have killed him if it wasn't for you."

"It didn't happen, Gracie, so put those thoughts out of your mind, okay?"

She looked up, her eyes suddenly bright with tears. "Frank killed Jordan," she said in a trembling voice.

He nodded. "Steve told me." He took a long breath. "I wish I had been there, Gracie. For Jordan, for Julia and above all...for you."

"You were here for Andrew. That's all that counts right now."

Coop looked at her hands, which were clasped on her lap. He wanted to take them in his and tell her he loved her, that he had never stopped loving her, but she was already standing.

"I guess I'd better go. We all need some rest." She bit on her lower lip, a habit he remembered well. "If you'd like," she said a little awkwardly, "I mean...I was wondering..." She cleared her throat. "Maybe you could come for dinner on Sunday? Andrew and Julia will be there. And so will Steve."

This time Coop made no effort to stop the tears that filled his eyes. "I'd like that, Gracie." He swallowed. "I'd like that a whole lot."

The sight of Penny's ravaged face when she opened her door the following morning had Julia fighting tears again.

"Oh, Penny."

With a sob that caught in her throat, Penny threw herself in Julia's open arms and wept hopelessly. "I didn't know, Julia. I swear I didn't."

"Shh. I know." Julia patted the thick mane of hair. "I know."

"I'm so...sorry."

"What Frank did is not your fault, Penny," Julia said gently as she led her friend to the living room. "He liked money and beautiful things. He always did."

"I should have known." Penny sank onto the sofa. "I'm his wife. I should have realized something was going on. When he started bringing me expensive gifts, claiming the money came from a bonus, I...should have known."

Julia sat close to her. "You trusted him."

"If I had been more suspicious, I might have stopped him in time, before he..." She buried her face in her hands. "Oh, Jordan. Poor Jordan."

Julia bit her lip and looked away. The realization that Frank had arranged for Jordan to be killed by Vinnie's men in such a cold, calculated way hurt her more than anything else. The three of them had been as close as any three people could be. They had been best friends, soul mates, confidants. On the day of Frank and Penny's wedding, Jordan had been best man and Julia matron of honor. Any one of them would have laid down his life for the other.

One had.

But Penny was not to blame. Gently, Julia took her friend's hand. "Jordan wouldn't like it if he knew you blamed yourself."

Penny pulled a tissue from a box on the coffee table and blotted her eyes. "No, I guess he wouldn't." She looked up. "Frank heard us talking last night, didn't he? That's how he knew about Andrew's extra cassette."

Julia nodded and told her what Detective Hammond had learned later from Frank. "He called in sick to the station and drove to the cabin. He knew there was a backup copy of the tape somewhere because Paul had told him, but like me, he didn't realize where it was hidden until he overheard us talking."

Penny stared at her with stricken eyes. "He wouldn't have hurt Andrew. Please tell me he wouldn't have hurt Andrew."

Julia looked down and didn't answer.

"Oh, my God." Penny stood up and went to stand by the window. It was a while before she spoke again. "The night he...killed Paul, I wanted to know where he was going. He said he had to visit a sick friend." A dry sob shook her shoulders. "I believed him."

"You had no reason not to."

"I even told him to make sure to wear his raincoat, the one with the hood, because it was raining."

That's why Eleanor had been so confused, Julia thought. With the hood and the raincoat, she hadn't realized the person she saw walking into Paul's house was a man. And with the black Lexus and the black Volvo looking so similar to her, she'd never had any doubt.

"Oh, Julia," Penny said as she turned around. "How could I have been so wrong about him?"

"You loved him," Julia said simply.

"I still do," she said fiercely. "That will never change, Julia." Walking back to the sofa, she sat down again. "What's going to happen to him?"

"He didn't tell you?"

She shook her head. "He won't see me."

"He's ashamed, Penny. Give him a couple of days."

"He's going to need an attorney."

"I already talked to Michael Rumson."

Penny looked startled. "You did that? After all...that happened?"

"I did it for you, Penny. You're the one who matters now."

Penny blew out a long sigh. "I'm so scared for him, Julia." Then, as if realizing others had suffered, too, she asked, "How's Andrew?"

"Better. I had to explain to him about Frank. I had to, Penny," she added, when her friend closed her eyes. "He would have heard it in school."

"Of course." Penny started pulling the fringe of a small pink pillow until it began to unravel. "How did he take it?"

"He was confused, angry, hurt. He asked a lot of questions. I answered them as best as I could."

"I hope he doesn't hate me."

Julia shook her head. "He could never hate you."

"And Coop?" She looked worried. "I heard he was hurt when...Frank hit him."

"He has a mild concussion and had to spend the night at Memorial, but he'll be fine. You know what a tough guy he is. Now he's proven it." She glanced at her watch and stood up. "I've got to go. I don't want to spend too much time away from Andrew." She kissed Penny on the cheek. "Okay if I stop by tomorrow?"

Penny shook her head. "Thanks, but...if it's all the same to you I'd rather be alone for a few days. I need to...sort things out, make decisions..."

"I understand. Just promise me not to make them too quickly. That's what you always tell me, remember?"

Penny gave her a wan smile. "I remember. And I promise."

Halfway down the driveway, Julia turned around, but Penny had already closed the door.

Steve and Julia sat on the stone bench, frosty glasses of iced tea in their hands. A few feet away, Andrew was giving Jimmy a detailed, slightly embellished version of what had happened at the cabin.

After picking up a few things at the Monterey Arms, Steve had returned to The Hacienda, but Julia wasn't sure if he had done that for Andrew's sake or because he truly wanted to be here.

There was so much she wanted to tell him, but she couldn't find the words. What if it was too late for them? What if, as Penny had pointed out a couple of days ago, she had just thrown away the best thing that ever happened to her?

Unaware of her turmoil, Steve nodded toward the two boys. "Look at Andrew, will you?" he said with something resembling fatherly pride. "Aren't you just amazed at how resilient this kid can be?"

"Amazed and grateful. He had a hard time understanding, and accepting, what Frank did at first, but we talked it out and I think he's going to be all right. Your little man-to-man talk while I was at Penny's didn't hurt, either," she added. "By the time I got back, he was a different kid." She smiled. "What *did* you say to him?"

"Actually, not much. I let *him* do all the talking."

"Well, whatever you did, it worked. Thank you." After a while, Julia cleared her throat. It was now or never. "Steve?"

He sipped his tea and continued to watch the boys. "Hmm?"

"I was thinking...I said some very unkind things the other day. I mean...I jumped on you, perhaps unfairly."

She glanced at him again. He was still sipping, still watching Andrew and Jimmy.

He wasn't going to help her one bit, she thought in dismay. She would have to do it all. "What I'm trying to say is that I'm sorry." She bit her lip. "I hope…it isn't too late for us."

Steve took another sip of his tea. His features, usually so expressive, revealed nothing.

"I'm making a fool of myself, aren't I?" she asked.

Another long silence stretched, more awkward than the one before. "Will you say something?" she whispered angrily. "If you don't think we can salvage what we had, then tell me. But for God's sake, say something."

"I'm crazy about you."

Her heart tumbled in her chest. "What?"

"You asked me to say something, so I'm saying it." He turned his head, and the look she saw in his eyes had her trembling. "I'm crazy about you," he repeated. "So much that I can't imagine my life without you. I want you near me, Julia—*with* me," he corrected. "Not just as a lover, but as…my wife."

The pressure in her chest was almost unbearable. "Is that…a marriage proposal?"

His smile spread slowly. "Can you handle it?"

"Can you?"

He nodded. "Oh, I can handle it." In the sunlight, his dark eyes shimmered. "Of course, we'll need to work out a few details."

"What kind of details?"

"Where do we live, for one. Monterey or Fort Lauderdale?"

"Oh." She fought back a grin. "That's the easy part. I have a business to run, a child in school. Therefore Monterey should be our home."

"But I'm the man," he deadpanned. "And you're the woman. The woman *always* follows the man."

She laughed. "When did you turn into such a chauvinist?"

"Since I started imagining you stretched out on the deck of the *Time Out* in a string bikini."

"Not a thong?"

"Thongs leave nothing to the imagination."

The baseball Andrew had been tossing up in the air as he talked to his friend rolled to her feet. She scooped it up and tossed it back. "I couldn't spend twelve months of the year in a bikini. Bad for the skin."

"Could you do it for, say..." he pursed his lips "...three months?"

"Three months?"

His expression grew serious. "You, Andrew and I could spend summers in Florida. You'd both help me crew. Then when school starts again, Jesus could take care of the boat and we would come back here. You need a full-time handyman, anyway, don't you?"

A lump formed in her throat. "You would do that for me?"

He kissed her mouth. "I would do that. And much more."

"What about The Hacienda while we're in Florida?"

"Maybe we could ask your mother and Penny to run it."

What a wonderful idea, Julia thought. Penny would love that, especially now that she had to readjust to a life without Frank.

Julia stared at Steve through misty eyes. "It looks as if you thought of everything."

"I didn't want to give you any reason to turn me down. And if you're worried about how Andrew will feel about us getting married, I already talked to him. He's thrilled."

"You talked to Andrew about us?"

"Of course. You don't think I was going to propose to you without checking with my buddy first, do you?"

"Is that why the two of you went for a ride early this morning? To discuss marriage?"

"No. Andrew and I had a little errand to run."

Her curious nature kicked in. "Where to?"

Steve reached into his pocket. "We went to see your friend Monsieur Garnier."

"My, aren't the two of you getting chummy." She tilted her head. "What did you need from him this time?"

"This."

He produced a small black velvet box and handed it to her.

With trembling fingers she opened it. Nestled in white satin was the most exquisite antique ring—a small, square-cut emerald surrounded by twelve baguette diamonds. She had admired it in Monsieur Garnier's case many times, had even tried it on once.

"How?" She swallowed. "How did you know I loved this ring?"

"I didn't." He took the ring out of the box. "But I had a hunch Frenchie might have something suitable. He showed me this and swore to me it was a perfect fit because you had tried it on once."

"I had no idea he'd remember that. Or that he still had it."

"Fate, darling. I'm a great believer."

Steve took her left hand and slid the ring onto her finger. "Well, what do you know? Frenchie was right, after all. It is a perfect fit."

"It's beautiful, but..." She shook her head. "It's too much."

He laid a finger on her lips. "No, it's not, so not one

more word—except, of course, for the word I need in answer to this question." He looked deep into her eyes. "Will you marry me, Julia?"

"Say yes, Mom! Say yes!" Andrew had stopped bouncing his ball and was jumping up and down. "Say yes, say yes!"

Jimmy joined him and soon the two words became a chant, broken only by the boys' happy laughter.

Julia giggled. "I guess I'm outnumbered."

"I'm still not hearing a yes," Steve said. "Are you, boys?"

"No!" they shouted in unison. "Say yes!" they chanted again.

"All right, all right! The answer is yes! Yes, yes, y—"

The rest of her sentence was drowned in an explosion of cheers and laughter.

CHRISTIANE HEGGAN